THE EYE OF VERISHTEN

K. E. BARRON

FFF

The Eye of Verishten

K.E. Barron

Foul Fantasy Fiction, an imprint of Bear Hill Publishing
P.O. Box 50088
Edmonton, AB. T5Y 2M9
Canada
foulfantasyfiction.com

This is a work of fiction. Names, characters, places, and incidents either are the product of the author's imagination or are used fictitiously. Any resemblance to actual persons, living or dead, events or locales is entirely coincidental.

For Tyson

*Were it not for you, all of my books would be in the
Cloud where no one could find them*

Ingleheim

The Höt Eakes

Crystal Lake of Rainmier

Village of Rainmier

Untevar Mountain Range

Fae'ren Province
(of Del'Cabria)

City of Untevar

River Sleban

Town of Luidfort

Nordenheim Mountain Range

Frost Woods

City of Nordenheim

University

Volcano of Venishten

Verishten's Wrath

Iron Mines

Deschner Mountain Range

City of Deschner

Luidfort Mountain Range

Glacier Peaks

Fortress of Mortlach

Barrier of Kriegle

Kensloche Mountain Range

Town of Kensloche

Breisenburg Mountain Range

Village of Eerichstag

The Crags

Pass of Halberschtag

Kingdom of
Del'Cabria

The Steinkamp Mantra

To fight means to kill; to kill is mercy

The Steinkamp Pledge

We hereby pledge to uphold the Steinkamp mantra at all times. We pledge to never waver and never retreat; to defend the defenseless and punish the wicked; to never cause undue suffering to our enemies and to leave no trace of ourselves behind. From the darkness we are born, in the shadows we fight, in the name of justice we kill, and in obscurity we die. We are the faceless and the nameless; we devote our lives, our blood, and our spirit to Ingleheim and the Mighty Führer as one heart, one mind, and one force.

We are Steinkamp.

Ode to Golems

Golem, take me to your land
Spare me from your powerful hand
Give yourself to me, then we shall be free
Golem, find me, here I stand.
Golem, your eye, I see through
Let me show you what we can do
Blessed by Verishten, you are of my kin
Golem, hear me, I am you.

1
PERSONS OF INTEREST

Kommandeur Wolfram and his two comrades came upon the old farm property a few miles north of the Crags. *This is it,* Wolfram thought. *This is where the Earl of Kensloche is hiding, the last Golem Mage in Ingleheim besides the Führer.* The kommandeur dismounted from his steed and tied the reins to the old wooden fence post. His comrades followed suit.

Wolfram pushed aside the gate and took one purposeful step onto the dirt path that led to a quaint little farmhouse. He stood still for a moment with his hands folded in front of him. His comrades, in full black armor and all their specialized weaponry strapped to their hips, back, and legs, waited behind him. With a deep breath, he took in all the scents of Ingleheim pastures. Wolfram had been born and raised in the high-end Eastside of the City of Deschner where the smell of sheep and their refuse was nonexistent. The smells of the countryside tended to nauseate him. Despite that, he did enjoy the lower-altitude, ash-free air of the Kensloche Mountain Range. He was going to miss the clarity and vigor it had provided during his last month on assignment.

With a short sigh and a lick of his lips, the kommandeur began his trek up the long, dusty path with his comrades tailing behind.

"Wait for me, Kristoff!" called a small child from the sheep fields to his left.

"Don't call me that!" chastised another boy just as all three soldiers snapped their heads in the direction of the children's voices.

A lanky boy, appearing around eight or nine, sprinted from the herd of heavily woolen sheep with a playful shepherd dog prancing at his heels. Following behind the child and his dog was a much younger boy, about five or six years of age, who struggled to catch up to his older playmate.

One of the boys we seek is also named Kristoff, Wolfram thought, becoming ever more confident that he found the right place. Yet, Kristoff was a common name. Wolfram couldn't let himself get too excited.

The boys ran across the path of the three soldiers and halted their sprint upon taking notice of the looming figures approaching. They gazed in dreadful awe at the two shapeless and faceless figures at Wolfram's side. Their eyes dilated, trying to discern an identifiable facial feature within the soldier's protective masks, fashioned from thin yet durable metallic mesh and enchanted by a light-absorbing magic. As a kommandeur, Wolfram no longer had to wear the mask and belted uniform of his comrades, although he too was dressed head to toe in black to convey the dominance of the Steinkamp soldier.

Wolfram tipped his square military hat, "Greetings, young herrs. I can appreciate how startled you must be to see Steinkamp soldiers in the daylight, but we will not be here long. I don't suppose your father is home. We have come a long way to speak with him."

There was no need for the boys to fetch their father, for he had already left his house and made his way down the path. Dust billowed into the air with each step he took toward the soldiers. His dark hair was slick with sweat, his beard and mustache wiry and unkempt. His dirt-stained wool smock was worn loose at the neck and rolled up at the sleeves, revealing the muscular forearms of a laboring man. There was nothing to distinguish the man of the house from the rest of the shepherds Wolfram had observed on his mission—a far cry from a highborn, much less an earl.

"Good day, herr," Wolfram said with a subtle melodiousness in his voice to help keep the sheep-shearer at ease for the time being. The two men shook hands, and the kommandeur continued, "Please do not be alarmed by our unannounced visit. I am Kommandeur Wolfram, and these are my comrades. We have come on behalf of the kanzler of this range, Herr Waldemar, in service to our Mighty Führer. If we could take a few minutes of your time, you will be able to return to your work momentarily."

The sheep herder's steel gaze only left the kommandeur for a brief moment to look at his boys. Wolfram caught a flash of concern behind the man's eyes as he would expect to see when Steinkamp soldiers came sniffing around. The sheep herder nodded and allowed the kommandeur to continue.

"We have come all this way in search of persons of interest to the Regime, and we were hoping that perhaps you might have some information." The kommandeur concluded with a warm smile.

Unlike the Steinkamp foot-soldiers he brought with him, Wolfram's specialized training went beyond the battlefield. He was a man talented in the fine arts of persuasion, intimidation, and subterfuge, all for the purposes of gathering information. Moreover, he knew that a friendly grin often went further than a well-aimed crossbow bolt.

"Boys, get inside now," the father said without removing his eyes from the soldiers.

"What is going on, Father?" the oldest boy asked.

The younger boy hid behind his brother, chewing on one of his dirt-stained fingers as he stared up at the daunting strangers.

"Do as I say—go help your mother."

The two masked comrades stepped in front of the children so that they couldn't go anywhere.

Wolfram interjected, "There's no need for the children to be absent. We only want a few moments of your time."

Past the bearded shepherd, a fair-haired woman in a plain dress stood at the doorway of the house.

"Ah, and that must be their lovely mother. I would like for her to join us as well if you don't mind." Wolfram waved her over with a warm smile on his face.

Upon noticing the Steinkamp Kommandeur and his masked comrades, her posture became rigid. She hesitated as she looked to her husband and the boys. The husband gave her a curt nod, and she slowly walked along the path to join them.

"Is there anything we can help you with, offiziers?" the woman asked, keeping her arms crossed and then stepping just behind her husband.

Wolfram removed his hat and placed it on his chest while extending a hand to her in greeting. Wolfram was sure to rub his thumb across the top of the woman's hand, as was the customary greeting of respect among ladies of high status. She curtsied in response, yet her smile was quick and tight-lipped. *She could easily be the wife of an earl, perhaps Frau Anja herself,* Wolfram thought. If they were the last Golem Mage family on Wolfram's list, then the coveted promotion to Kapitän of the Steinkamp force would finally be his.

Formal introductions were made, revealing the names of the husband and wife to be Ferdinand and Frieda. Wolfram turned to the boys and asked them for their names, but they looked up to their father with large, questioning eyes. Their father nodded.

"My name is Ernst," the eldest boy said, placing his arm around his little brother's shoulder, "and he is Hans."

"Ernst and Hans, strong names for soon to be strong men," Wolfram said.

He eyed Ernst carefully. It was common that the eldest son inherited the Eye of Verishten, the mark that indicated the abilities of a Golem Mage. Usually, the Eye manifested in the oldest son when he reached ten; then it was a year later before he would learn to control golems. Occasionally the Eye appeared on more than one son. On the rarest of occasions, a daughter may bear it. Sometimes it wouldn't manifest in any child only to reappear in a future generation. Such abnormalities were the reasons why the Führer ordered the entire Mage family to be executed lest any member left alive grow up to challenge him.

Turning back to the parents, Wolfram got right down to business. "The Regime is in search of particular persons of interest—a family of five. The husband and wife would be middle-aged like yourselves, the man with dark hair and gray eyes, and the woman with light brown hair and brown eyes, although they may have taken measures to change their appearances. They would be traveling with two boys, years eight and five, and a girl of thirteen."

"What is this family guilty of, Kommandeur?" asked Ferdinand.

"I am not at liberty to divulge that information, I'm afraid," Wolfram replied without pause.

The couple looked thoughtfully at each other again then looked back at the kommandeur. Ferdinand's eyes remained cold and severe.

"I don't know what to say, Kommandeur, but we have not seen this family of five—at least nobody who sticks out in our minds . . . Dear?"

Ferdinand nudged his wife, and she responded with a shake of the head. Their answers did not surprise the kommandeur in the least. He knew he was not about to get a confession out of them, and he didn't need it. The Kanzler of Kensloche gave him all the authority required in this mountain range. Wolfram's strategy was to gauge Ferdinand and Frieda's reactions when he described the similarities between them and his persons of interest.

As they stood in silence, beads of sweat began to form on Ferdinand's forehead.

In the past, other Steinkamp Kommandeurs used more stringent methods in hunting down Golem Mages. It was easier, in the beginning, to kick down doors and storm estates without question or warning, but those tactics only worked so well for so long. The Mages grew more careful. They went deep into hiding and often used decoys to help them escape. The Regime could no longer rely on brute force to bring the Führer's enemies to their knees. Instead, it would rely on the honed skills of its most methodical and vigilant officers. Absolute certainty was a necessity for Wolfram in hunting and bringing down enemies of the Regime.

"Very well." Wolfram sighed. "If I may review your identification papers quickly before I go, that would be much appreciated."

"May we ask why?"

Wolfram adjusted the sleeves of his long, black military jacket. "For me to ascertain that you are who you say you are, and to provide evidence for my superiors that you have been questioned."

"Yes, of course, Kommandeur." Frieda nodded and went back to the house to fetch the papers.

"And documents for your children as well, if you please," Wolfram called after her. She nodded and disappeared inside the house. "Our Führer is quite fond of his checks and balances," the kommandeur commented with a smile. Ferdinand strained one of his own, nodded, and scratched at his thinning hair.

Wolfram could hardly contain his excitement at the possibility that he was standing before Earl Sigmund of Kensloche. Wolfram wondered where on his body he bore the Eye of Verishten. It was commonly known that Earl Sigmund had it; the only question was if Ferdinand was that same man.

Soon enough, Frieda returned and handed a bundle of papers to Wolfram. He unraveled the ties that held the documents together and unfolded them. Reaching into his inside coat pocket, he pulled out his reading spectacles. He was a man in his prime and hardly required lenses to read, but he quite enjoyed the duality of being a kommandeur in the deadliest military force in the world while appearing as a harmless intellectual at the same time.

The identification papers for the husband and wife read as expected. A middle-aged married couple named Ferdinand and Frieda, both born and raised in the Village of Leichstag in northern Kensloche Range.

It was the children's papers Wolfram was most curious about. When Herrscher Heinrich took power as Führer, he had enacted a law that required children of the same family to be registered on a single document to keep parents from hiding sons required for military service. It came in handy for times such as this.

"I see a Yolanda listed here. She is your daughter, yes? Is she in the house?" Wolfram asked.

"Yes, she is in the kitchen helping me prepare for tonight's meal," said Frieda.

"You've reared her well, I see," Wolfram commented. "My little Kriemia is just a babe. I can only hope she will be as helpful as Yolanda is when she gets to be that age."

"Congratulations to you," Frieda said.

"Thank you, frau," replied Wolfram. "When I am finished here, I may get to finally return to my wife and child. I have been stationed all over Ingleheim so long, I missed the birth"

Wolfram honed in on the names of the children: Yolanda, Ernst and Hans. They were the same age and genders as Rosalinde, Kristoff, and Siegfried, the children belonging to the Earl of Kensloche. *This is no coincidence.*

Handing the papers to Ferdinand, Wolfram said, "Thank you for your time, herr, everything appears to be in order. We will not bother you any longer."

Wolfram shook the hands of the couple and turned to leave while his comrades remained planted for a moment. Before the family made their way back to the house, Wolfram called out a name.

"Siegfried?"

He looked back just as the youngest boy whipped his head around in response to his true name.

"Herr Ferdinand, I ask that you remove your clothing," Wolfram said.

"If it's the Eye of Verishten you seek, Kommandeur, you will not find it. If I were a Mage, I'd have legions of golems upon you before you three had a chance to dismount from your horses!" Ferdinand's top lip quivered, but his steel-gray eyes were severe.

"In that case, what is about to happen will work out in your favor." Wolfram's voice took an icy tone that contrasted strongly with the friendly one he had been using up until now.

The kommandeur signaled for his black-clad comrades to approach, one to restrain the wife and the other to subdue the husband. Wolfram stepped toward the boys and placed a hand on each of their shoulders to keep them from running away.

Pulling them closer to him, he whispered, "You boys should look away now."

Ferdinand reflexively moved to attack the soldier whose intent was to grab hold of his wife. The other Steinkamp, anticipating the husband's reaction, had already drawn a cudgel from his belt and drove it hard into Ferdinand's abdomen. Frieda screamed and struggled as the Steinkamp pushed her face-first against the western wall of the farmhouse. The other comrade shoved her husband against the wall alongside her.

In rapid fashion, they bound the couple's hands.

"Strip him!" Wolfram ordered.

The boys screamed as Wolfram held them in place.

He crouched down to offer them some comfort under the circumstances. "If your parents are truthful, they will be just fine. But if they lied . . . well, you should both look away, as I've suggested."

Wolfram and the boys watched the soldiers slash away Ferdinand's shirt and slacks. Wolfram's spine tingled with anticipation, coupled with a slight fear of what he would or would not find. If somehow his hunch were wrong and this man was not a Golem Mage, Kanzler Waldemar would severely reprimand him. Furthermore, news of what happened to the poor sheep herders would spread throughout the range, possibly driving the real earl and his family deeper underground. However, the ramifications of leaving the farmhouse without being absolutely sure would be far worse for his future under the Heinrich Regime. His hunches had never been wrong before. All he needed now was to view the undeniable proof somewhere on the earl's body.

"Shall I strip the wife as well, Kommandeur?" asked the comrade holding onto Frieda.

"There is no point," replied Wolfram. "The husband is the only Mage in the family. We have to execute her regardless, so it makes no difference if she were to bear the Eye as well."

"Please, you can't—" Frieda cried as the other Steinkamp cut away the last of her husband's clothing.

"Kommandeur, I found it!"

The Steinkamp pointed down towards the man's leg.

At the back of Ferdinand's hairy calf was a circle, surrounded by three triangular burn-like marks. Wolfram exhaled euphoric relief. *It is finally over.*

With the side of his bearded face still pressed against the stone wall, Ferdinand started to beg, "Please understand that I have never acted against the Führer. We just want to live out the rest of our days in peace— show mercy for the sake of our children!"

"I'm afraid it is outside of my jurisdiction to offer such, Earl Sigmund of Kensloche. If you had come forward, the kanzler might have arranged an alternative for you and your family, but you chose to flee, to position yourselves as enemies of the Regime. I am under a strict directive to bring you in, dead or alive . . . preferably the former."

"Sigmund . . ." Frau Anja sputtered before the kommandeur gave the order to dispose of them both.

Anja was the first to meet her end by a Steinkamp skewer knife through the base of her skull. Her death was over in an instant. Sigmund and his sons screamed upon watching their mother's lifeless body hit the soft earth. The dog's shrieking barks came soon afterward.

Wolfram swallowed hard as he kept his grip on the boys. It was not ideal to kill parents in front of their children, but the alternative of killing the children in front of the parents was unusually cruel, even if the parents' end would follow shortly thereafter. The Steinkamp mantra was not about cruelty; it was about mercy.

"Go into the house and find the girl." the kommandeur ordered the Steinkamp, wiping Anja's blood from his blade.

The herding dog continued to yelp. Wolfram looked around briefly, eye twitching, but couldn't locate the animal. Nonetheless, the barking eventually ceased.

The other Steinkamp executed Sigmund in the same manner as his wife, and he was on the ground a second later. Wolfram pushed the oldest boy ahead. "Kill this one first."

"Yes, Kommandeur."

As the Steinkamp soldier approached the eight-year-old, the elusive dog lunged at Wolfram from behind, taking his arm into its jaws and violently pulling it down. Kristoff managed to squirm out of Wolfram's grasp, duck behind him, and snatch the younger boy away. The kommandeur cursed while taking his skewer knife and driving it hard and fast through the canine's eye. It died as quickly as the earl and his wife, not having enough time to puncture Wolfram's thick leather sleeve.

The boys ran several feet into the pasture and stopped at a rock cluster in the grass, much to Wolfram's surprise. Kristoff picked up the loose stones and threw them at the advancing soldier. The small rocks deflected off of the Steinkamp's armored chest.

"Get to Rosy, Siegfried!" Kristoff yelled.

Little Siegfried's face was red from crying, his vigorous trembling keeping him in place.

At that moment, the rock cluster near the boys suddenly moved on its own. A humanoid figure made of stone stood up in guard of Siegfried and Kristoff. The creature was over seven feet tall, its misshapen arms nearly dragging on the ground. It had short and stumpy legs with bits of moss and dirt lodged in the cracks between the boulders that formed its massive torso. A crag golem, native to Kensloche. It was of the smaller, man-sized variety, but still dangerous in its own right.

This is preposterous—surely Kristoff is too young to control golems, Wolfram thought.

The golem swung its long limbs at the soldier, only to miss on account of the soldier's superb reflexes. Having had no luck in finding the daughter inside the house, the other comrade ran out to assist.

"Kill the boy, and the golem will be released from its command!" shouted Wolfram.

The golem protected Kristoff unshakably and neither of the Steinkamp soldiers could get past its massive reach, its solitary eye shining with a green light from the middle of its lopsided head of rock.

Siegfried finally found it in himself to run away. One of the Steinkamp ducked the golem and ran after him only to be met by another, even larger. As it rose from the long grasses, the golem knocked Siegfried onto his hands and knees and the Steinkamp onto his backside. The golem raised one stone leg, caked with dirt and moss, and brought it down hard on top of the man lying on the ground. The snapping of the bone in his leg was loud enough for Wolfram to hear from where he stood a dozen feet away.

His other comrade fared better. The Steinkamp managed to duck the golem's next swing and catch up to Kristoff, who was running for Siegfried. Kristoff and the Steinkamp were now between the two crag golems. The Steinkamp drove his blade clean through the boy's chest, much to Wolfram's relief.

Kristoff's lifeless body hit the ground, but the golems did not fall into two dormant rock piles as expected. They still had the lone Steinkamp surrounded and were ready to pummel him into the earth alongside the earl's eldest son.

He is not the one controlling the golems!

Looking around frantically, Wolfram's eyes soon fell upon a small figure at the base of the Crags to the south. A young girl no older than thirteen stood still, her ashen braids and white apron flapping in the breeze. The girl stared at the golems protecting her brother, her eyes red, raw with rage that Wolfram could see even at such a distance.

"It's the daughter—kill the girl!" Wolfram bellowed while pointing across the field. He felt a pang of guilt as he thought of the comment he made earlier when he'd hoped his own little girl would grow up to be like the one he had just ordered his men to eliminate.

The Steinkamp left standing took out his small dispenser of blast gel. He rolled toward the golem to avoid the swing of its arm and sprayed the clear gel all over the golem's torso and legs. Diving to the side, the Steinkamp clenched his gloved fist to activate the fire magic infused in the gel. It ignited rapidly and exploded. The sound of splitting rock shook the air, and the golem dropped to the ground, absent its legs.

The larger golem, rather than engaging the Steinkamp, turned, scooped up the fallen Siegfried and bounded toward its master. The Steinkamp jumped to his feet and began to give chase while Wolfram jogged over to his injured comrade.

"Can you get up?"

"No . . ."the comrade grunted, holding onto his left leg, bent unnaturally at the knee.

Wolfram clenched his fists, arms stiff at his sides. "Find something to bind that leg."

There was no time to help the Steinkamp mend his broken knee. The golem and Siegfried had already made it to the Crags. The stone creature raised Siegfried above its head, while Rosalinde reached down and pulled her brother up by the arms onto the rocky ledge to join her. If Wolfram and his last standing comrade didn't catch up to them, they could chance to lose the children in those rigid shale cliffs forever.

The kommandeur growled in frustration. Leaving the injured comrade behind, Wolfram ran to the base of the Crags where Rosalinde had been standing just a moment before. The other comrade had already sprayed the second golem with more blast gel and detonated it, blowing its stone body apart.

The Steinkamp leaped off a large boulder that had once been part of the golem's torso and grabbed hold of the ledge above. Pulling himself up with ease, he turned to assist his kommandeur onto the ledge with him. The two men continued their rapid climb up the treacherous shale inclines, their footing increasingly uncertain the farther they went. The girl and her brother were nowhere in sight.

Adrenaline pumped through Wolfram's veins as worrisome thoughts played out in his mind. *We have to find them before the girl summons any more golems or, Verishten forbid, Cragsmen find them first.* Cragsmen were lawless men and parentless whelps who lived in the Crags to avoid Regime authorities. They made their living pillaging the surrounding villages. *Perhaps if the children do run into a clan of them, the commotion could help us locate them easier,* Wolfram then thought.

Once the soldiers turned up the rocky path, they heard the faintest of squeaks. He halted and held out his arm for his comrade to do the same. The two men stood still and silent. A muffled cry came from behind an outcropping on the path above. Wolfram pointed it out, and his comrade went to investigate.

The Steinkamp stealthily climbed the outcropping, crouched on top of it, and peered down the other side. Wolfram watched as he pulled out his retractable sword from the short sheath strapped to his back and slowly extended the thin steel without making a sound. In the blink of an eye, the comrade reached down, and a shrill scream bounced off the shale cliffs. Rosalinde kicked and shrieked furiously in the Steinkamp's grasp right before his blade silenced her permanently. Blood sprayed from her throat as her arms and legs ceased to move. Wolfram winced, wishing they could have arranged a cleaner death for the girl.

Continuing up the path, Wolfram arrived at the outcropping. What he found was a mess of blood soaking into the dirt and amassing between the cracks in the shale. Rosalinde's body was wedged between two large rocks that had served as her hiding spot.

"Where is the boy?" Wolfram asked his comrade.

"He was here, but he ran when I grabbed the girl," he replied.

"Ran where?"

"Your orders were to kill the last Mage and now it is done. What does it matter if the youngest boy escapes?"

"Because *my* orders are to make sure every last Mage, including their kin, are disposed of. Our Führer will accept nothing less," said Wolfram.

The soldiers split up to cover more of the most logical paths. The echoing sound of shattering shale led Wolfram down an incline where he came to a lengthy chasm in the ground. Siegfried was there, clinging to a ledge as if trying to climb into it.

If he falls into that crevasse, it will take hours to get his body out. Wolfram approached carefully to keep from startling the boy.

"Little one?" called Wolfram.

Siegfried looked up from where he hung on for his life, his eyes red and swollen from crying.

"There you are . . . Siegfried." The kommandeur bent down and offered the boy his hand. "I know that after what you have witnessed you must be very scared, but I urge you now to take my hand."

Siegfried shook his head, quietly sobbing. Small pieces of shale below his feet came loose and shattered off the crevasse walls as they fell. With his tiny hands, Siegfried tried to edge further away. The masked soldier, suddenly appearing beside Wolfram, startled the boy. He attempted to move again. His right foothold fell away, and his high-pitched screams echoed down into the crevasse.

The Steinkamp reached for the crossbow strapped to his back, but Wolfram put out his hand to stop him. "Not until we get him away from this chasm," he whispered sharply to his comrade.

Siegfried pressed his little body harder against the rocks.

"Don't be foolish now." Wolfram stretched his arm even farther toward him. "Attempt to flee this way, and you will surely perish."

Siegfried shook his head again.

"You might think me a monster, but I assure you, I am not. What was done to your parents, your brother, and your sister was an act of mercy. It was not our intention to do it in front of you, but it had to be done."

"Mercy?" Siegfried sobbed.

"Yes, my boy, mercy is precisely what it was. If you take my hand now, I promise, you will not suffer. I can take you anywhere you want to go."

"I want to go home," Siegfried murmured through whimpers.

"Then that is exactly where we will go."

The boy didn't move a muscle.

"Tell me, little one, do you like running and climbing? I know lots of little boys who love to climb."

Siegfried sniffed back tears and nodded.

"I happen to know a place where boys like you can run for miles and miles and never get tired. You will be able to run faster than Kristoff. There you can climb the highest cliffs and never fall. If you come with me, you will be able to do all those things, but if you don't, your little legs will surely break at the bottom of this chasm, and you will never be able to run or climb ever again. I know you don't want that to happen. Take my hand, child, and I promise you will be able to run faster and climb higher than anyone. Wouldn't you like that?"

The boy remained stationary. Realizing his persuasion tactics were not going to work, Wolfram motioned for his comrade to circle around the rock that Siegfried clung to. The Steinkamp lunged for him, but Siegfried reacted without thought. His left foothold broke off, and he was holding on by only his little arms. Siegfried's five-year-old hands were too weak to support his weight and he lost his grip.

"Shit!" Wolfram's curses echoed off the chasm walls, joining Siegfried's high-pitched shrieks as he fell into the blackness.

"Comrade!" Wolfram barked. "Go after him!"

Before the Steinkamp could follow his kommandeur's orders, the entire crags began to quake. Both men fell to their knees. Large chunks of shale cracked off the cliff sides and slid into the crevasse. Rocks and dirt flew toward Wolfram as he tried to get out of the way before it buried him alive.

"Comrade!" he bellowed.

The Steinkamp was nowhere to be seen. The shuddering crags separated them. Wolfram was determined to see his new daughter and held no interest in losing his life for the sake of a five-year-old boy—one who would likely never grow to bear the Eye anyway.

Kommandeur Wolfram struggled to his feet and ran for his life.

2

ODE TO GOLEMS

(Twenty years later)

"Why again, Professor, are we freezing our danglers off to study golems outside that we already have in the laboratory?" Klemens complained.

"Not all of us have danglers to freeze off," muttered Katja as she trudged ahead of him.

Klemens pushed his spectacles up his nose. "I should be back in the library."

"It would do you some good to get your head out of those dusty, old books every now and again," Katja rejoined.

"It is important that we study these creatures in their natural habitats," said Professor Ignatius, trudging up the snow-laden path with his two best students in tow.

"Then why must their natural habitat be in the thick of Frost Woods?" Klemens said.

Ignatius chuckled. "These woods are close enough to the university to make a day's trip and happen to be teeming with golems, most of them still untouched by the Führer. If we are ever going to conclude that people like you and I can communicate with golems, we best figure out how with the ones found out here."

He stopped at a fork in the road and checked his map. Lightly falling snow sank into his white mustache and bushy sideburns that stuck out from his fur cap. It seemed to Katja like yesterday that his whiskers had been dark brown and his thick eyebrows even more so. She could not decide if Ignatius was a young man who was graying before his time or an old man finally starting to look his age.

"So you really believe that the golems out here have never been dominated by the Führer?" Klemens asked.

"The Führer can dominate any golem anywhere," Katja added. "Or so they say."

"Perhaps his power cannot stretch as far as these woods," Ignatius surmised. "More likely though, it can, but he just hasn't bothered. He'd have no use for them this far north." He rolled his map back up and headed east. "There is a clearing up this way where I believe we will find some man-sized golems to study. If we are extremely lucky, maybe even a giant one." Ignatius looked back to his students, his brown eyes sparkling.

Katja adjusted her wool scarf to keep out the frigid breeze and followed the professor up the icy incline. Unlike Klemens, Katja treasured any time spent away from the lab or the library—rather, any time spent outside of four walls. Her whole life, she had lived within the confines of one castle or another. Her few brushes with nature had been within gated and locked gardens where no outside eye could ever catch sight of her. Such was the lot in life for many young highborn women like Katja.

Klemens jogged ahead of her. "It's slippery here, Kat. Feel free to take my arm if you wish."

Just as he turned to offer Katja his hand, his left foot slid out from beneath him. Klemens sat in the snow, grumbling at his own clumsiness. Katja gave a wry chortle while stepping past her wet and cold classmate.

Turning back to Klemens, she offered him her hand. "I'll take that arm now."

Klemens grabbed hold and hoisted himself to his feet. "Well, at the very least you could crack a smile. Some laughter would be fitting."

Katja gave Klemens half a smirk. "I'm laughing on the inside, Klem, always on the inside."

It was a running jest between the two of them that Klemens would make her smile before the year was up. To him, Katja's passing grins or sarcastic smirks didn't count. All throughout adolescence and into adulthood, people commented on her sour face, saying that she would be so much prettier if she just smiled more. More often, she would politely tell those people to shove it in some fashion.

When you smile, all I see is how Verishten has blessed you, for he's given you intelligence beyond your years and beauty beyond measure. The memory of those words made it seem as if the man who had once spoken them whispered them now into

Katja's ear, sending shivers up and down her spine.

As the group continued up the snowy mountain trail, the path widened enough for Klemens to walk next to her. Before he could utter a word, Katja said, "Hope that fall didn't break your flute."

He took the long wooden wind instrument from his bag to make sure it was intact. "Still good, although I doubt it will matter much. I know you said the golems in the lab responded to the noise, but I just don't think these flutes are going to work."

They had both read corroborating historical references that people thousands of years ago used flutes and other such instruments to communicate with golems. They theorized that regular folk used them to subtly influence the ones not under Golem Mage control. Once a Mage had a golem under his or her command, no other Mage could take it over until it was released. After the Golem Studies team had uncovered the ancient texts alluding to regular people communicating with golems, it offered a potential opportunity for humanity to share a little in the power that now only the Führer possessed.

"I'm with you, Klem. That's why we're out here. The answers are clearly not in the texts, so we take our hypothesis, however negligible, and experiment until something works."

"Katja is right," Ignatius joined in, still walking ahead. "We know the flutes have some effect on golems. We find out what effect it has on the untouched variety, and if it's the same or stronger, then we direct our research accordingly. If there is minimal to no effect, then we go back to the texts and find a new lead."

The research team finally reached the top of the hill. A small creek bisected the snow-filled clearing, trickling softly against the silence of winter. Katja frowned. This was her last year in Nordenhein before she earned her doctorate and set off for home. If she were in Deschner, the pure, white snow that fell around her now would be replaced with gray volcanic ash raining down from the Volcano of Verishten.

"Well then, shall we start playing?" Ignatius said.

"Are there even any golems here, Professor?" Klemens wondered. "It's far too quiet."

"No matter. Dormant golems are no different from stone and ice in these parts. There's only one way to know if they're here. We wake them."

Ignatius blew three sharp notes into his flute that cut cleanly through the crisp winter air. Nothing stirred in the wilderness. Katja and Klemens joined their flute songs with Ignatius, but still no sign of the scores of golems he claimed were there.

"Perhaps we should fan out a bit more," Ignatius suggested.

"Come with me, Kat. There might be some this way." Klemens beckoned as he made his way toward the stream.

Katja couldn't help but be a little annoyed by Klemens's attempts to be alone with her. The two had studied closely together for the last two years after Klemens transferred from Military Studies with the Führer's approval. Since then he was hardly ever far from her sight. Earlier that day, Klemens had requested to stay behind and catch up on his historical readings—until Katja expressed a keen interest in accompanying Ignatius, and suddenly a winter stroll didn't seem so bad anymore.

There was nothing she found particularly unattractive about Klemens. He was clearly from good highborn stock—polite, well-spoken, and his intellect was unrivalled among scholars at his level. With his spectacles, wavy brown hair, sideburns trimmed short, and a clean-shaven face of friendly features, a highborn lady like Katja could do much worse than him. However, she held no interest in marriage or starting a family. Only golems mattered to her; colossal, powerful, and ageless wonders of Verishten's creation that had served mankind for millennia.

"I think the professor meant that we *each* fan out." Katja waved her hands in a fanning motion.

Not waiting for a response, she ducked through a thicket and slid carefully down a snowhill to find a peaceful clearing cut off from the rest of the team. She held onto her thick woven skirt with one hand while steadying her descent through the deep snow with the other. To Katja's relief, Klemens didn't follow. She felt sorry for the way she'd dismissed him, but today she needed some distance, not just from Klemens, but from the professor as well.

She had an experiment of her own to conduct, but she was afraid to let the others in on it, especially if it happened to work. Klemens had a point that playing randomly on musical instruments to communicate with golems was not enough. The people in the Age of Man had to be playing a specific song, and Katja thought she might already know that song.

When she was a girl, she had stumbled upon an old book of sheet music in one of her father's libraries. She had learned to play each and every song on her cello until they were second nature. Her favorite was the *Ode to Golems*. Eventually her father had found the sheet music left out in her music room and chastised her for taking it from the library without permission. He informed her that those songs were forbidden under the Regime, and she should never play them where outside ears might hear.

Katja walked until the others' flutes were whispers through the leafless birch trees surrounding her. There, she began to play the *Ode to Golems*. She loved the simplicity of it, yet its hauntingly dark melody filled her with both solace and sorrow. It was sad, yet hopeful—such were the ancient songs of the Age of Man. She became lost in a melody she hadn't played since she was twelve until she caught a shadow in her periphery.

Startled, she spun around to find nothing but a mess of trees and snow-covered rocks with icicle fingers connecting to the ground. She carefully inspected a cluster of soapstone, finding nothing unusual. She continued to play the *Ode* again while wandering around the clearing. When the song finished for the second time, the formation she had just inspected moved. The icicles shattered as one of the snow-covered soapstone boulders rose up and stood on two legs.

Katja gasped in both shock and delight. There, just a dozen feet away, was a frost golem. It was an inch or two taller than her, about six feet in height. Sweat formed under her woolen scarf. She stood mystified. This frost golem was leaner than the others of its type in the laboratory. The soapstone that made up its shape was darker in the areas not covered with snow and bits of ice. Its elliptical eye shone blue like a glowing icicle between its rigid shoulder blades. The light flashed bright, dimmed, and lit up again.

The golems in the lab do a similar thing when interacting with each other, Katja thought. This one was trying to communicate with her, but like in the lab, she couldn't figure out how to communicate back. The golem turned away.

"Wait, come back," she squeaked. She tried to play her flute again, but her mouth was suddenly too dry.

The creature of ice-tipped soapstone bounded away through the pine trees and disappeared more stealthily than anything of its size should be allowed. It took her breath away to watch it move so effortlessly for having a body made entirely of rock. *These beings should be respected in fellowship with man, not dominated by them.*

She let out a defeated sigh. Then the shadow returned to her periphery from her other side. She spun around to find nothing yet again. The hairs on the back of her neck stood on end.

"Is someone there?" Katja called out. Her shivering voice billowed as a white mist into the frigid air. *Could there be wolves this close to the university?*

"Is that you, Kat?" called Klemens from afar.

Katja stared into the white stillness for a time, but without another golem to jump out at her, she decided she no longer wanted distance from her research team. "Yes. Wait there, I'm coming to find you!"

When Katja climbed back through the thicket she was met with Klemens's smiling face, his spectacles dotted with fallen snow.

"Find any?" he asked.

Katja wanted to jump for joy with a resounding *yes*, but she would have to explain how she managed to awaken it with a forbidden melody of the Regime. "No. How about you?"

Ignatius, approaching from the north, chimed in, "Thought maybe for a moment I'd seen one, but it turned out to be a collapsing snowdrift."

"Either this experiment was a failure, or there just aren't any golems around here," Klemens said, taking off his spectacles to wipe his lenses.

"Oh, there are," Ignatius said. "I've snuck up on an entire group of them before. I know they lie here in dormancy during the winter months. If we didn't see them, it means these blasted flutes don't awaken golems in their natural habitat."

"Then what's our next step, Professor?" Katja asked.

"You two return to the library and find another clue in the history books, and I'll see what I can discover in the lab."

Ignatius placed his flute back in his satchel and led the team down the mountain trail with every bit the spring in his step he'd had on the way up. The professor never seemed to get discouraged, and Klemens lit up as well with the prospect of reading more history books. Katja, on the other hand, couldn't decide how she felt after this excursion. She may have just discovered the secret behind the flutes, but it was a secret she could not divulge without bringing undue suspicion onto herself as to how she found the forbidden melody . . . although, she considered, it may have been a coincidence that the golem awakened right after she played it. Maybe it was the shadow in the woods that stirred it.

I have to come back and try again on my own, she thought.

Upon their return, the three researchers parted ways in the university atrium. The University of Nordenhein was an ancient stone structure built with the assistance of golems in the Age of Man, and then modified during modernization efforts in the Age of Kings. The more recent upgrades, within the last twenty years, made the university now resemble a small fortified city to keep out enemies of the Regime.

The atrium was one of the few places where remnants of the old architecture were displayed in breathtaking force. Massive marble pillars presented each hallway, giving Katja a glimpse into the Age of Man. The elongated green and violet stained glass windows built into the grand vaulted ceilings depicted the likenesses of renowned scholars of old and dressed the atrium in the light of the Age of Kings. The university was the perfect example of what the City of Nordenhein was known for. It was Ingleheim's center for education and culture, and that fact was showcased through countless paintings and sculptures on every wall and in every great hall. Not even in her father's castle back in Deschner could Katja marvel at such artistic and architectural grandiosity.

Katja walked through the green and violet beams of light made by the stained-glass windows on her way to the information desk. She checked with the clerk for any confidential messages.

"No messages have been left for you, Fraulein Katja, but you do have a visitors notice. In fact, your guest arrived thirty minutes ago and has been escorted to the Brendt meeting room, down the hall, two doors to your right." The kind older woman handed Katja a key.

All visitors had to come in secret and wait in guarded meeting rooms for security purposes. The process kept rebel abductors from walking into the university, asking to visit a student, and making off with that student unseen. Many things had changed since Katja's parents attended the same institution. None of the students enrolled with their true names anymore, and their family ties remained hidden from all other students and staff to lessen the risk of kidnapping.

Who would visit me here without prior warning? Katja wondered. Surely *Father would never risk such an appearance.*

Then she thought of another man—one not as well-known, but who possessed almost as much power. Her insides began to curdle at the thought of Meister Melikheil coming to see her again. He had left her father's service to offer magical aid to the Kingdom of Del'Cabria in the Desert War. It had been almost two years since he visited her last, and she'd hoped that she would never see him again. Could he have returned from the desert already?

Katja removed her scarf and hat as she walked down the marble hallway. After smoothing out her wavy brown hair and refastening it with a clip, she inserted her key into the lock. She took a deep breath, silently praying that it would not be Melikheil behind the door. Her heart almost leaped out of her chest as she opened the door and entered the meeting room. It flopped instead upon seeing that the Spirit Mage waiting for her was not the darkly handsome one she'd expected, but another just as dangerous.

3

LITTLE DOVE

"Katja, how grand it is to see you," chimed the woman waiting in the Brendt meeting room. "Love the name you've chosen, by the way."

She sashayed over to her and gave her a light hug followed by a quick peck on the cheek. Katja returned the greeting without a thought.

"Brunhilde, whatever brings you here?" The last person she had expected to see was her stepmother.

Brunhilde was ten years older than Katja but dressed as a woman only entering her prime. Long ago, Katja had been jealous of her honey blonde locks and delicately striking facial structure, not often seen among the average Inglewoman. She wore her curls tied up in an outlandish style, held in place under a hairnet adorned with jewels and a black, lace fascinator. Her gown was made of a gorgeous red wine silk with a wolf fur cape dyed black to match her headwear.

"Don't look so excited to see me, Little Dove," Brunhilde said, making Katja flinch. Little Dove was the pet name Melikheil had given her once upon a time, and Brunhilde decided to keep the name alive after he left for war. The sound of it always made the blood curdle in her veins.

"Did my father send you, or are you here on your own volition?" Katja crossed her arms in front of her chest.

"Your father misses you dearly, I assure you, but he did not send me. I volunteered to make the journey. The City of Nordenhein is the place of my birth, you know. It has been too long since I've taken in the ash-free air. How are you finding the winters here?"

"Cold," said Katja dully.

"I can see you are eager for conversation today." Brunhilde rolled her eyes.

"You took a three-day journey from Deschner in the middle of winter to pay me a visit after six years . . . just for conversation?" Katja raised one eyebrow.

"Well, forgive me for wanting to catch up a little before getting down to the task. I don't see why the two of us can't just attempt to enjoy each other's company once in a while," Brunhilde huffed. "Your father and I are curious as to how your thesis is coming along. I understand it's about communicating with golems without Mage intervention. Whatever made you choose such a bold topic?"

Katja grazed her fingertips across the cushioned frame of one of the sofas. "Quite an obvious reason, really. If something ever happens to the one and only Golem Mage, the golems and their contributions will be lost forever."

"And what do you think is going to happen to the last Golem Mage?" Brunhilde's eyes narrowed.

"Why, anything at all. Our nation is at war with rebel armies wishing to dismantle his regime. There are threats from a desert warlord to decimate our entire nation, not to mention the fact that all men age—and die. Worse still, he stands to leave behind no son bearing the Eye of Verishten. So you can see how my work is needed."

Brunhilde shivered in her black fur cape. "Yes, well, I suppose that is why you are the Golem Expert." She twisted her onyx marriage bracelet, her lips pursed with irritation. She had yet to bear Katja's father an heir, and he was getting quite old indeed. "Your work is needed more than you know," she went on. "The Regime has recently stumbled upon the Alpha Golem that once guarded the Pass of Halberschtad."

Katja hardly noticed her own mouth gaping, and her arms fell straight to her sides as she struggled to catch her breath. "Y-you found the Golem of Death? It can't be . . ."

"Oh, if only you could see it. You will have never laid eyes on a creature so gargantuan."

"Where was it found?" Katja asked.

"That is classified. Only the highest offiziers of the Regime, myself included, know of its location. War golems are guarding it day and night, and lava golems from the mines are working to unearth it as we speak."

"What is to be done with it once it's uncovered? No Mage in history has been able to dominate an Alpha. They are not for any man, but for the Mighty Verishten alone to command."

"They are to be for our Mighty Führer now," Brunhilde said, her sparkling hazel eyes betraying her excitement. "He has sent orders to your professor to see that your research is directed toward his end."

"Toward what end, exactly?" Katja asked. She could hardly believe that her research would actually be used for something so crucial to the Regime, for something as dangerous as the Golem of Death. She was afraid to hear her stepmother's answer.

"To be the first Mage to dominate an Alpha, and use it to end this silly rebellion. Why else?"

"And he will be the last to do so if he thinks he can dominate the Golem of Death," said Katja.

"Hush now, Dove," Brunhilde cooed. "It is your father you're talking about, and his orders are final. Curtail whatever research you have going on currently. Start looking into how Alphas can be awakened and anything else you can find out about them."

"I've studied golems for six years, and now I'm supposed to find out everything there is to know about Alphas in just how many? One?" Katja sputtered.

"Hopefully, yes. But if it takes longer, then I suppose we will have to wait, though not forever, mind you."

"Tell them to leave it where it is," Katja warned.

"That is not for us to decide. When your father has his mind set on something—well, we know how that can turn out."

"Are you referring to how he systematically murdered all the other Golem Mage families so he would remain completely unimpeded?" Katja said, crossing her arms in front of her chest again.

"To put it bluntly . . . I suppose," replied Brunhilde, twisting her marriage bracelet a second time.

"Even you can see this is madness!"

"I will hear nothing more of it," Brunhilde said in a sharpened tone. "Starting tonight, you and your team officially work for the Regime. All you need worry about is how to wake the Golem of Death, and garner some insights as to how it can be dominated. Truthfully, none of us know if the Mages of old ever *tried* to control one. It might be easy. Your father suggests studying regular ones, and hopefully they can lead you to another

Alpha lying dormant somewhere. Do whatever you scholarly types do and figure out how to wake it up. We expect status reports on a biweekly basis. Do you think you can manage that?"

There was nothing else to say. Katja knew better than anyone that once one was deemed to be an instrument of the Regime, there was no backing out without severe consequences. She had to think of the safety of her team. They were a part of this too.

"Of course. I will do whatever I can to aid the Regime in this endeavor," Katja's eyes drifted to the floor.

"You always talk of the Regime as if you exist outside of it, when in fact you are every bit a part of it as your father," said her stepmother.

"You and I both know that I am no more a part of this regime than the ghosts of the kings that were slaughtered under it. Father hardly registers my existence anymore." That's all she had ever been to him, a wandering spirit in his dark castle halls, growing lonelier and more vulnerable with every passing day.

Brunhilde sighed heavily. "Oh cheer up, Little Dove. Think of all the discoveries you will make as a result of this assignment. Your thesis will dominate all others in your field."

Katja nodded in agreement, even though all she could think was how impossible the task before her was going to be. Her thesis was the least of her worries now. The Regime was attempting to awaken an Alpha, and the Golem of Death at that. Admittedly, Katja had not studied Alphas much, being that up until now they were thought to have disappeared. But if the lore were correct, the one who controlled the Golem of Death would have the power to destroy anyone and anything at will. It was not only going to be the rebels that suffered under its destructive gaze, but all of Ingleheim and the kingdoms beyond. It was complete folly, and Katja wanted no part in it.

Brunhilde dismissed herself and went to the door. Katja thanked her for coming by, even though her thoughts were fervidly opposed to her words.

"Wait, there is something else you should know," the Spirit Mage turned back to Katja, her hand still on the doorknob. "You mentioned desert warlords earlier, which reminded me of something I had neglected to tell you."

"What is it?"

"Meister Melikheil . . ." Brunhilde struggled to appear stoic, but continued in a wavering voice. ". . . is dead."

Katja felt as if a bag of bricks had struck her right in the midsection. The news of such a powerful sorcerer being dead was almost as much of a shock as learning that an Alpha Golem had been found. "H-how . . . how did he . . . ?" she sputtered.

"Well, you remember that silly deal he made with the King of Del'Cabria to eliminate the Overlord of Herran, Nas'Gavarr? It turns out the Great Melikheil was not great enough."

"But he was so powerful," Katja murmured.

"You don't have to tell me. I've seen no other Mage wield both essence and spirit as effortlessly as he did. He should have been able to defeat that desert serpent." Brunhilde's delicate jaw clenched, and she couldn't continue.

Katja nodded, trying her best to appear unaffected by the news. "When did all this happen?"

"When the Del'Cabrians first marched on Herran, Melikheil went with them and never returned. Our Meister–Apprentice rapport allows me to stay connected with him, and that connection was . . . brutally severed. It would seem that Nas'Gavarr's proficiency with flesh magic won him the day."

"That was almost a year ago. Why did you wait until now to tell me?" Katja asked shrilly.

"I'm sorry, dear. It didn't cross my mind to tell you at the time. You were so busy studying, and things are always hectic in Deschner considering the rebellion and everything. Honestly, I didn't think you'd care so much. How close *were* the two of you really?" Brunhilde let out a slight huff at the rhetorical question she posed.

You, above all others, knew exactly how close we were, Katja fumed within her mind. She still couldn't believe what her stepmother had told her. *Am I finally free of him?* Brunhilde could be playing some cruel jest, but to what end? She may be the queen of deceit, but something about how distraught she sounded told Katja she was not lying. It was enough to bring a relief that she never thought she would ever get to feel, not since the day she met the iniquitous sorcerers.

"Now, I really must be going. I don't know when I will see you again. You will need to remain here to work over the break. Hopefully you will finish soon and you can join your father and me in Breisenburg when it comes time to awaken our Alpha. Goodbye for now, Little Dove."

A weak utterance of a goodbye was all Katja could manage in reply.

Brunhilde closed the door behind her while Katja flopped down onto the sofa, trying to keep her thoughts straight. She couldn't decide whether to feel long-overdue relief in knowing Melikheil was gone or frustration over the impossible research project she was just assigned. Her confusion about the whole situation soon led to anger.

How dare she come to my school with her wolf furs and fake niceties to drag me back into the insanity that I have been free from for six years, she seethed inwardly. In Nordenhein, Katja's gifts could be put to a noble purpose. Here, she was more than just an isolated highborn girl without a true friend to be found. She was the university's top Golem Studies acolyte, soon to be an expert in her field, powerful in her own right and earned on her own merits.

It was at that moment when Katja made a decision. She would sooner see the Regime fall to pieces than let that witch decide how she would make her mark.

Meister Melikheil is dead now, she thought. *Do you really think you can control me in my world, Brunhilde? You say I should curtail my current research, but it is far too important to let go.* She would continue to investigate ways an average human could influence golems and with that knowledge, man and golem will live the way Verishten intended. With golems on the side of all mankind, her father's power over the people would wane, and his regime would fade away into obsolescence.

Now all Katja had to figure out was how to do that while pretending to do what the Regime had ordered her to do.

4

HEAR ME, I AM YOU

The sound of the pen scratching on the paper in her journal was one of the most satisfying sounds Katja could think of. The smell of the smooth, black ink as it flowed off her quill always put her at ease. It was week's end, and she had the library all to herself early that morning.

"What're you writing there?" Klemens asked from behind her.

With a screech, Katja snapped her leather-bound book shut before Klemens could make out what she scrawled. She cringed upon realizing the ink probably smudged. She wasn't alone in the library after all.

Katja took a risk, keeping a journal in a Regime where truth was more destructive than a thousand war golems. If anyone were to read what she had written over the years, it would implicate her as an enemy of the Regime. However, that knowledge never deterred her, for she would quickly descend into madness holding all her thoughts inside her head.

"Something private, I assume." Klemens circled around the large oak table and sat across from her.

"Um . . . not really, I was just taking notes from this tome that references writings over two thousand years old," Katja said.

"Really?" Klemens leaned over to peek at the book Katja had in front of her. "Where did you find a tome with references that far back?"

"I got it from that crate of books brought in by Regime offiziers four days ago," she replied. "They are being kept under lock and key in Ignatius' office for our use only." Katja motioned to the stack she had signed out on the table.

"Find anything that will lead us to an Alpha?" Klemens asked.

"Nope." With a sigh, Katja closed the tome. "Even in these forbidden volumes written thousands of years ago, Alphas are barely mentioned. This assignment is ridiculous."

"I agree that the Regime is putting a lot of pressure on us, but I for one am honored that the Mighty Führer gave us this opportunity to better it."

Katja cringed. Every day she heard people praising her father and expressing undying loyalty to his Regime. She wondered though, how many of them actually meant it.

Klemens took a couple books from the stack and joined Katja in studying. For the next half-hour they lost themselves in the ancient texts and reference papers.

Then Klemens spoke up. "All of these writings refer to Mage abilities more than golems themselves. This may be more relevant when we look into how to wake an Alpha, but we have to find one first."

"All the lore can tell us is what we already know. There are six Alphas, one for each mountain range. If the Golem of Death was found in Breisenburg, then we can safely assume the others will be found in the remaining five," said Katja.

"So for example, frost golems are native to Nordenhein, so their Alpha would likely be lying dormant somewhere in this area?"

"Yes. And the Alpha of the crag golems would be in Kensloche Mountain Range, and the Alpha of the crystal golems in Untevar Range, et cetera."

The six golem types possessed characteristics resembling the rock formations most common to the mountain ranges from which they hailed. Near the active Volcano of Verishten in Deschner Range, lava golems could be found. The crystal deposits in the Hot Lakes of Untevar were home to thousands of crystal golems, and the stormy granite cliffs of Luidfort Range is where winged golem sightings were most frequent.

"But where specifically in the mountain ranges are we to find them if the Regime doesn't divulge exactly where they found the Golem of Death?" asked Klemens.

"I don't think knowing the exact location of one Alpha will lead us to another. We should look to regular golems as the Führer suggested."

"Why would he suggest that?"

"Legends say that in the Age of Golems, the Alphas cared for their own, up until mankind came along. So they must have a connection to each other."

Klemens nodded in agreement and started searching through one of the other tomes from the pile. After another hour of gaining no new insights, the researchers decided to switch books. It was a trick they used often to help them see something the other may have overlooked. The switch eventually paid off when Katja found an excerpt that mentioned the Alphas' exodus into dormancy thousands of years ago.

"Here it mentions that the Alphas abandoned mankind during the Age of Man, taking much of the Mages' power with them, but nobody knows where they went or why they left." Katja rose from her chair and went around the table to show the excerpt to Klemens. "What power did the Alphas take with them, do you think?" she asked after a second or two.

Klemens finished reading through Katja's paragraph, then excitedly pointed out one from his own text. "I think I just read the answer here. It suggests that the first six Golem Mage families had a connection that stretched across all golem-kind, all over Ingleheim—just like the Führer can today."

Now we are getting somewhere, thought Katja. *No wonder Father felt the need to keep these volumes hidden until now.* These texts could possibly reveal to the people how he came by his unique abilities, which allowed him to control golems without needing them in his sight. This skill gave him a distinct advantage over the other Mages he went up against.

"Could that be it?" she wondered aloud. "The first Mages had the power to control all golems en masse, and then the Alphas left, limiting their command to only the golems in their sight. Now an Alpha has been found—some twenty years after Herrscher Heinrich has uncovered that power."

When Katja had asked her father why he was so much stronger than the others, he would tell her that he was the only true Golem Mage blessed by Verishten, while the rest were weak and unworthy. They needed to be eliminated for the good of Ingleheim. That was the same rhetoric the public received to convince them to accept the horrible things he did to protect them and usher in the current Age of Order.

Klemens nodded and opened up one of the books he had brought into the library. "I keep coming back to the tale of the First Steinkamp and his climb up the Volcano of Verishten. It was there he confronted the Golem of Fire and where Verishten rewarded his bravery by searing his Eye into the man's flesh, granting him dominion over golem-kind."

"Yes, the tale is told in the Golem Mage tomes as well. The first one, known as Siegfried, speaks of the Golem of Fire who caused the First Eruption and ushered Ingleheim out of the Age of Golems and into the Age of Man. The tomes mention a covenant between Verishten and man, one that allowed mankind to settle in the mountain ranges of Ingleheim in return for holding dominion over golem-kind, as he once had. Every scholar interprets the tale a little differently but they all agree that Siegfried faced the Alpha of Lava Golems at the top of the volcano and returned with Golem Mage abilities."

"Well, from that tale, along with our hypothesis that the Alphas reside in each of their own mountain ranges, it is pretty obvious where we'll find the Golem of Fire. Right where the hero Siegfried found it," said Klemens.

"Eureka!" Katja cheered sarcastically, slumping against the side of the table with her arms crossed. "Let's assemble the team and climb to the top of an active volcano in hopes Verishten will bless us for our bravery."

"Most likely scorch us from the inside out for our stupidity, much like what happens to those silly pilgrims," Klemens snorted.

The pilgrims would stop climbing once the heat and the ash overwhelmed them, but the fanatical few would persevere until they suffocated or their lungs burnt away. Even with masks, nobody was known to have made it all the way to the top and back.

"I don't know, is it silly for people to climb a deadly volcano in order to be closer to their god?" Katja asked hypothetically.

"Hey, maybe that's how the Führer got his power. Wouldn't that be something?" Klemens muttered.

The thought of her father climbing to the top of an active volcano made Katja shake her head. If he had accomplished such a feat of endurance, he would have made sure everyone in Ingleheim knew about it. "How he got his power doesn't matter. He's not a god. He cannot control an Alpha, only Verishten can," Katja said.

"If anyone has a chance in controlling the Golem of Death, it's the Mighty Führer. Besides, it's not for us to question him."

"But doesn't it bother you that he wants to awaken something that could destroy us all? How can you not question it?"

"I understand your concern. I too have read the lore surrounding the Golem of Death, but we need to remember that if it wasn't for the Führer uniting the ranges under one rule, the kings would still be fighting amongst themselves and ripping Ingleheim to shreds. We are lucky to be living in this Age of Order and in the peace that it has granted us. In return, as citizens, we must trust his judgment."

Returning to her seat at the other side of the table, Katja tried not to engage. It always disheartened her to listen to Klemens speak so fervently in support of the Regime, even though she couldn't expect any different from someone of his rank. *If more people of high standing admit that there is something wrong with the Regime, no one would have to fear it anymore,* she thought. "You know better than anyone, Klem. War is inevitable, but a few battles every other generation is preferable to the systematic slaughter committed by this regime every day. The Mages fought at times, but that does not justify the mass genocide of an entire group of people, their women and children—"

"You don't know what you're talking about," Klemens said while looking around the library for eavesdroppers who were not there. He continued more quietly, "The rebellion is seeking to destroy everything we hold dear. They wish to divide us, to render Ingleheim to rubble. We can't even tell each other our real names or parentage without the risk that some traitorous ingrate abducts us and holds us for ransom. Our Führer must do everything in his power to make sure people like them don't win. We must do everything in our power to assist him."

"Rebellions don't just rise up without a reason. They represent the plight of the common people. If the order provided by the Regime actually benefited them, why are so many willing to risk everything to oppose it?"

"And what would a woman like you know of the plight of the *common people?*" Klemens scoffed.

He had a point. Katja lived a sheltered life, completely separated from Deschner's impoverished sectors, those of which she only heard about in passing. Furthermore, journalists were never allowed to write on the subject, courtesy of the Regime's Censors.

"No more than you, but rebellions such as the one we are facing today never existed in the Age of Kings," she concluded.

"Blast the Age of Kings!" Klemens slammed his fist on the table, and she jumped in her seat. "Katja, your words are becoming treasonous. Just for listening to you, I'm obligated to turn you in."

"If the Regime were acting in the best interest of its people it wouldn't need to imprison them for speaking the truth as they see it!" Katja raised her own voice.

"Katja, shut up!"

"Or what? Will you report me? Will you have them send me to the Iron

Mines? I am not afraid of them."

"You should be," Klemens said in a low, stiff voice.

The doors to the library groaned open and both Klemens and Katja abruptly stopped talking as Ignatius entered the library.

"I hope that all of this shouting means you two are getting close to finding a lead," he said sternly but with a hint of facetiousness.

"Not exactly," Katja muttered. "I'll let Klemens fill you in."

She picked up her journal and inkwell, then swiftly exited the library. Klemens told Ignatius to wait a moment, and got up to go after her. He caught up to Katja in the empty hall.

"Kat, I'm sorry, I didn't mean to insult you," he said when he stepped in front of her. "I just don't want to see anything bad happen to you. The things you say sometimes—if anyone were to overhear, they could report you."

Let them report me! Katja screamed within her mind, but instead, she gave in. "I've hardly slept since we were put on this project. Please just forget what I said."

"You know I would never actually turn you in." Klemens placed a warm palm on her shoulder. "I'd hate for you to be afraid to share your opinions with me, but some opinions are very dangerous to have . . . you must be more careful."

Katja knew Klemens was trying to help. He was afraid, just like so many others living under the Regime. Katja, however, was tired of being afraid. She was tired of people more powerful than her telling her how to think and what to feel. As long as she was in control of her own mind, she would think and act by her own mind, and nobody else's. "Thank you for your concern, Klem. I think I should lie down for a while."

"That sounds like a good idea. Feel better, alright?" Klemens nodded and headed back to the library.

Katja wanted so badly to sleep, but she would never be able to until she returned to Frost Woods and attempted to awaken a golem using the forbidden song one more time. She needed to wait until such a time where her team was preoccupied and would not look for her.

It was early enough in the morning. She could make a quick trip to the woods, a few miles north of the university, and still return before dark.

The horse's hooves crunched against the packed snow of the northern university path. With her scarf wrapped tightly around her neck and face, Katja raced her bay mare toward Frost Woods in an attempt to make good time.

She couldn't believe the gatemen had just let her go without an escort. As a researcher for the Regime, Katja had an all-access pass to the university and its grounds. She was allowed to leave the premises anytime she wanted, but for security to let her ride into the woods unaccompanied seemed a little too lenient. She had been prepared to threaten the gatemen with telling Gustaf, the Kanzler of Nordenhein, that they were inhibiting her research if they made her wait for a forest ranger. Luckily for everyone, such action was unnecessary.

Katja reached the woods in a little over an hour. She rode a mile or so farther until the frozen shrubbery grew too thick and the snow too deep. She dismounted and tied the mare to a sturdy branch, took her things from the saddle bag, and continued on foot.

With a map and compass in hand, Katja navigated through the winding paths and found her way to the clearing at the top of the hill. She continued through the thicket to where the frost golem awakened a week prior, then decided to venture farther through the pines where it had disappeared. It took ten minutes for Katja to find another clearing, but once she had, she felt like going farther still. She trudged through deeper and deeper snow, some of it falling into her boots, but her wool leggings kept her skin from freezing.

Katja continued on, pushing through snow-covered branches until she came upon a third clearing where a small waterfall fed into a stream. *This is it.* Her gut told her that a dormant golem would be here.

She took out her flute and played the forbidden melody. When she finished the last note, she waited, and waited some more. The only stirring in the woods was the trickling waterfall.

This just has to work. She played the *Ode to Golems* four more times, and as she came to the final bars, she swore she heard a deep and distant voice sing along, bringing the song to life. She immediately stopped playing, and the singing voice finished the last bar.

"*. . . hear me, I am you.*"

Spinning around, Katja expected to see a forest ranger or perhaps even Klemens behind her.

No one was there.

Katja gulped. Who could possibly know the words to the *Ode* if even she didn't? *Would a rebel know? One could be camped out here, hiding from the authorities. What if I get kidnapped? No one would think to look for me for several hours.* Katja's mind raced. Her father would never negotiate with rebels, even for his only child. They would have to kill her.

Before panic truly set in, the ground underneath Katja trembled. Mounds of snow fell from the rock formations just left of the waterfall. They began to move and fast. She screamed and backed away from the creek.

Katja gaped, her breath frozen in her throat. Snow poured down from a cliff face that was taking on a new form right before her eyes. The cliff lumbered slowly toward her, shaking the ground, and stopped just shy of the creek separating them. When the last of the snow fell away, a blue light flashed near the top of the towering soapstone creature. Ice, coating the light source, shattered away as it shone even brighter. It was a gigantic blue eye.

Katja strained her neck to look up at the giant frost golem she'd awakened. She held her breath, but still shivered profusely. The size of it petrified her. She had seen war and winged golems plenty of times, but they averaged to only fifteen feet tall; this one was closer to twenty. It was shaped similarly to its much smaller cousin she'd awakened the week before, with long limbs compared to its torso. The shoulders were positioned higher than its head, resembling jutting icicle spires. The head itself protruded from its upper chest and possessed a single elliptical eye that shone with a brilliant blue light.

For what felt like an eternity, the golem stood as frozen as the ice that coated it, staring down at Katja. Her heart raced as a smile slowly formed. *How do I address this massive stone being now that it's awake?*

Like the human-sized version, the golem's shining blue eye dimmed and brightened again. The golem then turned its back to Katja just as the last one had. The ground shuddered beneath its weight as it walked into the bush, the sound of cracking ice echoing off the crisp winter air.

"No!" She sprang to her feet and ran toward the golem, stopping short of the creek. "Don't go!"

Her mind went blank as she watched the unstoppable colossus cleave through the foliage. The vibrations of its footsteps grew weaker the farther it went, and the woods were silent once again.

At that point, her bearings returned. She knelt down into the snow, took out her notebook and inkwell, and quickly jotted down her findings.

Observation week 2: Giant frost golem awakened after the song was played through 4 time—

Katja stopped writing. She had almost forgotten about the singing voice. It wasn't until actual words were sung that the golem had risen.

Adrenaline of a more urgent kind took hold of Katja upon remembering she was not alone. She hurried to collect her journal, quill, and inkwell, and swiftly turned to leave before whoever it was showed themselves. *Maybe the golem scared them off,* she hoped.

When Katja began her trek through the dead underbrush from whence she came, a figure stepped out into her field of vision. She froze. A man, wearing black from head to toe, stood as still as the thin birch trees sprouting through the snow several feet away. He stared her down with no eyes. No nose, no mouth—no face. A shapeless black mask covered it entirely.

Her alarm turned to pulse-pounding terror. A Steinkamp soldier. It didn't make sense. *Why would the Regime send an assassin after me? Father would never sanction such a thing. But what other reason is there for a Steinkamp to be in these woods if not to kill me?* Whether in the Age of Kings or the Age of Order, Steinkamp soldiers were trained for only one thing. *To fight means to kill!*

Without another thought, Katja took off into the bush. It didn't matter where she ran or if she got lost. If a Steinkamp soldier were sent to kill her, he would find her eventually—that much was certain.

The soldier sped along the snowdrifts, so light the snow hardly came loose, so fast he was a shadowy blur amongst the trees' white and charcoal bark. As soon as Katja emerged from a mass of pine tree branches the Steinkamp was in front of her. She screamed so loud the crows took from their perches and flapped and cawed overhead.

"Don't run." The Steinkamp's voice was strangely temperate for someone who was about to murder a woman in the woods.

"If you're going to kill me, just do it!" Katja meant to say those words with fortitude, but her voice quavered like a lost child's.

"If I were here to eliminate you, you'd be dead before you ever caught sight of me," the Steinkamp replied, his tone almost mocking. But she knew, as they say, *to face a Steinkamp is death assured.*

"What do you want?" she asked, still wary.

"I've been charged to provide the security for you and your team," stated the Steinkamp.

"So you're here to protect me . . . not to kill me?" Katja began to breathe normally again, but her body still shook.

The Steinkamp nodded. Katja discerned no features from behind his black mask of metallic mesh armor. It was as if all the light around it were absorbed into an inescapable void. For the few seconds she stared into the mask, her eyes ached.

"Fitting that my father would send one of you to guard me," Katja commented. "A Steinkamp soldier for security detail is quite overzealous."

"My orders come from the kapitän, which flow through my kommandeur. I am not at liberty to question where the command originates, whether it is from your father or the Mighty Führer himself."

Katja's spine tremored. She realized that this Steinkamp soldier, obviously sent by her father, witnessed her awaken a golem with a forbidden piece of music.

"How long have you been following me?"

"Since your first expedition to these woods one week ago—the same day you were put on your assignment," the Steinkamp replied. He enunciated is words extremely well, yet his phrasing was fluid with no distinct dialect. That made it impossible for Katja to guess which range he was originally from.

"You were watching me that day." She bit the inside of her cheek. *Is he obligated to report on everything he saw?*

"Affirmative." He nodded. "It is often that a Steinkamp can better protect his charges without them being aware."

"You don't say. Then why show yourself to me now?"

"Your suspicious behavior has forced me to." The Steinkamp's voice grew deeper as he took one step closer. She reflexively took one step back, the pine needles from the tree behind her getting stuck in her braid. "Where did you learn that song?" he asked.

"The song is no concern of yours." She stepped away from the tree and brushed the pine needles off her fur collar. "Our methods of research are top secret. You are here to protect, not to question."

She heard a quiet grunt from behind the Steinkamp's mask. "So top secret you came to these woods alone without your colleagues knowledge? Could it be because you play works forbidden by the Regime?"

"The Regime has no qualms about me using forbidden works if it helps to serve their interests. I hope to inform my colleagues as soon as I deem it appropriate. Again, it is not your place to comment on how I conduct my research." Katja slung her bag over her shoulder and walked away from the nosy Steinkamp.

"If you were going to tell your team at all, you already would have," the Steinkamp challenged as he followed her through the forest.

"Is that so?"

"As soon as the Regime demanded your services, nobody would care how or why you knew that song if it worked. It's not the song you wish to hide from them, but the fact that you might have been successful in its use. The question that remains is why?"

This Steinkamp must have been the one who sang the last few bars of the Ode, Katja thought. She turned around sharply to face him. "I've never known Steinkamp to talk so much. I've also never known them to sing, especially forbidden songs of which no record of the lyrics exists."

For years she wondered what the lyrics were. She had searched the entire library at home, but no such thing had ever turned up. Over time she had made up her own words, trying to imagine what people must have sung to golems during the Age of Man. She continued, "I am a well-regarded Golem Studies major working on a top-secret project, and my clearance allows me to see what the Regime has censored. I've seen more forbidden documents in the last week than most high standing offiziers have seen in their entire careers. You knowing the words to such a song, however, is truly suspect. I'm sure the Führer would be interested to know how my protector learned them."

"What are you proposing?"

"I don't tell the Regime that one of their soldiers knows the words to a song long suppressed, and you won't inform your superiors or my colleagues what you saw here today," Katja said.

"As you wish," the Steinkamp replied, and he continued walking.

Katja then realized that she would need more than just his word not to tell. "And you shall teach me all the lyrics to the *Ode to Golems* before we return to the university."

"My orders do not come from you, fraulein," the Steinkamp said dully as he walked ahead of her, pushing aside some low-hanging branches and ice-tipped foliage to clear their path.

"That's a pity. I suppose I will have to inform the Führer that the Steinkamp sent to protect me is hampering my research more than he is helping it. Given the importance of this project, he won't take kindly to that, and then you won't be taking orders from anybody—"

Before Katja could take her next breath, the Steinkamp spun around and grabbed her by the elbow.

"The only reason the gatemen allowed you to leave on your own today was that they knew I was already attending to you. One word to the security offiziers and you will be prohibited from ever leaving university grounds for the entirety of your attendance. If I must, I will report to my kommandeur that you act against the interests of the Regime, and they will take you away where your highborn relatives will never find you. . . . All I need to do is give them this."

The Steinkamp raised his free arm and revealed Katja's journal clutched within his gloved hands. She gasped and patted down her bag to find its volume significantly lacking. "Give that back!"

The soldier held fast to her arm until it ached, but all she cared about were her innermost thoughts and insurrectionist ideas being exposed at that moment.

Finally, he released her and handed the book back. She snatched it and placed it back in her bag. How the Steinkamp was able to take it without her being aware frightened her more than his menacing reaction to her meager threats.

The Steinkamp said, "I won't do any of the aforementioned things, but I won't just recite to you the lyrics either, not while that book is in your possession. Do you understand?"

Katja nodded begrudgingly while rubbing her elbow. She had to remember this man was not some ordinary security guard from the university. This man was Steinkamp. He would not hesitate to take her head off if commanded.

"I have no choice but to continue my research unimpeded, despite what you say," said Katja.

"The way I see it, I have something you want, and you have something I want," the Steinkamp said. "So, I will offer you this. Instead of telling you the lyrics, I will simply escort you on your secret excursions. I can then assist you in raising golems to your heart's content, provided you never write the lyrics in that book, and you never tell anyone of our interactions henceforth."

"That is all I want," Katja agreed. "But tell me. What exactly do *you* want out of this?"

The Steinkamp, in a staunch voice behind his unmoving mask, said, "That is not for you to know at this time."

"Well, then how am I supposed to trust you?"

"I don't much care if you trust me at all."

"Then I cannot accept this arrangement."

"By all means, reject my offer to help you, and see how far you get the next time you decide to leave university grounds alone," the Steinkamp said gruffly.

"Not if I turn you in."

"A Steinkamp has been ordered to protect you; it doesn't have to be me. However, *I'm* the only one that knows the lyrics you seem to need so badly. So make your choice, fraulein."

He turned from Katja once more to continue the trek, leaving her stunned. *Why does he insist on getting in my way?* Unfortunately, it didn't matter. She had to know if the words sung in conjunction with the notes would work in waking a giant golem again.

Sighing with frustration, she followed the black-clad soldier down the path. "Alright, Steinkamp. You may accompany me to these woods at the same time next week . . . and have your singing voice ready."

"Already looking forward to it," he muttered under his breath.

5

BLUE LIGHT

"Do you have a name, Steinkamp?"

Katja and her bodyguard had been riding silently upon the northern road toward Frost Woods for the past hour. Week's end had come again, and she was able to break away from the rest of the team to make another trek.

"I am nameless," was his only reply.

"So none of you have names? How does your kommandeur give you orders?"

"Our superior offiziers know our names."

The conversation ended at that.

The Steinkamp had required no warning of Katja's arrival at the stables earlier that day. As soon as her horse had set hoof on the northern trail, he appeared on his own horse right next to her. Even with the winter whiteness all around them, the soldier, dressed head to toe in black, could easily be mistaken for Katja's own shadow. His uncanny ability to approach unseen made her even more uneasy around him.

He rode ahead of her, his posture unfaltering, his every movement made with calculated intention. He made the act of sitting on a horse appear as athletic as sparring or climbing. Never having seen a Steinkamp this close before, Katja took this time to study the meticulous craftsmanship of his armor. It was designed to protect every inch of his body without appearing bulky and ungainly, even with the various weapons he wore. Among them were a sword and crossbow at his back, a circular throwing blade at his hip, a cudgel at his leg, and a knife at the other. She could only guess what else hid in his various pockets.

The crossbow made her curious. She was familiar with them, as her father's personal guard had taught her how to use one at thirteen. The Steinkamp's however, appeared much more advanced. It was compact as to not weigh him down, and capable of holding three bolts in its barrel instead of one.

A bulky, cylindrical apparatus strapped to the Steinkamp's left forearm irked Katja the most. To relieve some of the discomforts she felt just having him there, she decided to ask, "What is that thing on your arm?"

Glancing down at it, the Steinkamp replied, "It's a splitting blade dispenser."

"All that just to dispense a blade?"

The Steinkamp lifted his arm to let her get a better view. "It's not just a blade. It is attached to a chain, wound up inside the base here," he pointed to the largest section of the dispenser. "Then when the catch is released here," he indicated the lever on the underside of his forearm, "the blade fires, similar to how a crossbow does. It is designed to fan into three blades at the hilt upon impact so it cannot be removed from its target easily."

"Whatever for?" Katja asked with a grimace, starting to regret asking about it at all.

"It can be very useful in eliminating a target from a distance if it needs to be retrieved after," the Steinkamp stated matter-of-factly.

Bile rose in Katja's chest upon listening to the Steinkamp speak of his targets as if they were not human beings. "Do you really think you need something like that out here?"

"A Steinkamp should do his best to avoid leaving a weapon behind when he goes out on a mission. I keep replacements for almost everything in my saddle bags."

"I suppose one cannot be too prepared," she commented, although she still thought such weaponry was over the top for the mission he was on.

Katja couldn't stop shivering as the fat snowflakes fell around them. The flakes landing upon the Steinkamp's uniform melted instantly, while piling on the shoulders of her own tawny overcoat. Her long brown hair was pinned back and tucked away under her fur hat, but it did little to protect her from the winds that blew the snow into her face. She tightened her scarf around her neck. "Aren't you cold?"

"It has been years since I felt the cold," he answered. "All Steinkamp complete their survival training in the most extreme environments of Ingleheim, one of those places being the Glacier Peaks of Nordenhein. Temperatures drop to such dismal levels, that more than half of novices don't make it through."

"You lose that many . . . in training?" Katja was baffled.

"That's why it's called *survival* training. A Steinkamp who cannot face his own impending demise has no right to inflict such on his foes."

"Even when those *foes* are innocent children? When does a Steinkamp train in that?"

Katja didn't know why she asked him such a thing, but the Steinkamp's presence was beyond vexing and she couldn't help but lash out. *Why would Father send the same type of soldier to protect me that he used to slaughter children during his rise to power?* she wondered. *And how in Verishten's name does he know the Ode?*

The Steinkamp replied to Katja's sharp inquiry, "A Steinkamp's kill training begins at the age of thirteen. We are taught to kill every manner of man and beast, but children are not among them."

Katja's brow furrowed as she contemplated his answer. The Regime required all boys to serve a minimum of ten years in the military when they reached sixteen. It helped to strengthen Ingleheim's military machine and keep young men off the streets during their most tumultuous age. Katja's father had said to her once that *'idle hands in a regime will work to unravel it.'* Boys that skirted this crucial responsibility were often hunted down and killed by Steinkamp soldiers. Of course, there were exceptions among the wealthy and educated, like Klemens, who could petition a ruling from their kanzler that would allow them to better serve through scholastic or mercantile pursuits.

"Do they not still require novices to execute military dodgers as a part of their kill training?" Katja asked.

"Yes."

"Are they not children?"

"If the Regime deems them man enough to fight for Ingleheim, they are man enough to suffer the consequences for not doing so."

Katja shifted uncomfortably in her saddle as they rode into Frost Woods. "What do you have to say about the atrocities committed by your fellow comrades in the slaughter of hundreds of families, including innocent women and children?"

"I don't know anything about what my comrades did twenty years ago nor do I care." The Steinkamp's voice was curt. "My mission is to see to your protection, not to kill you, murder children, or anything else you've imagined me and my comrades doing through the ages. Now drop it."

Katja sighed with frustration. "Just give me the lyrics."

"That's not happening."

"I promise I won't report you."

"The day I take the word of a spoiled highborn girl like you is the day I jump into the Mouth of Verishten."

"Then, by all means, take the infernal leap. It would certainly simplify things."

Katja kicked her horse and galloped ahead, her head spinning. She needed some distance from the faceless soldier.

The Steinkamp didn't stay behind for long. He kicked his jet-black steed into a gallop and turned it in front of her. Katja's horse danced backward to get its bearings. Fortunately for her, she was able to get the spooked mare under control rather quickly.

"What are you doing?" she huffed.

"I'm here to help you, you know."

"You know what would really help me right now? You, returning to the shadows so that I can be blissfully unaware of you again!"

The Steinkamp maneuvered his horse across the path so that Katja's couldn't move past him. "I would love nothing more, but here we find ourselves."

"Get out of the way."

He tilted his head. "You have nothing to fear from me, fraulein."

"I am not afraid of you."

"Well, you're certainly afraid of something. Is it the Regime or something else?"

Do they teach Steinkamp to read thoughts as well? Is this another Mage sent to use my mind as his plaything? Katja thought. She grew weary of the Steinkamp's intrusions and since regretted antagonizing him in the first place. "Leave the analysis to the researcher. Just keep to what you are trained for."

She leaned forward in her saddle and swung her right leg over the back of her horse just as a cracking branch under the other horse's hooves spooked it. The mare shifted its weight so suddenly Katja lost her balance and fell head-first off the right side of her saddle.

Faster than she could take a breath, the Steinkamp leaped off his horse. He caught her around the waist as she fell diagonally into his arms. He then swiftly and gently twirled her into a snowdrift. The Steinkamp held her there for a moment, looking down at her with what she imagined was a smug grin behind that dark metallic mesh.

"What I'm trained for, according to you, is slaughtering children." The Steinkamp released her once she was able to steady herself.

Katja brushed the snowflakes from her coat and scarf while reddening with embarrassment. "Perhaps I can concede that not all Steinkamp soldiers are child murderers."

"A highborn lady, willing to concede? This is news to bring back to my comrades," he mocked.

He continued to stare at her as she shook the snow from her hat and put it back on. Though she could not see his face, she couldn't stop imagining a mocking grin, and it unnerved her not to know if it was really there.

It would be nice to put a face to his lack of a name. With that thought, Katja approached the Steinkamp and reached for his mask in a weak attempt to rip it from his face. Without a glance, he snatched her wrist with lightning speed and held it still.

"What do you think you are doing?" The Steinkamp's voice was husky.

Katja's skin flushed. "I wish to remove your mask so that I can wipe that smirk off your face!"

"Steinkamp don't smirk."

"Fine." She yanked her wrist away and went to grab her things from the saddle bag. "Keep it on, then. It will make it easier for me to ignore you."

"That's what we count on."

The Steinkamp and Katja finished tying their horses to a couple of low branches and continued onward down the snowy path.

They trudged through Frost Woods in relative silence. Within several minutes, they arrived at the creek where Katja awakened her first giant frost golem, and like she did on that day, she felt it prudent to venture farther.

That week's heavy snowfall had filled any tread marks the golem left behind. Numerous times, she consulted her map and compass so she might locate another clearing close by.

The Steinkamp sighed. "Put those away and follow me."

In half an hour, they emerged from the thick foliage above a snug valley amongst a bunch of pines growing along an icy ridge.

"Down this way," the soldier urged as he gracefully began his descent.

The way appeared dangerous, and Katja didn't dare move. The Steinkamp turned back and offered her his hand. She hesitated, but on his second urging, she grabbed hold of his arm, and he brought her safely to a snow-covered platform below. The remainder of the way down was a sheer drop to the snow-filled valley beneath them.

"Are you ready?" asked the Steinkamp, reaffirming his grip on Katja's arm.

"Ready for what?"

Without replying, he leaped from the ledge, taking Katja with him. She screamed and cursed as they free-fell. But the fall and her screams were cut short when her feet abruptly made contact with the deep snow. Both Katja and the Steinkamp became buried up to their waists in the soft, fluffy flakes that she had thought were several feet down, but in reality, were not that far below the platform. Then came unfettered laughter. That laughter was Katja's, and she was completely unprepared for it.

As quickly as glee had overcome her, she stopped laughing and cleared her throat awkwardly upon noticing the Steinkamp's silent, masked stare.

"Oh, I suppose Steinkamp don't laugh either."

"Only on the inside."

Katja paused. They were words stolen straight out of her own mouth, said so many times before to Klemens. *Strange that I break down in a laughing fit in front of a masked soldier of death whom I just met, instead of the classmate I've known for years.*

He easily climbed out of the snow. Katja tried to do the same but only sank deeper. In her frustration, she simply looked up at him—his shadow cast over her—and said, "You put me in here, now get me out."

The Steinkamp grunted as he tugged Katja out of the snow by her arms. She couldn't tell if he were annoyed or amused. The two of them then slid down a snowy incline to the bottom of the valley where the snow was not as deep and they could walk across the top.

The snow in the valley was light, the smell of it crisp and clean. Katja never wanted to leave Nordenhein and return to the ashen gloom of Deschner. *Would Father ever consent to me permanently residing in Nordenhein Range?* She wondered.

"This place is as good as any to find dormant golems, I think," she said.

With her flute in hand, Katja first played the *Ode to Golems* without the words as a control experiment. As she predicted, no golems—giant or otherwise—appeared to them.

"I wonder why I was able to awaken that human-sized golem with only the notes, but the giant one needed the words," Katja mused.

"I sang the words that day too," the Steinkamp confessed. "I was a bit farther away, so you probably couldn't hear me over your flute."

"Well, that answers that question." Katja brought the flute close to her lips again. "I guess it's time for you to start singing then."

The Steinkamp cleared his throat, seeming nervous all of a sudden. She surmised singing was not an art form Steinkamp were trained in, but he had insisted on being the one to do it. He crooned along to the flute's melody, his voice low and unmelodious. Katja strained to hear it.

"Golem, take me to your land.
Spare me from your powerful hand.
Give yourself to me, then we shall be free.
Golem, find me, here I stand."

Katja stopped playing for a moment. The lyrics were not what she'd expected.

The Steinkamp turned to her. "Does my singing voice offend you, fraulein?"

"N-no, not at all . . . keep going."

With the next verse, his voice grew a little more confident. She couldn't believe a Steinkamp could sing so well.

"Golem, your eye, I see through.
Let me show you what we can do.
Blessed by Verishten, you are of my kin.
Golem, hear me, I am you."

Katja found herself overwhelmed with wonderment. It was what she had always dreamed it to be. The *Ode* had not been written by people who wanted to dominate golems, but by people who thought of them as their kin, something that was a part of them, something they could experience the world through. Her research to find a connection between golems and humanity felt more possible than ever. *Finally, the words to my favorite melody.*

When the song ended, a strange yet calming silence enveloped the space between Katja and the Steinkamp.

"Where did you learn that song?" she asked softly.

Before the Steinkamp could formulate a reply, a shudder of falling rocks erupted from behind them. They both spun around to witness the stone platform they had jumped from earlier detach from the rest of the rock face. A giant frost golem lumbered around to face them.

"It worked! It's not a coincidence!" Katja exclaimed.

As the golem took steps toward them, the deep snow parted before it like a cold white wave. Katja took a few steps to meet the advancing colossus, her arms held out in front of her as if to brace it. She began to sing the *Ode* in a shaking voice, but having only heard it once, hadn't memorized the words yet.

"Steinkamp, start singing, please."

"What are you trying to do? Unless you're a Golem Mage, you can't control it," he said.

"There is historical evidence of people in the Age of Man being able to communicate with golems. I know I can't dominate it, but . . ."

The golem, standing about twenty feet tall, stopped a few paces away. She took another step toward it.

"Fraulein, stay back!" The Steinkamp took hold of Katja's shoulder and pulled her back to him.

"It's okay, let go," she demanded.

The golem stood before them for a moment longer, flashed its blue light, and then began to turn around like all the other ones before it. *I have to keep its attention this time.* Katja couldn't allow yet another golem to walk away without giving her something to document.

As the golem was leaving and the perceived threat lessened, the Steinkamp let her go. She dashed around the golem until she was again in its line of sight. It halted its stride, its blue eye flashing once more.

"Katja!" the Steinkamp barked.

"Sing the words!" She fumbled in her bag for the flute and brought it up to her dry lips.

She hardly had the chance to sound a single note when the frost golem's blue eye shone upon her—so bright, she could no longer see. She stopped playing and shielded her eyes with her arm. A cold penetrated deep into her bones.

A shadow suddenly blocked the blue light of the golem's eye, and shoved her to the ground. She lifted her head with a mouthful of snow and turned to witness the Steinkamp collapse in front of her, stiff, unmoving—his uniform white with frost. Lying face down, his frozen hand clutched his crossbow as if prepared to shoot.

"No!" Katja screamed.

The massive golem turned toward her again.

What just happened? Why did it attack?

Its eye shone almost white, hurting Katja's eyes once more. The cold returned in a wave.

With adrenaline pumping fiercely through her, she leaped up from the snowdrift and dove behind a pair of large pines. The freezing cold cloaked her, taking the wind right out of her lungs.

The sound of crackling ice deafened her. Glistening, crystalline ice coated every last pine needle of the trees at Katja's back. The ground shook as the golem drew nearer, stopping just behind the trees and causing parts of frozen branches to shake loose into the snow. Katja looked up to find the golem's eye shining high over the top of the pine's icicle tips, ready to freeze her on sight. She would never make the climb out of the valley before the golem reached her; she was hopelessly trapped. *Why is it so hostile? Man and golem have been at peace for over two thousand years. Only when a Mage commands a golem to attack a human will it do so!* Since the only Golem Mage left alive was her father, Katja never had to worry about golems attacking her. She was utterly unprepared for this.

A giant stone arm shattered the frozen pine trees that Katja hid behind. She dove to the side with a shrill screech. The golem's eye flashed again, and she reacted without a second thought. She ran between its legs, frantically searching for a way out of the enclosed valley. *There's nowhere to go!*

Directly east looked the most promising except for the mounds of snow hills that Katja couldn't hope to run through fast enough. She looked west to where she and the Steinkamp had come. There she found something she didn't expect to see. The dormant golem had blocked an opening in the cliffside. With the snow around it set aside, she could easily slip through it in hopes it would take her out of the valley.

But if not—I need a way to bring it down.

Katja knew that the eye was the golem's only known vulnerability, but damaging it often required skill in projectile weapons that few people possessed.

Before the golem could turn its massive form around, Katja took a risk and dove to retrieve the Steinkamp's crossbow from his frozen grasp. He wouldn't need it anymore. There was nothing Katja could do for him now. She sprinted west toward the crevasse, the snow still deep enough to slow her down. Once again she felt the penetrating cold at her back, her heart humming with dreadful anticipation of it being frozen in her chest. She reached the cliff just as the stone all around her became coated with ice, but she kept moving. The cliff walls grew tighter and tighter until Katja couldn't fit between them anymore. For all she knew, there was a dead end ahead.

The earth shook and the golem approached. Its blue eye shone through the crack in the cliff. For a moment she could make out the detail of it. There was no iris or pupil, but circular maze-like patterns with lines like crystal ice against brilliant blue. Katja was as captivated as she was terrified, but she had to keep her wits about her.

Pressed between two slabs of ice-coated rock, she cocked the crossbow with more ease than she'd expected, courtesy of a smaller cranequin, which didn't require her to use a foot stirrup for leverage. She edged closer to the golem, the crossbow aimed and ready to release. When the blue eye lit up again, Katja squinted from the brightness and pulled the trigger.

6

CRUELTY BREEDS
LOYALTY

The unbearable chill of the golem's eye pierced through Katja's body. The light made it impossible to see where her crossbow bolt went. She could only hear its release, and a second later, ice cracking.

Katja was so cold she feared it was the sound of ice crystallizing on her body. One more second passed before the light went out and the freezing air dissipated. She opened her eyes to see her crossbow bolt sticking out from the golem's eye. The ground shook as the giant creature collapsed against the cliff wall, slid down, and landed on its side.

Gasping for air, Katja's breath was a frigid white mist. The golem moved no more, but she knew it wasn't dead, only forced into dormancy. Her mind raced as frantically as her heart. *I just shot down a golem all on my own, and the Steinkamp barely stood a chance.*

Katja's breath seized. She may have miraculously survived the ordeal, but the one assigned to protect her did not. He died to save her life, and she didn't even know his name. *Calm down, Katja, he may still live,* she told herself.

With the crossbow in hand, she slowly approached the fallen golem that blocked her path out of the crevasse. It would not reawaken as long as the bolt remained in its eye. As she came closer to it, Katja could clearly make out the fine cracks that made up the strange pattern within. She would have to study it some other time; right now she needed to check on the Steinkamp.

After several attempts, she finally climbed up the golem's slippery

soapstone back and slid off the other side into the open valley. She ran to
the fallen soldier whose black armor was made white by a frost coating.

Her heart thumped in her throat as she turned the Steinkamp onto his
back, his mask caked in ice. She removed her gloves so she could find his
pulse but quickly realized she'd feel nothing through his thick leather neck
brace. Before she could figure out how to take it off, the Steinkamp jerked
awake, coughing and taking in violent, gargled breaths like a man who had
nearly drowned.

"You're alive!" She gasped and brushed the ice crystals from his mask.

He struggled to sit up, the ice from his uniform cracking but ultimately
keeping him from moving. The Steinkamp's breathing grew more forced
and frantic, mist bursting from behind the mesh.

"Are you all right?"

The Steinkamp's reply came out as chattering spurts, and was barely
intelligible. "H-h-hot spring . . . n-not far."

"Where?"

"East . . . h-h-help me . . ."

Katja didn't waste time asking more questions. She left the crossbow
in the snow and positioned herself behind the shivering Steinkamp. With
all her might, she lifted and pushed him to a seated position, ice chunks
shattering off his torso. Katja put his left arm over her shoulder and used
all her strength to lift him to his feet. More ice broke away from his legs as
he rose to a standing position. Her knees buckled under the Steinkamp's
weight, even after he dropped his sword and splitting blade dispenser.

With a grunt, Katja pushed forward, using both their momenta to
continue moving ahead. The Steinkamp kept some of his weight off her as
they ventured onward, but it was barely enough. The snow was too deep,
and her arms and legs tired trudging through it. The Steinkamp shuddered
more violently against her as she half-dragged him through the snow,
following his weak directives to go right, then left, then through some
trees. The map she had with her didn't indicate where the hot springs
were located, although Ingleheim had no shortage of volcanic landmarks.

Just when Katja felt she would give up and let the Steinkamp freeze
to death, she became immersed in a humid fog. The snow beneath their
feet turned into a thick slush, its translucence making the mud and dead,
flattened grass visible beneath. Precious warmth wrapped around the pair,
and the Steinkamp took his first few steps without aid. Katja rubbed her
sore shoulders as she followed him down a slushy embankment leading to

a steaming pool cradled in a ring of dark soapstone.

The ice frozen to the Steinkamp's uniform began to melt off as he stepped more assuredly toward the water. He threw himself into the hot spring, becoming completely submerged, then resurfaced. He floated for a while, shaking the water out through the mesh of his mask.

The steam swirled above the teal blue water, and Katja yearned to jump in with him and soothe her aching muscles but decided against it. It was better for her to stay dry. Instead, she stood holding her arms to her chest at the edge of the hot spring, watching the Steinkamp until, at last, he gained the strength to stand upright in the waist-deep water.

He then began to undo his clasps. "I have an extra uniform in my saddle bag. I need you to retrieve it for me. I cannot make it back with a wet suit. Do you think you can find your way to the horses on your own?"

The man had already removed the top armored layer and tossed the pieces onto the embankment, revealing a black undershirt of thinner material that better showcased his well-muscled forearms.

Katja swallowed. "Y-yes, I think so . . . I mean, of course, wait here."

She clambered back up the embankment and out of sight of the Steinkamp. *Now, how to get back to that valley where I left my map and compass?* she thought with cold sweat beading down her back. It took her so long to come upon the valley again that she worried she'd taken a wrong turn and gotten lost. She located her shoulder bag from where the Steinkamp had shoved her into the snow. The frost golem was right where she had left it as well. *I actually took down a giant golem by myself!*

With the help of her map and compass, Katja found an alternate path out of the valley and back to the horses. Almost two hours passed from when she left the hot springs to when she returned with the spare uniform in hand. At first she couldn't see the Steinkamp in the pool. Maybe he had grown impatient and decided to set off with a wet uniform after all. Then she found his entire suit in a heap on the embankment along with his mask.

Unless he set off into the winter cold in the nude, he has to be around here somewhere, Katja surmised. "Steinkamp?" she called.

Then, from behind one of the larger rocks that formed a small cave on the far side of the pool, she heard his quietly assertive voice. "Set it upon the stone and look away."

Through the steam, Katja could make out the rudimentary outline of a shirtless man, his bottom half obscured behind the soapstone formations, his back to her so she could not see his face. She crept toward the rocks and carefully placed the uniform bundle on the flatter stone surface as instructed. She didn't turn around right away, though. The closer she got, the more she could make out his form, and the more distinctive the muscles of his bare back, shoulders, and arms became through the thermal haze. It was known that Steinkamp soldiers were the strongest climbers in Ingleheim, and it was apparent by his definition that this one was no different. Katja let her eyes wander about him more. She noticed his closely shaved hair was light and ashen where for some reason she had expected it to be as black as the mask he wore.

"Katja, turn around and do not look my way until I tell you," the Steinkamp demanded.

"What does it matter if I see your face now?"

"It is important for me to remain faceless just as it is for your parentage to remain secret. It protects us both. Now turn around." His voice was harsh.

Katja had no desire to test the Steinkamp's patience further so she did what he bid. She listened to him move through the water, snatch the uniform from the rock, and put it on without a word.

The two of them returned to the valley to collect the Steinkamp's weapons. It was there where he finally broke the tension-filled silence. When he laid eyes on the fallen frost golem, he muttered, "How did it . . . ?"

"You may want to check your crossbow. You're missing a bolt," Katja said.

The Steinkamp did so and looked back to her, cocking his head to the side. "How does a highborn woman like you know how to use a crossbow so well?"

"Never mind that, wait until you see what the eye of a frost golem looks like." Katja motioned for him to follow her.

But the Steinkamp held onto her arm fast. "Don't go near it!"

"Don't worry, it won't rise again until the obstruction is—"

"If we don't start heading back now it will be dark before you return to your dormitory!"

He was right to be concerned. At nightfall, the Dormitory Monitors knocked upon each door to ensure every student was where they were supposed to be. If Katja was not back before then, she could forget about ever coming back to these woods without her team.

She nodded while edging toward the golem once again. "I agree, but first I have to examine its eye in case it's not here by next week's end."

"I said no!" The Steinkamp was brusque, clutching her arm tighter.

"Let go of me. You are not to interfere with my research, remember?" She pulled against the Steinkamp's grip but it did not falter.

"You've done enough research for today." He tugged her arm.

All she could do was look back to the golem helplessly. *If anyone comes upon that golem and removes the obstruction from its eye . . .*

"Wait . . ." was all Katja could utter.

The Steinkamp pulled harder, practically dragging her behind him. "My mission is all that matters to me right now, and that is to keep you alive. I ask you, how is one supposed to protect a woman with a death wish? If I had been any slower, that ice beam would have hit you dead on. If it weren't for the fact that it only grazed me and my uniform's propensity to withstand extreme temperatures, I would not be alive to talk some sense into you right now!"

Katja stopped struggling. "I don't have a death wish. But this research is too important. You have to trust me on this."

"You're asking me to trust you?" The Steinkamp finally let go of Katja and blared at her. "You won't even tell me why you keep your research to yourself."

"Don't you think I want to tell someone? Anyone? How can I be sure you won't report this to your kapitän or some rebel?"

"So you don't want the rebellion to know either," the Steinkamp muttered. Katja looked at him with confusion, and he continued, "The fact that a Steinkamp has been assigned to protect you is an indication that you are vital to the Regime, and yet you speak of that Regime with about as much disregard as you have for your own safety. Your inflammatory opinions combined with your propensity for ranged weaponry suggests you may have rebel ties, but you have no intention of sharing your research with them either. Who do you actually work for?"

Katja's heart throbbed in her ears. *This Steinkamp was not sent to just protect me but to investigate me, to test my loyalties.* She wasn't sure how much she believed that. She found herself desperate to trust him, but she froze.

Truthfully, she was working for no one but herself. She rebelled against her father, against Brunhilde, and the Regime for the sake of her own research. The danger was that her findings would potentially assist the Regime in awakening the Golem of Death. Katja couldn't let anyone find out. All of this, she wanted to divulge to the man in black. Under the circumstances, however, there was only one answer she could give to satisfy his curiosities and keep him from finding her out.

"I told you, I work for the Führer," she declared.

"If you are so close to the Führer, then turn me in," the Steinkamp challenged.

"For what?"

"For knowing the forbidden words to the *Ode to Golems*. One word from you and I will disappear, and a more obedient comrade will be assigned to your detail, and then you can continue your ever so important research unhindered."

"Who sent you to me?" Katja asked instead.

"I told you, my orders come from my kommandeur," was his only reply.

If he had been sent by Brunhilde, the Steinkamp would never tell her, even if he wanted to. That sorceress had ways of coercing others to keep her secrets through magical and other means. Katja hated the uncertainty, she hated the secrecy, but she didn't know what to do about it.

"You know who my father is, don't you?"

"I assure you, I do not know, nor do I care who your father is."

From behind the mask, Katja could never guess if he was lying, but if he had known who her father was, he would certainly care.

"It is time to head back," she said, exhaustion weighing heavily on her. She needed time to think.

During the ride back to the university, Katja felt like a lifetime had passed since the morning when she and the Steinkamp set out.

So much was on her mind. What were the Steinkamp's true intentions? Would she be able to study the felled golem next week? Through all of that, Katja had almost forgotten that she could have been riding alone right now, worrying about how she would explain away the death of her protector on their first excursion together. It could have been her frozen into a block of ice had it not been for the faceless man that she'd wished had never been assigned to her in the first place. *A Steinkamp is sworn to defend the defenseless, to never waver; never retreat. Maybe this one had no choice but to put himself in front of that beam, but would any man, even a Steinkamp, risk his life for a woman he would later see harm to?*

Katja stared at him for a moment, sitting not as straight on the saddle as before, his movements more listless, the condensed vapors of his breath blowing more forcefully out from his mask.

"Are you injured, Steinkamp?" she peeped. "You were nearly turned into a human ice sculpture back there."

"Rest is surely needed after today," he admitted, "but I will live. Believe it or not, I've felt colder during my winter survival training."

"How *did* you survive it?" She nudged her mare forward to ride next to him.

For a moment, he didn't reply. Katja figured that was a story she would not get out of him today, until he began, "I almost didn't. The other novices and I were flown by winged golem to Nordenhein's highest peak. We were left there with no supplies, no food, and nothing more than the clothes on our backs; none of which were particularly suited for winter. Many lost their lives within the first week. We spent the entire winter living off the land, but food was scarce, and ultimately all the novices in my survival group starved to death or died of exposure."

"Verishten have mercy," Katja murmured.

"I spent another month alone in those woods," the Steinkamp continued. "I would have gone the way of the others had I not stumbled upon the hot springs. The ground there was warm, so I made camp, and I stayed until spring. When I was strong enough to explore the woods again, I heard the sound of a distant bell toll. I followed the sound, and I soon found the City of Nordenhein. Only Verishten knows how long I would have wandered through those woods if it weren't for that clock tower to guide me out."

The Steinkamp paused for a moment and then continued quietly, "You see . . . I didn't want to survive. I never wanted to be a Steinkamp soldier. I longed for death, but cold kills far too slowly. That clock tower was a sign from the Mighty Verishten that I was meant to be of this world."

Sighing deeply, he went on, "About a quarter of the novices placed upon that peak had made it down before or after me. We had proven ourselves to be of true Steinkamp ilk. When our strength returned, we were subjected to two other survival tests before we were permitted to start our kill training in Breisenburg."

"Wait, didn't you say your kill training began at thirteen?" Katja asked, her mind still reeling from the Steinkamp's horrible accounts.

"Yes."

"Then that means you were only . . ."

"I was eleven," he stated.

Breathing suddenly didn't come easily. "What other harsh environments did they subject you to afterward?" she asked, though she wasn't sure if she wanted to know.

"Next, it was the storm-ridden peaks of Luidfort Mountain Range where it rained nearly every day at that time. We were forced to survive by climbing slippery cliffs and huddling in caves. The storms were so violent that lightning repeatedly struck down. The Peaks of Luidfort are named by the town's people as Verishten's Wrath for good reason."

Katja tried to lighten the subject by adding, "Yes, that peak was named after the Alpha of the Winged Golems, or the Golem of Storms. Legends say it had caused the great storms that shaped the Luidfort valleys during the Age of Golems. The great springs in the cliffs are fed by those storms. There is a religious sect unique to Luidfort that incorporated the Golem of Storms in their worship of Verishten. They believe that their prayers keep the storm waters pure for human consumption."

"The fresh rain water was probably why we only lost one-quarter of the novices on that excursion. It was our trip to the Volcano of Verishten that really tested our resolve. We could hardly breathe up there. The ash covered everything in sight and snuffed out all life, making it impossible to find food. There was no respite from the heat or the starvation. To survive, we had to descend from the mountain as quickly as possible without falling to our deaths or slipping into a lava pit. I still have the scars on my hands and knees from crawling along the burning rocks. The cold comforts of ice and snow are welcoming after experiencing the blaze of the volcano. Even far from the reach of the ash clouds our welts would not heal, our eyes would not stop burn—"

"Please . . . stop."

The Steinkamp turned his head to her. "Does my story bother you, fraulein?"

Katja didn't answer the question for a time, then said, "A Regime that would require the suffering of children to protect it is not a Regime worth protecting."

"And yet you risked your life with that golem in service to such a Regime," the Steinkamp countered. "Funny how cruelty can breed loyalty."

The quiet rigidity in his voice as he said those words brought Katja a painful realization. This faceless soldier assigned to her protection was every bit a victim of the Regime as those murdered under it. She thought of the accusations she made earlier that day and felt sick to her stomach.

Katja took a chance when she chose her next words. "My research must *appear* to better the Regime. However . . . the results they are looking for, I cannot allow them to have. It is still important for me to continue my own research and the Regime can never know. Neither can my team. I cannot put them in that position. Can I trust you will not report back what I've just said?"

The Steinkamp continued looking down the snowy road where the walls of the university stood in the distance with the sun sinking below them. Katja began to sweat beneath her scarf despite the chill of dusk. *Did I just make a horrible mistake? Is he still going to report me despite everything that happened today?*

"Cruelty breeds loyalty," the Steinkamp finally replied, "but I understand better than most that there are some cruelties in this world we cannot forgive."

Katja let out a sigh of relief. The risk she took in telling him the small amount she did may have been worth it. She then made another choice. "I do hope you will come with me again at week's end . . . to study the golem eye."

The Steinkamp snapped his head around as if he couldn't believe she would suggest that again after the verbal thrashing he gave her earlier.

"But only if you deem it safe," she quickly added. "And if I don't wake up in a traitor's cell tomorrow, I may tell you what my research is and why we must keep it secret."

"I will escort you, but only if you agree to do *everything* I say, to not approach a golem without my word, and if you ever so much as set foot or hoof on this road without me beside you—"

"Not to worry," Katja interrupted. "I will heed your every instruction. You have my word. That is, unless you'd rather jump into a volcano than accept the word of a highborn girl."

"The hot spring was hot enough for me," the Steinkamp said without pause.

"I bet it was luxurious. Next time, I should be the one to take a two-hour dip while you run back to the horses. Better yet, you should carry me there, it's only fair." Katja gave him a sidelong glance.

The Steinkamp snapped his head toward her once again. She imagined him glaring at her from behind the void of his mask.

Not looking to ruffle the faceless man any further, she gave him a smirk and kicked her horse into a canter. The Steinkamp followed close behind.

7

FIGHTING BLIND

In the dead of night, a lone Steinkamp soldier snuck through the unkempt gardens of the abandoned manor once belonging to the Earl of Deschner, one of the first Golem Mages wiped out under the Heinrich Regime. The men standing guard of the manor's perimeter had already been dispatched, allowing the Steinkamp to approach the west window leading into the main entryway.

The old architecture from the Age of Kings gave the building a cathedral-like appearance, with a stone tower sprouting from a vaulted roof. Sigurd could only imagine what this once great house looked like in the days of its use. It had been recently taken by a band of insurgents who called themselves the Kings' Remnants. They had abducted the Kanzler of Breisenburg on his way to Deschner to meet with the Führer. To gain recognition from his kapitän, who personally took charge of this critical mission, Sigurd convinced his kommandeur to allow him temporary leave of his ongoing assignment in Nordenhein, and a winged golem quickly flew him to Deschner.

Sigurd recalled the debriefing he received from his kapitän shortly after he had arrived in the City of Deschner.

"Remember, comrade," Kapitän Wolfram said, "Herr Volker is not only the Kanzler of Breisenburg, but the Regime's Chief Military Strategist, and a close personal friend of Herrscher Heinrich. The kanzler has been privy to extremely sensitive information. If it falls into rebellion hands, it will be disastrous for the Regime."

"How long has the kanzler been their prisoner?" Sigurd asked.

"Almost four days now, so there's a good chance that he already revealed such information. He could be dead, or kept alive for possible ransom. Your mission is not to rescue him, but to determine what the Kings' Remnants know and to prevent any further secrets from being leaked."

"Will I be accompanied on this mission?"

"No," Wolfram replied. "Due to the sensitive nature of the information at stake, I intend on keeping the details of this mission between me and one other comrade."

"I am honored that you have chosen me for this task, Kapitän." Sigurd took to his knee out of respect for his superior. He was excited to complete this assignment. It would bring him one step closer to becoming one of the kapitäns personal comrades. Just as him agreeing to the top-secret security detail at Nordenhein University got him noticed by the kapitän in the first place.

"Here is the floor plan of the manor where we believe the Kings' Remnants are holding Volker. Find him, eliminate him, and bring me back any rebels that may have information." Wolfram handed Sigurd a roll of parchment for him to memorize.

Sigurd then asked, *"Does the Führer not prefer his friend alive?"*

"Our Führer does not tolerate weakness, especially in a military leader. Friend or not, Volker is too high of a security risk. See that you show him a Steinkamp's mercy."

To best follow those orders, it was imperative that Sigurd clear the entire house quickly and without detection to avoid alerting the rebels holding Volker. He couldn't chance any of them fleeing the premises.

As he carefully peered through the ash-stained window into the manor's great entryway, Sigurd counted six figures standing guard inside. There were two at the front doors, and four more wandering about the large open space. Candle-lit chandeliers hung above them, coating the foyer in a soft glow. Light was the Steinkamp soldier's greatest adversary when it came to the art of stealth warfare. Twilight canisters fixed that problem.

Sigurd grabbed a small metallic canister from one of his front pockets while pulling open the window. He tossed the item into the foyer, where it struck the ground and cracked open. Every source of light was invariably shrouded by an inescapable darkness. The soldier leaped through the window, disappearing into the impenetrable shadow, his thin retractable steel blade extended and primed for the kill.

The light would begin to seep back into the room after a while, and the rebel guards were already alarmed by the sudden blackness, so Sigurd had to eliminate his targets with haste. Fortunately, being a Steinkamp not only made him an expert at vanquishing opponents more quickly and efficiently than other regime soldiers, but he could also fight blind, a highly specialized skill instilled into every comrade from the moment their training began.

Sigurd's sword cleaved effortlessly through the flesh of the two rebels guarding the front doors. Without his sight to guide him to the rest of his foes, he relied fully on his other senses. He heard their surprise, felt their panic, and smelled their trepidation. Each body dropped at his feet just as he proceeded to feel out his next opponent. Sigurd listened carefully to every man's croak, groan, or grunt, and when one's cries drew out too long, he was sure to cut them off with a well-executed stab to the throat or back of the neck.

Before entering the foyer, Sigurd had counted six men, and he had since counted six men dead by his sword before the light faded back into the room. He raced up the west staircase so nimbly, the warped, old wood had little time to creak under each of his carefully placed steps. He waited at the double doors at the top of the stairs to listen for movement behind them. From the mutterings of an occurring conversation, he inferred that at least two rebels were guarding those doors on the other side.

After carefully picking the lock of the double doors, Sigurd silently entered a wide hallway. He crouched down and crept forward until he was a few feet behind the two yapping rebels. He extended his retractable blade, careful not to make a sound. Without the guards noticing the shadow below them, Sigurd stood up quickly and thrust his steel through the back of the nearest man's neck. With two hands, he ripped the sword free and swiftly slashed the throat of the second guard in one motion.

The men hadn't had the chance to make a peep, and the others in the large room beyond the hallway were not alerted. Sigurd dragged each dead guard into an adjacent room and continued on. Another rebel guard, armed with a crossbow, approached the hall. Keeping to the shadows behind a pillar, he waited for the guard to pass. As he did so, Sigurd grabbed him around the mouth and chest, pulling the man back into the darkened hall with him. There, the Steinkamp plunged his blade into the back of the guard's sternum and through his heart. He lowered the body and dealt with it just as he had the others.

Not hearing footsteps approaching, Sigurd took stock of the room beyond the hallway. From the floor plan he had studied, he knew he had come to the upper balconies wrapping around a grand dining room on the first floor. He remained crouched, looking down through the balcony railings to the dining area below. There, an old oak table stood on a number of dusty frayed rugs. Four men enjoyed a meal, but from where Sigurd was positioned he couldn't be sure if there were others. On the top floor with him, there were three more men. They would have to be dealt with first.

The Kings' Remnants wore the old-fashioned military uniforms issued during the Age of Kings. They had long brown and red buckled coats that reached their ankles, with trousers that fit tight around the legs and buttoned down the sides, accommodating their boots, worn underneath rather than over the top of them. Upon their heads, they wore large brimmed hats with one edge fastened to the side.

These people can't be comfortable in those, and they look so unreasonably cumbersome, Sigurd thought with a shake of his head. He figured that rebels likely didn't care about the utility of their uniforms. It was what they represented; ghosts from the past, forever haunting the Regime that had destroyed them.

When the path was clear, Sigurd swiftly moved around the upper floor balcony, keeping to the shadows, ducking and rolling behind decorative pieces of furniture or sliding into alcoves along the walls. He successfully dispatched all three men on the top floor without any of the rebels below becoming aware. Sigurd now needed to clear the dining area, but even when peering through the balustrade he still couldn't see every man at the table. He needed a vantage point that put him at the center of the room.

Dangling directly in front of him hung one of two massive chandeliers above the dining table. It looked like it would provide adequate cover while allowing him full visibility of the room. The only disadvantage was that he would draw attention, which meant he would have to eliminate every man in the dining room fast. A Steinkamp had various options at his disposal to make such things happen.

Taking a deep breath, he made a running leap off the balustrade and grabbed hold of the chandelier. He used the momentum from his jump to swing his legs underneath it and crouch up inside. The jostling alerted the rebels as expected and they all looked up at once.

Wrapping his legs around a brass coil at the bottom of the chandelier, Sigurd hung upside down. Now able to see in every direction, he counted six men in the room, three aiming crossbows at him, two armed with knives, and one bolting for the hallway at the south end of the chamber.

Sigurd grabbed his small circular throwing blade, infused with wind magic, from his waist belt. With a backhand toss, the wind essence within the spinning blade activated, making it appear as a small whirlwind disk in flight. In this state, the blade was receptive to the Steinkamp's every whim.

Like all their Magitech equipment, a Steinkamp's gloves were connected to the essences infused within them and were therefore the most crucial part of the comrade's uniform. The gloves also ensured that only a Steinkamp could activate and utilize their Magitech.

By indicating directions with one hand, Sigurd guided the wind blade in a circular sweep of the dining room, slitting the throats or cutting off the heads of the men with the crossbows first. Sigurd pointed to the man running for the hall and the blade sharply changed course in response. It found its mark, and Sigurd subsequently pulled it back into the dining room to take off the heads of the final two guards with the knives. He then summoned back the wind blade, its wind dissipating as it neared him, and its speed reducing so that he could grab it with ease. Since the blades were limited in their wind essence and could only be refueled by a Wind Mage, it was imperative that Sigurd did not resort to using the dangerous weapon unless it was absolutely necessary.

Sigurd put the blade away and switched from hanging upside down by his legs to hanging right side up by his arms. He swung back and forth on the chandelier, creating the momentum he would require to leap to the balcony railing on the other side of the room. Unfortunately, the noise resulting from his prior stunt was enough to draw the attention of someone in the next room. He made his leap and took hold of the bottom of the railing just as the north doors opened and one rebel guard entered the dining room. Sigurd hung just below the rebel's line of sight.

"What's going on in here?" the guard called. "Where is everyone?"

Upon walking up to the railing, the guard let out a gasp of horror, undoubtedly catching sight of the bloody display in the dining room below. Sigurd could feel fear gripping the man in that vital moment. Steinkamp soldiers learned how to pick up on the subtle cues of hesitation. It was easy to take advantage of the human inability to process the sight of death, and utilize his own serenity with it, as one who lived and breathed death from the age of ten.

Before the guard could say another word, Sigurd vaulted over the balustrade with his dagger in hand. He drove the long skewer-shaped blade cleanly through the guard's throat, silencing him permanently. A voice then came from the opened door, followed by footsteps. He pressed his back against the wall just outside and waited for another guard to walk past and investigate what became of his partner. Before the man could react to the body slumped against the railing, Sigurd snuck up behind him, wrapped one arm around his neck in a stranglehold, and clasped the other around his mouth to muffle his cries. In one smooth movement, the Steinkamp snapped his neck to bring the rebel to a quick end.

After dragging the bodies away, the Steinkamp silently walked through the north doors into an empty hallway. He could hear more voices, but they were muffled as if coming from an attached room. Sigurd looked up to find the ceiling having rotted and peeled, exposing a few rafters. The hallway was narrow enough for him to jump off both sides of the wall, grab one of the rafters, and pull himself up. From there, he found his way to the room where the voices originated.

"When do you think the witch will crack him?" said one of the rebels.

"She's been up there with him for two days straight," said the other guard, motioning upward with his head. "I don't think the kanzler is going to talk."

"I still say good old-fashioned torture should do the trick. Volker wouldn't hesitate to do it to one of us if he was in our position," the first man replied.

"Well, I've been told that spirit magic can be every bit as torturous as a hot poker up the ass."

"Who told you that?"

"Gregor," the guard motioned up again.

It appears the rebellion has gained a Spirit Mage just as the Regime has lost its own, Sigurd thought. He made a note to be on the lookout for a woman, in case she happened to be the Mage in question.

"What does Gregor know about spirit magic, anyway? Although I could believe his ass has felt a hot poker or two," the first man said.

The two guffawed. Sigurd decided he would get no more useful information from them. He took out his crossbow and shot a bolt into each of their necks.

A Spirit Mage has been with Volker for two days, and he has yet to talk, he thought. That was good news for the Regime, but Sigurd was unsure if this changed his mission objective. *Should it be a rescue mission at this point?*

After reloading his crossbow, he went ahead and cleared the upper rooms. The floor plan had revealed that the manor didn't have an attic. The tower, however, could be accessed from the outside.

There was a lit fireplace in one of the rooms Sigurd had passed. Fishing into one of his vest pockets, he pulled out a packet of ice powder. He emptied the small sack of white powder, infused with water magic, into his right palm. While clenching his left fist, he cast the powder into the flames. The water essence activated with a clench of his gloved fists. The heat coming from the fireplace turned frigid and in one second the fire was out.

With ease, he climbed up the chimney and onto the rooftop of the manor. The light of the double full moons revealed the ash that coated the roof from years of neglect, but Sigurd was not bothered by it. Ash just made it easier for a Steinkamp to blend into his surroundings.

He found the tower at the north end of the manor where he took out two strands of earth bindings, the most useful of all magical items at a Steinkamp's disposal. In their normal state, earth bindings appeared as ordinary leather straps. When squeezed tightly within a Steinkamp's gloved palm, the earth magic within allowed the bindings to mold onto any surface they came in contact with, be it stone or human skin, with the exception of the Steinkamp's uniform—save the belt. Only a Steinkamp or an Earth Mage could return it to leather again.

Using the bindings as secure handholds upon the ash-stained brick, Sigurd scaled the tower. He reached a thin ledge and balanced along it until he found a small window at the tower's southern side.

Sigurd sensed movement inside. The multi-paned window was already unlocked. He ever so carefully opened one of the small panes at the bottom. Now he could hear the mutterings inside, over the groans of pain coming from Volker.

He took out his crossbow while he listened. There were at least two other people in the room with the kanzler, a man and a woman, who Sigurd assumed was the witch.

"We've got to get a move on, Jenn," urged the man, his voice deep like someone larger than average. "They likely know where we are by now."

"Stop distracting me. His mind is strong, but I almost have him," said the woman. She sounded younger than Sigurd expected. The hard *t* and the strong *s* in the witch's dialect revealed her to be of Deschner Mountain Range, but the guttural sound of her words indicated she was far from highborn.

I can never decide what sounds more irritating—the haughty, sanctimonious air of the highborn lady, or the aggressive grating noise of the commoner, mused Sigurd. Thoughts of Deschner dialects reminded Sigurd of Katja, back in Nordenhein, but he quickly forced himself to regain focus.

"That's it, Kanzler," cooed the witch after a few minutes of silence.

"You know where the Golem of Death is, don't you?"

Sigurd wondered, *Golem of Death? Could this be what the Regime has Katja researching?*

"No . . . I can't tell you. . . ." Volker murmured through rattled breaths.

"As your Führer, I command you to tell me!"

"You've tried this several times already," whispered the other man in the room who Sigurd presumed was Gregor. The witch ignored him.

Sigurd waited on the ledge for a long time, trying to uncover what the rebels already knew before he made his move.

"H-Heinrich . . . is that really you?" rasped Volker after a time.

"Yes, my friend, I have you now. Where are you guarding the Alpha?" Jenn asked, less harsh but no less forceful.

"Don't you know?"

"I need to know that you know. This is very important, Volker," Jenn pressed.

Sigurd had never witnessed a Spirit Mage at work before. He knew that unlike Essence Mages, who manipulated the six essences, fire, water, earth, air, light, and life force. Spirit Mages manipulated spirit itself, the energy that made every life form sentient. They were very rare and incredibly dangerous. They had various specialties such as the art of mind reading, brainwashing, spiritual projections, and memory manipulation, among other terrifying talents. The Great Melikheil was the only Ingle Spirit Mage Sigurd knew of, and it turned out the rebellion had now found another, but of lower birth, right here in Deschner.

"But . . . wait, you're not—get away from me, witch!" Volker pleaded.

"Shit!" Gregor spat.

"Calm down. I can do this," Jenn said with determination in her voice.

A few more moments passed with Jenn frantically whispering to Volker, or Gregor. From where Sigurd was perched, he couldn't make out her mutterings, but he did not dare peer through the window in case he cast a shadow into the room and alert them.

"Are you ready to cooperate, my friend?" Jenn then said in a commanding voice once again.

"Of course, Heinrich. Of course, I will tell you."

Sigurd now had two choices in completing his mission. Since Volker had yet to talk, he could kill Gregor and the witch, and escape with Volker alive. Or he could continue with his original orders and eliminate Volker before he revealed the information, kill Gregor, and then take Jenn back to be interrogated for any other secrets she may have learned during her two days inside Volker's mind.

Sigurd was inclined to follow his orders exactly as his kapitän delivered and gain his favor. However, he knew that killing Volker ensured his secret died with him. I want to know what this Golem of Death is. *Since Volker revealing that information was something the Regime already expected, what did it matter if it happened anyway? At least he would then have a better idea of what he protected back in Nordenhein.*

He waited outside the tower window and allowed Volker to talk.

"East Breisenburg . . . the Alpha is under war golem guard in the eighth sector. No number of men can get past them."

"You mean the abandoned Fortress of Mortlach?" Jenn asked.

"In the caverns underneath, it is buried under mounds of earth and stone," Volker finished.

"Thank you, my friend." Jenn was breathless.

She asked no further questions regarding what the Golem of Death was or what it could do. It appeared the rebellion already knew that much.

It was time for Sigurd to act. Aiming his crossbow through the open window pane, he shot a bolt straight into Volker's aorta, killing him in his chair. He shot his second into Gregor's forehead before bursting through the glass. The sorceress screamed curses and attempted to make a run for it, only to have Sigurd catch her around the neck with an earth binding and pull her hard onto her back.

He had used too much force, not realizing how light the witch was. Underneath her old military jacket, made for a man twice her size, was a mere slip of a girl. Her dark hair was chopped short like a man's, her face narrow and cheeks sunken. She looked like a starving, street urchin. She grasped for the bindings molding to her neck's flesh.

"Do not struggle. You'll only rip the skin and bleed out," Sigurd warned.

Before he could tie another set of bindings around her wrists, Jenn somehow removed the one around her neck, rendering it to leather. *She must be an Earth Mage . . . who is also a competent Spirit Mage!*

Jenn rolled backward and returned to her feet. Before Sigurd could restrain her, she waved her arm sharply, and the tower room erupted with a penetrating light. Sigurd's black mesh absorbed much of it so he was not blinded by the sudden brightness. *She's a Light Mage too! The only other Mage that can manipulate more than one essence, as well as spirit, was the Great Melikheil. This girl is a rare find.*

Sigurd didn't hesitate in taking out his last twilight canister and breaking it on the floor. As the Magitech device sucked the piercing light from the room, he had the advantage once again.

Jenn ran for the staircase out of the tower as the room turned pitch black.

"Steinkamp! Steinkamp!" she screamed.

It was no use. Sigurd had already killed every last rebel on the property.

He caught up to her in a few strides and locked both of her spindly arms within his, so that if she struggled too hard she would chance to break one of them. In the dark, Sigurd found the window by following the cool draft and the sound of breaking glass under his feet. He backed himself up to the opening only to feel a blunt force against his shoulder and head, sending him and Jenn tumbling to the ground. Jenn cursed, but being the thin waif she was, slipped out of Sigurd's grasp and made a run for it.

Before he could get up to go after her, a large male figure swung in from outside the window. Jumping from his back to his feet, Sigurd extended his retractable sword. The unseen foe attacked with such guile that he was only just able to deflect his dual knife blows. In the darkness, no man was a match for the Steinkamp soldier's speed, agility, or accuracy, yet this man was countering all of Sigurd's moves as if he saw each one coming a second before execution. It was reminiscent of his blindness training. *I'm fighting a fellow comrade!*

From the moment a Steinkamp soldier began his kill training, they were taught to defend themselves against it. It was inefficient to fight another Steinkamp with the intent to kill if such attempts were constantly undermined. Sigurd had to change tactics. The rebel Steinkamp was at a slight disadvantage, as he was not wearing the flexible body armor and metal mesh mask. A blitz attack was Sigurd's best option.

Instead of going for the obvious mortal areas, Sigurd retracted his blade in preparation to use his fists and attack one specific region. He caught his opponent's knife-wielding arm and twisted it, then struck the other, completely disarming him. After throwing the blades aside, Sigurd leaned into his rebel opponent and went straight for his left kidney, punching and kicking so feverishly he eventually broke through the rebel's defenses, rapidly laying one punch after another.

The rebel Steinkamp grunted in pain and bowled hard into Sigurd with his shoulder. Sigurd was pushed backward for a moment, but he regained his stance and continued his onslaught. Sigurd's bombardment of attacks abruptly came to an end when the rebel's knee smashed against his mask, making the very distinctive clank of metal against metal. The force was enough to knock him fully upright. The rebel then performed a jumping roundhouse kick with the same leg, his foot impacting Sigurd in the chest with as much force as a steel hammer. The blow took the wind right out of him as he flew out the door and smacked hard against the wall at the top of the stairs, cracking the plaster boards against the underlying brick. *Is this man wearing steel-plated armor under his pants?*

Sigurd shook off the jarring hit and raced back into the room that was beginning to lighten again. Through the fading darkness, a large auburn-haired man ran for the broken window from whence he came. Sigurd took note of the man's slight limping gait as he ducked through the window and disappeared into the night, his long brown and red coat fanning out behind him. *Dammit . . . all he wanted to do was keep me from taking the witch away, and he succeeded,* Sigurd thought to his own chagrin.

It was then that Sigurd smelled smoke coming from the bottom of the stairs. Somewhere, a fire had started. With his knife, he cut the ties that held Volker to the old wooden chair and used that rope to tie the dead body to his back so that he had use of both hands to escape the burning building. If he wasn't able to take the witch as a witness, Sigurd had to return to his kapitän with something else to prove he'd completed his mission.

In a little over an hour, Sigurd arrived back at the Deschner Steinkamp headquarters and laid the corpse of Herr Volker on the table in the middle of Kapitän Wolfram's debriefing room. Kneeling before his superior officer, Sigurd removed his mask and gave the Steinkamp salute, placing his first two fingers vertically to the top of his forehead and nodding stiffly.

"The Kanzler of Breisenburg, retrieved from rebel custody, Kapitän," he announced.

Wolfram put on his spectacles and inspected the body. "How much did he say?"

"That, I could not ascertain," said Sigurd. "I found him right as he was about to talk, so I kept that from happening, as was my directive."

Wolfram's eyebrow raised, as if Sigurd's report came as some kind of surprise. "His close personal friend will want to know what information he managed to share with the rebellion before you saw your crossbow bolt into his heart," he said.

At his words, the corners of Wolfram's mouth curled into a slight grin through his close-trimmed salt and pepper beard. Such an eerily jovial expression in the presence of Volker's corpse made Sigurd curious as to the thoughts running through his kapitän's head. As it stood, Wolfram would likely be in the running to be appointed the next Military Strategist, which often came with the Breisenburg Kanzlership.

"Did you kill the rebels that were with him, or bring them in for interrogation?" Wolfram asked.

Sigurd shook his head. "There was a sorceress with the kanzler. She would not have gotten away had it not been for a rebel with Steinkamp training."

With his hands held tightly behind his back, Wolfram sighed heavily and nodded. "It is as I've feared. The Rogue Steinkamp was behind the abduction. To succeed in such an endeavor, it would have to be planned and executed by someone with his training. It's the only thing that makes sense."

"A Steinkamp has gone rogue?" Sigurd asked, wide-eyed. "How is it that I'm hearing of this after my mission instead of prior?"

"The Rogue has to remain classified," Wolfram said sternly. "It would not serve our comrades to know that one of their own has defected and gone to join the rebellion. A Steinkamp always stands for the Regime, never against it. The Rogue is a disease in our midst that I am ashamed to admit I could not cure, and now he has returned to make me pay for that shortcoming—that is, unless you come bearing news of his demise?"

Wolfram looked hopeful until Sigurd answered, "He lives—for now."

"Pity." Wolfram sighed. "For ten years now, that rogue thorn in my side has eluded justice. Obviously, you're aware of the consequences faced by military dodgers, but do you know the punishment reserved for a Steinkamp soldier who defects?"

Sigurd nodded. "A Steinkamp defector can only receive Verishten's justice. He is flown by winged golem to the top of the volcano and dropped into the infernal Mouth."

"But our pledge states that we may never cause undue suffering to our enemies," Wolfram challenged.

"A Steinkamp defector is beyond our enemy. He is a deadly infection, the lowest form of humanity. He is unredeemable by the laws of men and therefore only the Mighty Verishten can keep his soul," Sigurd spouted off with obedient fervor, just how he knew Wolfram would like it said.

The kapitän stared at him for a moment before he smiled broadly and nodded. "Very good, comrade. Despite your inability to retain the sorceress in question, you've done well." Wolfram looked down at the late Kanzler of Breisenburg again, still with the devilish glint in his eye.

From hearing about Wolfram through kommandeurs and other comrades who have worked under him over the years, Sigurd learned what made him unique from other Steinkamp Kapitäns. Wolfram had volunteered to undergo the torturous survival training that those of his high birth normally did not have to endure. This made him a truly dangerous man, and he was an ambitious one at that. He proved his drive by going from foot-soldier to kommandeur to kapitän in a span of only a few short years. After being kapitän for over two decades now, Wolfram's unsated ambitions for a promotion long past due permeated the air around him.

The kapitän motioned for Sigurd to rise. "I've been watching you for a long time, and I've played with the thought of you serving alongside me in this coming war."

It gave Sigurd pause to hear Wolfram's desire to advance him so quickly. He'd expected his inability to retrieve the witch and kill the Rogue to reflect poorly on him. "You honor me, Kapitän." Sigurd bowed his head, giving the Steinkamp salute once again.

"Nas'Gavarr and his hordes are marching toward Ingleheim." Wolfram turned to the map hanging on the wall behind him.

Sigurd stepped up beside the kapitän. "So the Herrani are officially declaring war on us."

"Yes. After Meister Melikheil's crushing defeat, the Overlord of Herran took the Ingle Mage's presence as an act of war from Ingleheim as well as Del'Cabria. He will not stop until we too are under his vicious rule."

"Was that not the reason for Melikheil pledging allegiance to the King of Del'Cabria and renouncing Ingleheim citizenship? So that both nations could see an end to the serpent's campaign, and Ingleheim wouldn't have to take up arms?"

Peace had been achieved between Ingleheim and Del'Cabria for the first time in centuries. Ingleheim would finally get to extend its borders into the untouched and resource-laden lands of Del'Cabria's Fae'ren Province in exchange for Ingleheim's most powerful weapon to extinguish the Herrani threat in the far west. That weapon was the only Mage known that could stand against Nas'Gavarr, or so everyone had believed.

"Melikheil failed, Del'Cabria lost the war, and now the desert dogs are occupying the lands King Tiberius promised to us. However, Tiberius's castle remains standing, and his great cities left unmolested. That can only mean the Overlord and the King made a treaty of some kind. He grants him our lands for the safety of his kingdom. Now it is up to Ingleheim to defend itself and take back what was promised."

"Why would Nas'Gavarr pass over the abundance of wealth and resources in the Del'Cabrian Kingdom for just the forested lands of Fae'ren Province?" Sigurd inquired.

"Nas'Gavarr's reasons for not taking Del'Cabria do not concern us at the moment. All we need to know is that he has his sights set on Ingleheim and will use the disputed borderlands to invade it. However, even if the Herrani take all the lands surrounding us, no army could hope to invade without going through the Pass of Halberschtad. It is heavily guarded and far too narrow for his vast numbers to get through."

"The Overlord must know this. So then, how does he plan on getting here?" Sigurd asked.

Wolfram replied, "We theorize that he will use his naja to do what his men cannot. They will climb the Barrier of Kriegle to enter Luidfort and raze the villages there." Wolfram pointed out the supposed route on the map. "From those areas, the naja will have access to our military strongholds in Breisenburg to the east, our farmlands in Untevar further north, and quite possibly our commercial center, the City of Deschner to the northwest."

"How many naja are we talking about?" Sigurd was surprised. "Aren't those humanoid reptilians near extinction?"

"On the contrary," replied Wolfram. "Somehow Nas'Gavarr has amassed an entire force of them."

"Will you have me and my comrades battle them, Kapitän?"

"No, the Führer will deploy his winged golems from Luidfort for that. I have another strategy in mind. Each naja is brainwashed so that they will bend to the will of their master, much like how a golem obeys the will of our Führer. Unlike our Führer, Nas'Gavarr is not controlling them all by himself. He has delegated their manipulation to lesser Spirit Mages in his employ—Naja Handlers. These Handlers cannot venture too far from their beasts lest those beasts escape or massacre the wrong side. I will select my best comrades, including you, to infiltrate the enemy encampments and eliminate the Handlers while our infantrymen and golems take care of the creatures on the ground."

"You honor me with this opportunity, Kapitän, but what of my current assignment?" Sigurd asked.

"Ah yes, I think we can both agree that you have grown beyond the world of security. How is your assignment going, by the way? Your kommandeur tells me the woman may be a challenge."

Sigurd made sure not to say too much to his kommandeur about Katja and her suspicious behavior until he found out more. But what the kommandeur thought he knew of her was a mystery to him. Though, he wasn't wrong. Katja was more of a challenge than Sigurd would have ever expected. Killing Naja Handlers in enemy territory sounded like a more straight-forward mission than the one he was currently on. Sigurd was curious about golems and the effect of the Ode that awakened them, and in turn, awakened something in him. Hearing Katja play that song brought back childhood memories with such force, he couldn't resist making himself known to his charge, something he rarely ever did by choice. His desire to learn more about golems and his curiosities regarding the Golem Expert he protected were pulling him in strange and conflicting directions.

"She is no trouble, Kapitän."

"Good. Then hopefully you can manage to remain at your post for a while longer. I plan to ship out in a little over a month. We require more time to gather additional information on the whereabouts of the Naja Handlers." Wolfram took Sigurd by the shoulders and began to lead him out of the debriefing room.

"I will return to Nordenhein and await your orders," Sigurd assured his kapitän.

"Take this assignment and you will be working underneath me for the foreseeable future. Show me what you're capable of, and I may deem you fit to be a kommandeur someday. You know what that means, don't you? You can be a man with a name and a face again, marry, and bring sons into the world. What Steinkamp does not dream of that for his future?"

The truth was that Sigurd had never imagined much of a future. He was forced into the military life as many orphans were. Nobody asked Sigurd what he wanted, and there was no purpose for boys like him in Heinrich's Regime, other than to be used as killing tools.

"With all due respect, Kapitän," Sigurd began, "I have no desire to lead. I only wish to serve until I am forced to stop, be it by death or age."

"That's a shame. I think you could go far in the way of Steinkamp leadership, but nevertheless, your devotion is admirable," Wolfram said, still with an eerily gentle smile on his face.

From behind his spectacles, Sigurd could sense that the look in his eyes was not entirely genuine.

"You are dismissed, comrade."

Sigurd nodded and touched the top of his forehead in salute before securing his mask upon his face and walking out of the debriefing room.

The kapitän offered Sigurd a tempting opportunity, not because he desired all the perks Wolfram just proposed, but for desires solely unique to him. For the first time since he became a Steinkamp soldier, Sigurd finally had the opportunity to work directly underneath Kapitän Wolfram, giving him the best possible access.

His will to overcome the trials of his training came to him when he looked upon that clock tower in the City of Nordenhein. However, it wasn't until his graduation day when he took the Steinkamp pledge that he discovered the reason why Verishten guided him from those woods. It was then he had seen Kapitän Wolfram for the first time in thirteen years. It was then he realized that all of the pain, anguish, and torture he had been put through to become the thing he hated most had been for a higher purpose.

It was from that moment Sigurd knew he would have the vengeance he had craved every day in the orphanage where he was so alone, unwanted, and ignored, and every moment in the military academy where he was beaten and spat upon. After all the survival training he endured, and all the atrocities done to him and those done by him onto others, there was finally a reason for it all. The reason was to mold Sigurd into the instrument of vengeance that would make Wolfram pay.

You've now made two fatal mistakes, Wolfram. One is allowing me to accompany you to war; the other was not making sure I was dead in the Crags twenty years ago.

Sigurd hummed the *Ode to Golems* quietly to himself. The song soothed him, brought his hatred down to a steady rhythm, and kept his rage from overpowering his faculties. It allowed him to buy his time, and the time was drawing nigh. It was not an uncommon thing for a soldier to find misfortune in the midst of war, and Sigurd would soon be in a prime position to ensure that misfortune found Wolfram.

Take my hand, child, and I promise you will be able to run faster and climb higher than anyone around. Wouldn't you like that?

Yes, my kapitän . . . I would like that very much.

8

KILL THE MAN

It was still dark when Sigurd took shelter at a Steinkamp haven in Deschner's run-down Westside, a strategically placed accommodation for Steinkamp soldiers during missions. There, Steinkamp could find food, bedding, transportation, medical aid, extra weapons, Magitech, and uniforms. After nearly being frozen solid a few days prior, exhaustion weighed heavily on Sigurd. It was taking longer for him to recover than he'd expected. He was glad there were still a few hours of dark so that he could rest before dawn.

He left his black gelding in the haven's stables and showed his wrist branding number to the clerk.

"Welcome, comrade," said the older man with a lumbering stature. "You will find an empty room on the third floor, two doors to your right." Sigurd nodded curtly as the clerk continued, "I haven't had the chance to fully stock it yet. It needs more Magitech."

"Just bring it up at first light," he muttered as he climbed up the stairs, left of the clerk's desk.

Once Sigurd entered the dark, windowless chamber, he removed his mask and armored vest along with the attached weapons and let them drop to the floor in the corner. There was a small table near the door to his right upon which Sigurd found a lamp. He smelled that there was some oil left in it, so ignited it with a switch at the base.

With the room dimly lit, he turned around, expecting to see a modest bed to collapse onto. The bed was there, as was a tall man in his mid-forties sitting in the chair beside it with the long brown and red coat and the large brimmed hat of a rebel. He had one leg crossed casually over the other, hands resting comfortably on the arms. It was the Rogue Steinkamp, but Sigurd didn't know how he got into a room with no windows. *He must have been let in somehow.*

"Hello, comrade," the Rogue grinned, raising his thick auburn eyebrows mischievously.

Sigurd lunged for his sword upon the floor and extended the blade. The Rogue Steinkamp remained seated, putting his hands up languidly, still with a smug grin on his face. A Steinkamp must refrain from killing while not on duty unless it is in the interest of self-preservation. If the Rogue didn't wish to fight, Sigurd had no grounds to kill him—at least not yet.

"What do you want, defector?" he asked, lowering his weapon.

"Ah, so your kapitän told you all about me," the Rogue said. "I suppose he had to tell you something. It has been a while since I've battled another Steinkamp that lived to run home to tell Papa Wolf. How is that old bloodhound holding up these days?"

"You snuck into my haven just to ask me how my kapitän is faring? Come to your point quickly or be on your way."

The Rogue crossed his muscular arms over his chest and looked straight into Sigurd's unmasked eyes. "You're right, I couldn't care less how that bastard is doing. What I'm really interested in right now is you. May I call you by your name?"

Sigurd remained silent and stone-faced.

". . . Right, I almost forgot. You are nameless. Well, my name is Rudiger, and I was watching you back at that tower. You were waiting there for quite some time, listening to my team extract classified information from Herr Volker, which you had ample opportunity to stop. Why did you let him talk?"

Sigurd was caught off-guard. "I cannot divulge the details of my mission to you," was all he felt the need to reply.

Rudiger rose from his seat. "What mission entails letting highly sensitive information fall into rebel hands before executing your Führer's Chief Military Strategist? I've seen how effectively you cleared that mansion; my kidneys have experienced your combat technique first hand." Rudiger winced while touching the middle of his back. "You are not an incompetent soldier, so I will ask again. Why did you wait until after Volker talked before putting a bolt through his heart?"

This man was hiding in wait at that tower, preparing to strike me down before I could stop the interrogation. Waiting for Volker to talk may have saved my life, Sigurd realized as he felt himself breaking into a cold sweat. "I was acting on the orders of my kapitän, nothing more," he stated. It didn't matter what a defector said, the mask of the Steinkamp gave Sigurd complete deniability. His mission was executed to the satisfaction of Kapitän Wolfram, and that was all anyone would know.

Rudiger huffed. "Hmm, a pity. Just like all the others."

"Others?"

"When I defected ten years ago, I managed to take a few close comrades with me, but Wolfram has kept a tight leash on the rest of you ever since. I've been unsuccessful in corrupting another," Rudiger said with a cheeky grin.

"So you think you can corrupt *me?*" Sigurd scoffed.

"Every Steinkamp I've tried to recruit has sworn absolute and vehement loyalty to Papa Wolf, and I see that you are no different. I will not bother you any longer."

Rudiger headed for the door and stopped to say, "Although, your behavior tonight struck me as odd. I had this feeling that you were not entirely acting in the best interest of the Regime, that maybe you had a directive all your own."

"You'd be wrong," said Sigurd.

Rudiger shrugged, scratching at his trimmed auburn beard. "Come to think of it, it does make sense that Wolfram would want the kanzler removed to secure the man's position for himself. It's not like he hasn't done such a thing before. You see, when I referred to Wolfram as a bastard earlier, I meant it in the literal sense. He cannot inherit a single schlept of his family's wealth. His only means of upward mobility is through the use of his unique skills and invaluable service to the Regime. Of course, you being one of his personal comrades, you're probably aware of how he managed to reach such heights despite his illegitimate birth . . ."

"I am not his personal comrade."

I have to shut down this interrogation, Sigurd bit his lip.

"Again, my mistake. Such an important mission, involving such sensitive information, I assumed would be handled by a Steinkamp of Wolfram's top selection. Now I am even more curious as to why you were there at all. Maybe it is not you who acts against his kapitän, but your kapitän who acts against his Führer. That would make you"—Rudiger pointed at Sigurd—"the scapegoat?"

"If you are trying to make me suspicious of my kapitän so that I will reveal details of my mission to you, it won't work." Sigurd's voice wavered.

Admittedly, he hadn't thought too hard about the fallout from that night's mission. Wolfram was adamant that the Führer approved of Volker's elimination to protect the Regime's secrets, but if the Führer ever learned that those secrets could have been kept and that his friend could have been saved, would he change his mind? Heinrich could hold Wolfram accountable, who could then turn around and punish the comrade for acting against his orders—orders that he could simply change after the fact. The Rogue was right. It wasn't the first time Wolfram lied to the Regime about the details of a mission. The fact that Sigurd was alive was proof of that.

"You're right, it won't work, because you already are suspicious of your kapitän." Rudiger grinned, coming closer. "In fact, it is clear by the look in your eyes that you are more than suspicious of him. You don't much care for him at all."

Sigurd blinked and brought his gaze down for a moment. *What does this man want from me?*

"When one spends all his days hiding behind a mask, he forgets how to wear one after he takes it off. You hold no love for Kapitän Wolfram or this regime any more than I do," Rudiger pressed.

"You want him dead," said Sigurd. "That comes as no surprise. Your ridiculous hat says it all."

Standing only a foot from Sigurd, Rudiger let out low, droning laughter. "It's rare to find a comrade with a sense of humor still intact . . . well, intact enough." He went to sit back down in the armchair. "Yes, in order for the Kings' Remnants to return Ingleheim to the glory that was the Age of Kings, Wolfram, like many offiziers of this regime, will have to die. But as you know, killing a Steinkamp requires a Steinkamp to do it. You already took care of Volker, so I just thought—"

"That I'd kill Wolfram for you too." Sigurd had to admit, it was a convenient proposition.

"Eventually, but I need Wolfram alive for the time being, and I need someone on the inside to keep tabs on him, among other things."

"You want me to be a mole for the Kings' Remnants."

"We have moles everywhere else, why not amongst the Steinkamp?" said Rudiger. "Not to worry, though, I won't ask you to wear a silly hat, only your mask."

"I do not have time for rebellion vendettas," Sigurd said dismissively. "Say you're right and that I want Wolfram as dead as you do. Why would I agree to keep him alive for your cause, which doesn't concern me, and miss any opportunity I have to see him fall?"

Sigurd only wanted to focus on Kapitän Wolfram's downfall while still assisting Katja in her golem research. Furthermore, he wanted to go to bed.

"Why go after one offizier? If the objective is to kill a man, a Steinkamp will not waste his energy cutting off limbs when he can just cut off the head. The same goes for a regime. Wolfram is an arm that can grow back, but Herrscher Heinrich—"

"Is a head that cannot be cut off—he is untouchable," Sigurd reasoned.

"No man is immortal. The late and great Melikheil has proven that," Rudiger argued. "Heinrich's wizard is not around to assist him anymore. The time to act is now. If we wait any longer, the Golem of Death may be awakened, and Verishten help us if that ever happens."

If I can get him to tell me more about the Golem of Death and what the Remnants are planning with it, it may give me more leverage in the event the Regime comes down on me for letting the location slip. "Volker said the Alpha is in the Fortress of Mortlach surrounded by war golems. The man you want to kill happens to have control of those golems and all the golems in Ingleheim. How do the Kings' Remnants hope to get past them and hold the fortress for any length of time?"

"Before I tell you that, I should tell you why we think the Führer can do what his deceased counterparts could not," said Rudiger. "The theory goes, Melikheil was somehow able to combine his spirit magic with the spiritual aspects of Heinrich's abilities, thus amplifying his reach. This is consistent with when Heinrich started displaying these powers, around the same time Melikheil was appointed the official Mage of the Regime."

Sigurd only knew of Meister Melikheil through his work designing and supplying the Steinkamp with their Magitech weapons and uniforms. He had no knowledge of what the Mage did for the Führer. Herrscher Heinrich was an extremely secretive figure. Only the most senior officials claimed to have ever seen him on a regular basis, and even they could not attest to where he was at any given time—which castle he lived in, which mountain ranges he visited, whether he had children or even a wife. This mystery surrounding him only added to his mythos, which was perhaps the real reason he had remained in power for so long. For all Sigurd knew, the Führer could be long dead or dying, his power and authority nothing more than an illusion. The Censors did well in hiding everything regarding the Führer that weren't tales to inspire loyalty and or fear.

Rudiger continued, "With Melikheil dead, there is a chance that the Führer doesn't have the same control of his golems as before. We know that once a golem is commanded by its Mage to do a task, it will complete that task regardless of where the Mage is, but he must return to it to issue new commands."

"Except Heinrich can issue commands from anywhere in the world to as many golems as he pleases," Sigurd inputted.

"Yes, but if the theory is true, then all we have to do is dismantle the golems currently guarding the Alpha and hope that he will be unable to send more right away. He would have to personally activate and command the new ones."

"Okay, that's for taking the fortress, but how will you hold it after?" Sigurd asked.

"In the last twenty years, the Kings' Remnants have recruited many talented individuals. One of them you had the pleasure of meeting. Jenn's power has been growing stronger every day. Her earth magic abilities may be adequately robust in physically dismantling them, at least the smaller ones."

"That won't be enough," Sigurd stated.

"That is where we could use your help."

"Count me out. I am growing weary listening to this folly. Now if you'll excuse me, I need to rest," said Sigurd.

Rudiger sighed, looking as though he had reached the end of his tether. After a thoughtful pause, he said, "I take it Wolfram never told you *why* I defected."

Sigurd groaned quietly to himself as he started toward the bed. *If I have to fall asleep to this man's yapping, then I will.*

Rudiger took the lack of response from Sigurd as permission to continue. "The truth is that I was wrongfully accused of treason by Wolfram."

Sigurd snapped his head up. "What reason would Wolfram have to brand one of his own soldiers a traitor?"

"Men who are not used to making mistakes, like Wolfram, tend to overcompensate when they finally do. It all began with a mission twenty years ago," Rudiger began.

Sigurd's breath seized, and his heart began to pound into his throat. *What mission twenty years ago?*

"I will never forget it. We were fresh out of the Academy, my comrade and I, and we were assigned to accompany a *Kommandeur* Wolfram to hunt down the last Golem Mage family in existence. It was the day we found them that everything changed, and I paid a dear price." Rudiger placed his left foot on the arm chair and rapped his knuckles on his shin. It sounded like knocking on a metal plate underneath the skin.

Sigurd's head spun, his blood instantly boiled. Images from the past ripped through his mind. The tall and daunting faceless soldier in black, sword in hand, marching toward Kristoff, ready to put that sword through his chest. Sigurd could still remember the sharp crack of the Steinkamp's leg breaking under the weight of the golem that stomped on it.

Without another thought, he leaped from the bed and tackled Rudiger off the chair. Sigurd had no weapons handy, only his bare hands. He bashed the Rogue against the wall, cracking it down the middle. He then tripped him to the floor, wrapped his hands around his neck, and squeezed with all his might.

As he pressed his left knee into the older man's midsection to hold him down and strangle the life from him, Sigurd imagined all the things he used to fantasize about doing to the Steinkamp soldiers who carried out Wolfram's commands. Sigurd had never been able to track them down. Such was one of the advantages of being faceless and nameless.

Rudiger didn't stay down for long. He was heavier and stronger than Sigurd and soon pried Sigurd's hands from around his neck and met the young Steinkamp's face with his forehead. Sigurd fell back violently as Rudiger returned to his feet and lunged to tackle him. Using the other man's momentum, Sigurd redirected him hard into the wall, nearly putting a giant hole through the old plaster.

He immediately started in with a barrage of punches, but Rudiger was prepared for that this time. He ducked out of the way, and Sigurd put his fist through the wall. Rudiger grabbed the old wooden chair and smashed it against Sigurd's side. He was down, growing more exhausted despite the anger that coursed through him. However, he would not rest until Rudiger lay dead at his feet. He sprung up with new fervor, but the defector knocked him back down with an uppercut. With a throbbing jaw and blood pouring out of his nose and mouth, Sigurd finally submitted long enough for Rudiger to speak.

"I don't believe it. It's you!" he panted, wiping the blood from his mouth and spitting more out on the floor. "You're the Crag boy, the Earl's lost son. I thought that telling you of Papa Wolf's crimes would somehow break your loyalty to him. And here we are. Verishten, the sick bastard that he is, allowed that boy in Kensloche to survive the Crags and grow up to be the very thing that killed his family. You may be more valuable to our cause than I realized."

"My only cause right now is to bring you death!" Sigurd clambered to his feet and attacked Rudiger again, unfocused and sloppy from mixed rage and fatigue.

Rudiger quickly overtook him and cast him into the plaster head-first. Sigurd slid down onto his backside and rested breathlessly against the wall.

"Not tonight, my friend," Rudiger said, sitting down on the bed. "Although I don't believe it absolves me of my trespasses against you, I was young and green, following the orders of psychopaths just like you've been doing ever since you took that pledge."

Sigurd knew deep down the man was right, but he didn't want to let go of the only thing that had kept him alive for so long. The Steinkamp were a perversion of what they used to be. The pledge meant little these days. Sigurd said the words, but he only lived by one code; kill *for* the man so that someday you may *kill* the man.

With a shake of his head, Rudiger asked, "How did you survive that day?"

"I've been asking myself that for twenty years," Sigurd said feebly.

"I couldn't follow you and your sister into those Crags, obviously." Rudiger placed his hand on his metal-plated knee. "Later that day, Wolfram reported that you fell into a chasm. Before anyone could look for your remains, a violent earthquake caved in much of it. Searching for you after that was far too risky. Though, Wolfram wouldn't dare return without the expected number of bodies, so he and my comrade went to the orphanage in the Town of Kensloche and found a boy that matched your age and size. Wolfram presented all five bodies to Herr Waldemar, proving that all Golem Mages and their offspring were dead. Less than a year after that he was made kapitän."

Rudiger picked his hat up from the floor near the bed and fiddled with it rather than look Sigurd in the eye. "Wolfram became insecure in his new position and paranoid that the truth would someday be revealed. He was confident that you would not have grown up to be bear the Eye, but the fact that his job was left incomplete kept him up at night. Only the other comrade and I knew the truth, and that fact made us vulnerable. Wolfram grew so paranoid that we would reveal his secret, he made arrangements to silence us. My comrade was allowed to retire early and take on a highly held position in the Regime in return for his silence."

Placing his hat upon his head again, Rudiger finally met Sigurd's gaze. "I, on the other hand, desired nothing like that. I had nothing Wolfram could hold over me. All I wanted was to be a good little soldier and forget about the horrible things we'd done to get Wolfram that promotion. He set me up on the mission that would brand me a traitor and I was arrested. Three of my closest comrades knew what really happened and came to my aid. Without them, I would be dead today. They helped me escape my fate, and a few years later we joined the Kings' Remnants in hopes that someday," Rudiger clenched his fists, "we may topple this corrupt regime and return the Steinkamp to honor, to make our pledge mean something again."

"Say I believe you. Say you are truly repentant for your part in my family's death. Why should I agree to help you when all I can think of is your severed head at my feet?" Sigurd hissed through gritted teeth.

"Because you need help, and who can a man like you trust in a regime built purely on lies? Trust must go both ways, or it cannot exist. To do that there can be no secrets between us, and I've told you mine. You need an ally in your quest, and I need a man on the inside to direct focus away from us. Then, when the time is right, we exterminate Wolfram. I promise, you will have your revenge but only if you help us." Rudiger rose to his feet.

"You ask me to trust the man partially responsible for the slaughter of my entire family? Are you mad?"

"I cannot bring them back, nor can I expect your forgiveness. I can only assure you that I am far more useful to your cause alive than dead." Rudiger went to the table, the only piece of furniture left standing after the brawl, and fished out paper and a quill from the drawer. He started writing as he said, "If you need more convincing, then so be it. I can't offer you my severed head at the moment, but I will offer you this."

He handed the page to Sigurd. The words, written in rigid and shortened handwriting read:

Kommissar Vaughn
54 Kentin Road
City of Nordenhein

"This will prove how important your trust is to me. In two weeks, I will approach you wherever you may be stationed, and if you still wish me dead, you are welcome to try at that time," said Rudiger.

"Who is this?" Sigurd asked warily.

"That man is the Kommissar of the Karl precinct in Nordenhein and is all-around corrupt—as Karlmen tend to be. As you know, Ingleheim's national police force is meant to find and neutralize the underground criminal organizations that have sprung into existence, courtesy of Heinrich's unreasonably harsh trade restrictions. Over the last several years they have assisted powerful smuggling rings all over Ingleheim by looking the other way. Under their kommissar, the squadron in Nordenhein has taken their corruption to the next level. They deposed the kingpins there and are now getting filthy rich off illicit trade and prostitution, while making life very difficult for small-time merchants. Nobody would shed a tear if such a man were to meet an abrupt end."

"I am not your killer for hire." Sigurd attempted to hand back the parchment to Rudiger, unsure why the man thought it was supposed to please him. "If you want him dead, kill him yourself."

Rudiger smiled in such a way, it caused the hairs at the back of Sigurd's neck to stand on end. "I would, only that, I thought it would be far more satisfying for you to kill him instead."

"Why?"

"On that paper is the name and home address of the man that killed your father, your brother, your sister, and a five-year-old orphan boy that should have been you."

Sigurd stared at the parchment, his heart racing. He let the name and address singe into his mind. *The other Steinkamp.*

After giving Sigurd a few moments to process his words, Rudiger asked, "So? Where will you be stationed for the next two weeks?"

"Nordenhein," Sigurd muttered, still staring at the sheet of paper.

Patting him on the shoulder, the Rogue said, "Perfect. I'll see you in two weeks then, Siegfried of Kensloche."

Rudiger left the room where Sigurd remained, clutching the parchment in his trembling fist.

9
BEHIND THE MASK

"By Verishten's mercy, it's still here!" exclaimed Katja as she ran for the fallen golem.

Sigurd followed closely behind. It felt like almost a lifetime had passed since he had been to the snow-filled valley one week prior. "Don't go near it until I've inspected it," he cautioned the overeager Golem Expert. Upon seeing the crossbow bolt still sticking out from its eye, Sigurd allowed Katja to proceed.

The two of them climbed over the golem's body and into the crevasse on the cliffside. Katja kneeled before the giant eye, absent its freezing blue shine. She opened her journal and started drawing what she saw, furrowing her brow and biting the inside of her cheek in concentration.

Looking over Katja's shoulder, Sigurd watched her thin charcoal pencil swiftly move along the paper, sketching smooth and immaculate lines. She was so absorbed in her composition she didn't seem to notice Sigurd behind her.

When she appeared finished, he started, "So that's what a golem eye really looks like."

Katja made a pitched cry, dropped her charcoal into the snow, and reflexively cursed in a way highborn ladies weren't known for. Her surprisingly brazen language amused him, but he managed to hold in his laughter.

"Yes," Katja sighed as she fished the charcoal out of the snow. "There does not seem to exist a detailed diagram of a golem's dormant eye. It's strange since you'd think Mages would have ample opportunity to view one when they're building their war golems."

"I always wondered where war golems came from," said Sigurd.

"Earth Mages tear human-sized golems apart and remove the eye. They are then embedded into massive, iron-supported stone monuments. The eye's power animates the man-made titan as if it were a real giant golem, but with the tactical advantage of having a miniscule eye relative to its body.

"However, war golems can only be animated through the commands of a Golem Mage, and when released, they are rendered dormant. The reason being," Katja's voice stiffened, "that they are not alive like other types. Removing the eye from a golem effectively kills it."

Sigurd returned to the original topic. "They probably didn't feel the eye's appearance was important for their purposes. So, why do you?"

"The giant eyes are aligned with five of the six essences—frost golems with water, crystal with light, crag with earth, lava with fire, and winged with wind. But, the eye is also the golem's soul. For all these years I've been studying the behavior of these beings without studying the very thing that makes them what they are."

Sigurd found it interesting that she referred to them as *beings*. They weren't merely creatures to her.

Katja rose to her feet and turned to the previous page in her book. "Yesterday I felled a frost golem in the lab in order to draw its eye and . . ."

She stopped talking as she flipped the page over then repeatedly flipped back and forth between it and the previous. Upon releasing an excited gasp, Katja ripped the one page from her journal so she could directly compare it to the other.

"These are identical, the shape and the design of the eye. Both this giant frost golem and the smaller version have exactly the same eyes!" Katja pointed to certain areas of her drawings where the two were alike and then pointed out a dark splotch in each drawing. "And even here, what I thought was a flaw, occurs in the exact same place on both."

"Is that not normal?" Sigurd asked.

"I don't think so." Katja shook her head. "I mean, human eyes all look very similar in size and shape, but when inspected closer we find that, physically, every pair of eyes is unique, in not only color but design. These frost golems are unique in their body shape and size, but their eyes are identical."

"Do you think all golems in the world have the same eye design?"

Katja's amber eyes sparkled. "That's what I intend to find out."

Sigurd bent down to look into the dormant golem eye himself and found the network of cracked lines hypnotizing. "Are you ready to climb out of here now, fraulein?" he said, straightening.

"Of course not, we can't leave it exposed like this. We should remove the bolt from its eye," Katja stated casually, still studying her journal page.

"I'd advise against waking this golem while we're trapped in here."

"Not to worry, it takes about twenty minutes for a golem eye to heal after an obstruction is pulled out," the scholar replied.

"Good. That will give us plenty of time to get far away from here."

"This might be the only opportunity I have to try and communicate with it. Pull the bolt out, and let's wait here for it to reawaken. If it gets testy, you are in prime position to shoot it with another."

"We shouldn't risk it," Sigurd insisted.

"Trust me. It will be fine . . . this time."

Sigurd gave her a tilt-headed glare. "You are unbelievable."

"It's as I've told you before, my research is to discover how regular people can communicate with golems. Looking at these eyes reminds me of an observation I've made early in my studies of how they communicate with each other. Their eyes flash bright and dim to nothing when one approaches another. In the lab, we've tried to replicate those light patterns ourselves, but nothing worked, and the experiment was abandoned. I think I finally know why. It's not the light of their eye that they use to communicate—it's the eye itself."

"How did you reach that conclusion?"

"In the lab, we observed golems of the same type gather together while golems of different types tend to ignore each other. Such behavior makes sense for when they would have banded together to protect their mountain ranges before mankind came along. I hypothesize that they dim their lights to read each other's eyes. That's how they can tell if they are the same type, which leads me to predict that every golem has an eye design unique to its own type," Katja said, all the while furiously writing in her journal with the quill.

Sigurd felt his spine tingle. Uncovering golem secrets with Katja made him think of his sister and how much fun it was to watch her play with crag golems so many years ago. To satisfy his own burning curiosity, Sigurd yanked the bolt free from the golem's eye. The bolt was in good enough condition to be added back to the quiver, strapped to his lower back. He then grabbed his crossbow, already fully loaded, aimed it at the golem, and waited for it to heal.

To pass the time, he asked, "So, fraulein, why do you *really* want man to communicate with golems?"

Katja laid her quill between the pages and looked up from her book. "To ensure that Ingleheim doesn't fall into another Age of Golems. When the Führer inevitably passes on, there will be no Mages left. What will happen to golem-kind then? Will they seek to destroy us like this one tried to? Or will they simply fall into a permanent slumber like their Alphas? We cannot abide by either scenario."

Although he was curious as to how she knew Heinrich had no heir bearing the Eye, her mentioning the Alphas perked his interest more. "Alphas? Like the Golem of Death?"

"Yes. What do you know of it, Steinkamp?" Katja's voice quavered.

"I know where the Regime has it and that the rebellion wants it. What they want with it is beyond my clearance," said Sigurd.

"T-then how did *you* find out about it?" Katja asked in near whisper.

"Through some rather unconventional channels. I'd rather not get into it." Sigurd sensed Katja's disquiet and regretted bringing up the Golem of Death.

"Did a sorceress named Brunhilde tell you about this?" Katja's voice housed an accusatory tone.

"Who?"

"Tell me the truth, Steinkamp. Otherwise, I can no longer share my research with you."

"I do not know a witch named Brunhilde. Everything I know of the Golem of Death was learned from a member of a rebel group," Sigurd confessed, hoping in doing so he would put his charge more at ease.

"How do I know you're not lying?" Katja clutched her journal to her chest.

"I just told you I've had contact with the rebellion, which appears treasonous. Lying about something like that to a woman with connections like yours puts me in a very compromising position. If I wanted to lie, I would choose a story that doesn't pose as much of a risk to me."

"I suppose." Katja slowly let her arms down. "That is very risky of you."

"No riskier than purposely keeping your research details from the Regime," Sigurd stated. "I suppose we best continue to keep each other's secrets, then." After a few more minutes with the golem still not fully restored, he said, "While we wait, how about you tell me what exactly the Golem of Death is."

Katja began, "The only references historians have of it are in the books of legend from over two thousand years ago. They tell of how it stood guard of the Pass of Halberschtad, the one and only entrance into Ingleheim. Mankind, being directionless nomads in that age, badly wanted the lands the golems protected so fiercely. These nomads sent their strongest warriors into the Pass, and the Alpha destroyed them all before they could take a single step."

Taking a seat on a protruding rock within the crevasse, Katja went on, "They say the Golem of Death's eye is large, its gaze endless. Every soul it looks upon falls under its judgment, said to be the infallible judgment of Verishten himself. Its death stare has the power to inflame the life force within a man and turn him to cinders within seconds. Entire armies were sent to the Pass and all of them perished. Even women and children were put before it with hopes that their innocence would appease the Alpha, but they too died. A violent and covetous people who would send their most vulnerable against the Golem of Death were not worthy of Verishten's favor."

Katja put her journal back into her bag and got up to stand closer to Sigurd on the other side of the crevasse. "It soon dawned on mankind that large assaults were not going to work, but they were a stubborn people. So, they searched high and low for the bravest, strongest, and most honorable men among them to face the Alpha's judgment. From all the clans, only six men were deemed noble enough to send into the Pass. These men named themselves the Steinkamp Warriors. The word Steinkamp actually derives from the ancient language to mean bravery and humility combined as one."

"Interesting," Sigurd murmured.

Katja wandered over to the golem to study its eye again. "The six Steinkamp faced the Golem of Death at the Pass of Halberschtad. The first man to enter its death gaze was deemed very honorable, but he'd had past sins, and although he had atoned for them, he was not worthy. Right before his life force was burned within him, the other five Steinkamp offered their lives for their one comrade. The Golem of Death found their sacrifice truly noble and as a result, it spared all six of them. It was then that the journey of the first men into Ingleheim began."

It surprised Sigurd that he had never heard that part of the story of the first Steinkamp before, or what the word even meant. It was likely because such tales were not conducive to kill training and deemed a waste of time by the Academy. But, it was nice to hear that, at one time in history, the Steinkamp stood for something more, that they were not born of darkness and death. They were once the best mankind had to offer.

"It is not known when the Golem of Death went the way of the other Alphas into dormancy, but in Breisenburg, the Regime managed to stumble upon it. You mentioned that you know its location, so how did the rebellion find out—"

Katja's words were cut off. The golem eye flickered to life, now fully repaired. The ice-tipped soapstone titan slowly rose to its arms and legs and peered into the crevasse. Sigurd aimed his crossbow, keeping Katja behind him. She shoved her way next to him and held the drawing of the eye out for the golem to see.

Does she think the golem will recognize a depiction of its own eye?

Katja stood still, not taking a single breath. Sigurd peered over to her to make sure she hadn't been frozen in place. He decided to sing the first verse of the *Ode* hoping that it would keep the creature calm.

The light in the frost golem's eye dimmed, revealing the delicate lines in full detail. Sigurd finished the song, and it was silent in the valley once again. Katja's arms quivered. Standing so close beside her, Sigurd could hear her heart beating as fast as his.

The twenty-foot golem rose on two legs and moved aside, leaving space for Katja and Sigurd to edge carefully out of the crevasse.

With Sigurd keeping pace ahead of Katja, they eventually came before the golem. She still held the drawing out in front of her as if it were a shield that could deflect an ice beam. The golem then took to one knee, shaking the ground and spraying the snow outward. It stretched a snow-covered limb toward them and laid its hand on the ground at their feet—like a ramp up to its back.

"I think it expects us to crawl onto its shoulders," Katja whispered. "With your permission, I would like to do so."

Sigurd had once seen how Regime soldiers climbed onto their war golems that way. "Have you ever ridden a golem before?"

"No, but how hard can it be? If you come with me then you can ensure that I don't slip off," she pressed.

I probably shouldn't let her ride it, but how will I ever get to ride a giant golem myself unless I take her with me? Sigurd thought, feeling the excitement of such an endeavor bubble up inside him. Without further protest, he turned to face Katja while taking out a long tether of earth bindings. "If you are so set on riding this thing, then you do so while attached to me the entire time. Understood?"

Katja nodded as her face lit up with eager anticipation. Such enthusiasm, Sigurd fully shared with her. He told her to unclasp her winter coat, and he swiftly tied the end of the bindings around her waist just above her thick woven skirt. It surprised Sigurd how petite Katja actually was underneath her bulky coat. She had the tall, willowy build of the typical Deschner-born woman but possessed more of a feminine curvature than most.

Once Sigurd ensured Katja's ties were secure, he tied the other end to his belt and activated the earth magic to mold to it. Leaving ample leeway so he could move freely while still attached to the researcher, Sigurd stepped up onto the golem's arm first while keeping hold of her by the elbow with one hand and the slack of the tether with the other.

When the two were safely perched upon each of the golem's shoulders, it slowly rose to a standing position. What might have been a controlled elevation to the golem was a jolting ascent for the people sitting on top of it. Katja screeched and held on tight to one of the icy spires sticking up from the golem's right shoulder.

The giant golem set off to an unknown destination. It stepped effortlessly up steep mountain ridges, cleaved through the pines and birches and glided across the snow-filled valleys. Several minutes later, the trees became sparse, and soon enough, they left Frost Woods behind. The golem headed toward the Glacier Peaks, but still quite a few miles from where Sigurd had been dropped during his survival training. This place had nearly killed him when he was a child, but from twenty feet up it looked perfectly serene, with sparkling glacier ice and blue-gray stone jutting through the snow. Flakes of which, swirled around them as the winter winds picked up pace. The cold was bracing up so high, but the exhilaration of being there made Sigurd feel swelteringly hot beneath his armor.

Katja must have felt it too because when Sigurd looked to the golem's other shoulder, she had removed her hat and unbound her hair. Carefully standing up and gripping the spire, she let the wind sweep through her dark brown waves. It had become somewhat frizzy from being under her hat, but that only made Katja look more natural and less like an uppity highborn lady.

Sigurd realized that he hadn't taken the time to honestly look at her when they'd first met, at least no more than his mission required. She possessed the impressive bone structure often found in Deschner-born people of high status. Usually, pronounced cheekbones and strong jaw lines were traits more suited for men, but those features on Katja didn't take away from her femininity due to fuller lips more commonly found on women from Luidfort Range.

He watched her spread out her one free arm and drank in the cool winter breeze, taking in its chill before letting out exhilarated laughter, her smile so big that her eyes were nearly squeezed shut by her own cheeks. It was strange to see Katja's previously sullen and uptight features glow with such carefree bliss. *Is this even the same woman?* Sigurd felt a smile of his own creep in from behind his mask. It felt stranger to him than seeing one on Katja, but luckily, she didn't have to witness the awkwardness of it.

"I can't believe this is happening!" Katja exclaimed, practically jumping up and down upon the golem's shoulder. She then pointed downward. "Steinkamp, look!"

Dozens of man-sized frost golems emerged one by one from beneath the snow mounds as the larger one passed. "They're awakening in response to the giant one, and see—" she pointed again. "They're communicating just like they do in the lab!"

Sigurd saw for himself how the golem's blue lights flashed and then promptly dimmed as they recognized their own. They continued to follow along, some of them even latching onto the larger one's legs.

"I want to come to the other side with you. Hold onto my rope," Katja said.

Carefully edging her way across the golem's icy shoulders, she suddenly slipped. Ready for that eventuality, Sigurd held fast to her bindings. She screeched while swinging across the golem's back, but Sigurd quickly pulled her up and onto the left shoulder alongside him.

"Whoa there, fraulein, are you all right?" Sigurd asked.

Katja could barely form a reply through her gasps for air mixed with fits of laughter. "I can't remember a time I've ever felt better!" she giggled, casting back her heaps of tangled hair without a care. Like Sigurd, she sat facing out behind the golem, and they watched the parade of man-sized frost golems trailing behind, more popping up from under the snow as they went.

"It astounds me that a young lady like you is not more scared of being this high up on a moving colossus," Sigurd said.

"I'm flattered you think I'm that brave," Katja replied. "I am *terrified* to be up here. But I don't care. I've dreamed of this ever since I was a little girl. I've spent countless hours imagining what it would be like to be a Golem Mage in the Age of Man. Golems would be my loyal friends and guardians. . . ."

Katja's grin faded somewhat as she continued to look out to the parade below. "You see, I wasn't allowed to have any real friends as a child. My father kept me from everyone and everything. Back then I dreamed of giant golems descending from the volcano to take me away from my loneliness and boredom. In a way, that dream did come true. Golems, or the study of them, took me out of my father's house and brought me here."

Sigurd hadn't realized just how alike he and Katja were. He grew up vulnerable and exposed as an orphan, not protected and isolated like her, but both of them were without a friend to call their own, and both had once dreamed of golems coming to take them away.

Her father must be a powerful man to have felt the need to keep her as isolated as he did, Sigurd thought. For the first time, he found himself worrying about who Katja's parents might be. He already figured she was from Deschner where the Regime's most powerful and wealthy lived. Her father could be a kanzler, possibly Volker. News of his kidnapping and subsequent death had been suppressed for the time being. She would not be aware of it yet. Sigurd cast that thought from his mind—*far too unlikely.*

"Will you listen to me going on and on?" Katja shook her head. "We, regular human beings have successfully communicated with a golem, without Mage assistance, for the first time in two thousand years, and I'm talking about how boring my childhood was."

"You should be proud of this achievement," Sigurd commented.

"I can base my entire thesis on this . . . that is, if I publish these findings, which I cannot." She sighed, her body slumping over in defeat. "Mighty Verishten, if I tell anyone about this, it could potentially lead to awakening an Alpha, and I can't let that happen. How do we achieve cooperation with golem-kind if I can't share this discovery with the world?"

"At least you have one other witness to it."

"I wish that were enough." Katja's usual dour disposition returned with a vengeance. "Everything I've done up until now won't matter in the end, not as long as this regime still exists and that Golem of Death is unearthed. Something must be done."

"And why must it fall upon you to fix this nation, fraulein?"

"Because I'm too close to it. I can see the damage it is doing, and I'm not talking about the violence and the corruption. I'm talking about all the secrecy that props it up. The Regime's lies have caused more death and despair than any Steinkamp soldier can ever inflict. So many secrets . . . well, I am sick of them!" Katja began to stand up again.

Sigurd shortened the tether and kept her close. "What are you doing?" he asked, concerned.

"Look where we are." Katja presented the vast winter scene of Nordenhein with a wave of her arms. "Who is going to hear our secrets up here?" She faced the Glacier Peaks and yelled out at the top of her lungs, "Hear me, Ingleheim! My name is Kriemhilde II of Deschner. I am riding a golem, and I am not a Golem Mage!"

"Kriemhilde?"

Katja rolled her eyes. "I know what you're thinking: *'why, you're not an old woman.'* Well, fear not, I was named after my great-grandmother."

Hearing that name brought a startling thought to Sigurd. He was aware that many girls named Kriemhilde often went by a modern version of the name in childhood since such an old-fashioned name didn't suit the young. A well-known variation of Kriemhilde was Kriemia.

"My little Kriemia is just a babe. I can only hope she will be as helpful as Yolanda is when she gets to be her age." So many details of that day were forever etched into Sigurd's memory, and now this one gave him a chill of which the winter winds were not responsible. Could Katja be Wolfram's daughter? It would explain her uncanny knowledge of Steinkamp soldiers and skill with a crossbow. But how many Kriemhildes were there? Old-fashioned names like that were common among the highborn.

He studied Katja standing beside him, looking for some resemblance or mannerism that could possibly have come from Wolfram, but he found nothing. Having the same name and relative age as Wolfram's daughter was in no way proof of his paternity. There were also Katja's anti-Regime sentiments that a man like Wolfram would never tolerate.

Words spoken by Wolfram the week before came to mind. *Your kommandeur tells me the woman may be a challenge.* It never made sense to Sigurd that his kommandeur would have reported anything about Katja back to Wolfram. It was likely Wolfram already knew Katja would be a challenge because she was his own headstrong, opinionated daughter. Perhaps reporting nothing of note to the kommandeur was actually more suspicious because he would expect her to be difficult. Something didn't feel right, but Sigurd couldn't let himself believe that Katja was the daughter of his worst enemy without more evidence.

Her voice broke through his worrisome thoughts. "I'm glad I got to choose an alias when I enrolled in university. I named myself after the last known female Golem Mage, Katja of Breisenburg. Both she and her husband, who also bore the Eye, were killed by the Heinrich Regime."

The last female Golem Mage killed by the Regime was my big sister Rosalinde of Kensloche, Sigurd thought bitterly. *If you were Wolfram's daughter, would you not know that?* It brought him more feelings of anger and hatred to know that his sister was not even a footnote in history. The Censors made sure of that.

Finally, the golem stopped when it reached a massive, icy cliff face. The smaller golems following them also halted. Katja screeched again as the golem bent down and lowered its arm to the ground.

"Why does it want us to stop here?" She frowned.

Sigurd and Katja safely slid down the arm and back onto the ground. Afterward, the golem stood, flashed its bright blue eye to them and turned away. Katja waved goodbye as the immense stone creature faced the cliffside, and before their eyes, became one with the ice and rock. The other golems all followed suit and went dormant along the cliff and surrounding hills. Katja quickly took out her journal to document the strangeness of all of them going dormant at the same time and in that one spot.

"It's going to be a long way back to the horses now, fraulein. We should get going," Sigurd suggested.

While packing everything away, Katja replied playfully, "But you have yet to share a secret with the Peaks."

"The Peaks don't need to know my secrets," said Sigurd while untying the earth bindings from Katja's waist.

"Well, maybe they don't, but I do."

Sigurd shook his head dismissively. He then began walking down the snowy mountain toward the woods.

"Come on, that's hardly fair," she pressed while trundling behind him. "I've told you about my research, the Golem of Death, my childhood dreams, and my real name. Can I at least know yours?"

Sigurd let out an annoyed groan realizing that, in the interest of getting her off his back, he'd have to tell her something. He'd already broken the Steinkamp pledge numerous times, what did it matter if he told one civilian his name?

"My name is Sigurd," he relented.

Katja's eyes widened with delight. "Sigurd? That's interesting."

"What's so interesting about it?"

"Sigurd is a derivative of the name Siegfried, a name even older than mine, if you can believe it. Siegfried was the first Golem Mage and the first Steinkamp. You must know the tales."

Everyone knew the legendary tales of Siegfried, but since they had so far to go, he allowed Katja to tell him the story anyway.

"Well—continuing from where we left off—the six Steinkamp Warriors traveled through all the mountain ranges looking for lands fit for settlement. But in every range, they came across golems and their Alphas, all fiercely committed to keeping humans out. Five of the Steinkamp perished, and it was Siegfried who was the last. Believing he had failed, he decided to leave the mountains to their golems. But while traveling through Deschner Range, he heard a mighty voice calling to him from the volcano.

"Following the voice, Siegfried climbed the treacherous mountain where he survived numerous lava golems determined to cast him down. He made it all the way to the top and requested an audience with the source of the voice calling to him. The voice was that of Verishten. Offended by Siegfried's arrogance and angry that a mere human survived his trials, Verishten opened the very mountaintop, causing the First Eruption. Still, Siegfried survived. So, from the mouth of the volcano, Verishten sent one of his greatest weapons against him. The Golem of Fire.

"Siegfried fell to his knees before the great Alpha who called itself Verishten's Voice. He could only grin with elation. The Golem of Fire asked him, 'Why do you smile, human? Do you not know that you are about to die?' and Siegfried told it, that although he feared Verishten in all his infinite strength, he was glad to be in his presence, happy to have been given the chance to better his people. Siegfried thanked the God for allowing him to make it as far as he did, and he gave his soul to him to do with what he willed. For, he trusted no other with it as long as Verishten did right by his people.

"Verishten, so touched by Siegfried's courage and humility, decided not to kill him and instead burnt his Eye into his flesh, signifying a sacred covenant between Verishten and man, and man and golem. The first-born sons of the other five men that perished were also given the Eye so that they all could pass the gift on through their line. And on that day, the Age of Man began."

"So Golem Mages and the Steinkamp used to be one and the same,"

Sigurd said. "I wonder what changed."

"I've read recently that after the Alphas had left, much of the Mage abilities went with them. Enough of it remained to allow the Mage families to rise as rulers in their own kingdoms. Being so powerful, they didn't need to fight their own battles anymore, and instead created armies of golems and man to enact war on each other. I imagine at that point, the kings required a more brutal form of soldier, where golems would not be practical. What were once the bravest, most honorable of warriors slowly, over time, became faceless and nameless killers for a nation that had forgotten what the sacred covenant once stood for."

Sigurd mulled over Katja's theory and found himself agreeing with it, despite the fact that he was a product of the new type of less honorable Steinkamp. "You must strip a man of his identity and of everything that makes him human. From there you have a broken shell that can be filled with whatever it is you desire. He can be your perfect soldier, your instrument of death, or your unfaltering protector . . ."

Katja didn't respond to Sigurd's morbid viewpoint. She simply shivered then tugged her hat more firmly over her head.

To prevent the demise of their conversation, Sigurd asked, "So, why do you think the Alphas left?"

After a moment, Katja answered, "It's funny that you ask that because I've been thinking about it ever since I heard the lyrics to the *Ode*."

"Really?"

"In the Age of Man, legends tell that the first Golem Mages were powerful enough to influence golems from anywhere, like our Führer can. I believe in those early days, Verishten allowed for a broader spiritual connection between them as part of the covenant he made. A thousand years later, the Alphas disappeared. The writings suggest it caused the Mages to lose that connection.

"I've started to wonder. What if it was not the Alphas that severed the connection by leaving, but the Mages, giving it up in the interest of dominating golems, which in turn, caused the Alphas to leave," theorized Katja.

"You mean like a trade off?" Sigurd inputted.

"Exactly. The Mages discovered they could dominate a golem in their immediate vicinity rather than subtly influence them from anywhere. So, by the end of the Age of Man, Mages had taken all the power to influence golems away from the common people by keeping them under their complete control. Inducing golems from anywhere in the world would no longer make sense if another Mage could command them away."

"Instead of enjoying a fellowship with golem-kind, man chose to exact control, turning them into their mindless slaves," said Sigurd.

"Yes, and now with only one Mage left, we have a better chance at finding golems untouched by him and rediscover the art of cooperating with them through their own free will. The *Ode* suggests that mankind was entrusted to care for golems as kindred. They should only dominate them when absolutely necessary. But mankind eventually succumbed to the urge to control everything around them, it seems," Katja concluded.

"So the Alphas just left all the Golem Mages to it? Verishten doesn't seem like the kind of god to let mankind off that easy," Sigurd said.

"I'm not sure he did. The Second Eruption occurred at the dawn of the Age of Kings, demolishing the City of Deschner and most of the City of Untevar. The Mages' part in repairing what was lost contributed to the separation of Ingleheim into six different kingdoms. So much of what we knew in the Age of Man was lost during that time. We can never really know why the Alphas left, but I think their absence is what has prevented the golem and man connection from ever returning."

"Except with the Führer . . ."

"No." Katja shook her head. "He has been able to dominate golems from all over, evidenced by the fact that the other Mages couldn't command them away from him. His abilities are far more mysterious than we know."

"There is a theory going around that the Führer uses spirit magic to expand his reach. Since the Great Melikheil's death, he hasn't been seen dominating golems the way he used to."

Katja didn't answer Sigurd for a long time until she murmured, "Interesting theory."

The conversation between the two of them ended at that, and Sigurd wasn't exactly sure why, but he didn't move to end the silence this time.

On the ride back to the university, the sun had set, and the light of the double full moons were all that lit the way. The heavy ash fall in mountain ranges like Deschner and Breisenburg often shrouded them, making Sigurd forget how large and bright they could really be, even on an overcast night such as this.

The university is going to be put on high alert when Katja is not found in her dorm. I will have to sneak her into her room through the window to make it look like she was there all along.

"Sigurd . . ." Katja's softened voice interrupted his internal strategizing.

"Yes, fraulein?"

"What you were saying before—about having no identity and being molded into whatever the Regime wants you to be—I hope you know that you are more than just their conditioned killer."

"What makes you so sure?" Sigurd challenged.

"To the ignorant many, golems appear as mindless shells waiting for a Mage to give them purpose. But I have always believed that they were more than that and today we proved it. If a golem can be something more, so too can a Steinkamp soldier," Katja concluded.

"And what exactly can a Steinkamp soldier be, other than what he is trained to be?"

"Anything he wants. You don't have to let them steal your identity. You may have to hide it from them and everyone you serve . . . including me, but surely you are not nameless or faceless in your heart."

Sigurd's uniform felt unusually constricting as he and Katja rode on. He said, "I lost my identity long before I started training. The Regime didn't have to take it from me because I never had one for them to take."

"I don't believe that."

"Stop trying to read me, Katja," Sigurd said curtly. "It won't get you anywhere."

She sighed sharply. "I suppose after hours of looking into that black void you call a face, I'm starting to see things that aren't really there."

"It is a common mistake." Sigurd could tell Katja was frustrated with him, but he couldn't afford to let her pry any further.

The two soon arrived at the university. They tied their horses within a cluster of trees with the intention of Sigurd coming back to get them later. They continued on behind the tree line to avoid being noticed by perimeter guards. Soon they found an opening to approach the wall. Sigurd took out a lengthy set of earth bindings and quickly tied a makeshift harness around Katja's legs and waist. He then strapped her to his back and molded part of the bindings to his belt for good measure.

"Hold on tight," he instructed while he used a set of smaller bindings to act as handholds.

When he began to climb with Katja strapped to his back, she made a gasp and wrapped her arms around his chest even tighter. It reminded him of when he'd tied Volker's corpse to his back in a similar fashion. Needless to say, Katja's warmth and scent were more than preferable, and Sigurd found himself enjoying the climb and the subsequent descent.

Eventually, they reached Katja's dorm room window on the third story without being noticed by security. After carefully setting Katja down on her narrow window ledge, he had to sit somewhat astride her in order to untie her harness. The Dormitory Monitors were probably asking around for her by now, assuming she was studying late somewhere, but it wouldn't be long until they checked her room again and put the school on lockdown.

"You know, I'm starting to see how being without an identity would have its advantages in this day and age, when a highborn lady has to be smuggled into her own school," Katja whispered while Sigurd continued to untie her. "If I were nameless like you, I wouldn't have to worry about security guards and rebel abductions."

"Be careful what you wish for, fraulein," he replied. "You can wear your own mask and try to be no one, but no matter where you run or where you hide, you can't get away from who you really are. Take it from me." He ground his teeth beneath his mask, thinking of how his parents paid dearly for that same mistake.

When Katja was free of her harness, Sigurd paused for a short moment. Amber eyes looked straight through his mask and met with his own. Her eyes were thoughtful and softer than he had ever expected. There was a fragile vulnerability in her gaze, there was fear, but more than that, there was understanding. Katja's gaze left him feeling raw, and he was compelled to look past her.

She shouldn't be able to see me through this mask, he thought as he went to work on the window to get it open from the outside.

Once unlatched, Katja was safely within her dorm room, but she didn't go to her bed. She remained standing before the window, directly in front of Sigurd, who still crouched on the ledge outside.

"Is there something else, Katja?" he asked in a near whisper.

"If there is nowhere to run and nowhere to hide . . . then why bother wearing a mask at all?" Katja gently placed her hand upon the seam of Sigurd's mask and hood as if she were about to take it off.

Normally, his reflex would be to pull away, but for some reason, he didn't move a muscle. What if he just let her remove it right then? What if she saw him, not through the metallic mesh, but truly?

A reply to Katja's question was not forthcoming. She then leaned over the window sill and pressed her lips to Sigurd's mask where his own lips would be. The sensation of her kiss was lost on him. His face felt only the warm moisture of her breath through the mesh. His heart beat wildly in his chest, and he broke out into a sudden sweat inside his uniform. Sigurd didn't know why she was doing this, but he now felt incapable of leaving the window ledge.

Katja's lips left his mask, but she remained close, her hand still touching it. Her voice was quiet and breathless as she spoke. "Hide behind your mask then. Maybe you need it more than I do."

"I . . ." Sigurd couldn't think, let alone speak.

Katja released him and backed away, the warmth of the air between them quickly dissipating. After a long pause, as if she expected him to speak first, Katja said softly, "Thank you for everything, Sigurd. Goodnight."

"Goodnight, fraulein."

She smiled before closing her window and drawing her curtains.

It took several moments before Sigurd found the wherewithal to leave Katja's ledge that night.

10

ASHEN RAIN

(Nine years ago)

In the libraries of Deschner castle, Kriemhilde waited with unbearable anticipation for Meister Melikheil to summon her. *He has been here for hours already, why has he not called for me yet?*

She sat in the plush sofa near the fireplace, watching the rain pelt against the stained-glass window. Wet ash splattered upon the depictions of Ingle warriors and trickled down each pane. Once dried, the ashen rain would form into crackled black sludge the groundskeepers would have to scrape away when the rains ceased.

After another hour absent Melikheil's presence, Kriemhilde tried to read one of the books she had on the side table, but it was as if she'd forgotten what the letters meant. Her ability to focus had all but left her.

I will come to you soon. Kriemhilde held Melikheil's promise in her heart as she continued to wait.

She had almost dozed off when the sorcerer eventually entered the library at nightfall. Trembling, she jumped from her chair with a start. There, standing in the doorway was the man she loved—the man she would die for.

Melikheil closed the door behind him without removing his gaze from her. As he slowly approached, she stood paralyzed by his masterful image, from his near black locks of shoulder-length hair to immaculately trimmed facial hair along his chiseled jawline. The intensity of his dark brown eyes made her quiver to look into them.

"How is my Little Dove doing today?" Melikheil's deep voice was as eloquent as it was foreboding, and Kriemhilde lived to hear every word he spoke. It took everything for her not to run into his arms, but Melikheil didn't like spontaneity. Only at his word would she dare move toward him.

Curtseying respectfully, she replied, "All is well, Meister . . . now that you have returned."

"That is good to hear," he said.

Melikheil sat down in a chair near the fire, crossing one ankle casually over his knee without letting go of his brass staff that he always had with him. He gently and dexterously caressed the brass raven, holding a sapphire in its talons at the top of the staff. What Kriemhilde wouldn't give to be that raven-shaped adornment right then . . . *Please, Meister, just tell me what you want of me, and I will do it!* her mind pleaded, but was too afraid to voice it to the ineffable Mage.

Finally, to her relief, Melikheil spoke. "I am weary from my travels, but your presence does much to stave it off. Come here."

She walked straight to him without a moment of hesitation. "What do you require of me, Meister?" she asked dutifully.

Melikheil put his staff aside and started unbuttoning his burgundy waistcoat, revealing a fine white shirt beneath. "Remove your dress."

Kriemhilde didn't hesitate. She unbuttoned her bodice and pulled her dress down. Melikheil watched her strip to her undergarments with a satisfied half-smile upon his face.

It excited her to see how pleased he was with her, but before she could untie her lace bodice, she paused, ill at ease. She knew being with Melikheil this way was wrong. Looking to the doors, Kriemhilde feared her father would walk through them and catch his young daughter in the midst of exposing herself to his Regime Sorcerer.

Her gaze quickly returned to Melikheil. Lightning flashed through the stained-glass window behind them and cast his magnificent features in blue and red hues. *He is so beautiful,* she thought. Nothing else mattered when he was with her. She would let nothing get in the way of their love. It was not like her father or Brunhilde ever ventured down the wing since they considered it Kriemhilde's living space.

With a deep breath, she slid out of her undergarments, letting them fall to the floor in a ring of lace around her feet. Her entire body was exposed to the great sorcerer; the comforting heat from the fire in the hearth was cast away by a chill ripping through her.

Melikheil's eyes hungrily draped over her naked form as he reached out and brushed her hair off her shoulders. She closed her eyes and focused on his hands, hot and cold all at once, lightly drawing across her shoulder and down her left arm. Melikheil's every finger on her body made her shiver. She could think of nothing more than him taking her, over and over again. Kriemhilde yearned for the Mage to pull her forcefully against him, to feel the heat of his skin flush with hers while taking her in a passionate kiss, but he did not.

"Meister . . . please . . ." *Why does he always make me beg?*

"Please what?" He gave Kriemhilde a small tongue-biting grin.

She craved for his being to devour her own, if only for a moment, but she found it so hard to express anything in Melikheil's consuming presence. There was no feeling Kriemhilde could think of that was more torturous than being this close to him and yet not being *with* him.

"Grant me your touch," she said breathlessly.

Melikheil gently grazed his hand down Kriemhilde's other arm. "Like this?"

It was not enough, and he knew it. Kriemhilde broke out in an eager sweat, the aching of her loins growing unbearable. "Take me. I want to feel you, Meister . . . please."

"You've become quite greedy in my absence," he teased.

Kriemhilde's voice trembled as she felt herself growing more desperate. "I'm sorry, Meister, I don't mean to be, but I've missed you so much, I—"

Placing a finger on her lips to silence her, Melikheil said, "I may oblige you, Little Dove, but only if you truly love me."

"I do, more than anything in this world—"

"Prove it."

"I can—I will, just tell me what you want from me," Kriemhilde said in a shaking voice.

Melikheil put his hand out toward the fireplace. A burst of flame leaped from the hearth and formed a crackling ball in his palm. Kriemhilde watched the flames dance between his fingers, never to touch them. Witnessing how easily Melikheil could manipulate essences like fire fascinated Kriemhilde as much as it terrified her.

"If you can withstand the burning pain of this flame, then I will know how much you really love me."

Kriemhilde's heart raced and her stomach lurched. This wasn't the first time Melikheil had requested that she take extreme measures in proving her love to him, but never had he requested she physically harm herself.

But what was she to do? Disappointing him was something she could not abide.

Staring at the flame, Kriemhilde slowly moved her right hand toward it. The flames licked her fingertips, stinging her, but she didn't stop. Melikheil smiled, encouraging Kriemhilde to push past the pain. Tears wet her eyes as she struggled to keep from crying out. Her skin began to sizzle as she bit her bottom lip until it bled.

It wasn't until her tears began to stream down her cheeks that Melikheil snuffed the flame with a squeeze of his fist. "That's enough for now. I believe your devotion to be true." He pulled Kriemhilde onto him and kissed her fervently.

Her burning hand quickly became an afterthought.

Katja awoke on her stomach, practically smothering herself with a pillow, her head pounding. She groaned hoarsely as she rubbed the sleep from her eyes and sat up in a daze.

Even in death, that damn sorcerer continues to taunt me.

Looking down to her hand, absent fingerprints, left her with a dull ache in her gut that she still carried with her after all this time. *He's dead now,* she reminded herself. A part of her didn't believe Melikheil was really gone, but rather that he was still out there somewhere. There were some moments when she felt like he was right beside her, this moment being one of them. She shivered despite the warmth of her bed sheets.

Katja rubbed her aching temples, trying to push the sickening memories from her mind. Doing that pulled certain other memories to the surface, memories of kissing her Steinkamp's mask the previous night.

Collapsing back into the bed, she moaned into her pillow, "Verishten have mercy, what's wrong with me?"

The exhilaration she'd experienced with her new discovery, combined with the thrill of sneaking past university security, had caused her to get carried away. The truth was Katja had never felt so alive, and this time, the feeling was real. It was not contrived by an emotionally sadistic Spirit Mage.

Katja hoped that she hadn't made it awkward between her and Sigurd. Thinking about the kiss, she smiled to herself. She had to admit there was something exciting about kissing a man whom she had never seen before;

to get so close yet remain so far away. It was different than when Melikheil had kept her at a distance, because this was on her own terms.

Stop it, you're being stupid! The man is a killer and your bodyguard. He cannot be anything more than that.

Somehow Katja's heart disagreed. *Killer or not, Sigurd may be the one true friend I have right now. That will have to be enough.*

She decided that it was best not to dwell on flights of fancy with a Steinkamp soldier. There was a whole new world of research to do after yesterday's revelation. She sat down at her desk and opened to a new page in her journal where she wrote down further details of her findings. In particular, she made note of the strange way all of the golems had decided to go dormant together at the edge of the Glacier Peaks. But the more she wrote, the more anxious she felt.

Ignatius and Klemens needed to know what happened, but the professor was obligated to share his knowledge with the Regime in the bi-weekly report. *How can I face my colleagues today and pretend I didn't revolutionize human and golem interaction yesterday?*

Tossing her quill into the inkwell, Katja slumped back in her desk chair and sighed. Her head still pounded incessantly. Grabbing her quill again, she took a loose page of notepaper from the drawer instead and wrote a message for a Dormitory Monitor to deliver to Professor Ignatius. She would be too ill to research today.

(Two nights ago)

"Y-you can't!" Kommissar Vaughn screamed.

Sigurd dragged him across his own yard at fifty-four Kentin Road in the middle of the night. He had already broken both of Vaughn's arms so he could not fight back. It surprised Sigurd how easy it had been to sneak into the mansion and overpower a Steinkamp-trained Karlman. *Years of living in affluence earned by your illicit activities have made you careless, Herr Vaughn,* he thought.

When they reached the gate at the front of the kommissar's property, Sigurd lifted him up and held him to the steel bars by his neck.

"A Steinkamp can never cause undue suffering to his enemies!" Vaughn croaked, a terror sweat dripping down his flaccid features.

"That's correct, Kommissar, but your suffering is long past due."Sigurd's retractable blade sank easily into the soft flesh of Vaughn's midsection.

"W-Why?"he gasped, barely audible.

"I've been asking that question since you sliced open my sister's throat," Sigurd snarled. He twisted the blade.

"Wha—no!"Vaughn gargled blood as it rapidly filled his mouth.

Sigurd pulled his blade down hard, causing blood and viscera to pour onto the grass at the two men's feet. He wasted no time molding earth bindings around Vaughn's forearms and stringing him up to hang from his own gate. Sigurd was sure not to hit any major arteries—it would take hours for the kommissar to bleed to death from his gut wound.

Sigurd watched for a moment while Vaughn struggled, hanging by his arms, his insides exposed to the cold night. The smell was putrid, putting Sigurd off despite such scents being part of his everyday life.

One man gone, two to follow.

Sigurd turned and left the kommissar alone to bleed out.

Sigurd lay on the cot inside the Nordenhein haven with his head resting on his hands, listening to each bell toll as if it were a beautiful melody. There was nothing like being stationed in Nordenhein, to hear the sound of his salvation reminding him of why he still lived.

He had been up for hours before the morning light appeared, reminiscing of his most satisfying kill from the night he arrived back in Nordenhein. Vaughn had suffered far more than Kristoff and Rosalinde combined, but Sigurd believed that the violent acts committed against children should be returned tenfold.

I suppose I should check on Katja's status.

Sigurd wondered what kind of mood she'd be in after the last night. He hadn't been able to stop thinking about her kiss, and she hadn't even touched his lips.

The decision to begin the day was made for him by a series of knocks upon his door.

"Who's there?"he called out.

"I'm here to determine whether you are friend or foe," said the man behind the door.

Sigurd opened the door, not bothering to put on his mask. There stood

Rudiger, wearing typical civilian attire consisting of a gray and white vest and trousers. He grinned, removing his bowler hat, his hair slicked back. "The fact that you greet me in your undergarments is a good sign you don't plan on slaying me."

Sigurd motioned for Rudiger to come in. "It's only been one week," he said as he went to unlock his weapons cupboard where a clean uniform was stored.

"I gave you two weeks to follow up with that name and address I gave you," Rudiger replied while setting his lofty frame into a chair. "I did not expect to find him strung up and gutted three days after we last spoke."

"I don't believe in wasting time." Sigurd put on his undershirt and pants and reached for his armored vest.

"That, I should have guessed. It certainly looked like you got your frustrations out. I hope that whatever you imagined doing to me a week ago was exhausted on our unfortunate kommissar."

"He got what he deserved," was all Sigurd said in response.

"And making it appear as if *I* did it. That wasn't your way of sticking it to me a little bit, then?"

Sigurd was fastening his uniform's straps on his vest when he turned to Rudiger with a raised eyebrow.

"You made it too obvious that a Steinkamp murdered Vaughn. The streets of Nordenhein are rampant with hearsay about Steinkamp going rogue. Papa Wolf won't like his little secret getting out," said Rudiger with a shake of the head.

"No, he certainly won't." Sigurd nodded. "Maybe that will teach him to keep a better eye on his killer dogs."

"A more vigilant Wolfram is the last thing we need! Only four men know about the body of little Siegfried having never been found: Wolfram, Vaughn, me, and you. Of course, Wolfram is not aware of you. So now that Herr Vaughn is confirmed dead by Steinkamp soldier, he will deduce that I am the only one connected to him who is capable of doing such a thing. Wolfram will understand it as a tactic of mine to draw him out. That is not good for us."

"I know you preferred for me to make Vaughn's murder out to be a like a rebel committed it, but I want the world to know a Steinkamp did it. I want Wolfram to be scared of his own comrades turning against him, to weaken his position among them and the Regime. Only that will make him vulnerable," Sigurd said while pulling the snug black hood over his head.

"Everything I did for the Kings' Remnants could have been executed by any one of my comrades that defected with me. With Vaughn, it hits a little closer to home for Papa Wolf. Because of you, he is now positive that I am still out there, wreaking havoc," Rudiger complained.

"Better to keep his focus on finding you than for his suspicions to fall on me. This way, he is sure not to see me coming."

Rudiger stood up from the chair, fuming, his snarky expression turning into legitimate frustration. "Curse you, Siegfried. I told you that our objective is more than just putting down the Wolf. This is no longer a solitary mission. We work together or we do not work at all, and trust me when I say, the chances of getting what we both want are much higher if you agree to the former!"

"Refrain from using the name Siegfried. He was a legendary hero who dominated golems and faced a god, none of which are attributes of mine," said Sigurd in an icy tone.

Rudiger sighed, arms crossed. "Then what should I call you?"

"Sigurd."

"Sigurd? That's strangely close to Siegfried."

"That's the idea. In the event that I inadvertently answer to my real name, it becomes plausible that I misheard Siegfried for Sigurd as opposed to Siegfried for Hans . . . for example."

"Many a grown man has fallen for Wolfram's tricks," said Rudiger. "You were only five."

Sigurd could barely look at Rudiger right then. *I am not about to speak of that day with him if I must refrain from killing him.* He turned to his weapons cabinet. "You're getting ahead of yourself. I never agreed to join your foolish rebellion. First of all, you still haven't told me how you plan to capture and hold the Fortress of Mortlach. I don't believe your little witch is powerful enough to do it all by herself."

"You're right about that," Rudiger replied. "Our advantage comes from many sources. Before I let you in on that, however, I must ask of your current assignment. How long will you be stationed here in Nordenhein?"

"Not for much longer. In less than a month I will be joining my kapitän on the front lines to fight the incoming Herrani forces."

"I see." Rudiger frowned, and then suddenly he slapped himself on the metal-plated knee. "Wait a minute. You are joining Wolfram's unit? You might be exactly what I need, and exactly where I need you!" Now with Sigurd's interest fully captured, he continued, "You're familiar with how to take down a golem, I presume?"

"A bolt through the eye will do the trick. However, war golem eyes are too small and are protected by an iron grating. No crossbow has the range, and no man has the skill to hit such a mark," Sigurd said.

"Yes, crossbows are certainly useless in that regard, but a longbow will do quite nicely. Our neighbors to the southwest have the most renowned archers in the known world. My sources speak of a young man who fought in the Desert War whose archery prowess is unmatched. They say he has never missed a mark—not even during training. Some are calling him Gershlon Reborn."

During his tactical training, Sigurd had been told of the various wars fought between the kings of Ingleheim and Del'Cabria. The bloodiest among them were the Urling Wars. It was during that time the legendary Great Gershlon, Champion of Archers, was recorded to have felled so many war golems in such a short amount of time that he singlehandedly won Del'Cabria the war, and the disputed lands in Fae'ren Province for them. They were the very same lands offered to Ingleheim more recently, before Melikheil met his untimely end.

"And this Del'Cabrian soldier is just going to volunteer his services to Ingle rebels?" Sigurd raised an eyebrow while collecting his weapons from the cupboard.

"He's not a soldier—well, not anymore. Stories of his mastery come from my Herrani sources. They speak of a Fae'ren who turned his back on his contingent and ran away with a Herrani woman in the middle of duty."

"And you would trust such a man to aid you in your cause?"

"Don't judge the lad too harshly. Many young men have been rendered powerless by the insatiable whims of the Herrani woman. I can attest to that." Rudiger made a soft grunt and ran his tongue over his teeth.

Sigurd didn't need to know how the Rogue knew what he knew about Herrani women. He imagined Rudiger likely bedded more women now that he was free of Steinkamp discipline, which forbade intimate relations of any kind while they were faceless and nameless—not that that stopped many Steinkamp or even Sigurd from time to time. He was reminded again of Katja's kiss, but he quickly pushed the image out of his mind.

"Anyway, I'm digressing," Rudiger said. "The archer in question has been running with a band of desert thieves for the last year and has auspiciously joined Herran's forces in Fae'ren Province, laying siege to the Barrier of Kriegle."

"So a year ago this man fought with Del'Cabria, then became a desert thief, and now he has joined with the enemies that occupy the land of his birth? What kind of barbarian are we dealing with here?"

"My sources say that he's not fighting with the Herrani, but that he's under the guise of a Herrani warrior to gain access to Ingleheim. He intends to find and sack a Steinkamp Magitech cache in west Breisenburg." Rudiger took out a map from his vest pocket and rolled it out on the small dining table for both of them to see, pointing out where the cache was located. "My guess is he wants to steal Steinkamp weaponry and sell it to the enemy. A full cache of Magitech is worth around sixty thousand schlepts. I'd say that could pay a thief's way for quite a few years."

"Well, good luck to him in getting through the Pass of Halberschtad," scoffed Sigurd.

"He won't need it. You're going to help him while you're out there. You will find him, see him safely through the Pass, and take him to the cache without incident. In return for your generosity, he will agree to lend us his talents to take the Fortress of Mortlach."

"You really expect a traitor and a thief to risk his neck for you?" Sigurd asked.

"We're all traitors here, and as for thieves, I expect them to follow their self-interest every bit as much as I expect you to follow yours. We give the thief something to show that we are men of our word, and promise much more upon his cooperation. We can give him a chance to hone his archery skills, and truly become the great Gershlon Reborn. With all that, as well as a massive supply of Magitech, he will not refuse, provided that you do your part and get him to me."

His words rang true in Sigurd's mind. Rudiger had done the same for Sigurd with giving him Herr Vaughn tied up in a bow and promising Wolfram's head on a platter, but would he keep his word to either Sigurd or this Fae'ren archer? There was only one way to know for sure.

"So I deliver you the traitorous archer, and that's it?"

"For now."

Sigurd nodded and fastened his mask. "I must be off. I'm late in reporting for duty."

"Those Golem Experts hardly require Steinkamp surveillance while behind university walls," Rudiger commented in levity. "At any rate, I will return here by month's end to provide you further instruct—"

"I never told you my assignment was guarding the Golem Experts. Do you have a mole among the Steinkamp ranks after all?"

Rudiger blinked a few times and grinned slightly. "You'd be the only one. You already told me your assignment was in Nordenhein. I made an educated guess, and your reaction just confirmed it."

"That was some guess. Why would you even think the research team would have a Steinkamp detail in the first place?"

Scratching his beard, Rudiger hesitated. "I probably shouldn't tell you this, but it just so happens the Remnants have a mole on the research team that you've been protecting. That mole made me aware of a Steinkamp on their security detail, which led me to wonder if it was you."

Katja? She told me she wasn't working for the rebellion, but she is acting in a rebellious way . . . It made Sigurd sick to his stomach to think that she may have lied to him, but he calmed himself, cursing his overcautious nature, and asked, "Tell me who this mole is."

Sigurd reported to his post later that morning and received status reports of the research team from university security guards. Since Katja had indicated how excited she was to start studying golem eyes, Sigurd was surprised to find that she had not yet left her dorm room. Her being there actually made his task easier. Now he wouldn't have to find a way to speak to her privately within the university. He was anxious to inform her of what he'd learned from Rudiger.

The morning sun never shone on Katja's window, so it was still coated with a thin layer of frost when Sigurd climbed up to it. He gently scraped off a small circle with the grips of his gloves to peer inside.

You'd better not have gone to the woods without me after everything that happened. Sigurd's fears were put to rest when he saw the scholar at her desk, scribbling away in her journal. Her hair was partially clipped back to keep it out of her face, save a few wavy strands that she wrapped around her fingers as she wrote. Sigurd was entranced by how every strand fell about her shoulders with abandon. He imagined running his hands through it, entangling it further. It was then he realized he'd been gazing at Katja for far too long. *I'd better make myself known before she notices a shadow man peeping through her frosted window.*

He rapped lightly on the glass, and Katja snapped her head around in fright. He looked away from the peephole he'd made, hoping Katja wouldn't notice it, and waited for her to open the window.

"Sigurd, what are you doing here?" Katja held her robe tight across her chest even though she was fully clothed underneath.

"Apologies for coming to your room like this, fraulein, but I must speak with you in private."

Katja stood hesitant, holding the window partly open to either keep out the cold morning air or the Steinkamp crouched on her ledge. After nervously glancing around her room, she moved aside. "Um . . . come in."

Sigurd could tell letting him into her room made her uncomfortable even though she seemed all too comfortable with him the night before. *Maybe she regrets what happened between us,* he thought.

"What is this about?" Katja said once Sigurd climbed into the room and closed the window. She shivered and tightened her robe around her.

"Is there something amiss, fraulein?"

She wouldn't look directly at him. "I didn't sleep well . . . too much excitement, I suppose," Katja ran her hand through her hair and brought it over one shoulder.

"I expected to find you in the library studying after the discoveries we made yesterday."

"Me too—I want to—but if I uncover anything more, I won't be able to keep it secret from my team," she admitted. "I don't know where to go next."

"I think I do," said Sigurd. Katja finally looked at him dead on with hopeful eyes. "It's what I came here to tell you. Your professor is a mole for the rebel group known as the Kings' Remnants."

"What?" Katja gasped, her eyes widening in shock. "How long have you known?"

"It has just been brought to my attention."

Katja nodded. "Your rebel contact."

"Yes. He told me Herr Ignatius has been submitting falsified reports on your progress to the Regime in order to stall them. He's also supposed to report to the Remnants any pertinent information gained from your research that can assist the rebellion."

"What do the Kings' Remnants think they are going to do with the Alpha?" Katja asked.

"They want to take the Fortress of Mortlach where it is being guarded and hold it for themselves. However, I don't think they want to awaken it—just take it from the Führer."

"Whatever their intention is, we can't allow my research to fall into their hands. You haven't told your rebel contact anything about our excursions, have you?" Katja inquired sternly.

She's not taking this as I expected, thought Sigurd. "No, Katja. I told you I will keep your secrets just as you keep mine," he reassured her.

"Of course, I don't mean to doubt you, it's just . . ." Katja sighed, looking away and hugging her arms around herself. "I don't like this. It feels dangerous. Ignatius being their spy explains how the rebellion found out about the Alpha, but who told them the location? Only those with the highest clearances would know of it—unless—"

Before Katja could voice her theory, Sigurd said, "The public is not aware of this yet, but members of the Kings' Remnants abducted Kanzler Volker and tortured the information from him."

"The Kanzler of Breisenburg?" Katja gasped.

"He's now dead."

"Herr Volker is dead," Katja repeated, trying to process it. "This does not bode well for the Regime."

Unless Katja was an expert at hiding her emotions, which Sigurd didn't believe her to be, her reaction to the kanzler's death was not one of grief. Herr Volker was definitely not Katja's father. Sigurd let out a quiet exhalation.

"Hence their reason for keeping it from the public, I presume. It would be disastrous for the people to know how close the rebels are getting to hurting the Führer. By taking his closest allies right out from under him," Sigurd said.

"Volker was Steinkamp-trained. His military pursuits made him a man harder than the iron in the mines. What kind of tortures could they have subjected him to that caused such a man to talk?"

Sigurd frowned. She knew much about the senior officials of the Regime. If her father was not Volker, it was a man that knew him well enough. This worried him more.

"The Remnants enlisted a talented Spirit Mage, who extracted the information." Katja's lip quivered at his words. "What is it?"

"Melikheil . . . ?"

Katja's voice was so small Sigurd could barely hear her; only her mouthing the sorcerer's name gave him any indication of what she'd said.

"It's a young woman—a commoner, and a real up and comer, they say."

Katja breathed deep, hugged herself tighter, and nodded. She cleared her throat. "Thank you for telling me this, but how is this going to get me out of my dilemma?"

Sigurd took a few steps toward her and she reflexively took one step back, though still allowed him to get closer.

"You can't shoulder this on your own, Katja. Ignatius can be your ally."

"You're asking me to tell a man with rebel ties about my research?" she asked warily.

"You told me, and I have those same rebel ties. Talk to him. He may be able to help you. At the very least, he is one other person on your side who won't sell you out to the Regime."

Katja looked away and sighed heavily. "I suppose that's better than not telling anyone at all."

"Find a way to gauge his loyalties, then inform him of whatever you feel comfortable with."

Katja nodded. "I will, thank you."

"Oh, and in case Ignatius denies his involvement with the Remnants, tell him Herr Rudiger entrusted the information to me."

Sigurd then excused himself and went to the window. Upon him opening it, he got halfway out before Katja said, "Be careful."

He turned to face her. It was always implied that a Steinkamp soldier would take the utmost caution on his missions so it never had to be said. Having someone say it to Sigurd though, gave him pause; it grounded him.

"I don't trust the Kings' Remnants any more than I trust the Regime. Their mission to capture the Golem of Death is folly, and you should not involve yourself in it."

"I use them for information, nothing more," he assured her while stepping out onto the ledge.

"And one more thing." Katja walked up to the open window where Sigurd stood just outside, "Do not trust that sorceress they have."

"Do you know of her?"

"If she is, in fact, a Spirit Mage, then I don't have to. They are all dangerous. They will fill your head with lies, and you will never be able to trust your instincts when they are around. Just promise me, if you come across her . . . do not engage."

"I will take that under advisement, fraulein. Good day to you."

With that, Sigurd dropped to the ledge below and made his descent down the dormitory building.

Katja knows Meister Melikheil well enough to be afraid of him. That could mean he worked very closely with her family. He worked very closely with Wolfram too . . .

A gnawing discomfort formed in Sigurd's gut. He thought about looking into other possible offiziers that contracted Melikheil's services to find clues into Katja's parentage. He needed to rule out Wolfram.

It will change nothing. Wolfram must die. In a few more weeks I will leave Katja and her research behind, and she will never know it was me who had done it anyway. Sigurd's logic was sound, but something inside him lurched at the idea of causing Katja any kind of pain, even if he wouldn't be there to witness it.

11
RIGHTEOUS IDEALISM

The next morning Katja felt more in control of her situation.

She found the professor in his office. After locking the door behind her, she strode up to his desk where he busily wrote in his journal. Her blouse collar suddenly felt hot and constricting. Now that she was here, she wasn't sure how to broach the subject.

"What can I help you with, Katja?" Ignatius asked without looking up.

"Professor, I know about your ties to the Kings' Remnants!" Katja blurted.

Ignatius smudged the words he wrote as he snapped his head up to look at her. "I don't think—"

"It's okay if you are," Katja cut him off. "I might be in a position to help you, but only if you promise not to divulge anything to them about what I am going to tell you."

"For Verishten's sake, Katja, how did you find out about this? Who else knows?" Ignatius set down his quill and closed his journal.

"Only me and the Steinkamp," Katja answered in a hushed voice.

"What Steinkamp!?" Ignatius's eyes widened as he stood up from his desk chair with a start.

"The one assigned to our security. It's all right, though. We can trust him."

"A Steinkamp soldier on our security detail?" Ignatius was shrill, but remained hushed. "If he knows what I am doing, then it is all over."

"If he were going to report you, he would have already. Herr Rudiger thought it acceptable to tell him about you, so he must be a man they can trust."

"So, Rudiger got another Steinkamp to defect. Most interesting," Ignatius muttered.

"What do you mean, *another* Steinkamp?"

"There are at least four other former Steinkamp soldiers, including Rudiger, who are now members of the Kings' Remnants."

Sigurd forgot to mention his rebel contact was a former Steinkamp. Maybe that's how he made his acquaintance, Katja surmised inwardly. "Have you met any of them?" she asked.

"Only Rudiger, but I did hear a rumor that one of them was responsible for the murder of the Karl Kommissar here in Nordenhein recently. Steinkamp Magitech was used, but the gruesome manner in which he was killed suggests the one responsible has renounced the pledge not to cause undue suffering."

The notion of Steinkamp defectors out there, completely unrestrained and free of the pledge, gave Katja a chill.

Ignatius stepped out from behind his desk. "So how do you propose to help me?"

"Before I get to that, I need to know—why would a man in your position join the rebellion?"

The professor walked over to his office window and stared at the tiny snow hills accumulating between the panes. "In my younger days, I was the staunchest supporter of Herrscher Heinrich. As you know, I was a Golem Studies acolyte at this university. It was here where I met who at that time were my closest colleagues: Herrs Volker, Bachman, and Heinrich."

Katja's eyes widened. Two of those men had become kanzlers and, of course, Heinrich became the Führer. Together they, with her father at the helm, had carved out the Age of Order.

"Bachman studied economics; Volker, military strategy; and Heinrich, politics. The three of them came up with the brilliant initiative to unify Ingleheim by centralizing the rule of authority to Deschner, under Prince Heinrich—a Golem Mage, and the heir to Deschner's throne.

"Heinrich took me into their group since Golem Mages and Golem Experts often went hand in hand. They were all admirable in their own way—Volker in his unbreakable resolve, Bachman's unparalleled intellect, and Heinrich with his righteous idealism."

"The Führer was a righteous idealist?" Katja scoffed.

Ignatius huffed and turned from the window. "Time changes all men. Righteous ideals become bitter realities. When they were young, their dreams of a united Ingleheim were not only obtainable but necessary. None of us doubted that the Prince of Deschner was the man to see it done, but no one could foresee the cost of those actions until it was too late. Their well-intentioned plans to see an end to the never-ending bloodshed of warring kings brought with it more pain and suffering than any of us could have imagined."

Taking a seat at his desk again, Ignatius ran his hands through his white whiskers. "When I learned what was happening to the other Mage families, I tried to reach out to Heinrich—tried to reason with him. He thought I was attempting to gain insight into his mysterious abilities, which admittedly I was researching at the time, unbeknownst to him. He threatened to remove me from my position, destroy all my research, even go as far as have me arrested if I insisted on getting in his way. I made a choice to protect my life's work. . . . "

"And now you rebel against him. What changed?" asked Katja.

"I could no longer sleep at night," Ignatius sighed. "My choice to do nothing was made out of fear, and that fear ensured Ingleheim's future under a cruel and tyrannical government. A few years after the Regime established itself, its offiziers broke into my study and stole my research anyway, in particular my research surrounding why Heinrich can do what no other Golem Mage has done for thousands of years. That's when I decided to do something about it."

The professor rose to his feet again and paced around the office, eyeing his impressive collection of leather-bound tomes and historical documents upon the polished oak bookshelves. "Since then, I have been secretly rebuilding my notes from memory. After a time, I approached the Kings' Remnants and shared with them all I knew about Heinrich's abilities, but I could not prove my hypotheses without the help of another Golem Mage or someone close to the Führer who could study him in secret. That turned out to be impossible, so I did what I could from here to aid the rebellion. My focus now, though, is keeping the Regime from making any further progress with that blasted Golem of Death."

Katja couldn't believe that her own professor actually knew all those men when they were young. It was an entirely different time, when students didn't have to hide their identities as they pursued higher education. So many more questions swam around Katja's mind. She hardly knew what to ask first, but there would be time for scholarly inquiries later. "How long do you plan on stalling?"

"Katja. I don't want to drag you into this. It could mean your death," Ignatius warned.

"I'm already in too far as it is. Neither one of us is going to make it through this with our heads attached if we don't start helping each other."

Ignatius sighed heavily, then nodded. "I plan to stall the research project until the Kings' Remnants take the Fortress of Mortlach. In a few more months, the Remnants will have enough archers to bring down the golems guarding it and hold it for however long is necessary."

"And then what?" Katja said in a harsh yet quiet voice. "They wait there to be crushed by the Führer's entire stock of war golems?"

"That's where my old research comes in." Ignatius picked up his notebook and flipped through it. "I theorized that Heinrich's abilities were being amplified by Meister Melikheil during and after his rise to power. Since Melikheil's death, we have seen no evidence that the Führer is giving golems commands from miles away. While the rebels hold the fortress, we may be able to witness golems awakening from all over. If that happens, then we'll know he can control them from anywhere, but if they don't, and he doesn't send his stock until much later, then it is an indication that he needs to be present to give them commands."

"Your experiment will put too many lives at risk." Katja was shocked that Ignatius would go so far, but then again, she understood where he was coming from. The thrill of experimentation and the urge to uncover golem mysteries often superseded all other things, no matter how important.

"Not if my theory proves true. The Führer will be revealed as a regular Golem Mage, no different than the ones he had murdered. The people will be more likely to rise up."

"Even if it is true, it does not mean the rebellion will win. Melikheil may be dead, but the Führer has other Mages in his employ. If you look hard enough, you could probably find plenty of examples of him giving golems commands without being present. You don't need to take a fortress to find that out."

Now it makes sense why Father has been so secretive over the years. Hardly anyone is aware that his wife is a Spirit Mage or that she even exists, thought Katja.

"The Kings' Remnants have other plans that I'm not privy to—"

"I don't care what their other plans are," Katja snapped, causing the professor to raise a bushy eyebrow. "We can't depend on them. The rebellion is going to lose and the names of everyone that assisted them will be brought to light. The Führer won't care about your past friendship when he finds out you were involved."

"I made up my mind long ago. I know well the risk I take. I've chosen the path in which I can prevent the Golem of Death from awakening, giving the rebellion a fighting chance at creating a better Ingleheim."

"Not if the Regime kills them all."

"You have yet to tell me how you can help. I suppose you have a better idea?"

"I think I might."

"Well, let me hear it, for Verishten's sake!"

"You keep stalling for a little while longer, and in the meantime, we delve into researching golem eyes. Now that the two of us can control the flow of information to the Regime, there is no reason not to start searching for Alphas to better our own knowledge," Katja said.

"Pardon me?" Ignatius furrowed his brow in confusion. "Golem eyes— Alphas? How are these two things even connected?"

Katja quietly informed her professor of everything learned on her excursions with Sigurd. "If golems of the same type have the exact same eye, then we can predict that their Alpha, too, has the same eye," she concluded.

"So to look in the eye of a golem is to look in the eye of its progenitor," Ignatius said. "But how will that help us find one?"

"That, I don't know yet, but it's the best lead we have, and it's one I can no longer investigate without you," Katja admitted. "I need the full support of you and your faculty resources."

"Very well, but say we do find an Alpha. What then?"

"We find out everything we can about it and what connection it has to other golems. We report back to the Regime anything that will convince them controlling an Alpha is impossible and that awakening it will be suicide. This means that from now on, all of our research notes and reports, every piece of paper that leaves this university will be falsified. If they insist on using lies and secrecy to advance their agenda, so shall we," Katja said.

"And what agenda might that be, exactly?" Ignatius crossed his arms over his chest.

"The covenant between golem and man was not exclusive to the Mages, but was meant for everyone. Over time, the Mages' insistence on dominating golems stripped mankind of their connection with them. I say we uncover the secrets of the Alphas to rediscover that connective power and give it back to the people. If we can do that, neither the Regime nor the Kings' Remnants can use the Golem of Death for their own purposes."

"That is a risky plan. What if it takes years to uncover the secrets of the Alpha Golems? Years of reporting failures to the Regime will not be tolerated. They'd sooner replace us than let the project die—and by replace, I mean drag off to the mines, or worse, put on the wrong end of a Steinkamp's blade. I wouldn't be surprised if this Steinkamp on our detail was here more to ensure our compliance than to protect us. At least with the Kings' Remnants, there is a chance the Regime will be toppled before we are ever discovered."

Katja could appreciate the professor's reservations. He, unlike Katja would surely lose his life if they were ever found out. "The Steinkamp is no friend to the Regime nor is he one to the Kings' Remnants, and I think that is where we should stand as well. I for one am not going to sit here and watch Ingleheim enter another Age of Golems. This Regime will fall, the rebellion will fail, but the people of Ingleheim must remain. Only through golems do they have any hope of surviving this."

Ignatius nodded and scratched at his whiskers while studying Katja. "You know, you really remind me of him sometimes."

"Who?"

"Heinrich."

"I remind you of the Führer?" Katja was aghast. *I am nothing like him! I can't be like him!* Her stomach lurched.

"Not the Führer—the idealistic young man I once knew and admired. He was very headstrong in his principles, persuasive to a fault. He got his way by convincing others that it was their way too. He'd get the same look in his eyes that you get when you speak of your passion for golems."

"Is that . . . a good thing?" It irked her to be compared to her father, even in his youth.

"When I knew him, Heinrich loved Ingleheim. He deeply cared about his people, and he had the means to make real change, but he lacked the humility that is paramount to a true leader. He thought he was better than the people he wanted to rule and because of that, surrounded himself with sycophants who stifled his growth into the leader I believe he was meant to be. His ideal Ingleheim became a realm of fear because he himself was afraid. I see a lot of Heinrich in you, Katja, but what I don't see is his lack of humility and courage. I think you have what it takes to excel in whatever it is you want to do, but you won't have to worry about falling prey to your own shortsightedness like he did."

Katja hadn't noticed that Ignatius had placed his hand on her shoulder until he finished speaking. She felt tears threaten to surface, so touched by Ignatius's words, but she blinked them away and smiled instead. She wished, at that moment, that Ignatius was her father instead of the Führer. She was supremely gladdened to have confided in him. For the first time in a long time, Katja could breathe more freely than the thin mountain air of Nordenhein had ever allowed before. "Thank you, Professor. I don't know what to say."

"How about you and I get to the lab?" Ignatius suggested, giving her shoulder a pat.

By the following day, Katja had a complete set of golem eyes drawn onto separate sheets of paper. She and Ignatius had shown all of the golems in the lab the eyes, and each one responded as predicted, following the researchers around the cages. Showing an eye from a different golem type had resulted in them ignoring it. Katja had made a note that the human-sized golems followed the person that showed them their eye in the same manner that the frost ones had followed the giant one in the woods. But the question remained, where had the frost giant been leading them?

Katja was now in the library with Klemens to get his take on how the eyes were connected to their Alphas. Due to his Regime loyalties, Katja and Ignatius kept a lid on their prior day's discussion, but they couldn't keep him completely in the dark. If they were going to find an Alpha, they would need his help. Katja decided to tell him about the *Ode* since he would find out sooner or later. She also told him she and Ignatius discovered that golems communicate by their eyes in the lab. Katja felt it best to leave out anything regarding the Steinkamp, only casually mentioning that one would accompany them on future excursions as mandated by the Regime.

"I hope you're not upset that the professor and I made these discoveries without you," said Katja.

"Are you kidding? I'm just glad that we finally have a real lead. You know I don't care for the lab work anyway," Klemens replied. He studied all five eye drawings scattered about the table. It was after dark, so the library was empty, giving them use of the entire space. "You're pretty good at drawing, Kat. These eyes really are identical."

"Yes, and I hypothesize that these eyes are also identical to their Alphas'."

"You're brilliant. You know that, right?" Klemens flashed her a proud smile.

"Do you see anything unusual, any patterns emerging?" she said, trying to brush off the compliment.

"I don't see any patterns, and *that's* what's unusual. Life forms are basically symmetrical, but these designs, however you look at them, appear random." Klemens adjusted his spectacles and brought two drawings up to his face for closer inspection. One was the frost golem Katja had copied from her journal, the other a lava golem.

"I found that strange as well. The only things that are common in all types are these large spots." Katja pointed to the flaws in each picture he held.

"You mean those aren't inkblots?" he asked in surprise.

"No, I drew these exactly as they were."

Humming and hawing, Klemens set the drawings on the table again and started arranging them in a way Katja couldn't quite figure out, but she let him work in silence. He had always been better at recognizing patterns than her.

After at time, she blurted, "What are you doing, Klem? You look like a general contemplating war tactics on a map."

"Wait a minute," Klemens murmured, holding up a finger. ". . . A map."

He briskly walked around the table and went to the back wall where he pulled down a large canvas map of Ingleheim and tied it down. He returned to the table and after a moment of staring at the sketches, he snatched the crag golem eye and took it over to the wall.

Katja's heart picked up pace as she sauntered to the map to stand alongside Klemens. He analyzed the drawings and the topographical depictions of Kensloche Mountain Range for an excruciatingly long time. When she couldn't take the silence any longer, she said, "Klem, what are thinking?"

Klemens pointed to the map of Kensloche, tracing the patterns of the Crags with his finger, then he pointed to the drawing. "This collection of cracks in the eye . . . it's not random at all. The lines match almost exactly the outlines of the Crags here. See? Look. The Crags are very distinctive and so are these lines in the golem's eye."

Snatching the paper out of his hands, Katja tried to see what he saw. It didn't take her long to notice the pattern of the Crags matched the pattern of the drawing.

"Let's look at another one." Her stomach fluttered with anticipation.

Klemens rushed back to the table while Katja pinned the crag golem eye over Kensloche on the canvas. Once he returned with the drawing of a crystal golem eye, the two researchers looked to Untevar on the map, the mountain range farthest east of Deschner. Untevar Range was harder to compare to the eye. Its map had less rigid mountain lines, with the land being made up of many massive valleys suitable for farming. Even so, the eye of the crystal golem shared a shocking resemblance to Untevar's landscape.

"Are the eyes of a golem simply maps of the areas they derive from?" Katja twirled a loose strand of hair around her finger.

Klemens stood, growing fidgety. Katja pinned the crystal golem eye to Untevar, and both she and Klemens raced back to the table. They grabbed the rest of the drawings and dashed back to the wall, practically tripping over each other and almost falling face-first into the canvas.

After matching the landscape of Nordenhein to the frost golem eye and the map of Luidfort to the winged golem eye, they found themselves stumped when trying to match the lava golem's to Deschner Range.

"It doesn't match," Katja groaned. "Why does this one have to be different?"

"Wait. Where is the golem eye for Breisenburg?" Klemens looked back to the table to find it bare.

"There are no golems native to Breisenburg—only war golems, which possess the eyes of various other types," said Katja.

"Of course!" Klemens exclaimed, clapping a hand to his forehead. "Breisenburg Range is technically a part of Deschner Range. It was not until a few centuries ago that what is now Breisenburg broke away from the Monarchy of Deschner."

Klemens took the picture from Katja and studied it and the map again. When Deschner and Breisenburg were treated like one range, the eye of the lava golem matched the landscape as perfectly as the others.

The two took a step back and looked at their map of golem eyes.

"It's incredible!" Klemens said in complete awe.

"You are incredible," Katja gushed. "I've been staring at these pictures for days, and they looked nothing like maps to me."

He blushed. "Well . . . during my years studying military history, I would see maps every time I closed my eyes. I never imagined my hunch would be correct, though."

She and Klemens continued to study the maps for a time until he announced he was going to retrieve Ignatius to share their findings with him.

"Klem, wait," she called. "Look at the flaw on the lava golem's eye. Look where it is on the map of Deschner Range."

Klemens returned and peered closely at the splotch in the lava golem's eye. It was right in the center of the Volcano of Verishten—right where legends said the Golem of Fire resided.

"If the cracks in the eyes represent the mountains of Ingleheim, then these spots could represent the locations of their Alphas," Katja theorized.

"Or the locations of volcanic activity," said Klemens.

"No." Katja shook her head. "Because in Nordenhein, the eye's spot is way out in the Glacier Peaks, and the hot springs are several miles away."

She pointed to the location of the Nordenhein hot springs where a splotch was absent. The spot around the Glacier Peaks struck her. It was only a few miles from where all the frost golems mysteriously went into dormancy together. Could they have been trying to take Katja and Sigurd to their Alpha, only to realize it was deep in slumber and could take them no farther? Perhaps golems not dominated by a Mage felt the need to follow their Alphas the same way man-sized golems followed their giant counterparts.

Was that giant frost golem trying to tell us something? she pondered. It was as if the golems wanted humans to find their Alphas, suggesting that humans might be the key to awakening them. The question, of course, was how.

"So what do you think, Kat? Could these splotches really be Alpha Golems in dormancy?" Klemens looked to his research partner still staring at the strange dots on the paper.

"There's only one way to find out for sure. We go to one of these locations, and we find ourselves an Alpha." She then met eyes with Klemens.

"That sounds like quite the excursion." He wiped away the nervous sweat forming on his brow with his sleeve.

Katja couldn't help but squeal in delight. Their discovery, late at night in the library, was almost as exhilarating as getting to ride the golem in Frost Woods. "We did it, Klem! We're going to find an Alpha Golem, and it's all thanks to you. You're a genius," she gushed, suddenly finding her arms around him.

She pulled herself off him quickly and tried to keep her wits about her. Lately, she found it hard to contain herself with all these new discoveries.

"You're the genius," Klemens returned, his face reddening. "It was your intuition that led us to the golem eyes in the first place. Your thesis is going to change the world, Kat."

Katja exhaled, smiling so wide her cheeks ached from the effort. Klemens's jaw dropped, and she immediately closed her lips and placed her hands over her mouth.

"You're smiling." He pointed at her face.

"No, I'm not." Her words came out muffled in her hands.

"I told you I'd get you to do it. You're smiling!" Klemens guffawed.

She shook her head back and forth, giggling into her hands. "You're mistaken, herr."

"Let me see—you have to let me see!" Klemens reached out in an attempt to take Katja's hands from her mouth.

Unable to stop laughing, she turned away. Klemens reached from behind her and tried to grab her arms again, but she spun around and started running. She covered her mouth any way she could as Klemens tried with all his might to peek at her laughing face.

"Get away, you lunatic!" she squealed.

Klemens finally caught her by the arm and spun her around playfully.

"Ugh, you are relentless." Katja came down from her laughter and leaned back against the canvas map in exhaustion.

"Show me," Klemens begged, caging her against the maps, trying to view her snickering as she turned her head to the side.

Katja was so embarrassed to smile in front of him. She was losing a two-year power struggle, but she was too tired and elated to keep up the sullen façade any longer. Katja revealed her smile, shaking her head all the while.

To her surprise, Klemens took a hold of her chin and turned her head to face his. He then leaned in close and kissed her on the mouth. Her whole body became rigid. Klemens leaned in more and Katja, with her back against the wall, had nowhere to go. She simply allowed the kiss to run its course.

When Klemens pulled away, he respectfully stepped back, allowing her to stand up straight. She immediately fixed her hair and adjusted her blouse even though neither had gotten overly tussled. Her stomach fluttered grievously, making her ill. *Why did I let that happen?*

"Apologies. I was caught up in the moment." Klemens pulled at his cravat, his face redder than ever, more out of breath than Katja was.

"That's all right," she murmured.

"Well, I'm glad for it," Klemens replied then took her hands in his. "You're probably aware that I have feelings for you because I'm so awful at hiding them. Thank Verishten the Führer approved of my transfer to Golem Studies, because—"

"Klem, I—"

"I do hope that after this project or after graduation, whichever comes first, you will consider me . . . I mean—I hope you will agree to . . . uh . . ."

Katja knew the words Klemens was trying to sputter out, which made her chest so tight she was afraid she'd pass out before he stumbled upon them.

"I'd like you to be . . . my wife."

And there it is, Katja groaned inside. What she wouldn't give to be a Del'Cabrian noblewoman at that moment. In Del'Cabria, would-be couples of high status often underwent long, drawn out courtships before ever agreeing to marry. Ingles, however, weren't fond of wasting time when it came to such things. If one found a suitable match, it was best to propose quickly lest someone else get there first. The only thing required to make it official was for the bride to put on the marriage bracelet presented by the groom to show she fully consented. No months of anticipation or outlandish celebrations.

"K-Klemens," Katja stuttered, finding it hard to speak, "I . . . we don't even know each other's real names."

"You needn't worry about that. I assure you, I come from a very wealthy family. My inheritance alone will see us and our children—and our grandchildren—to a very prosperous future. It doesn't matter where your family stands. They could be paupers for all I care."

The library faded in and out of focus as she struggled to respond. "You don't know me."

"Nonsense, we've been working together for two whole years. So what if I don't know your real name or your parentage? What I do know is that you love golems because you secretly wish you were a Golem Mage. I know you write in your journal, not just to record your findings but to get your frustrations out. I know you hate smiling because you think it gives your power away, and that's okay. I think you're beautiful even when you scowl at me. I'm sure there are many things about you I don't know, and frankly I want to spend the rest of my life finding out what those things are—that is, if you will give me the chance."

Katja's heart flopped and her guts tied in knots. He knew her so well, but not nearly well enough. *I love golems because they are the only things I was able to identify with growing up. I write in my journal to let my frustrations out about a regime you support unfailingly. I hate smiling because it caught the attention of a Spirit Mage who turned me into his love slave before shattering my soul into a thousand pieces with a wave of his hand. And yes, there are many more things you don't know about me, Klem. Like how I am indirectly assisting a rebel group that according to you wants to turn Ingleheim to rubble. Oh, and I'm harboring a strange erotic fixation on a faceless, nameless killer, and possible defector. Do you really want to spend the rest of your life learning more about me?*

Those were the words Katja wanted to yell at Klemens. Of course, she wouldn't dare.

Katja swallowed the lump in her throat and said, "Klemens, you are highly intelligent, and I find you very sweet. Trust me when I say—"

She was interrupted by a messenger bursting into the library. "Message for Herr Klemens."

"I am him, but can it wait? I'm in the middle of something here." His eye twitched.

"I'm afraid it cannot wait. The message is of an urgent nature."

"Well, just tell me then, if it's so important." Klemens's hands grew even clammier as he continued to hold Katja's.

"You may want to take this message privately, herr. It is dire news regarding your father."

Klemens looked to Katja, his face tense with sudden worry. "Excuse me." He strode toward the door and took the parchment from the messenger who bowed and swiftly exited the library. Klemens unrolled the piece of paper and read it. His usual blushing face immediately paled to the hue of cream.

It felt like several minutes of Klemens staring at the note before Katja said, "Klem, is everything all right?"

"No." It seemed like it took all of his energy to say that word. "My father is dead."

"Verishten have mercy." Katja's heart stilled. "What happened?"

"Killed by rebels." Klemens started to wander away, unable to meet Katja's eyes. "I have to go."

She helplessly watched her deflated research partner slip out of the library like a disembodied spirit. When he closed the double doors behind him, her legs gave way, and she dropped to the floor in shock. Katja knew of one man who had been abducted, tortured, and killed by rebels—Kanzler Volker.

12
LOOSE SHALE

One week later, the research team set out for the Crags of Kensloche in search of their first Alpha. They chose the Golem of Stone in Kensloche Range first because it was closest to the university other than the Golem of Ice in the Glacier Peaks. Since Kensloche was far warmer in winter, it was the obvious choice between the two. Discovering the Golem of Ice would have to wait until the summer months.

Kensloche was the lowest-altitude range in Ingleheim, whereas Nordenhein was the highest. As a result, the team experienced some minor headaches and lethargy during their travels, but after the third day they grew accustomed to the thicker air. The Steinkamp kept to himself for most of the trip and spent his time scouting ahead to find the quickest and safest paths. He had indicated that the Crags of Kensloche could be treacherous since the Regime did little to police them.

The team had left their horses at the stables in the Town of Kensloche, and Sigurd had left his at some other location he referred to as a haven. It was there where he switched out his crossbow for rope and a pulley for rock climbing. He had told Katja once that a Steinkamp never left a weapon behind, but this time the crossbow would have to be sacrificed in the interest of carrying a much more useful apparatus. From there, the team continued their hike up the rugged trails and reached the Crags on the third day.

Klemens had been quiet for much of the ride to Kensloche Range. He had told the team earlier he'd been instructed not to return home, but instead continue with the assignment, which the Regime assured him was more important.

Katja caught up to her distraught friend who was growing paler as the hike progressed. "How are you faring, Klem?"

"Fine," he muttered, though he didn't engage her any further. They had barely talked since he had gotten the news about his father. There was still that unanswered marriage proposal dangling between them, and Klemens was likely not in the right state of mind to handle any kind of response from her just yet.

"You know you didn't have to come with us. We would have understood if you wanted to stay behind and grieve," Katja said.

"What good would I be to you and the professor sitting in my room thinking about my father? I still have a duty to the Regime and to my family. I am more determined now than ever to find out how to awaken the Golem of Death so this wretched rebellion can be wiped out of existence once and for all." Klemens's jaw was taut.

Katja cleared her throat and murmured, "Again . . . I'm so sorry."

There was nothing else she could say. She could not allow the Regime to succeed, but her heart bled for Klemens and his loss nonetheless. Guilt gnawed on her insides for lying to him about her and the professor's real intentions. This Alpha, if found, was not going to wake up, and that was what they were going to report to the Regime, one way or another.

A few hours into the hike, the team met Sigurd at the base of a humongous jagged cliff face.

"The quickest way to the Crags is over this cliff here," he said.

"I thought we were in the Crags already," returned Klemens.

"This is just a lowly mountain trail, herr. Up there is the Crags." Sigurd presented the looming vertical cliff with his arm.

Both Ignatius and Klemens gulped in unison.

When Sigurd showed them the rope and harnesses they each would be using, Katja piped up, "Excuse me, but am I not going up there strapped to your back?"

"Whatever gave you that idea, fraulein? You will be going up on your own, just like them." Sigurd nodded toward the men.

Katja felt the fool for almost revealing her previous experience with him. The idea of scaling such a daunting wall of rock without his assistance made her break out into a cold sweat.

Sigurd helped everyone strap into their harnesses and came to strap

Katja in last. She was glad she wore hiking slacks, paired with a vest and cravat under her leather lady's frock coat, even if doing so meant receiving some curious glances from her male counterparts. As Sigurd crouched to fasten the harness around Katja's thighs, her entire body flushed, imagining what his hands could do while he was down there. *Stop it, Katja.* She could feel a drop of cold sweat drip down the back of her neck. An even colder breeze swept by, sending shivers through her, making her almost regret wearing her hair tied up and off her neck in a loose bun.

After tightening the final strap around her waist, Sigurd stood and said in a low husky voice that only she could hear, "You'll be fine. I don't expect any of you to climb such cliffs on your own." He stepped away and said to the rest of the group, "I will go first and lift you all up with a pulley when I get to the top."

"You're going to climb that entire thing on your own?" Katja asked, her neck straining to look up at it.

"We all do our climb training in these Crags. There is nothing to it."

Sigurd gathered the ends of all the ropes and hooked them to his belt underneath the pulley apparatus strapped to his back. The research team stood and watched the Steinkamp scramble up the rock face with the ease of a squirrel running up a tree. Katja bit her lip for several minutes until he finally disappeared over the final ledge.

A few moments later, Sigurd set the pulley and started lifting the team members up one at a time. Ignatius went first, smiling and waving down to his acolytes as he ascended. *Nothing can ever get the best of the professor, it seems.* Next was Klemens, who asked Katja to wish him luck as he wiped sweat from his brow and pushed his spectacles up his nose. The poor man looked petrified, but it was not long until he was at the top, and Katja began to feel her own rope tighten.

She thought she'd be more scared, but as long as she kept her eyes forward on the rocks in front of her and didn't look down, she felt fine, other than the discomfort of the harness biting into her thighs. When she finally reached the top, Sigurd lifted her up by the arms and set her down safely. She let herself glance over the edge to see how far she'd come and her legs quaked at the distance. Sigurd, sensing her anxiety, took her by the arms again and led her well away from the edge before packing up his pulley. Katja noticed that it was sealed to the ground by solid rock at its base. As soon as Sigurd touched it, the rock reverted back into the leather bindings that he had used to hold it in place.

After a quick meal, everybody was ready to continue. Sigurd kept ahead of them as before.

"Now everyone, watch your step on these cliffs," he called back. "There is a lot of loose—"

Just then, Klemens nearly slipped down an incline were it not for the professor keeping him upright. Chips of stone broke free and slid down the hill and off the cliff, shattering as they hit the jagged rocks below.

"—shale. So make sure your footing is solid before putting your full weight down," Sigurd finished.

"Sound advice," Klemens agreed as he collected himself.

The four travelers trekked downhill most of the way, and each step across the rugged trail opened up to the breathtaking landscape of Kensloche Range. Katja marveled at the sights of the cutting, gray shale ridges against seemingly smooth remnants of rockslides alongside them. Gnarled trees grew sideways out of the cracks in the rock. Mosses of every imaginable shade of green lined the path at their feet. Looking onward to the horizon, the team took in rolling snow-specked hills and luscious green pastures miles below that stretched toward the setting sun.

It was not long into dusk when the party arrived at a plateau where they could camp for the night. They set up their tents around a shallow cave, where a nearby stone outcropping served to shield them from the winds. It was nowhere near as cold in Kensloche at this time of year as it was in Nordenhein but it was winter nonetheless, and on the Crags the wind still brought with it an icy bite.

Sigurd went to work on building a fire using trace amounts of blast gel and kindling he had collected. The rest of the team worked on setting up their compact tents and bedrolls. By nightfall, the camp was nearly prepared, and the Steinkamp took off to secure a perimeter around them, whatever that entailed.

It was so strange for Katja to be out on an excursion with her entire research team again, and so far away from Nordenhein. Even stranger was having the Steinkamp with them and pretending she hadn't met him before. She wondered if Sigurd also felt odd acting like he didn't know her, though it seemed effortless for him, not that she'd be able to tell.

Klemens decided to take all the canteens to a spring they had passed earlier and refill them. He grabbed a lantern and set off while Katja and the professor went to feed the fire. When Klemens returned, he suddenly fell forward and rolled down the loose shale until he reached the plateau.

"Klemens!" Katja cried out, running to him. "Be careful, we almost lost you once already today!"

Klemens shot up and glared behind him as if the rocks he had tripped on committed some terrible offense against him. "I didn't trip. I-I was pushed—someone was behind me!"

Katja wanted to chalk it all up to Klemens's clumsiness until she heard the crunch of shale from where he had fallen. Four figures sauntered from the shadows into the lamp light, snickering amongst themselves. They were men, wearing old fur or leather smocks and outworn breaches with holes in the knees. They appeared as if they'd lived in the wild for years, apparent from their tangled beards, unkempt hair, yellowed or cracked teeth, and deadened eyes. In reaction to the blunt weapons the men carried with them, the team backed up towards the flat-sided outcropping near Katja's tent.

"Who are you people, and what do you want?" demanded Ignatius.

These men, Katja could only assume, were Cragsmen. She had read somewhere that they lived in the Crags to hide from the Karl and made their living pillaging farms and villages in the area. Whatever it was these men wanted, it was not to share a meal by the fire.

The Cragsmen continued with their guttural laughter. One of them said, "You'll need to tend to those cuts, boy."

They began to close in on the three researchers. It was too dark to run, and if the researchers were to try, they'd risk twisting an ankle, tripping down a cliff, or worse. These men would know that.

Where are you, Sigurd? Katja screamed in her mind.

"Never mind him, what is it you want?" Ignatius said in a loud voice.

"What you got, old man?" said a bald Cragsman wearing a bloody handkerchief over one eye. His dialect was choppy and barely understandable.

"We have food, medicine, and not much else."

"Give it here, then." The one-eyed man motioned with his chin for Ignatius to go and get it.

Carefully, the professor went toward his sack of rations and exposed Katja who had been behind him. Only the one-eyed Cragsman followed the professor while the other three ventured closer to the outcropping. Klemens trembled, trying to push his glasses to his nose but found them missing. They were still on the ground where he had fallen.

"We have schlepts—lots of schlepts," Klemens sputtered.

"What are we going to do with schlepts?" said a Cragsman with a scraggly brown ponytail down his back but not much else on the top of his head.

"I don't know what I'd do with schlepts, but I know what I'd do with her," said the taller one with a haggard face and the tiny eyes of a shrimp. He made kissing motions with his lips toward Katja, making her shudder in disgust.

"I don't think she likes you, Lars," snorted a younger Cragsman wearing a makeshift hat made from animal hide.

"Don't matter much, never stopped me from getting my way," the thin-faced one named Lars said as he edged closer, licking his peeling lips.

"If you value whatever it is you call lives, you will walk away now!" Katja said as loud and forcefully as she could in her terrified state.

"Pretty lady wants a fight. Well, you'll get your fight," said the man with the ponytail.

Lars and Ponytail advanced toward Katja, while One-Eye clasped a hand over Ignatius's mouth before he could cry out. Klemens's reaction was to keep shaking. The hat-wearing Cragsman lunged toward him, took him by the shirt, and threw him down, then struck him with his mallet while he was on the ground.

Katja's scream echoed off the cliffs but it did nothing to deter the two men that came at her. Her back pressed against the outcropping as Lars grabbed her by the face. His hands stank of blood and excrement, causing her to wretch.

Before she could begin to fight back, Katja heard a sickening crunch. She stood wide-eyed as Lars's body shuddered jarringly. His throat rattled and blood streamed down his face from his hairline. Without warning, the point of a blade pierced out the front of the man's skull from the inside. Blood splashed, and Katja jerked her head away before any of it got into her mouth and eyes. Ponytail quickly backed away while everyone else stood frozen.

Leaping down from a protrusion in the outcropping above was Sigurd, holding the chain from his splitting blade dispenser. As he descended, Lars's body, acting as a counterweight, lifted up into the darkness by the chain. Lars was dead before the blade had split open, but his body twitched macabrely.

Sigurd made a controlled landing on the shoulders of the ponytailed Cragsman, wrapped the chain around his neck, then pulled hard and fast.

The crack of Ponytail's spine ripped through the night air. Sigurd jumped from Ponytail's shoulders, causing his body to fall forward. Lars's weight ensured that the chain around Ponytail's neck tautened before he hit the ground. Ponytail spun on his axis, the chain strangling his broken neck while Lars, the lighter of the two, continued to hang lifelessly above.

Feeling flooded back into Katja's limbs as her flight instinct took over. She bolted away and ducked into the cave, huddling there and watching as Sigurd dodged the swing of Fur Hat's mallet by taking cover behind Ponytail's half hanging body. The mallet made brutal contact with Ponytail's face, sending him flailing to the ground and jolting Lars above. With his corpse-shield gone, Sigurd rolled toward Fur Hat, extending his thin steel blade. One swing from Sigurd's sword sliced Fur Hat's throat wide open. A crimson waterfall poured from the man's neck, drenching his tattered coat before he fell dead onto his back beside Klemens, who paled to the hue of a ghost and recoiled away. Sigurd paid no mind to the body he just left behind as he turned to the final Cragsman left standing.

Ignatius had already squirmed away from One-Eye, leaving him there to face off with the Steinkamp by himself. One-Eye dashed down the rocky path. Katja was afraid he'd get away when Sigurd didn't speed after him. Instead, Sigurd tossed his circular blade, nearly invisible in the darkness, and it burst into a small cyclone that flew toward its fleeing target. One-Eye hadn't made it ten paces before his bald head toppled from his shoulders, rolled down the shale, and off the plateau.

Katja's hands were clasped around her mouth for several moments after all the Cragsmen were dead. She barely registered Sigurd returning to check if everyone was all right.

Once ensuring all three of the team members were relatively uninjured, he said, "I apologize for not getting here sooner, I was preoccupied by eight Cragsmen waiting to strike over the ridge there."

"There were twelve altogether?" Ignatius asked, rubbing his arm from having it been twisted so awkwardly.

"I eliminated the entire clan. No more should come upon you tonight. Cragsmen don't generally come up this high," Sigurd said as if he were spouting off a morning report. "All of you tend to yourselves. I will finish securing the perimeter."

"What about them?" Katja murmured while pointing to the bloody corpses splayed about the camp.

"I will dispose of them when I return. I will only be a few minutes,"

Sigurd replied, then disapeared into the night.

It was then when a cracking slurp echoed into the air. Lars's skull ripped free from the splitting blade; his body dropped to the ground with a splat. Klemens clambered to his feet and darted to the edge of the plateau to vomit. Katja felt like joining him but kept it down in favor of picking up a canteen and pouring it over her face to wash away the blood.

"There goes our drinking water for the night," Ignatius said. "Allow me to refill them at the spring."

Katja thanked the professor and handed him the now empty canteen. Once Ignatius had gone, she scanned the camp for Klemens's spectacles while trying to avoid looking directly at the bodies scattered throughout the site. She eventually found them broken in half down the center.

As promised, Sigurd returned a few minutes later. He offered a small piece of earth binding to mold the spectacles together again, making them as good as new, save the scratched lenses. Klemens was grateful that he could still see out of them at all. Sigurd then went to quietly dispose of the bodies over the side of the plateau. He was considerate enough to do it far from camp so that no one could hear the bodies splattering onto the rocks below. Katja didn't ask what he'd done with the eight others he had supposedly killed.

In the meantime, Katja sat with Klemens on blankets inside the cave, illuminated by a lantern. She applied disinfecting ointment to his facial wounds, some from his tumble and a few more from Fur Hat's mallet.

"You were right. I should have stayed behind. I'm not cut out for these expeditions. It's hard enough without barbarians clubbing me in the face." Klemens winced as she applied the ointment just above his eyebrow.

"Nonsense, we need you out here," Katja said consolingly, even though she wasn't sure why she should bother. He had yet to ask her if *she* were okay.

"Yeah, a lot of good I've been so far. Almost falling to my death earlier and then freezing when that Cragsman put his filthy hands on you."

'Filthy' was not an effective enough word to describe Lars's hands. Katja didn't want to imagine what those hands would have done to her had Sigurd not come to the rescue. "It's all right, Klem. None of us knew what to do. I wouldn't expect you to take on four armed men by yourself. That's why we have the Steinkamp."

"I understand that, but the fact remains, you're going to be my wife someday. I should have done something—anything to protect you,"

Klemens lamented.

Katja wanted to comfort Klemens, but she was irked by what he said. Even though she would rather talk about anything else, she needed to put an end to this. "Klem." She cleared her throat. "I never actually agreed to be your wife."

"What?" Klemens shook his head. "Oh no—I mean, of course—I knew that. I'm sorry. I'm not entirely in my right mind at the moment."

Klemens cradled his head in his hands then ran his fingers through his wavy brown hair. Katja wasn't sure if he was going to start crying or not. She suddenly felt the urge to add more.

"Just with everything going on right now, our research and your father . . . I think it would be best to put thoughts of marriage on hold for now."

Klemens brought his head back up with a snap, looking toward the fire. Katja became startled as well only to see Sigurd walk by and head up the hill, probably to the spring to wash, she assumed. He didn't seem to pay mind to her and Klemens huddled in the cave together.

Once realizing the shadow was only the Steinkamp, Klemens replied, "You're absolutely right as always. My proposal couldn't have come at a worse time for both of us. Right now, we need to focus on this project. As soon as we return to the university, I will take the time to mourn my father."

"That sounds wise," she said.

"It is not ideal, but it is for the best." Klemens placed a hand on her knee and rubbed it affectionately. "I do intend to take you as my wife, Kat, but not for a little while. I do hope you will wait for me."

Katja was off the hook for a time, but not completely. That made her uncomfortable still. Luckily, Klemens didn't wait for Katja to respond. He merely patted her leg and stood up, offering his hand to her to stand up as well. She took it.

"Shall we retire for the night?" said Klemens.

Sleep was something she desperately needed, but after the night's terror, she was afraid of what would happen when she closed her eyes. *So much blood.*

As if sensing Katja's reservations to return to her tent, Klemens held onto her hand and offered, "If you're too frightened to sleep in your tent all by yourself, you're welcome to join me in mine."

Katja gave him a shocked glare. She would never expect a man like Klemens to make such a forward suggestion at a time like this.

"You misunderstand, I don't intend to—I don't even want to—well, of course I want to, but—" He stopped himself before saying anything that would dig him into a deeper hole.

"That's very sweet of you, but I'm not tired anymore. I think I'll just warm up by the fire and retire to my own tent later."

He nodded, the blushing color returning to his cheeks, visible even at night.

"Very well, I understand. It just might be safer to have someone around in case . . . never mind. Goodnight, Kat." Klemens nodded and hesitantly ducked into his tent across from hers. She wondered if his offer was made more for his benefit, being scared to sleep alone, than it was for hers.

Sighing heavily, Katja let her hair down and hugged her coat around her. She walked to the fire and sat down on a rock. To her surprise, she saw Sigurd standing just on the other side of the flames, barely illuminated by the firelight. His own shadow cast onto the outcropping ahead was more distinctive than he was. *How long has he been standing there?*

After taking a few deep breaths to calm her nerves, Katja asked, "Find any signs of Cragsmen out there?"

"None, but I will keep watch, so not to worry."

"Do you ever sleep?"

"A Steinkamp must train his body to operate effectively while sleep-deprived."

"Right," was all Katja could say in response.

"What about you, fraulein? You should be asleep like the rest of your team. I hear Herr Klemens is keeping a spot warm for you in his tent."

Katja's face suddenly grew as red as Klemens's. *So, he did overhear us! Verishten swallow me whole.* "Hmm, well, the thing about Klemens is . . . he has the best of intentions . . . I think," she sputtered.

"I am most certain he does," Sigurd replied in levity. "However, after what happened tonight, are you sure you're all right?"

Katja was glad to know that Sigurd was concerned for her after the days of traveling together where he barely registered her existence. "What happened tonight was no more frightening than staring down a frost golem right before it's about to freeze you solid, or even the morning when we first met."

Remembering the sheer terror of that moment made her shiver, despite the warmth of the flames. The Cragsmen could not compare to that, and now the man who'd made her feel that way stood by the fire across from her, and she couldn't be more comfortable in his presence.

"But tonight was different," Sigurd continued.

"If you call a man's head exploding from a Steinkamp splitting blade different, then yes, tonight was very different," Katja quipped, her sarcasm sounding more hostile than she'd intended.

Sigurd didn't respond right away, but then said, "Not having my crossbow limits my ranged attack options."

"You made it look so easy . . . It really is like breathing to you, isn't it?"

Of course, killing is like breathing to a Steinkamp, you idiot! She mentally chastised herself. Knowing that, however, didn't help with her nausea. She could still hear the sickening crack of the man's skull being split open from the inside.

"Katja . . ." Sigurd released an irritated sigh. "Do you know what those men would have done to you had I not killed them? They would have forced you to watch them beat your professor and Klemens to death. Then they would have dragged you to where the rest of the clan was waiting and had their way with you, until you were bloodied and begging them to end your life. Trust me, those men will give far more to the world as rotting corpses."

"I know that," Katja said. "You gave those men a cleaner death than any of them likely deserved and we are all very grateful. But . . . that doesn't make it any easier to stomach. I don't have to like what you do, but I know I must accept it because honestly, Sigurd, you might be the only person in this world whom I trust with my life."

"Really?" he asked. "What about your colleagues, you don't trust them?"

"I wish I could, but if they knew certain things about me, they'd likely turn on me. They don't know me like you do. I trust you, Sigurd. Is that foolish of me?"

Sigurd shook his head in response and held out his arm. "Come with me."

She looked warily at him. "Where?"

"Just a second ago you said you trusted me more than anyone. Are you going to take my hand or not?"

"Very well." *I suppose I have a thing or two to learn about trust,* she thought.

Katja took Sigurd's hand. He led her away from the campfire and into the shadows of the night. Even walking directly in front of her, she could barely see him, only feel his cold, rough glove over her hand. Her step became more and more uncertain as they walked up an incline of shale, but she never slipped.

They finally reached a flat rock bed at the southern edge of the plateau where the light of the one-half moon and the more distant full moon shone down, casting the Steinkamp as a silhouette against darkness. Sigurd laid down on the rock with his hands behind his head, and motioned Katja to lie next to him. As cold as she was this far out from the campfire, Katja did as he bid more out of curiosity than anything else.

Once she faced the night sky, she gasped in awe. Scattered above them, thousands upon thousands of blinking white eyes stared down at them, endless in their variation of size. It was as if Verishten himself, after all the horrors they had witnessed over time, were trying to assure them of his benevolent purpose. Katja realized she hadn't taken a moment to look to the sky since the sun fell. Many Ingles went their entire lives without seeing the stars. Volcanic ash clouded the skies, in some places so thick it blotted out the sun and moons. Only in the mountain ranges farthest from the volcano was the sky clear enough to see the stars. Nordenhein was one of those places, but Katja had spent all her nights under the university roof for the last six years. She never thought about going out to see the stars on the few clear nights such as this, so busy with her studies and afraid to leave the campus. She almost forgot they existed.

"Oh, Sigurd . . ." Katja was breathless. "I never imagined them to be so dazzling."

"You must truly be Deschner-born to have never seen the stars before."

"Say what you want about our ashen sky, but we have resilient lungs for it."

"They'd have to be, they're blacker than obsidian."

"Oh, and you would know?" Katja challenged, and then suddenly realized that Sigurd would have seen the inside of a body once or twice. "Well . . . maybe you *would* know. And I suppose your lungs are perfect specimens?"

"Maybe if I had remained in Kensloche all my life, they would be," Sigurd said. "It is nice to return every once in a while. The air here is so rich it makes a man feel almost superhuman."

"So you were born here? Growing up, you must have seen the stars every night."

"I grew up in a Deschner orphanage, but I do remember when my sister would take me into the Crags nearest to our house and point out the constellations."

"Like the pictures people see in the stars?"

Sigurd pointed out a distinctive star cluster. "That there is the Cragsman's Club, see? Because it is in the shape of a club."

"That's imaginative," Katja scoffed then pointed out a group of stars in the shape of a bell. "What about that one to the north?"

"That one is called Frau Blomgren, although I'm not sure why."

"Oh, I know why. It's Frau Blomgren of Nordenhein, a famous painter from the Age of Kings. My father has a few pieces of her work hanging in his study." Katja had to stop herself from mentioning that many of the paintings had been pilfered out of Golem Mage homes after they were executed. She then pointed to a constellation southward. "What's that one over there that looks like a dog's face?"

"Ah yes, that one is the uh . . . Disgruntled Coyote."

"Disgruntled Coyote? That's ridiculous, who came up with that?"

"Me . . . just now," Sigurd admitted sheepishly.

Katja smacked his shoulder with the back of her hand playfully, and giggling ensued. "A Steinkamp soldier makes a joke."

"No, no, that wasn't a joke, that was me trying to trick you. There is a distinct difference."

"Shame on you, thinking you could pull one over on me." Katja giggled on. To her amazement, she heard a husky chortle from behind Sigurd's mesh mask. *Could this day be any stranger?* she thought, *I am sitting under the stars having a laugh with a Steinkamp soldier only an hour after he brutally killed twelve men!*

It was as the laughter died down when Katja felt one of Sigurd's gloved fingers brush up against the side of her hand. Her unconscious reaction was to shift her hand away from it. Had he meant to touch her? Perhaps she shouldn't have moved her hand.

Trying to break the odd tension beginning to form between them, Katja asked, "Sigurd, I still want to know something. How did you learn the words to the *Ode to Golems?*"

After a few moments, Sigurd replied with a sigh, "My mother sang it to me when I was very young."

Katja snapped her head around. "Really? Then how did she know it?"

"I don't know. She died when I was five," he replied darkly, not taking his gaze from the stars.

For Sigurd's mother to know the words to the *Ode to Golems,* she must have learned them before the Regime made the song forbidden. Even in the Age of Kings, that song was already over a thousand years old and wouldn't be commonly known, but it would be better known by Golem Mages.

Could Sigurd be a survivor of a Mage family? No, that's impossible. They were all wiped out. Every last one. Even through Katja's logical thoughts, she still felt a twist in her gut at the notion that Sigurd was made an orphan because his father happened to bear the Eye of Verishten. She wanted to grill him further about his family, but it was obviously difficult for him to speak of them, and she didn't want to her personal probing to end this night prematurely.

She decided to talk about her own experiences instead. "I'm sorry to hear that. At least you have fond memories of her. My mother died giving birth to me. She never even had a chance to name me. I often think the reason my father kept me locked away was less about protecting me and more to keep from having to look at me after she died. I've been told that I look a lot like her."

Katja was unsure why she told Sigurd the last bit. She did not intend for the conversation to take such a dark turn.

"Katja," Sigurd began, finally turning his head to face her. "Unless he hated your mother, I don't think he could keep himself from looking at you."

"Well, he hasn't . . . not for ten years now."

"Then he is blind."

Sigurd's finger touched hers again, only this time, she didn't move her hand away but edged it closer. Before she knew it, her fingers became entwined with his. Sigurd squeezed her hand until she felt every ridge of his glove's grips pressing into her palm. Katja could barely breathe. *How many people have these hands killed?* She couldn't help but wonder.

It was all Katja could do to not draw attention to the situation. Her stomach fluttered, and she was at a loss for what to do or say next.

"Your glove sure is rough," she blurted. Katja hoped Sigurd would take off his glove and maybe he would actually touch her, but he removed his hand from hers instead. She wanted to kick herself for opening her mouth.

It wasn't until Sigurd rolled onto his side to fully face her that Katja realized why he had let go of her hand. He used that arm to prop himself up. Her breath grew shorter, and her heart beat faster. *What are you thinking?* She wanted to ask, but she remained silent, as did he.

Sigurd reached his other hand out toward her face and lightly grazed his thumb just above her eyebrow. "You have a little blood . . ."

Katja's nerves were beyond shot. The night was cold, and she desperately longed for Sigurd's warmth. She grabbed his hand after he finished wiping the blood from her forehead, and finger by finger she removed his glove. He made no attempt to stop her. She then entwined her fingers amongst his, feeling the warm, scarred skin of his palm flush against hers. No irritating grooves. Only him.

Sigurd's breathing picked up pace as he examined Katja's fingers. *Can he see that I have no fingerprints on this hand?* Desperate to forget about the events that caused her to lose them, Katja brought Sigurd's hand to her cheek. From there he didn't need any more guidance from her. He continued to caress her cheek and then run his thumb across her bottom lip. Breathing deeply, she trembled at his touch, so purposeful but gentle in a way that made her weak.

Sigurd removed his other glove and cupped Katja's face with both hands, bringing his body so close to hers that she had to press her palms firmly against his armored chest. She found herself hating the Steinkamp uniform for separating them. Sigurd wore the cage, yet it was Katja who felt imprisoned by it. A surge of frustration crashed against her desire. Never before had she felt anything like this. She ran her hands slowly down his faceplate, his breath warming them.

Sigurd pulled Katja's head toward him and brought her forehead to his. He breathed heavily through his nose, his frustration building behind the thin steel mesh. Katja closed her eyes and imagined she was actually touching him. One of his hands ran through her hair while the other explored her neck, making her skin flush despite the cool breeze.

This is crazy! Am I really falling for a Steinkamp? Would I want him this badly if he wasn't wearing that blasted mask? There was only one way to know for sure.

"Take off your mask. I have to see you," Katja whispered, her forehead still pressed against his.

It was at those words that Sigurd's hands suddenly left her. *Please don't.* Her mind begged. It felt as if Sigurd were near frozen by a frost golem's ice beam again.

"I can't," he muttered and sat up.

"Why?" Katja sat up alongside him and placed a hand on his shoulder. The moment she did that he was up on his feet. "Did you hear that?"

"I didn't hear anything." Katja remained seated, realizing that whatever had been happening between them had run its course.

"I must patrol the perimeter. You should retire to your tent. Try to get some sleep." The Steinkamp's voice was colder than the icy chill of the breeze.

There was no use in arguing once Sigurd disappeared into the night, leaving Katja there alone. Luckily, the fire in the camp had not died out, and it guided her back safely.

When she returned to her tent, she was startled by a large blood and brain splatter on the rocks right in front of its entrance. Her nausea came back in a wave. The thought of trying to sleep in her tent with pieces of Cragsman just outside made her so ill that she considered taking up Klemens's offer and climbing into his tent to pass out next to him. Realizing she would have to step over the blood to get to her bedroll anyway, she decided to sleep in her own. She didn't want to send the wrong message to Klemens or Sigurd.

Katja tied up her tent flap and tucked herself into her chilly sleeping bag for the night. She lay there wide awake, freezing and frustrated. She had to hand it to Sigurd at any rate, instead of going to sleep with images of blood and decapitations in her head, it was the feeling of his thumb on her bottom lip and his warm hands caressing her neck that kept her from sleeping. She continued to imagine those hands doing so much more to her for the remainder of the night.

13

THE TIME IS NOW

The Steinkamp and the research team set off again early the next morning. It was all Sigurd could do not to think of him and Katja under the stars— how soft her hair was when he ran his hands through it, how warm her skin felt, and how badly he wanted to take off his mask to kiss her. It wasn't as if he were a stranger to the touch of a woman. Despite strict rules about Steinkamp having intimate relations, soldiers still had the needs of men, as broken as those men were. It was common for some women to throw themselves at Steinkamp soldiers who fulfilled fantasies of a dangerous and unidentifiable man having their way with them.

Katja wasn't one of those women. She had been disgusted with everything Sigurd stood for when they first met and yet she had invited him to touch her. She wanted to know the person behind the mask, unlike the other women who made a point not to think of him as a person at all.

On top of all that, she trusted him. *Nothing good can come of this,* he thought.

Looking to Katja following behind with the rest of her team, Sigurd hoped to gain some insight into what she was thinking or where things stood between them, but she hardly looked his way. The team appeared a little ragged after the events from the night prior and Katja was no exception, but it did little to change Sigurd's perception of her beauty. There was something about witnessing a highborn woman removed from her finery that gave him much-desired pause.

Eventually, the team came to a dead end of sorts. The path continued gradually downward and would take them to sheep-herding country, away from where they believed the Alpha to be. Katja and her team reviewed their maps again to realize that the Alpha would be on the other side of a high ridge, beyond a deep gorge in the distance.

"It will take several hours to climb that and days to go around," Klemens moaned.

"And according to the map, we will find no kinder terrain on the other side," added Ignatius.

Sigurd sighed to himself, exhausted from the night before and not looking forward to lifting three people up and down the series of cliffs and drops.

"Do we just turn back now or take the long way around?" Klemens asked.

Katja then spoke, "I have a suggestion. It might sound a bit mad, but if it works, we can be over that ridge in no time."

Sigurd had an inkling of what her suggestion might be, but he dared not hazard a guess in front of the other researchers.

"As we know, giant crag golems have the ability to manipulate earth with the light of their eyes. They can mold their bodies to other rocks much like the Steinkamp's leather bindings. This essentially allows them to march straight up cliff faces like that one."

"Are you suggesting we awaken a giant crag golem? What makes you think it will take us where we want to go?" Ignatius inquired.

"It might not, but what better way to practice influencing golems than in their natural habitat? Man-sized golems follow giant ones, so maybe giant golems follow their Alphas. It's worth a try, don't you think?" Katja said.

Does she think the giant frost golem from before was taking us to its Alpha? Sigurd wondered. He grinned behind his mask, excited to see if this hunch of hers would pay off like the last one.

"That's a bit of a stretch, even for you, Kat," Klemens said.

Ignatius rubbed his hands together excitedly. "Well, you know me. I'll give anything a try. Come on, you two, start singing."

Sigurd walked ahead of the researchers, listening to them singing the *Ode to Golems* behind him. After a quarter hour of walking and singing, the sound of rocks falling echoed off the shale cliffs. A giant crag golem broke free from the cliffside to their right. It proceeded to slide down the cliff, chipping off bits of shale as it went. It dropped into the gorge and out of sight. A moment later, the crag golem rose on elongated stilts of shale and effortlessly stepped out of the gorge. As it walked toward the team, the shale shed from its legs, reducing their length and the golem's height from what could have been thirty feet down to twenty.

Sigurd had to blink a few times to make sense of what he saw. Everyone gaped at the sight of the enormous creature made entirely of shale and other stone sediments. Ignatius held up the drawing of the eye, and the crag golem took to one knee and offered its arm for the three researchers.

The professor chuckled with giddy excitement. Klemens trembled and muttered curses to himself, and Katja—she was as radiant as she had been on that first golem ride. Sigurd twinged with envy that he couldn't join her up there, but he had to maintain his expected distance.

"Steinkamp, are you coming up?" Katja called down to him. The golem turned toward the gorge.

"That's quite all right, I will follow on my own."

"Nonsense, comrade. Climb on," the professor urged.

Sigurd decided that it was probably better to stay close to the team anyway as they made the potentially dangerous climb. He made a running leap, grabbed hold of a protruding rock on the golem's back, and hung on tight as it made its climb down the gorge.

Once the stone titan began its ascent up the cliff, Klemens's body stiffened even more, and he repeatedly muttered, "Oh dear, dear me, Verishten be good."

"Just don't look down, Klem," warned Katja.

That was precisely what Klemens did, and as a result, he grew even paler than he already was. Katja only chortled at his discomfort.

"Whatever happened to you laughing on the inside, Kat?" Klemens griped.

Katja glanced back to Sigurd hanging off the golem's back. The way she smiled at him made his heart beat obtrusively beneath his armored vest. He returned the smile, but she would never see it. *What would have happened if I had taken off my mask for her last night?* He pondered. A sharp pang of regret came upon him, and he was compelled to turn his head away.

The golem finally reached the top of the steep ridge and made its descent down the other side. It eventually reached another walking path where it let the researchers off and went into dormancy.

Ignatius consulted the maps again. "Great idea, Katja. The Alpha should be another mile north of here. I wonder why the golem didn't take us closer."

"Maybe its connection to the Alpha is too weak after its thousand-year absence," replied Katja.

"Or maybe the effect of the drawings only lasts for so long before the golem forgets where it's going and returns to dormancy," Klemens theorized.

"Take your time on this path while I scout ahead," Sigurd said, leaving the researchers to their analysis, as much as he wanted to keep listening. He continued down the thin rocky path heading west until he was out of sight.

The landscape became startlingly familiar. During his climb training, Sigurd had only explored the higher altitude areas of the Crags. He'd never been this low down, or so he thought until he came across a view that he never dreamed he'd see again.

Around a large outcropping, Sigurd found that the rocks formed a shallow nook. It was the very hiding place that he and Rosalinde had huddled in twenty years ago. It was so much smaller than he remembered, but there was no mistaking the spot.

Sigurd struggled to control his breathing as the same paralyzing fear he felt that day came flooding back. He remembered how helpless he was, pressed against dirt and shale with his big sister's hand clasped around his mouth to keep him from making a sound.

Running his hand along the moss-coated wall within the alcove, Sigurd could remember the horror of Rosalinde's blood coating the rocks after the Steinkamp sliced her throat, so fast that blood sprayed in every direction. Sigurd knew that the elements would have washed it away, but he swore he could still smell her blood where it had soaked into the dirt, pooling between the cracks in the shale.

In that moment, Sigurd felt justified in the tortuous method he chose to kill Vaughn. Throat-slitting, although an effective means to eliminate a foe, was hardly the least painful death a Steinkamp could offer someone. Vaughn chose to cut open the throat of a young girl when he could have offered the more painless death of a severed spinal cord.

If only Rosalinde had been able to find more golems after the other ones were demolished . . . but she and Sigurd had been too afraid to move from the nook. Rosalinde had just been learning to dominate golems. The Eye of Verishten had appeared on the back of her shoulder only a year before that day.

Sigurd's traumatic memories then led him to a shale incline behind him. It was there where he found the never-ending chasm from his nightmares.

The blackness of it pulled him in as if he were falling again. Sigurd held his left side, remembering the shock of his ribs shattering against the rock.

"I think the Alpha is here," said the professor from a distance, breaking Sigurd out of his painful reverie.

"No, Professor," Klemens began. "I believe the spot on the map is farther beyond that ridge over there, although I'm not sure where we are right now."

"You're right, Herr Klemens," Sigurd said. "You should continue on. I must inspect this area further—for safety."

Ignatius and Klemens consulted their maps again while Katja carefully made her way to where Sigurd stood near the open chasm.

"You think the Alpha might be down there, don't you?" she asked.

"I have no opinions on the matter one way or the other," Sigurd stated. "You should go with your team. I will follow shortly."

Sigurd returned to staring into the void below. All he could remember after falling down that hole was waking up at the base of the crags, miles from home with a broken arm and cracked ribs. He'd dragged himself to the nearest farmhouse where a ranching family took him in and tended to his injuries. When that winter came upon them, the family felt that Sigurd would take food out of their five children's mouths and had him sent to the orphanage. But the Kensloche orphanage had not been accepting any more children at the time. Sigurd was sent to Deschner to live out his childhood in the orphanage there.

The word *mercy* stuck in his mind. It made him sick to think of Wolfram's perversion of the Steinkamp mantra. *There is no mercy in the slaughter of children!*

Katja, having not yet left like Sigurd had told her to, quietly asked, "Is something the matter?"

"Go with your team," Sigurd ordered.

Katja turned to them, but to Sigurd's annoyance she said, "The Steinkamp wishes for you two to explore the area beyond the ridge while he and I check out this chasm."

Although Ignatius and Klemens seemed suspicious of the request, they put forth no arguments and continued out of sight and earshot.

"Katja, I told you to go with them!"

"Absolutely not! You know as well as I do that the crag golem has brought us as close to the Alpha as possible, just like the one that brought us to the Glacier Peaks. The Golem of Stone has to be here. I am curious why you sent the others away, though. Do you sense danger?"

"There is always danger," Sigurd muttered. As he continued to stare down into the darkness, the memory of falling played over and over in his mind. The Crags circled around him as the pit began to pull him down into it.

Katja's hands clutched at his arm and pulled him away from the edge. Breaking into a sudden sweat, Sigurd turned away and leaned against a boulder, struggling to breathe as his chest tightened. His uniform stifled him; he wanted nothing more than to rip it off, but a Steinkamp could never act on such an impulse.

"Sigurd, is something wrong?" Katja asked with concern. It never inspired confidence when a soldier showed signs of weakness. *Keep it together, comrade.*

Sigurd needed to know what was down that hole. He had to find out how he had survived, or he would be useless in his mission. Spinning around, he took purposeful steps toward the chasm again. "I'm going down there."

"Great, I'm coming with you."

Sigurd shook his head. "No!"

"If the Alpha is down there, I need to observe it," Katja argued.

"For once can you do as you're told, woman!" Sigurd snapped.

Katja took a few steps back. "I beg your pardon?" she huffed.

"You can't follow me down there because someone needs to watch the rope in the pulley to ensure it doesn't get caught," Sigurd reasoned in a more controlled tone.

"Oh—well, you could have just said that," Katja muttered.

Sigurd thought about apologizing but dismissed the idea. Just because the two of them shared a moment the night before, it did not give her license to order him around. She had to realize his primary duty was to keep her safe. *Is going down into the chasm part of keeping her safe?* He asked himself. He thought maybe not, but he needed to do it regardless.

After binding the pulley apparatus to the ground, Sigurd put on a harness and began his descent into the crevasse while Katja waited above. Before long, she was out of sight and darkness engulfed him. The lower he went and the farther the light of day got, the harder Sigurd's heart beat inside his chest.

Never had he felt so uneasy climbing before. In fact, he was beyond uneasy. He was downright terrified, almost as terrified as he had been as a boy. His head spun so much he never noticed how far down he had gone.

The shock of abruptly reaching ground jolted him out of his stupor.

It was total darkness at the bottom, the light from above completely cut off. Sigurd took out his cudgel. Steinkamp cudgels also acted as torches, with light magic infused at the base. He activated the light by squeezing it just above where he would usually hold it. The top portion of the cudgel shone brightly, and the chasm suddenly came into vivid detail, surprising him in how open it was.

The shale at the bottom of the chasm was more compacted, forming harder sediments. Sigurd released himself from the harness and ventured further into the chasm by foot. He had no idea what he expected to find—perhaps some indication of how he survived the fall or a tunnel leading out to the base of the Crags miles away. The eerie silence remedied only by his own footsteps started to get to him. He hummed the *Ode* just to hear his own voice echoing off the stone walls.

The first thing Sigurd found was a piece of Steinkamp uniform, made worn and gray by shale dust, amongst scattered bones and a human skull, barely intact. *Could a Steinkamp have fallen during climb training? Sigurd wondered. It really should be my bones down here.*

He then came to a cluster of boulders blocking what appeared to be a tunnel. He climbed the largest one, which took him to a flat stone platform. Beyond that was nothing more than a solid rock wall. It was a dead end. There was no way out of the chasm other than up.

Sigurd racked his mind trying to figure out how he could have gotten out of there with a broken arm and ribs. The only thing that made sense was that he had been rescued. Vaughn had to have come down here to collect his body, but why leave him at the base near a farmer's field and go on to kill an orphan instead? Rudiger had told him there was an earthquake that caved in part of the chasm, and they had decided not to go looking for him afterward. If they didn't come for him, then who did?

Without finding any answers, Sigurd decided to turn back. As he walked along the flat stone platform, the cavern suddenly ignited with a brilliant green light so bright it drowned out the white light from the cudgel. Sigurd grunted in pain, his eyes burning from the light emanating from below his feet, despite the protection of his mask. This was no ordinary light. Then, as suddenly as it ignited the chasm, the green light faded and Sigurd's eyes adjusted.

He looked down. The platform below his feet turned out to be a circular disk. It was adorned with glowing, vine-like designs etched into a glossy surface beneath layers of dust. The vibrant green energy twinkled, revealing a familiar pattern. It was the same design that the researchers had been looking at throughout the expedition. A map of Kensloche. A crag golem's eye!

"Siegfried..."

A low voice rumbled through Sigurd's body, the force of which brought him to his hands and knees. The glowing green platform vibrated and grew brighter, blinding him once again.

The chasm quaked, and Sigurd heard himself scream.

Katja wrote in her journal as she waited for Sigurd to jiggle the rope and signal that he wanted to come back up. *You can stay down there all day for all I care*, she fumed in her mind. She was unsure of how she should feel about him. It wasn't like she could have any sort relationship with him, so what could she possibly expect from him? The man was a killer for the Regime and probably the Kings' Remnants as well—two things Katja wanted nothing to do with. That didn't make what happened between them the previous night any less exciting however, or the icy wall Sigurd subsequently put up any less hurtful.

Attempting to think about anything else, Katja wrote down her most pressing research questions:

—*Why do giant golems take humans in the direction of their Alphas?*

—*Do giant golems take their smaller counterparts to the Alpha as well, but we just haven't observed it?*

She wrote a hypothesis to her first question: *Golem-kind wants us to repair the covenant we broke, but lost its ability to communicate with us, until now.*

An echoing grunt from afar suddenly distracted Katja from her note-taking. She looked to the chasm and waited for Sigurd's rope to jiggle, but it didn't. Satisfied that he didn't need her help, Katja started writing again, until her inkwell tipped over and spilled across the rocks.

"Shit." She put her journal down and tried to pick up the fallen inkwell, getting ink all over her hands in the process. Katja cursed again just as she began to feel subtle vibrations from under the rocks. The vibration soon turned into a low rumbling and quickly erupted into an earth-shattering quake. Katja screamed as chunks of shale slid into the chasm and the entire opening collapsed in on itself.

"Sigurd!" She dove for the rope and pulled. It took no effort to pull it up. Sigurd was not at the end of it. Katja let it drop, hoping he could still use it to get free.

The quaking increased in severity. The rocks moved violently beneath her feet. Katja shrieked as she was thrown onto her back. The ground elevated in spots and sank in others, and she watched her journal and inkwell fall out of sight. Spinning around, she pulled herself back to her feet and scrambled to escape the rapidly rising ridge. She slid helplessly down the shale and landed on a mossy ledge.

She ran. The Crags were tearing apart, and she could no longer determine what was solid ground or falling rock. *Ignatius, Klemens, where are you?* She couldn't see them anywhere.

Before long, the ground beneath her crumbled away and she was running on air. Screaming, she plummeted to the earth with rocks and debris falling all around her. Then suddenly, a giant stone precipice swept underneath, saving her from her freefall. She found a handhold and clung to the rock formation, seemingly floating about in mid-air. It was attached to another ridge that also appeared to be levitating. The entire Crags were coming to life!

She tried to crawl across the moving platform, not sure where she was headed but too afraid to stay in place. The ridge became increasingly vertical, and she nearly slid off the edge. She screamed, noticing how far up above the rest of the Crags she really was. Katja clung to the rocks with all her might, terrified to move any farther. She looked up, desperate for a lifeline. A few yards away, she found a shining green beacon breaking through mounds of stone. *A massive crag golem eye! The Golem of Stone!*

With that realization, Katja's bearings returned to her. She clung to the Alpha's left arm, which was attached to a massive torso made of sedimentary stone. It appeared to be stuck, buried up to its waist in the Crags themselves. A thunderclap of rocks splitting apart cracked through the air, and the mountain broke away to accommodate colossal stone legs stepping out of it. The Alpha walked from its Crag prison with ease as shale and dirt rained down from its body. Old tree roots ripped from the ground. The entire section of the mountain, that Katja thought had been *housing* the Alpha, actually turned out to *be* the Alpha.

Katja looked to the Golem of Stone's eye again, wishing to get closer to it, but she was afraid to move lest she slip and fall hundreds of feet into what was left of the terrain. The green light emanating from the eye coated the rocks below and parted them in the Alpha's wake. On the rocky surface of its head, jutting perpendicular from its massive torso, a black-clad figure slowly rose to a standing position.

"Sigurd!" Katja screamed, but her voice sounded small over the shattering of the Crag's destruction, and the quaking of the ground as the Alpha walked.

Sigurd noticed Katja anyway. Using his earth bindings in combination with his superb rock climbing skills, he hurried down the massive golem's shoulder. The next thing she knew he was beside her, lifting her up by the arms and taking her around the waist.

"Hold on!" Sigurd had to yell even though he was right beside her.

With the golem's arm swinging back and forth, it was impossible for them to find their bearings enough to tie her to his back. Katja had to settle for clinging to Sigurd with both arms while he used his to climb. Earth bindings acted as guaranteed handholds as he gradually made his way back to the shoulders. Up there it was more horizontal so the two no longer had to fear being thrown off.

Even at the top, Sigurd never let go. He took her back to the Alpha's head where they crouched down together. They both held on as the Alpha continued to move farther away from the Crags. The noise died down and it was finally quiet enough for Katja to hear hers and Sigurd's rapid breathing. Her adrenalin eased somewhat, and she became more aware of Sigurd's arm still around her, keeping her steady atop the massive moving mountain.

"You awakened it!" Katja said breathlessly.

"I only hummed a few bars of the *Ode*. It couldn't have been enough to awaken it. I think it woke itself up."

"If it had awakened itself, that means Verishten must have done it."

"Maybe the God of the Ingles will be the one to stop mankind's foolish plan to unleash the Golem of Death," said Sigurd.

The Golem of Stone headed into Kensloche sheep-herding country. The vibrant greens of the pastures below had a calming effect, and Katja let herself sink deeper into Sigurd's arms.

"There is one other thing," Sigurd said. "Before it awoke, it said my name."

Before she could respond, the Alpha halted, causing her and Sigurd to lurch forward, but he kept them both upright. A deep rumble vibrated through her entire body.

"There it is again!" Sigurd gasped in awe—or terror; she couldn't tell.

"There *what* is again?" she asked, unsure if Sigurd referred to the powerful vibrations running through them or something else that she could not hear.

"*Siegfried, remember where you came from and know why you were saved. The time is now,*" Sigurd said as if repeating something he just heard.

"I didn't hear that! What does it mean?" Katja gulped.

Sigurd didn't answer on account of the Alpha sinking to one knee and bowing down. She screamed as Sigurd tightened his grip around her. The two of them held on as the Golem of Stone lowered itself to the ground as far as it could manage, allowing them to descend safely down one of its gigantic shale arms.

Once Katja's feet felt the grass, her legs gave way. Sigurd let her down gently and finally released her. He turned to face the Golem of Stone, standing over a hundred feet tall. The size of it took Katja's breath away but left her petrified of what had now been unleashed.

"Where do I come from? Why was I saved?" Sigurd called up to the mountain-sized colossus.

Why did Sigurd ask it such a question? Is it really speaking to him, and I just can't hear it? Katja wondered.

The Alpha didn't respond. It turned away slowly and walked back toward the Crags.

Katja stood on unsteady legs and took stock of their surroundings. They were at an abandoned farmhouse with the roof completely caved in; only its crumbling stone walls still stood. The door was rotten, the fence old and rickety.

"Why did the Alpha awaken just to bring us here? What is this place?" Katja wondered aloud.

"Remember where I came from," muttered Sigurd to himself. "It's here."

She approached the murmuring Steinkamp. "What do you mean?"

"I was not born here, but it was here where I was created . . . where it all began."

"What is going on, Sigurd? What did the Alpha tell you?"

"Remember where I came from and know why I was saved. The time is now," Sigurd repeated. Had he just received revelation from Verishten, or had he lost his mind? Katja wasn't sure which scared her most.

Sigurd approached the farmhouse and stopped at the west wall. He stared at it, his body tense, his gloved fists clenching and unclenching repeatedly.

"Sigurd, why are you staring at a wall?"

"They were killed here," he seethed, his voice like gravel.

"They? Your family—this was your home." Katja finally understood.

Sigurd leaned forward, placed both palms upon the wall, and rested his masked forehead against it. His entire body shook in pain, shrouded in his rage. "I can still see the blood . . . I haven't forgotten. I know why you kept me alive, Verishten, I need not be reminded," he said through gritted teeth.

"If the Alpha was talking about you, why did it say Siegfried?" Katja asked softly.

Sigurd ignored her question. "I know what I have to do. I will find the man responsible. I will drag him to these Crags, and I will see him recoil in horror when I use the Alpha that saved my life to end his."

Katja's adrenalin gradually returned.

"But I will not stop there," Sigurd continued. "After he is crushed by the Alpha's mighty hand, I will hunt down every last person responsible for their deaths. It is not enough to sever one arm. I must cut off the head!"

They all had to die. *The time is now!*

Sigurd realized that he could not stop at Wolfram. The Steinkamp Kapitän was yet another man following orders. It was the Führer that propelled Wolfram on his hunt for the Golem Mages, and it was the kanzlers that oversaw Wolfram's operations in each respective mountain range.

The wall where Sigurd's parents were executed had become overgrown with weeds and had crumbled from decay. The stone appeared off-color as if stained with blood. Sigurd could still remember the deadened stare of his mother when she slid down that wall.

"So this is where it happened," Katja said in a solemn voice.

Sigurd pushed off the wall and marched into the field where his brother had been slain. A child of eight throwing rocks at armored soldiers had no chance of escaping, and Kristoff must have known that. He could have run when the golem came to his rescue, but he knew the Steinkamp were determined to kill him no matter what. Sigurd hadn't realized that at the time, but now he did. Kristoff stayed back so that Sigurd would still have a chance, and all he could do at the time was huddle in the grass like a frightened field mouse.

For Sigurd to view his last childhood home in a state of decay like an eternal relic of his family's death brought him to his knees. He tried desperately to overcome the urge to weep. *Don't lose control now, comrade!* Relentless guilt rained down on him just for being there wearing the uniform.

"I became the same monster that killed you. I didn't ask for this. I'm so sorry . . ." *If I hadn't have answered to my real name, would they have been spared?*

He thought to become a Steinkamp was a means to an end, but it was twenty years later and the men responsible for killing his family were no closer to their comeuppance. Only Vaughn had been made to suffer, but Sigurd had only found Vaughn because Rudiger sold him out. He couldn't even be sure the kommissar was the right man. He was so eager to enact his vengeance on someone, Sigurd never stopped to think if it could just be a ruse to keep him occupied. Smugglers and rebels were often at odds in their ambitions. Rudiger could have wanted Vaughn dead for different reasons and used Sigurd to carry out the execution with fervor.

"By Verishten," Katja gasped. "Your family was killed by . . . they were Golem Mages, weren't they? How did you survive?"

Sigurd kept shaking his head, all the doubt and guilt weighing him down. "I didn't," was his weak reply.

Katja was suddenly right next to him. She placed a comforting hand upon his shoulder. Sigurd didn't want her to touch him. He didn't want her to feel him shaking, but he made no attempt to move.

"We should leave here and look for the others," Katja whispered after a moment or two.

Katja was right, but he couldn't find the strength to stand. If he left right then, he would be failing his family all over again.

"Vaughn was inconsequential. My whole quest is meaningless. I took the pledge for nothing."

Katja took her hand off Sigurd and backed away. "It was you who murdered the kommissar!"

"Yes," Sigurd said, finally finding the strength to rise to his feet. "Vaughn deserved to die and so do the rest of them."

"You're not making sense. What exactly do you think you are going to do?" Katja shivered, hugging her coat around her as the breeze cut across the fields. He gathered that she wasn't shivering entirely because of the brisk air.

"I will end their lives with the Alpha Golem that saved mine," Sigurd stated bluntly. There was no other explanation for why he survived that chasm other than the Alpha having seen him to safety.

"The lore surrounding the Golem of Stone refers to it as Verishten's Grace. It makes sense that it may have saved you back then, but it cannot be used as your instrument of death now!"

"Don't you understand? The Alpha spoke to me. This is where I came from!" Sigurd bellowed, waving his arms in the direction of the crumbling farmhouse. "This is why I was saved!"

"Saved for what?"

"For vengeance—not just for myself, but for all of them!"

Katja shook her head and backed farther away, her eyes wide with a fear that Sigurd never wanted to see in them, but he had to make her understand. He swiftly approached her and grabbed her by the shoulders. "I've been given the means to end this murderous regime, Katja. I can make them pay for what they've done!"

"Who is going to pay?" Katja hollered.

"All of them!" Sigurd replied vehemently, squeezing her arms tighter. "Kapitän Wolfram, the kanzlers—the Führer!"

Katja's breath seized and her features stiffened. She squirmed sharply out of Sigurd's grasp. "Have you gone mad? Going after any one of those men is suicide."

"No harm will come to me. It is Verishten who champions me."

Katja shook her head, tears welling in her eyes. "Listen to yourself, this can't be you, Sigurd!"

"Vengeance is all I am. It is why I still live. It is the reason why the Alpha brought me here—to remind me what I have lost and what I must do. You of all people should understand why this regime must fall. It murdered entire families and subjugates hundreds of thousands of people. It has perverted everything the Steinkamp once stood for to justify the slaughter of innocents. I aim to fix that."

"You sound just like Herrscher Heinrich," Katja spat. "You're no better than them. You cannot singlehandedly topple a regime, and you cannot expect to repair the damage with more slaughter. But you don't really want to fix things. You just want your selfish retribution and to bring the Regime down with you!"

Sigurd felt the truth behind Katja's words, but the rage inside his heart would not heed.

Katja continued in a more controlled tone, "Nothing you do is going to bring your family back. But there is still hope for you and for Ingleheim. The Führer will die eventually. What is important now is preserving human and golem interaction for the future. We must repair the covenant!"

"The covenant no longer exists, Katja!" Sigurd yelled. "Only retribution! I'm sorry, but your way is not enough." He took a sharp breath then slowly exhaled before continuing, "That is not to say your research is unnecessary. You should continue your search for Alphas. We are going to need them."

"I will not get involved in this," Katja said, a tear running down her cheek.

That tear gave Sigurd a terrible feeling deep in his gut. He turned away from her and looked out toward the Crags, now nearly unrecognizable since the Alpha tore through it. It appeared to be returning to dormancy and hopefully in the same location as they had found it.

"I don't expect you to help me, Katja. But you should know I will be leaving soon," said Sigurd.

"Where are you going?" Katja asked, her voice hoarse as she choked back tears.

It was never Sigurd's intention to cause her pain, but there was no other way. He couldn't bear to look at her while saying what he was going to say. "The kapitän has granted me an opportunity to join him in the war effort against Herran. In the interest of bringing him to justice, I must take it. I am to ship out in four days."

"Four days from now? So, as soon as we arrive back in Nordenhein—"

"I will no longer be at your service."

"You always knew you were going to leave, didn't you?" Katja said accusingly. "You never even mentioned it. I was a fool to trust you!"

"Not a fool, just naïve," Sigurd said. "Betraying your trust was the last thing I wanted to do, but it is unavoidable. Regardless of my situation, it is in both of our best interests that I leave."

"Not if you die," Katja said with a defeated voice.

Sigurd clenched his fists in anger. *I thought she'd be on my side—why can't she understand?*

He then saw two people in the distance. The professor and Klemens had made it out of the Crags alive. The younger scholar leaned on Ignatius, appearing to have injured his leg, but miraculously managed to keep his spectacles.

"Oh no, Klemens," Katja cried as she ran past Sigurd.

"I'm okay, kind of . . ." Klemens moaned. "My foot was just trapped under a rock slide. That's all."

"That quake was something else," said Ignatius. "I was so busy trying to dig out Klem here that I barely saw what happened. Did the Golem of Stone awaken?"

"That it did, Professor," Katja replied, taking Klemens under his other arm to relieve some of the weight off of Ignatius. "But we will have to discuss that later. We need to get Klem to a doctor."

"How did you make it all the way out here?" Ignatius wondered.

"We were on the Alpha and managed to get off here," she replied.

Klemens's eyes widened. "Verishten have mercy! That must have been terrifying!"

Katja glanced back at Sigurd, still standing in place. Her eyes were wet with tears. "It was fine. The Steinkamp kept me safe—as is his duty." The coldness in her voice brought with it a sting meant only for Sigurd.

"What were you two talking about as we were walking up?" Klemens asked. "Something appears to have upset you."

"Of course I'm upset! I was absolutely beside myself with worry for the two of you," she said for the benefit of Klemens, flashing Sigurd one more pained look.

He realized at that moment that he was to face his fate alone as always. *Could it have turned out any other way?* It would not do Katja any good to be dragged into his world of violent retribution. She belonged in the safety of Nordenhein University with her studies and fellow scholars. If he stayed with her, there was no telling how deep his feelings for her would grow, and how far into the abyss she would fall alongside him.

It is better this way.

14

FALLING FOR A MONSTER

Because of Klemens's injury, the team decided to cut their excursion short and return to the university. The doctor in the Town of Kensloche splinted his foot and recommended he travel by coach the rest of the way. Luckily a merchant, already heading to Nordenhein, agreed to take him for a small fee. Katja volunteered to keep Klemens company while Ignatius rode alongside the coach with the other two horses on a lead.

Sigurd rode far ahead and out of sight. It brought Katja a small relief not to be in his presence for the long trip back. She wasn't sure if she could look at him the same way again. Even if he succeeded in killing the kanzlers, if he made any attempt to kill Herrscher Heinrich, he would inevitably fail and lose his life in the process. What was there for Katja to do other than to tell Sigurd that the Führer was her father in hopes he would rethink his drastic plans? She couldn't risk letting her secret out, not even to the man that she had trusted more than anyone. It scared her senseless realizing how much she didn't know about the Steinkamp with whom she had spent the last month. She couldn't remember another time she felt so foolish, yet her heart bled for him anyway. *What is wrong with me? The man wants to kill my father!*

A few days later when the travelers were safely behind university walls, the Steinkamp briefly wished them all good luck and informed them that he would be resigning from their service. All Katja could do was thank him for all the times he saved her life, but not much else. As if he were a stranger to her, he left without a proper goodbye, leaving her to her dreary thoughts and unanswered questions.

In an attempt to numb her pain, Katja put all her focus into helping Klemens. Traveling for three days with a splint had been hard on him, and she felt partially responsible. She should have gone to find him and the professor right after arriving at the farmhouse. Her guilt alone was enough to keep her from leaving his side.

Later that night, Klemens hobbled on his crutches down the men's dormitory halls next to Katja, holding his books and supplies. He opened the door to his room and held out his hand to take his things back, but she instead walked past him into his room. After setting the supplies on his desk, Katja helped Klemens sit down on the sofa and went to work plumping pillows so he would be as comfortable as possible.

"Katja." Klemens chuckled. "You know I cherish all the attention you've been giving me lately, but you don't have to keep waiting on me like this, and in my dorm room no less. It's not particularly appropriate, you know."

Katja raised an eyebrow. "And inviting me to share a tent with you was?"

"That was different. I was thinking only of your safety."

"And I'm thinking only of yours." Katja fanned out a thin wool blanket and placed it over his lap.

"Can you believe the adventure we had?" he said, dropping the issue and settling into the sofa.

"You're lucky to be alive, Klem." Katja took a seat beside him.

"Now do you see why I don't like to leave the library?"

She wanted to follow with a clever retort but found herself trapped in an endless internal reverie about Sigurd and when she might see him again—or if she would ever see him at all. Before she knew it, tears pooled under her eyes.

"Oh, don't worry about me, Kat. It's just a small fracture. The doctor said in two months or less, I'll be able to walk just fine." Klemens rubbed his hand across her back to comfort her.

She couldn't contain her sorrow any longer. Klemens was so close. It didn't take much for her to bury her face into his shoulder. "I'm so sorry."

"Don't be silly." Klemens held her head on his chest. "None of us could have foreseen the dangers of our scholarly pursuits. In fact, I'm beginning to wish I listened to my father and joined the military like my younger brother. There hasn't been a war in Ingleheim since Herrscher Heinrich took power. I'd probably still be in one piece right now." Klemens put his hand to his chin thoughtfully. "On second thought, there is that naja horde at our doorstep. If left to face the likes of them I'd most definitely wet my breeches. Maybe I'll stick with the quiet, scholarly life after all."

Hearing Klemens talk of naja made Katja think about Sigurd having to face them. This, in turn, resulted in her crying harder. She hated herself for caring so much about a man she barely knew instead of the one she cried upon—a man who truly cared for her.

Klemens wavered for a moment, but he did his best to cheer her up. "Don't worry. Our military is the finest in the world. Naja are just a few pesky reptiles to the Führer's war golems."

Katja lifted herself from his shoulder and tried to regain her composure. "Please, just stop talking."

"Sorry. . ."Klemens sputtered. "I've been diagnosed with foot-in-mouth disease, the symptoms of which always seem to flare up when you're around. Imagine that."

Klemens brushed a strand of Katja's hair from her forehead, which only reminded her of how Sigurd had touched her. With Klemens now silent, she looked into his dark blue eyes, so open and unrestrained. Here was a man whose face she knew, whose body she could touch, whose lips she could kiss, and he loved her.

Casting all thoughts of despair out of her mind, she took his face in her hands and joined her lips to his. A second later, Klemens kissed her right back. She fell into his arms and kissed him harder, desperate to feel something—anything but what she felt then. She couldn't help but imagine kissing Sigurd's lips and touching Sigurd's face. *I don't want this. Why can't I have these feelings for Klemens—sweet, clever Klemens?*

When Katja leaned into him further, Klemens yelped in pain. She stopped immediately. "Sorry."

"No, no, I'm okay, I'm okay," Klemens sputtered, almost pleading. "They're just bruises, they'll heal."

He pulled Katja into his arms again, but she knew going on like this wasn't right. *This isn't fair to him.*

"I'm sorry . . . I-I can't do this."She climbed off him and onto her feet.

In an instant, Klemens's smile turned into a grimace, the sudden change in expression made Katja's hair stand on end.

"Something is not right with you, Kat."His voice took on a dark tone. "Would I be wrong in assuming it has something to do with that Steinkamp?"

The pointed question hit Katja like a crossbow bolt to the gut. "What? Why would you ask me that?"

Klemens looked down at his fidgeting hands as he replied, "I heard the two of you talking that night after the Cragsmen attacked. I couldn't hear your conversation so I thought I'd join you since I couldn't sleep a wink. When I left my tent, I saw you go off with him. It worried me. I thought about following you, but I decided against it . . . I was afraid of what I might see."

"And what do you think you might have seen?" Katja asked carefully.

"I don't know—you tell me."

"What business is it of yours anyway?" she snapped. "Do you really think I'm the type of woman that would debase myself with a complete stranger, and a Steinkamp, no less?"

Katja felt guilty lashing out the way she did even though Klemens was clearly overstepping his bounds. She had on numerous occasions, since that night, imagined debasing herself with the Steinkamp in various ways—until she learned his vengeful secret.

"I don't want to believe you'd do something like that, but it wouldn't be the first time a woman has been swept away by a Steinkamp's dark and mysterious allure."

"Nothing happened!" Katja yelled. "How dare you compare me to one of *those* women!"

"I may be a fool in love, but I'm not an idiot," Klemens shot back. "For the entire expedition, I saw how you ogled him and how eager you were to stay back with him at the chasm. Something happened, whether it was that night or at the farmhouse where we found you, something that made you avoid each other for the entire way home. I can only think of two reasons for your behavior toward him. Either he is intimidating you into doing something you're not comfortable with, or you're trying to hide an infatuation with him. Which is it?"

"We're not talking about this anymore." Katja turned to leave.

"Please Katja. Tell me. I may not have a right to ask, but I need to know. Are you afraid of him or are you in love with him?"

Katja turned back to Klemens to view the desperation written all over his face. He was right. He needed to know. It was the only way he would move on, but she despised admitting the truth to him almost as much as admitting it to herself. Defeated, she drifted into the chair across from the sofa with a heavy sigh.

"Both, maybe . . . I don't know," she murmured.

Klemens recoiled in what Katja could only perceive as disgust mixed with heartbreak. Removing his glasses, he rubbed the bridge of his nose, letting out a pained groan. Once he had composed himself, he put his spectacles back on. "Not exactly the reply I was hoping for."

"I'm sorry, Klem," Katja whispered, tears welling up again.

"No, I'm the sorry one," he replied, not able to look at her. "You are the most brilliant woman I have ever known, but what you are doing is extremely asinine."

"That's not fair."

"You're damn right it's not," Klemens punctuated his statement with a dark chuckle.

Katja sighed, squeezing her hands together between her knees as she sat. "It doesn't matter anymore. The Steinkamp is gone. I won't be seeing him again."

"Good. Because you're better than this, Kat. You can't love something like him."

"Some*thing* like him?" Katja repeated, digging her nails into her palms.

"I know a lot about Steinkamp soldiers," Klemens began. "My father was their kapitän before my brother was born. Through him and my Military Studies I've learned much about the faceless and nameless comrades."

"So your father *was* Kanzler Volker," Katja muttered, finally having confirmation.

"Yes. I know I'm not supposed to tell anyone but the rebels already got to him, so what does it matter now?" Klemens's jaw tightened, then relaxed before he continued. "The Steinkamp are made up of orphans and boys of otherwise low birth. They live and breathe death from the moment they can hold a blade. They are shattered souls, Kat, and for good reason. They do for the Regime what no other man can do because they are not men at all—they're weapons. There is no humanity left in them."

"That's not true. Your father was one of them, and you believed him devoid of humanity?"

"Highborn men like him undergo a different kind of training, one that offers higher education and turns them into leaders. Only the lowest-born stock become the foot-soldier . . . like the Steinkamp you claim to love. So, tell me, how can you love someone that has no capacity to love you back? He will only bring you pain and grief, Verishten forbid, even death."

"He would never hurt me. You don't know him," Katja snapped.

"You don't know him!" Klemens barked. "I'm trying to help you! Your Steinkamp is a monster, just like the rest of them, and if he were ordered to, he would kill us all!"

"You're wrong! He's not like the others. You have to understand—"

"Katja, I think you should leave, I need to be alone right now."

"But Klem—"

"Just go!" Klemens snapped, making Katja jolt out of her chair.

It was no use. Just like there wasn't any use convincing Sigurd not to leave. Now she was about to lose two men she cared for greatly. Saying nothing more, Katja left Klemens to his heartbroken thoughts. She tried desperately to keep tears at bay as the men's monitors escorted her outside.

She hastily crossed the courtyard toward the women's building. The sun was already setting, and it would soon be dark on her side of the campus. The women's dorm monitors let her into the building. She ran up the staircase and entered her room before the tears burst from her eyes. Slamming her door and locking it, she turned to rest her forehead against the carved oak, her heart ripping apart inside her chest. Her first instinct was to take her journal out and start writing, but she remembered that she had lost it in the Crags—where she had also lost herself.

"Katja," a quiet, husky voice said from behind her.

With a startled screech, she spun around, her heart in her throat. There was no one in the room. Then, a shadow figure appeared in the darkest corner.

"Don't be frightened, it's only me."

She stood against the door, holding a hand to her chest and willing her heart to stop racing. "For Verishten's sake, Sigurd. What are you doing here? I thought you left."

"I leave tonight." He remained in the shadows of the unlit room. "I came here to inform you that Rudiger is sending an ex-Steinkamp to intercept my replacement. I advise you all to lay low in the university for a while. Your professor will be informed when the switch has been made. You are not obligated to share your research with him as you have with me, but you can count on him not to report any of your activities to the Regime at least."

After quickly wiping her tears away, Katja crossed her arms. "Thank you for the information. Is that everything?"

"No." Sigurd clenched and unclenched his fists. "I also came to ask you something, and it is paramount that you tell me the truth."

"And what's that?" Katja stood on guard, her spine tingling with anticipation of what he was about to ask.

"Is Kapitän Wolfram your father?"

The question made Katja's heart sink then proceeded to make her blood boil. "Are you serious? You came here to ask me if the man you're about to kill is my father?" She dug her nails into the sleeves of her blouse. "What if he is? Would that change anything? Would you be inclined to spare the man who murdered your entire family?"

"No," Sigurd admitted bluntly.

"Then why ask the question?" She finally let go of her arms and directed them toward Sigurd. "To ease your conscience? I never knew a Steinkamp to possess such a thing. You don't need my permission to kill. That is all you're good for, so go and do it!"

"Please tell me, Katja."

"No," she stated firmly.

"No, he's not your father?"

"No, I'm not going to tell you," Katja hissed. "That way, when you stick your blade into your kapitän's heart, you will imagine sticking it into mine!"

She could have lied and said *'yes, Wolfram is my father,'* and perhaps Sigurd would agree to let go of his lifelong hatred and remain in her service. However, Katja knew he would leave regardless of what she said, so she was not about to make it easier for him. She was not prepared to know that the man she trusted more than anyone was going to knowingly kill her father against her wishes.

"You told me that you accept what I am. You know what I do is necessary, and yet you stand in my way," seethed Sigurd. "What are you so afraid of?"

"You!"

"Me?"

"Yes! I'm afraid of what you are, of what you will become if you go through with this." Katja couldn't stop the words from pouring out. "I'm afraid that I will never truly know you, and that you will always remain this killer in the shadows. Just tell me that they're wrong about you. Show me that I'm not falling for a monster again—"

Katja stopped herself before she went any further. She once thought that she had been in love with Melikheil and it had almost killed her, but none of those feelings were real. For the first time her heart beat true for someone, and yet, she was terrified that *this* someone was just as devoid of humanity as the last. Looking to the shadows in the corner of the room, she searched him for any reaction that could prove Klemens wrong, that he did actually care for her.

Sigurd moved his hand to his mask as he said, "I never wanted to be the monster that I am, but sometimes a man must become what he fears most so that he may never know fear again."

"So that's what this is about. Your own fear is the reason you hide behind. . . ."

Before she could finish, Sigurd stepped into the slivers of light shining through the window's slightly parted drapes. He was now completely in view, a dark silhouette against the last shred of light from the setting sun. His hand was still over his mask. With an audible click, finally, the mask was off.

Katja found herself gasping for air as she struggled to comprehend what was happening. Sigurd slowly walked toward her, and the first thing she saw was his eyes, gray as steel and just as unyielding. He pulled back his black hood to reveal short ashen hair. With his unforgiving facial structure and prominent brow and chin, Sigurd looked like Ingleheim itself; he had a face that knew brutality but weathered it like stone. There was defiance in his jaw, fierceness in his eyes, and power in his lips. Katja couldn't believe that this was the face staring back at her through the black metal mesh for as long as she'd known him. Her knees buckled as Sigurd came nearer.

"It's true," he said. "I devoted my life, my blood, and my spirit to the Mighty Führer who ordered the death of those I loved. I let them turn me into the masked killer of my nightmares, and for a time the nightmares ended. I didn't fear a thing because all things feared me—that is, until I met you."

As Sigurd got closer, Katja leaned against her desk to stay upright. His quietly stern voice, spoken without the echo of his mask, disarmed her.

She could only look up at him helplessly as he continued, "Now I find myself scared of something I've never been scared of before. Our pledge states that 'in obscurity, we die.'" His eyes fell to the floor for a second. "I don't want to die nameless or faceless. I can't leave this world already forgotten."

He was so close now. Katja could smell the winter air from outside that still clung to his uniform. The next thing she knew, he had found the clip in her hair and removed it. She didn't move a muscle as her hair fell loose in front of her shoulders, and Sigurd proceeded to run his fingers through it, forming fists of it in his hands, now free of his gloves. Katja's body edged closer to him of its own accord.

"Don't you have to go?"

"It was the *Ode* that first drew me to you, Katja." The way Sigurd said her name was like he savored every last syllable. It made her heart flutter. "When I heard you playing it that day, it reminded me that I had been loved once. For that, I must thank you. Maybe I can't expect you to support me, so instead I ask you to remember me."

If all Sigurd wanted was to be remembered, that meant Katja would certainly never see him again. The thought angered her as much as it saddened her. "I will remember you, Sigurd." She unabashedly gazed up at him in a state of defiance. ". . . As an utter fool."

Sigurd's left hand cupped the nape of her neck. His other hand took her by the waist and pulled her against him. She sharply inhaled as he bent down and pressed his lips firmly to hers. The intensity of his kiss shocked her more than the action itself, and she was quickly overwhelmed. Pushing against his chest, she freed herself from his kiss so she could catch her breath. Sigurd, with his arms still around her, studied her as if gauging her reaction.

Shaking her head, Katja muttered, "It appears I'm the fool."

She threw her arms around his neck and returned the kiss. The passion between them multiplied as they edged toward the bed. She fell back onto the comforter, bringing Sigurd down on top of her. His lips left hers then trailed down her neck. His warm hands traced Katja's delicate curvature through her blouse before returning to cup her face and tenderly graze his thumb over her bottom lip.

Katja released a sighing moan as she wrapped her legs around his waist. "You don't have to go."

Sigurd brought his forehead to hers, his lips barely touching Katja's as he caressed her cheek. "I do," he whispered before devouring her in another kiss. He pressed his body against her so hard that Katja thought he might penetrate her if it weren't for his uniform and her thick wool skirt bunching around her thighs.

"Stay with me," she pleaded between kisses. "Just for tonight." Katja squeezed her legs tight around Sigurd with no intentions of releasing him. Her fingers traveled up the hard leather armor of his back, absent his weapons, then along his closely trimmed hair, ending at his clean-shaven face of firm features. She discovered in that moment that she loved that face, and her heart broke at the realization it was the first and last time she would ever see it.

Sigurd buried his face into Katja's hair, nuzzling into the crook of her neck and shoulder. Katja held him there for a time feeling his breath, heavy on her neck. She thought for a moment he would lie there all night until he murmured into her ear, "You know I can't stay."

A tear ran down Katja's cheek and she prayed he wouldn't notice. Sigurd pushed himself off her, but she held on, bringing herself up with him. She kissed him any place her lips could find, but it was no use. Sigurd took her face in his hands and kissed her soft and slow. She was completely weakened by the sudden tenderness and let her guard down. Cold air then wrapped around her in Sigurd's place. By the time she opened her eyes, he was halfway to the window.

"Stop!"

Sigurd halted his step at the window and Katja cast her legs over the side of the bed with the intent of running after him. She didn't. *There is nothing you can do to make him stay. He's made up his mind,* she told herself.

"You're making a mistake," she warned as tears continued to trickle down her face.

"You may be right," Sigurd replied, putting on his gloves and hood and securing his mask before turning back to open the window. "But, if not, I shall return."

"There is no returning from this, Sigurd." Her voice broke.

Sigurd had no rebuttal, he just turned his head partially toward her, but not enough to fully face her.

"Goodbye, Katja."

The Steinkamp leaped from the window. Katja's felt as if her heart had been pierced with a splitting blade and was now being dragged out the window at the end of his chain. *There is no returning from this? Were those really the last words I chose to say to him?* Katja raced to the window, cast the curtains back and leaned over the sill as far as she could. There was no sign of her Steinkamp. The night had swallowed him in shadow.

Her legs gave way, and she burst into tears. What she felt for Sigurd was stupid, but it was real, at least. That gave her some solace. This time, however, Katja couldn't decide which was more painful—the manufactured obsession for a Mage that turned her into a cold, empty shell, or this tangible, terrifying and useless love for someone who refused to be with her.

Can I just be empty again?

15

GODS AND WOMEN

(Two months later)

Sigurd crept unseen through a Herrani Warrior encampment in Del'Cabria's Fae'ren Province. The Herrani had clear-cut massive areas along the outskirts of its lush forest and made use of the wood to build their fortified camps and naja holding pits. Many people had been displaced, their small communes invaded and repurposed.

It made Sigurd think about the Fae'ren archer he was supposed to find. Before he had set out, Rudiger instructed him that the archer would be stationed at one of the naja camps, waiting for them to breach the Barrier of Kriegle. In the last two months, Sigurd hadn't found any sign of him, and he was starting to not care if he ever found him.

The Fae'ren archer and the plight of his people didn't concern him. He needed to focus on finding one of Nas'Gavarr's most prominent Naja Handlers within one of the hundreds of encampments. And this was the largest he'd been to yet.

He kept to the shadows, easily avoiding the many Herrani sentries, male and female, armed with trident spears. They were easy enough to spot with their white hair, eyebrows, and eyelashes contrasting with their dark skin. Their builds were muscular and rigid, but short. They wore loose-fitting pants and tight brigandine armor that covered their torsos yet left their arms bare, showcasing tattoos signifying the tribe they hailed from or desert deity they worshiped. *What an unnatural-looking lot*, Sigurd thought. *But, no more unnatural than those puny, pointy-eared urlings of Del'Cabria, I suppose.*

He soon came across a tent guarded by fifteen reptilian humanoids where he believed the Naja Handler slept. The naja would be able to smell him from several yards away, so he carefully approached the camp from downwind.

The armored reptiles roamed about outside their Handler's tent. Groups of them congregated around fire pits, ripping chunks of raw animal flesh from bone with their fangs. Sigurd wondered if amongst the scattered blood and entrails were human remains. It was rumored that Herrani defectors were executed by being thrown to the naja. *Not so different than Ingle defectors being executed in Steinkamp kill training,* he thought. Both regimes had monsters to feed.

When Sigurd got close enough for some of the naja to catch his scent, they began to stalk around the camp on high alert, roaming ever closer to his location but not yet pinpointing him in the dark.

Killing the Handler in his sleep would be Sigurd's preferred way of completing the mission, but naja were next to impossible to sneak past. Eliminating them was more important than not waking the human warriors that slept in tents nearby.

Sigurd brought in hand two wind blades and threw each one in opposite directions. Guiding the blades around the camp, he expertly lopped off the heads of each and every naja in the vicinity. Ear-shattering screeches echoed through the night air as bright orange blood splattered everywhere. Several tent flaps whipped open and Herrani warriors leaped into the night to investigate the disturbance. Both male and female warriors searched the camp equipped with large tulwars, dual scimitars, and bows. A few of them climbed atop a stone wall and nocked their arrows, ready to pick off any invaders.

With his crossbow, Sigurd shot down three archers in rapid succession. The sound of the bodies falling to the ground aroused further commotion. After putting away the crossbow, he extended his blade and ran swiftly into the camp. He dove, rolled, and sliced the heels of the first two warriors ahead of him then drove his sword into their necks once they were face-down on the ground.

Soon, the rest of the warriors in the camp became aware of the soldier in their midst and had him surrounded. Sigurd ducked the Herrani attacks and moved through them like a shadow, his sword's edge claiming a major artery with every slice. Not a single slash of his sword went to waste. *To fight means to kill.*

After dispatching the last warrior, Sigurd reloaded his crossbow and searched the camp thoroughly for the Handler. He didn't have to search long. A middle-aged man with a blonde beard braided to his midsection stepped out of one of the tents right in Sigurd's line of sight. He wore bright colored, loose-fitting robes and an elaborate headdress made of fabric wrapped around his head, attire common to desert Mages. The Handler's eyes widened with horror at the sight of the headless reptilian creatures amongst several dead warriors outside of his tent. He bolted.

You will not get far in those bright colors, Sigurd thought.

He aimed his crossbow for the back of the Handler's head. Before he could pull the trigger, an arrow struck Sigurd in the side of the neck, nearly piercing his neck brace. He faltered as he yanked out the arrow and checked his surroundings. There must have been an archer he hadn't seen on his initial approach. He cursed as he turned back to find the Handler had vanished.

Movement from his periphery alerted him to a Herrani warrior standing upon the rock wall with another arrow nocked. Before he could aim his crossbow, the archer let his arrow fly straight into Sigurd's breastplate above his heart. He staggered backward, feeling the arrowhead rip through the thick boiled leather of his vest, but thankfully not through his undershirt.

Sigurd grunted, but he made no move to take out the arrow this time lest he leave a vulnerable point in his armor for the archer to capitalize on.

The archer then spoke in a rapid, oddly cheerful dialect. "Does Steinkamp armor have any weak spots?"

"No," Sigurd replied, taken aback that the archer would ask such a question. He shot all three of his crossbow bolts at the man on the wall. The archer managed to leap away from each bolt, the last one just scraping across his armored chest.

"Not even here?" The archer quickly recovered and launched another arrow straight at Sigurd's face. The arrow hit the top left of his mask, denting the metallic mesh, the tip of the arrowhead scratching the skin above his left eyelid.

With a growl, Sigurd yanked the arrows out of his mask and chest. He then extended his blade and ran full-tilt toward the archer, who cursed and jumped down behind the wall and out of sight.

When Sigurd arrived on the other side of the wall, the archer was gone, only to reappear from behind him, armed with dual, sickle-shaped, scimitars. His attacks came so fast that Sigurd could barely block them. At such close proximity, he could gauge his foe more clearly. He was dressed in the loose-fitting beige pants and form-fitting charcoal brigandine of the Herrani warrior, but he was lighter-skinned, of much smaller build than most, and younger than Sigurd had first thought. Most notable was his abundance of light brown hair worn in long, matted sets and gathered up in a bundle at the back of his head. The only people he had seen to possess hair like that were the Fae'ren. Sigurd smiled to himself as he continued to clash Steinkamp steel against Herrani scimitar. *Now he shows up*, he thought, annoyed.

"You're the one they call the Desert War Traitor," Sigurd said, fending off attacks that seemed to be getting quicker.

"Great," the Fae'ren huffed. "I'm famous in Ingleheim too. Let me guess—you either want to take my head back to King Tiberius, or take me to your superiors and have them interrogate me for information on the death of your wizard."

The archer dodged each of Sigurd's attacks by a hair. Even if Sigurd was allowed to go for a quick kill, he didn't think he'd be able to on account of how superhumanly quick the Fae'ren was. It was beginning to irritate him as he tried to make sense of what the boy was saying.

"If you are referring to Meister Melikheil, it makes no difference. I don't much care what happened to him."

The Fae'ren made a jumping leap with his scimitars raised above his head. Sigurd acted to block them but was met instead by a knee strike to the ear, almost knocking him over. The archer flashed a cocky grin, and Sigurd seethed behind his mask. *What is he smiling about? Does he not know what I could do to him?*

"Then that must mean you're trying to kill me." The archer chuckled. "Doesn't really seem like it, though. They say that *'to face a Steinkamp is death assured.'* It looks like I get to put that saying to the test." The Fae'ren circled Sigurd, spinning his scimitars about flamboyantly.

He considered killing the archer right then. *How bad does Rudiger need him anyway?* "You're not the wisest fairy in the forest, are you?" Sigurd retorted while coming in for a series of attacks. He just wanted to cut him a bit, but the quick little Fae'ren blocked and dodged flawlessly.

"If you're trying to kill me, then shouldn't I be dead by now?"

Sigurd attacked with everything he had, only for the archer to duck and roll away just before his blade could meet flesh. Sigurd's steel only managed to claim a lock of hair.

The Fae'ren gasped. He caught the severed lock before it fell to the ground. "You cut off my fairy lock! Fun time's over, Steinkamp!"

With a holler of determination, the archer ran at Sigurd with a newfound confidence. He caught Sigurd's blade between his scimitars and tore it from his grip.

Nobody disarms a Steinkamp! At that moment Sigurd found his focus, and he was able to take advantage of his opponent's lack thereof. He grabbed the base of each of the Fae'ren's scimitars with both hands, holding him in place long enough to kick his chest with both legs. The Fae'ren was simultaneously disarmed and knocked back. As the archer tried to get back to his feet, Sigurd rushed him, kicking the young man back down flat on his stomach. Kneeling on the back of the archer's legs, Sigurd held down his head and arms, rendering him unable to move.

"So this is where I'm going to die," the Fae'ren rasped.

"No, this is where I let you live."

"Huh?"

"You want to get your hands on some Steinkamp Magitech, and I am the one that can take you to it." Sigurd released the Fae'ren, who then slowly rose to his feet, breathing heavily.

Furrowing his brow in confusion, he asked, "And you would do that because . . . ?"

"Because in return, you are going to help me kill my kapitän."

"But that's treason!" the Fae'ren said, aghast, then chuckled. "Except I obviously don't care about that. What you should know though, is that I have a rule. I have to look a man in the eye before I make a deal with him."

At the end of his tether, Sigurd grabbed the irritating Fae'ren by the shoulders and slammed his dented mask into his arrogant face. The archer fell backward, crying out in pain.

"Did you get a close enough look just then?" asked Sigurd.

Holding onto his bleeding nose, the archer groaned, "Yeah, yeah, alright, let's make a deal."

The Desert War Traitor returned to his feet. Then, after wiping the blood from his nose, he bolted away. Sigurd cursed and gave chase. Taking his earth bindings in hand, he gained on the quick-footed Del'Cabrian, leaped off the side of the rock wall and tackled him. He put all of his weight on the archer once again and tied his arms behind his back.

"Hey," the archer whined from the ground. "You Inglemen with your freakishly long legs. You have an unfair advantage." Sigurd yanked the Fae'ren up by the hair, making him cry out, "Ow, ow, ow, mind the locks!"

"Do you want the equipment or not?" Sigurd barked.

"Of course I do, but I'm a thief. I'm supposed to *steal* things, not have things *gifted* to me—it sort of defeats the purpose. Besides, a Steinkamp soldier wanting to give away his own magical weaponry? How could that not be a trap?"

"I'm going to level with you here. My time would be better spent hunting down Naja Handlers rather than escorting a Del'Cabrian traitor to a Magitech cache. However, there are people in Ingleheim who think you are something special and are willing to make a trade. All the Magitech your little thieving heart desires in return for your archery prowess. If that sounds like a trap to you—well, I can't help you there."

"And I'm to assume you all want to use my archery prowess to kill the Steinkamp Kapitän?"

Sigurd nodded, though that was not part of the Remnants' plan. For almost two months he had been sent out on one reconnaissance mission after another in search of Handlers. He never had a single opportunity to move against Wolfram or even a moment with himself to properly strategize. The Fae'ren archer provided Sigurd that much-needed opportunity.

The Fae'ren winced. "Yeah, you know, I'm flattered that you would consider me for such a monumental task. Any other day I'd be raring to help a fella like you. I mean, a chance to take out the kapitän of the Steinkamp? What an honor . . . but, uh . . . I have a lot to live for yet, so in the interest of not ending up dead—"

"Let's put it this way. Do as I say, and I won't kill you right now. I can find another way to kill my kapitän, and the Magitech can remain secure in its cache."

"What about your friends?" The archer gulped. "The ones who think I'm special?"

"A Steinkamp doesn't have friends," Sigurd stated bluntly.

"Oh, I'm sorry to hear that. D-do you want to talk about it, or—?"

Sigurd socked him in the face then bent down to pick him back up.

"Now to get through the Pass," said Sigurd, "you will have to play the prisoner. Do you think you can handle that?"

"Do I have a choice?"

"No."

"Then lead the way."

Sigurd roughly pushed his prisoner onward. "After you."

Sigurd rode through the Pass of Halberschtad with the Fae'ren archer, who had introduced himself as Jeth, tied up behind him on foot. They came across three war golems blocking their entry.

"Whoa," Jeth gasped, gazing all the way up their massive bodies of iron and stone, built like juggernauts, sixteen feet tall. These particular war golems were over twenty years old, judging by the Eye of Verishten symbol inscribed into each of their metal chest plates.

After Sigurd had spoken with the soldiers at the Pass, they ordered offiziers, one for each golem, to command them aside.

"I thought your Führer was the only one who could control golems?" Jeth asked.

"He is," Sigurd explained. "He has given these men proxy control by commanding the golems to obey their assigned offiziers beforehand."

With the echoing creak of the golems' enormous iron joints, the three of them turned to the side to allow the Steinkamp and his prisoner passage.

Once they passed through another line of war golems, Sigurd flagged down a messenger on horseback and gave him a note to deliver to the Steinkamp Kapitän. It read:

The Desert War Traitor has gotten through the Pass. I tracked him to the western Steinkamp cache. I believe he intends to rob it. I will capture him alive. He may have information regarding the death of Meister Melikheil. If you wish to interrogate him, meet me at the cache where he will be held.

Sigurd signed the note with his name and the number from his wrist brand and instructed the young messenger to take it to the kapitän forthwith. Wolfram operated from a Steinkamp encampment in Fae'ren Province where Ingle forces had managed to beat the Herrani back, giving Sigurd and Jeth a head start. There would be enough time to come up with a plan while traveling to the agreed-upon location.

Part of Rudiger's instruction involved a member of the Kings' Remnants meeting him and the archer at the cache. What Sigurd didn't know was whether the rebel would be waiting there for them to arrive, or if they would have to wait for the rebel to come to them. He would have to figure it all out when he got there.

It wasn't long until Jeth complained about his bindings and how much they hurt.

"They are part of your skin now," said Sigurd. "If you stop struggling to get out of them, they won't hurt so much."

Jeth scoffed. "You Inglemen and your magical weaponry. You know that's cheating, right? And those iron monstrosities back there? Overkill, if you ask me. Del'Cabrians have gotten by with nothing more than swords, shields, spears, and bows for thousands of years, and we still managed to keep you lot from invading, when by all rights, you could have clobbered us at any time. Why do you think that is?"

"Do you ever shut up?" Sigurd groaned.

"Not even in my sleep."

"Well, you should give it a try, perhaps right now."

Jeth did remain silent for a while, but they had barely cleared the Pass when he opened his mouth again. "So . . . why do you want to kill your kapitän? What did he ever do to you?"

Sigurd let Jeth's question stew for a moment before he said, "He murdered my entire family."

"Well, shit. From what you said earlier about Steinkamp not having friends, I figured that included families."

"We all had families . . . once." Sigurd cleared his throat. "But, this regime is an efficient producer of orphans who are then fed into the military machine."

As Sigurd spoke, the Pass of Halberschtad opened to the charred and ashen landscape of the greater Breisenburg Mountain Range. Once a thriving kingdom in the Age of Kings, the range now was a visage of Ingleheim's most recent battles from that time, from border skirmishes with Deschner Range in the north to the wars against Del'Cabria in the southwest. For that reason, the Führer turned Breisenburg into his regime's military industrial complex. Cities were transformed into training facilities, great castles repurposed into armored fortresses, and the landscape peppered with armories guarded by war golems. Breisenburg was the first range outsiders would see if they ever managed to get through the Pass. What they would find was an impressive display of Ingleheim's military might within a haunted shell of civilizations past. The scorched earth, mountains of ash, and barren landscape of gray, dead trees told those outsiders that only death flourished there. One best turn the other way.

"You know what an even better producer of orphans is?" Jeth said.

"Plagues. My parents succumbed to the one that ravaged my people, and it's making a deadly reappearance as of late."

"So, you're an orphan too? Figures. Who raised you, then? Wolves?"

"Hah, one can only dream." Jeth chuckled, then scratched his beard with his bound hands. "It was fairies."

Sigurd couldn't tell if the Fae'ren was joking or not. Surely fairies were a myth—although, a couple of months ago Sigurd believed the Rogue Steinkamp was a myth too.

"Where are your pointed ears?" Sigurd then wondered.

"What? You think because I'm Del'Cabrian, I'm supposed to be an urling?" Jeth replied. "I'm a human just like you. In fact, the majority of Del'Cabrians are humans. If you Inglemen weren't so Deity-forsaken isolationist, you'd know a thing or two about the people that exist beyond your mountains."

"I should gag you."

"Please don't. Only my girl Anwarr gets to do that to me." The thief chortled.

Sigurd was irked by the visual that Jeth forced into his mind. Never had he known a Del'Cabrian to be so brazenly crude. Most of them were uppity puritans that made highborn Ingles seem shameless by comparison. Sigurd surmised that the people of Fae'ren Province were a whole other type of Del'Cabrian, or Jeth happened to be the exception.

"Do you speak of the woman who you betrayed your king and country for?" Sigurd asked, though he wasn't sure why he was keeping the boy talking.

Jeth burst out laughing and wouldn't stop.

"What's so funny now?" Sigurd sighed.

"You know, it was for a woman that I joined the Del'Cabrian forces to begin with, and because of another I betrayed them. It is true what they say. Women rule us all."

"For a boy like you, maybe," Sigurd commented. His entire life had been ruled by the whims of men more powerful than him, and it was all he could do to fight back. The wiles of women had always been the farthest thing from his mind. They were beings that Sigurd once viewed as just another tool in man's arsenal to dominate everything around him, like golems or soldiers.

Had Sigurd heard Jeth's comment a year before, he would think him unsound of mind, but after having known Katja, he felt the notion was not without some merit. Leaving her service had affected him more than he'd anticipated. He felt as if his insides had been shifted about and laid to rest where they should not be. His whole body, mind, and soul longed to be with her, and yet he was taking steps to kill the man that might be her father and thus severing any possibility of that happening.

If Wolfram is her father, she would have told me that night. She was just upset and wanted me to stay. And how badly he wanted to stay, but how could he when the men that slaughtered his family were still out there, living their highborn lives and exerting their ill-gotten authority over the weak?

"I wouldn't expect a Steinkamp to understand, but I'm telling you, it doesn't matter how clever, how ordinary, or how monstrous the man—there is always a woman in his life calling all the shots, even a man as powerful as your mighty Führer," said Jeth.

"What about Verishten? What woman commands a god?"

"Are you certain your god is male? They say his spirit resides in the mouth of a volcano. From my experiences with women, my bets are on Verishten being female." Jeth snickered.

"What can your pitiful experience tell you of gods and women anyhow? You're practically a child."

"I have a beard—I'm far from a child!"

"I've seen twelve-year-olds with fuller beards than yours, and they stand a foot or two taller as well."

"Not all of us can be the towering, statuesque totem of masculinity that is the Ingleman," Jeth retorted in a brutalized Ingle dialect. "You're one to talk, anyway. For all I know you could have the face of an ogre under that mask. Just because the only time you've felt the touch of a woman was suckling at your mother's teats, don't assume my experiences are the same. You know, maybe if—"

Sigurd kicked his stallion into a sudden canter, pulling the mouthy Fae'ren off his feet and dragging him through the ash just enough for him to get a mouthful of it. Stopping the horse, Sigurd allowed the thief to stand again. "Sorry about that. You were saying?"

Jeth looked up at Sigurd sourly while wiping away the ashen mud and spitting black gobs of it from his mouth. He grinned, showing his ash-stained teeth, but he didn't utter a word in defiance.

———≈———

In a few hours Sigurd and Jeth came upon the Western Breisenburg Magitech cache. Like all caches, it had a fenced area protecting a bunker with a single iron door and a watchtower south of the front gates. Caches were normally guarded by one or two Steinkamp soldiers overseeing a modest contingent of military guards. Groups of Steinkamp couldn't be wasted on guarding their own caches, but even one comrade would prove to be a challenge for a member of the rebellion. Sigurd would likely have to clear the cache of all the guards before the rebel and Wolfram arrived.

To his surprise, the fence had already been compromised. A man-sized hole had been cut through the steel links and the edges were tipped with ice. It appeared as if ice powder had been used to break through. *That's odd,* Sigurd thought. *All Steinkamp can access any cache simply by showing their wrist brand—no need to break in unseen.*

Unless it is one of Rudiger's defectors that I'm supposed to meet here . . . but if any of them had access to Magitech, would Rudiger not have used it against me the night we first fought?

Sigurd told the archer to keep quiet as he led him through the hole in the fence. Crossbow in hand, he scoured the grounds and eventually found all six watchmen dead at their posts. There was still no sign of the Steinkamp guard, which made the hairs on the back of Sigurd's neck stand on end.

On the steps leading down to the door, he found the Steinkamp soldier slumped over with no blood on the body or visible wounds of any kind. The man seemed to have dropped dead for no reason at all. Sigurd's heart rate picked up considerably.

The cache door was ajar. Pulling Jeth on his tether behind him, Sigurd ventured inside. Through the door, a dark stairwell went straight down into an even darker pit. He took his cudgel in hand and activated it, casting light on the grimy ash-stained steps.

"Whoa, that's bright. I'm definitely taking a few of those for myself before we leave," Jeth's whispers echoed down the cache stairwell.

Sigurd shushed him as they continued into the bunker to find all but one shelf empty. That one shelf, to their immediate right, had on it everything required to equip a single Steinkamp. The only thing missing was a cudgel.

Turning to Jeth, Sigurd said, "I guess you don't get your torch today."

Jeth groaned in disappointment. "You brought me all the way here for a few scraps? Great! So, this is a trap." His eyes darted across the room. "And someone else is here."

Sigurd looked around, the torch uncovering every dark corner of the rectangular space. "Where? I don't see anyone."

"How can you see anything through that thing?" Jeth pointed to Sigurd's mask.

"I see just fine—" Sigurd then jumped at a small figure coming into form beside a shelving unit, as if materializing from thin air. He blinked a few times to bring the woman into focus. She wore the brown and red coat and buttoned pants of a Remnant. *Of course the rebel I'm supposed to meet here is the little witch.*

"There you are. Light Mage, right?" Jeth pointed at Jenn with a flick of his wrist.

"I'm much more than that." She turned to Sigurd. "Thanks for bringing him, Steinkamp. I'll take him from here."

Sigurd asked. "Where is all the equipment? How did you get by the Steinkamp guard?"

"How do you think? I've gotten past you once before."

"Only because Rudiger came to your aid."

"With or without Rudiger's intervention you would not have gotten me out of that tower." Sigurd huffed and Jenn went on, "I froze the fencing using water magic, which allowed me to break through it. A team of rebels I had brought with me came through the fence and killed the guards while I used light magic to hide in wait for the Steinkamp to investigate the disturbance. That's when I used powerful wind magic to siphon the air away from him, and he suffocated. That's the only way I know how to bring down one of you safely."

"Where is the rest of your team?"

"They loaded up the Magitech and have already left. They are using some of the uniforms to pose as Steinkamp soldiers making a delivery to a cache in Deschner. I've been watching the Pass closely, and when I saw you with the Fae'ren, I made sure to get here before you. My men had been camped nearby for months already. I thought Rudiger explained all this to you," Jenn shook her head in annoyance and brushed back her hair from her forehead. Although having grown out some since Sigurd last saw her, it was still extremely short.

"Can one of you tell me what in Deity's name is going on here and what you all want with me, exactly?" asked Jeth, his nose twitching before he rubbed it with the back of his hand.

"I'll debrief you on the way to Deschner. That is where the rest of the Magitech is," said Jenn.

"Why not just let me have it right now?"

"Because Rudiger has a request he'd make of you first. If you're not interested, then you are welcome to what we left behind and what you can get off the one I killed outside."

"So what does this infamous Rudiger want?" Jeth made a flamboyant gesture with his hand as he said the Rogue's name, almost making Sigurd chuckle.

"He wants to use your archery skills to bring down the golems guarding a certain fortress our rebel group wishes to take from the Regime," Jenn answered.

"Okay, and is that before or after I help him kill his kapitän?" Jeth bobbed his head over to Sigurd.

"Excuse me?" Jenn screeched. "Rudiger says it is not time for Wolfram yet. The archer is not for you to use for your idiotic revenge plot!"

"I don't take orders from you, witch," Sigurd retorted. "I am not going to waste the one opportunity I have to get my revenge by waiting for your Rogue Steinkamp to make up his damn mind. I've already sent a message to my kapitän to meet us here. He is no more than a day away. We will capture him upon his arrival."

"I told Rudiger that you would be unpredictable," Jenn griped. "Go ahead and meet your kapitän, but kill him yourself. My directive is to take the archer to Deschner and await further instruction."

Jeth gave Jenn a finger-wiggling wave. "The name's Jeth, by the way . . . if you wanted to know."

She took steps toward the archer, but Sigurd stepped in front of him.

"He's not going anywhere with you. Wolfram will not come alone. He will bring his personal comrades, and how many, I am uncertain. One way or another, it will be too many for me to take on by myself. I need both of your assistance in eliminating his guard and restraining Wolfram so that I can take him to Kensloche. It is there where I will kill him."

"Why? What difference does it make if he dies in Breisenburg or Kensloche?" Jenn threw up her arms.

"It makes all the difference," Sigurd replied. *Wolfram needs to see what he created in those Crags. He has to die where I was supposed to,* Sigurd fumed in his mind.

"We don't have time for this. Release the archer from your bindings or I will do it myself."

Sigurd remained planted. The slight-figured sorceress was almost shorter than Jeth and thinner than a sapling, yet she stood just as defiantly as Katja would have. Sigurd remembered Katja's words. *Just promise me, if you come across her . . . do not engage.* He wondered if Jenn could suffocate him the way she did his comrade outside.

"You will have to make time," Sigurd said. "In the letter I sent to Wolfram, I had to divulge certain pieces of information to convince him to leave his duties and meet me here."

"What information?" Jenn's whole body stiffened.

"I mentioned that the Kings' Remnants are planning something with the Fortress of Mortlach and that the Desert War Traitor may be their newest recruit. If I'm unable to kill Wolfram on my own, I may be forced to reveal more details to appease him."

"You just ruined us!" Jenn growled, making Jeth jump back. "Rudiger will have your head for this!"

"Not if Wolfram dies and you both help me do it. That way, everything he currently knows about the rebellion's plans will die with him. Help me take Wolfram prisoner and get him to the crossroads, then you and Jeth can go about your merry way," Sigurd offered.

Jenn's dark brown eyes went black with anger. "Damn you, Steinkamp. Rudiger's orders were clear. We can't touch the kapitän yet!"

"I promised Rudiger I'd get him the archer, and I've done that. He promised me my revenge. I'm just choosing to take it earlier than he would prefer. I'm sure he will understand, given our . . . shared history."

"Bullshit on your shared history, and I don't give a damn about your revenge!" Jenn's face contorted as if she were in pain. "The Kings' Remnants must succeed in taking down the Regime. My mother's life depends on it!"

Sigurd cocked his head. "What does your mother have to do with anything?"

Deflating, Jenn said, "My mother and I are indebted to a powerful smuggling ring. They forced her into prostitution, and me into using my light magic abilities to assist in trafficking illegal goods between Ingleheim and Del'Cabria. But no matter how many schlepts we made them, they never kept their word to free us. I could have gotten out, but they threatened to kill my mother if I tried to leave. Rudiger saved us and found my mother a temporary safe house."

Jenn clenched her small fists inside her large jacket sleeves and continued, "It is only a matter of time before the ring finds us and kills us both. Rudiger said that the rebellion acts to topple a regime that gives smugglers a reason

to exist. If the rebellion fails, then the smugglers win. Helping the Kings'
Remnants is all I can do to protect the only family I have."

If what Jenn said were true, Sigurd could relate, but he couldn't let
himself think of other people's plights at the moment. Only one thing
mattered to him, and that was feeding Wolfram into the chasm.

"Can I ask something?" Jeth piped up.

"What?" Jenn snapped.

"Why doesn't this Rudiger just pay off your debt to the smugglers so
that they will leave you alone?"

"Why does that matter?"

"Well, if he really cared about helping you, the easiest thing to do is pay
off the smugglers to get your mother out of immediate danger, then count
on your gratitude to aid him in the rebellion. Otherwise, it looks like he's
using her life to control you just as the smugglers did. Doesn't sound like
a very trustworthy guy. Clever, for sure, but a man of his word? I'm not
convinced."

"And what does a little thief like you know about being trustworthy?"
Jenn hissed.

Jeth straightened himself, taut as a bowstring. "Who are *you* calling little,
you twig?"

"Enough!" Sigurd barked, his voice ringing off the iron walls of the
bunker. Turning to Jenn, he said, "You will help us capture Wolfram, and
I promise he will be dead in four days. You can still deliver Jeth before
Rudiger discovers any change in his plans. The rebellion will continue, and
your mother will come to no harm. Do we have an understanding?"

Jenn and Sigurd stood before one another in a face-off. He knew Jenn
would have to fold. Even if she could perform some kind of spirit magic on
him and compel him to hand over Jeth, she wouldn't risk leaving Wolfram
alive with information of the Remnants' plans. Sigurd was bluffing, of
course, but he needed to convince the witch to help and give her a good
reason not to kill him.

As they stared each other down, Jeth spoke, "And I will get my full
cache of Magitech equipment, right?"

"Yes, you'll get your bounty . . . and the Steinkamp will get his revenge,"
Jenn said bitterly then walked away.

"Alright then," Jeth said, rubbing his hands together. "So what's our
plan in capturing this *Wolf-man*, or whatever his name is?"

16
MEN LIKE US

From the watchtower, Sigurd spotted Kapitän Wolfram with three of his personal comrades, arriving at the cache early the next morning. He raced down the tower and into the bunker where Jeth and Jenn had been waiting patiently.

"They're here."

Jeth sprang up from his seated position. "That was quick."

"He must have already been in Breisenburg when he received my message," Sigurd replied. He turned to Jenn who sat on the floor in the corner with her eyes closed. "What is she doing?"

"She's recharging her essences."

"Jenn, they're—"

She opened her eyes and instantly rolled them. "Yeah, okay, I heard you the first time."

"I hope you have enough wind essence for three Steinkamp," said Sigurd.

"It's all stored here." Jenn pointed to the sapphire adorning her brass bracelet.

"How do you Essence Mages do that?" asked Sigurd.

"We don't. For whatever reason, sapphire acts as a natural reserve for essence aura. Brass acts to transfer it from the sapphire to my body and back. This little blue gem can store and maintain the essence aura that my body would gradually leak out if left unused."

Sigurd nodded. He already knew aura was the energy that made up essences and that Mages could somehow see and feel it in order to manipulate those essences. What exactly that had to do with sapphire and brass had always been a mystery to him despite his years of experience with those essences in the form of his Magitech equipment.

Rising to her feet, Jenn continued, "Anyway, if you need me, I'll be outside suffocating more of you faceless goons."

Jeth looked to Sigurd, as if expecting him to react to Jenn's comment in some way, but Sigurd couldn't care less. Instead, he tied Jeth to a shelving unit and went to meet his comrades at the gate, glad to have already cleared away the bodies the night before and switched out his dented mask for the deceased Steinkamp's.

"Why is there no guard to greet us at the gates?" one of the comrades asked.

Sigurd saluted. "They are behind the cache, guarding the Magitech that we had to move out temporarily in order to keep our prisoner locked inside."

Wolfram walked beside Sigurd toward the bunker. "Good thinking, keeping him away from the equipment."

"Right this way, Kapitän." He opened the heavy iron door for Wolfram and one of his Steinkamp guards. The two others went to investigate the yard where Jenn was waiting for them out of sight. Sigurd, Wolfram, and the third comrade descended the stairs into the empty cache. Jeth was still tied up and on his knees.

"So this is the infamous Desert War Traitor," said Wolfram, removing his spectacles and putting them in his coat pocket. "He's smaller than I expected."

"No, I'm not. You are all just freakishly tall," Jeth grumbled.

"So, you witnessed the death of Meister Melikheil?" asked Wolfram, ignoring the comment.

Jeth nodded but didn't say anything more.

"It is told that you were on the task force charged with escorting Melikheil through the desert to face off with the Overlord. You fled before that could happen. How could you possibly have seen the Overlord take him down?"

"I was taken in by a band of thieves who told me to rob a Serpentine temple for my initiation. It was there the Mages' battle took place."

"And?"

"Your Mage was—for lack of a better word—pulverized."

"Hmm, so he *is* dead." Wolfram sighed and wiped his spectacles with his handkerchief. "A shame. The great sorcerer who helped to create all that once filled this cache, gone. Just like that. Ah well. What can you do?" He put his spectacles back on and turned to Sigurd. "Get him up, we are sending him to the Führer straight away. Thank you for stopping him before he made away with the Magitech. Show me that it is all accounted for, and you may return to your original mission."

"Yes, Kapitän," Sigurd said as he took Jeth by the earth bindings around his wrists and brought him to his feet. While doing so, he returned the bindings to their leather state. As quick as a flash, Jeth ducked forward and kicked Wolfram's feet out from under him. Wolfram's Steinkamp reacted immediately, but Sigurd dealt with him while Jeth went to work subduing the kapitän. The comrade's shock at one of his own attacking him gave Sigurd the advantage. He quickly thrust his skewer knife under the man's chin where the mask seam met the neck brace.

Wolfram bellowed for his other comrades just before Sigurd assisted Jeth in knocking him out. They tied him up and molded bindings to his wrists before removing his gloves and cleaning out his supply of ice powder as well. It took all of Sigurd's self-control not to kill Wolfram right then.

But he had to wait.

Jenn opened the door to the bunker and called down to the men. Sigurd and Jeth carried the kapitän up the stairs and out into the ash-filled morning air.

"Watch him," Sigurd ordered while he checked the vital signs of the other two Steinkamp lying on the ground outside.

One of them was still breathing. Jenn hadn't suffocated him enough. To ensure they were both put down for good, Sigurd removed the Steinkamp's neck braces and plunged his skewer knife into the base of their skulls. He felt a pang of guilt for slaying his comrades in cold blood, but he had never considered himself one of them anyway. Despite calling each other comrade, there was seldom actual camaraderie among Steinkamp. They were as nameless and faceless to each other as they were to the rest of the world.

When he returned, he saw Jenn kneeling beside Wolfram with her hands at the sides of his head. "What are you doing?"

"While he's unconscious, his mind is vulnerable. I'm putting him into a spiritual slumber," Jenn replied.

"I need him awake when I exact my vengeance," said Sigurd.

"Don't worry. He'll be out for a day or two and disoriented when he wakes. This way he will be unable to escape before you get him to Kensloche. By the time you get there, he should be conscious enough for you to exact whatever type of vengeance you desire."

Sigurd nodded and thanked the witch. He *had* been contemplating how he would get Wolfram all the way there without him finding a means of escape.

Meanwhile, Jeth had put on the spare Steinkamp uniform. Even though it was a smaller size than the average, it still didn't fit as snug as it should, but it would have to do. The team then hoisted Wolfram onto a cart. Jenn climbed in as well, and Sigurd and Jeth covered both of them in a shroud. Jeth hopped onto one of the other Steinkamp's horses while Sigurd hooked the cart to his own steed. From there, they set off on the northeast road. No one would pay mind to two Steinkamp soldiers carrying corpses on the back of a cart.

As they rode, Sigurd turned to Jeth riding alongside him. "All of Ingleheim believed that the Great Melikheil would defeat the Overlord of Herran, so you will have to forgive my skepticism. Did you make up that whole story you told Wolfram back there?"

"It's all true. Melikheil put up one hell of a fight, I tell you. Nas'Gavarr used sunfire against him."

"Sunfire?" asked Sigurd.

"A powerful combination of fire and light magic," Jenn's muffled voice said from the cart.

"What good would that do?"

"Well, it is told that sunfire is one of the few things that can harm the spirit within the body and can, therefore, be used to weaken Spirit Mages," said Jeth.

Jenn shot up from under her shroud. "Where did *you* learn that?"

"We have a Mage on our crew who explained it to me."

"Get back under your shroud, Jenn," Sigurd ordered. She grumbled and lay back down. "So sunfire pulverized Melikheil?"

Jeth shook his head. "That stuff was so hot I felt like my eyes were going to burn from their sockets just looking at it, but that Ingle Mage brushed it off like it was nothing."

"So it was a relatively even match, then?"

"I wouldn't say *even*. Nas'Gavarr is the only Mage in the known world who has mastered essence, spirit, and flesh. Melikheil only knew essence and spirit, apparently, because once Nas'Gavarr realized his adversary could protect himself from the sunfire, he settled for tearing him limb from bloody limb instead."

Jenn sat up again. "You witnessed the use of flesh magic?"

Jeth turned his faceless head toward her and nodded. Her skin paled, and she didn't ask anything more.

Sigurd decided to let the subject drop. He wondered if Ingleheim was now in real danger. If a Mage that could use flesh magic succeeded in breaching the Barrier of Kriegle or the Pass of Halberschtad, what could Ingles do to stop him? *Perhaps I should have made killing that Handler a priority instead of escorting this archer about*, Sigurd thought with regret.

By late afternoon, they reached the crossroads where the northwestern road to Kensloche split from the northeastern road continuing to Deschner. The plan was that Jenn would pretend to be a rebel prisoner of Jeth's, who would be posing as a Steinkamp. Sigurd would keep the cart so he could get Wolfram to Kensloche without suspicion.

"So if I go with you, I get a giant cart full of Magitech, right?" Jeth removed his mask and looked down to Jenn from his saddle.

"You have my word, but only after you help us take the fortress."

"Alright, but I need to return with my bounty soon. I'm looking for this to be my last job since—well, not that either of you care, but I'm going to be a father, and I'd like to retire from the thieving life," Jeth confessed.

"Don't worry, Fairy Boy. As soon as you meet Rudiger, you will be debriefed of our plan. Then, in no more than two weeks, we will have that fortress and what is held beneath it," Jenn told him.

Jeth nodded and turned to Sigurd. "Well, Steinkamp, good luck to you with all your revenge and that. If you need a place to lay low afterward, find me. I know a few places, outside of this ashen wasteland, where men like us can hide."

Sigurd seriously contemplated the offer. As irritating as the Fae'ren was, Sigurd would probably need a place to hide out after his revenge was complete. Truthfully, though, he half-expected to die in the attempt. If he did survive, where would he go? Back to Katja? Would she be waiting for him with open arms? He wasn't sure if he wanted her to wait for him. She deserved someone who could take care of her and support her scholastic pursuits. What kind of life could a man like him ever give her? He felt like a skewer knife was stabbing him through the heart in slow, clumsy thrusts. He was never going to see Katja again. He was never going to hear her annoyingly haughty voice. She would never again look at him with those amber eyes that had the power to pierce through all his armor, physical and mental. It was as if she had always seen him, even before he took off his mask, and that alone terrified him. *A Steinkamp should never be seen.*

"I appreciate the offer, but I don't believe there is a place in this world for men like us. I do wish you the best, though. I hope you always know freedom."

"Thanks, I hope you find it," Jeth said with a grin.

"Make sure you kill him, Steinkamp." Jenn gave him a warnful eye. "Because if you fail and word gets out to the Regime of what we are doing—"

"Don't worry. I never told Wolfram a thing about the fortress."

"You lied?"

Sigurd shrugged and turned his cart down the northwestern road. "Thank you for your help. Give my regards to Rudiger, and if he moves to stop me, tell him I will reconsider our truce. My revenge will end with him instead."

Jenn opened her mouth but said nothing. Sigurd didn't expect her to know anything about his and Rudiger's history, and she was smart enough not to pry. She nodded and climbed onto the back of Jeth's horse. They trotted off down the road to Deschner, and Sigurd continued toward Kensloche with the unconscious kapitän in his cart.

By the time they reached the Crags a few days later, Wolfram was conscious. He was able to walk by himself upon the loose shale ridges while Sigurd pulled him along behind. Like Jenn had said, her spell left Wolfram incoherent for most of the journey. He barely opened his mouth, not even to question where he was being taken or the meaning of his abduction.

It took a long time to find the chasm at the Crags after the Alpha had returned to dormancy. Much of the landscape had changed, but finally by midday on the second day since he set off from Breisenburg, Sigurd found the familiar location. He sat the kapitän down and molded his earth bindings to a stone outcropping near the chasm.

He then approached the opening and declared, "Golem of Stone! It is Siegfried. I have returned!"

Wolfram finally decided to speak, though he was still weighed down by exhaustion. "Oh, now I see, you're *insane*. That explains everything."

"Do you not recognize this place, Kapitän?"

"One gray shale cliff after another—they all start to look the same to me. Should I know this one in particular?"

"I fell down this chasm as a child, don't you remember? You said I'd break my little legs and never run or climb again." He slowly turned to face his enemy. "But as you can see, I can run and climb just fine, unfortunately for you."

"I'm sorry, comrade, but your accounts are not ringing any bells for me," said Wolfram with indifference.

Bright hot anger flared through Sigurd's body. He rushed his kapitän and walloped him across the face with the back of his left hand where he wore his splitting blade dispenser, giving the strike additional heft.

"That I don't believe." Sigurd clutched Wolfram's coat lapels. "Your attention to detail has always been your strength. You know exactly where we are, you know exactly who I am, and you know *exactly* what you've done!"

"I've done a lot of things." Wolfram's gaze turned to ice. "I've killed a lot of people during my career—as have you. Are you telling me you remember every life you have ever taken, every family you've torn apart?"

"You do! You are too meticulous in your duties to forget a single one."

Wolfram smirked and exhaled sharply through his nose, trying to laugh but still too weak. "You've always been one of my most talented soldiers. You know your kapitän better than he knows you. Yes, I remember this place well, how could I not? This is where my career catapulted to unprecedented heights. I had worked so long and hard to find your parents . . . I remember how shocked I was to discover that it was your sister who bore the Eye and not your brother."

"What else do you remember?"

"I remember following the youngest boy to this very crevasse and him falling in before I could reach him. The entire crag erupted in quakes. I lost a good comrade that day, and I barely escaped with my life. But somehow, against all odds, *you* survived." Wolfram grimaced as if he smelled something foul in the air. "How did a five-year-old boy survive the earthquake when a fully armored Steinkamp soldier could not?"

That Steinkamp didn't survive? Then Vaughn was not the perpetrator after all! So much for no secrets between us, Rudiger, Sigurd thought bitterly. He would have to deal with that later.

"You're about to find out." Sigurd let go of Wolfram and walked over to the chasm again. "Golem of Stone! I have here the monster that you rescued me from twenty years ago. I ask that you finish what you started and destroy this man!"

He heard raspy chuckling from behind him. "So you think it was the Alpha of the Crag Golems that saved you. Are you so arrogant to think that you can awaken an Alpha on your command? Your body may have come away unscathed, but your mind is far gone."

"Shut up!" Sigurd barked.

After ensuring that the kapitän was properly molded to the rock and unable to move, Sigurd took another set of earth bindings and used them to climb down the chasm to get closer to the Alpha. Using the light of his cudgel, Sigurd found the immense eye of the Golem of Stone, this time, positioned perpendicular to the bottom of the chasm but at a slight upward angle above Sigurd's head.

Before the dormant eye, Sigurd sang the Ode to Golems. Nothing happened, so he sang it again. *Last time I only hummed a few bars and it lit up the entire cavern, though I was standing on it then.* He stretched his hand out and touched the cold, glossy stone and sang the *Ode* once more. Still nothing.

"Golem of Stone, I beg you to awaken. Help me to exact my vengeance, to make what is wrong right again. I know you hear me. Is this not why I was saved?"

The great eye remained dark, and all that answered Sigurd's question was silence. The Alpha was right there at his fingertips, yet it was as dead as the sediments that made up its body.

His chest tightened and an overwhelming heat flowed through him. He lashed out at the gigantic eye with his cudgel, unable to cause even a hairline fissure upon it.

"Light up, damn you! Speak! This is Siegfried, and I demand you tell me what you want!" He fell to his knees and removed his mask to wipe the sweat from his brow. Breathing in the ash-free air caused his head to ache.

Katja had told him that the Alphas follow the commands of Verishten only. Believing that this Alpha would respond to him made Sigurd feel even more the fool. *But why, Verishten? Why use this Alpha to save my life and again to speak to me two months ago?* Sigurd began to wonder if everything he ever knew had been wrong. He was certain that revenge was the only reason he was alive. If Verishten didn't want Sigurd to exact vengeance on the ones that murdered the Golem Mages, then what did he want?

This is ludicrous. What does it matter what Verishten wants from me? I will kill Wolfram and all of the others with or without divine assistance.

Regaining his composure, Sigurd climbed out of the crevasse, becoming winded in the process but too determined to let it affect him.

"Did everything go okay down there?" Wolfram said almost melodiously.

Sigurd touched the kapitän's bindings and unmolded them from the outcropping. He then hoisted Wolfram to his feet.

"What are you doing?" Wolfram was shrill.

Sigurd could now finally taste the kapitän's fear. "I'm taking you to a place where you can run and climb for an eternity." He pushed Wolfram to his knees and brought him dangerously close to the edge of the chasm. "I managed to survive the fall. Perhaps you will too—but not after breaking every bone in your body."

"Wait, wait! Stop!" Wolfram begged as Sigurd nearly forced him off the edge. "Don't do it! My daughter needs me. I'm her only hope."

"No harm will come to your daughter. That is true mercy. Something you can't begin to comprehend the meaning of."

Sigurd was prepared to shove Wolfram into the pit until he cried out, "Stop! You don't understand! If I'm dead, there will be no one else who can exonerate her for the crimes of which she's been accused."

"What are you talking about?" Sigurd's heart beat wildly in his chest. Wolfram had a daughter, of that Sigurd was certain, but surely his daughter couldn't be Katja . . . although, she *was* guilty of crimes against the Regime.

"Not a moment before I received your message to meet you at the cache, I was visited by the Karl with a warrant for the arrest of my daughter in connection with the Kings' Remnants," Wolfram explained.

"Who do you speak of?" Sigurd bellowed.

"She is the woman you were assigned to protect two months ago. Her professor has been revealing Regime secrets to the Remnants, and she has been caught in the middle. I know she would never be so foolish as to consort with the enemy, at least not intentionally, but I fear the Führer will not see it that way. If I do not return to Deschner in one week to vouch for her innocence, she will be put to death!"

Sigurd roared and threw Wolfram backward, the brittle shale cracking beneath him. "What game are you playing, Wolfram!"

"If only this were a game," the kapitän said, defenseless against Sigurd, who now loomed as a menacing shadow over him. "To think that I trusted you to guard my Kriemia when the entire time you were plotting revenge against me. The irony is as sweet as it is disconcerting."

Even though he had suspected it all along, once Sigurd heard Katja's true name spoken from Wolfram's lips, his mind instantly rejected the notion. *Katja would have told me. This is a trick.*

"You can't be her father!" Sigurd raged. He picked Wolfram up by the bindings and punched him in the face until blood sprayed from his mouth. "If you *really* cared about her and she were really about to be arrested, why did you wait until this moment to tell me? Why did you meet me at the cache in the first place? Wouldn't going to Deschner and exonerating her be your first priority?"

"There was nothing I could have done to stop the arrest once the warrant had been issued." Wolfram spat blood. "First of all, I wanted to wait for you to reveal yourself, so I knew who I was dealing with. Secondly, I knew I had at least three days before my daughter arrived in Deschner, and another week before she faces tribunal. I would have had plenty of time to step in and free her. In the meantime, I was not about to let the Desert War Traitor fall through my fingers. He would have made an excellent bargaining tool with the Führer in exchange for Kriemhilde's freedom."

"You're lying," Sigurd hissed, letting Wolfram down harshly.

"I don't expect my daughter's fate to incite sympathy from the likes of you. I know it to be pointless to lie. If you require proof, read the copy of the warrant in my left inside coat pocket."

Sigurd propped Wolfram against a rock and fished for the document. He found the paper and read it. The document was signed by the Karl Kommissar at the Untevar precinct. It called for the immediate arrests of Herr Ignatius of Nordenhein and Fraulein Katja, Alias of Nordenhein University—true identity to be determined during tribunal. The charges: Treason.

There was no doubting the legitimacy of the document; Sigurd had seen many warrants like these throughout his career. Ignatius and Katja were going to be arrested and subsequently executed by the Regime unless someone did something to stop it. Could Sigurd let his worst enemy go in order to do that?

"Why in Untevar?" Sigurd muttered. His hand shook, still gripping the paper.

"I'm not sure," said Wolfram. "Likely they are on an expedition to research golems or something to do with rebel activity. Do you believe me now? I beg of you, if you are going to kill me, do it after I've had a chance to save my daughter."

"You're not going anywhere," Sigurd rasped. He picked Wolfram up and forced him to walk the rest of the way down the Crags.

"I know you are no longer charged with her protection, but oftentimes residual urges to perform past duties remain with a soldier even after a mission is completed. Find that sense of duty within you to help her now. Please," Wolfram begged, but his words sounded forced.

The two men eventually reached the dilapidated farmhouse that was Sigurd's childhood home.

"Why are you taking me here? Is this—?"

Sigurd shoved Wolfram through the old rickety wooden door, shattering it on impact. He then rearranged the earth bindings so that one of Wolfram's arms was free and proceeded to mold him to the stone wall. Wolfram sat beside a dusty wood stove where most of the smokestack had broken away from the rubble that had once been the home's roof. Sigurd took out a bag of rations that he had earlier collected from a haven in the Town of Kensloche and dumped the contents at Wolfram's feet. He also tossed his extra canteen on his lap.

"There is enough food and water there to last you about a week," said Sigurd. "You'll wait here until I return."

"You can't leave me here!" Wolfram wailed. "Where are you going? If you think you can save Kriemhilde yourself, you can forget about it. The Karl will have already arrested her. She will be arriving in Deschner any day now, and soon she'll be escorted to a holding cell to await trial. A lone Steinkamp cannot free her. Only with my political clout does she have any hope."

If Wolfram was telling the truth about Katja's pending arrest, as the warrant proved, he was at least dishonest about the timing of the event. The order was dated around the time Wolfram would have received Sigurd's message, which meant that the Karl could only have just arrested her in Untevar if at all. Depending on where in the vast range the arrest took place, it could take anywhere between one and four days to make it back to Deschner by prison coach. There was still a chance for Sigurd to intercept that coach on the road from Untevar to Deschner, but if he were too late, Sigurd would need Wolfram alive so that he may do right by his daughter and free her. If Wolfram was lying about being Katja's father, then there was nothing he would be able to do to help. Either way, Sigurd was the only one that could help her now.

He had to put his desires for revenge on hold momentarily. Katja's life was more important than that. He knew the shortest routes through Kensloche, and if he rode through the night, he could make it to Deschner before first light. Then it would be another two days to Untevar.

Verishten, if you're still listening, please let me reach Katja in time, and do not allow Wolfram to escape in my absence.

Sigurd rushed out of the farmhouse as the kapitän screamed after him, "Come back! Unmold me, traitor! You will burn for this!"

Sit tight, my kapitän, I will return after saving Katja. When she reveals that you are not her real father, I will kill you. But if you are . . .

17

REGIME HANDS

On one of Untevar's northern farm roads, Katja caught herself staring at Klemens and the new Steinkamp riding ahead. They seemed to be making conversation with one another, which struck her as odd. The Steinkamp whom Sigurd had arranged to accompany the research team for the previous two months was not one to engage in conversation, particularly with Katja. It would appear that Klemens would rather talk to a masked killer than to her these days. She didn't blame him for his distance under the circumstances. As guilty as she felt for hurting him, she was relieved to no longer have to worry about his feelings.

Watching the new Steinkamp on his black horse made her feel dull and listless. Even though Sigurd had been gone longer than she'd known him, she still thought about him every day. Having another nameless and faceless soldier around didn't help her forget him. All she wanted to do was set her mind to more important endeavors like finding the Golem of Light.

Ignatius trotted up next to Katja on his flea-bitten mare. "Is something bothering you, Katja? You've been unusually quiet on this trip."

"Everything's fine, Professor." She sighed. "It's just that . . . there is something more depressing about this expedition."

"Oddly enough, I agree," Ignatius replied. "The state of Untevar these days can make anyone depressed. I take it this is your first visit to the range."

Katja nodded as she adjusted her large brimmed hat and the facial netting she wore to keep the airborne ash off her face and hair. It was true that traveling through Untevar did not bring with it the same adventurous flair that the Kensloche journey had. The team had taken the east road around Verishten's volcanic regions to get to the City of Untevar. Because of their high status, the team had to rent a fully armored carriage to protect them as they made their way through the city. Over the years the once vibrant metropolis had fallen into a chaotic mess of poverty, crime, and disease. The coachman took them through the least affected areas of the city for their own safety, but Katja still saw muddy streets and ash-stained buildings with windows that no one had cleaned for what looked like years.

Crowds of people had swarmed around the gates of the highborn areas. Dirty, sunken faces stared at the passing carriages. Hundreds of them had lined up at those gates for handouts of foodstuffs and other incidentals. Some of them pushed and shoved to get to the front faster before the city officials closed the gates and sent them away to try another day. It had been a heartbreaking sight to see.

A day later, the team had crossed the River Sleban east of the City of Untevar, and they now took the more scenic farm roads on horseback. The view of the rural countryside was even more depressing than what she had seen in the city. They passed by one grain field after another with acres of unharvested crop left to rot, buried under mountains of ash without a farmer in sight.

"How could Kanzler Bachman allow his range to fall apart like this? For such an intelligent economist, he should be able to fix it," Katja commented.

"The irony is not lost on me either. When I knew Bachman, he never stopped spouting the benefits of free markets and international trade. His thesis was on how the economic stagnation during the Age of Kings was directly caused by the lack of free trade between the competing Golem Mage Kingdoms. This consistently put them in situations where war was the most viable means of wealth accumulation. He highlighted how uninhibited trade between the four provinces of Del'Cabria led to their unsurpassed prosperity. It was Bachman's dream to see Ingleheim take part in that growth. It paired well with Heinrich's dream of Ingle unification."

"Obviously, Bachman's dreams have not become reality. Ingleheim is more isolationist than ever before." Katja frowned.

"Yes, and Untevar suffers the most for it."

"Why is there nobody to farm these fields?"

Ignatius shook his head. "After Heinrich took power, there were talks about redistributing the great wealth of Untevar, accumulated during the

Age of Kings because of its hold on Ingleheim's most fertile lands. The Regime developed a new taxation policy that essentially forced farmers to sell their harvests for a pittance so that all of Ingleheim would have access to inexpensive grains. This meant that regardless of how much they produced or the quality of the grain, rewards to the farmers were roughly static. Farmers who did not agree with the Regime's new approach had their lands taken away or were imprisoned."

"That's awful." Katja's stomach knotted. "They're basically slaves."

"In a sense, yes. As a result, you have what we see here. Acres of food and not a thing to eat."

"This so-called Age of Order we live in," Katja muttered with a shake of her head. After passing by a few more ash-filled fields in silence, she changed the subject. "Professor, I've been wondering about something lately. You knew Herrscher Heinrich well, so you must have known his wife. It was told they wed out of university."

"Ah yes. Ilsa of Luidfort was her name." Ignatius smiled. "She was studying Monarch History if I remember correctly. I didn't get the opportunity to know her as well as the others did. You see, it was more taboo in those days for men to fraternize with women of higher status than they."

"Oh, right—I suppose she must have been of a very elevated station to have married the Prince of Deschner."

"The highest station a young woman could hold without being from a Golem Mage family. It was a good thing too, after what Heinrich went on to do to those families," Ignatius concluded.

"The Führer started killing them after her death, didn't he?"

"His move against the Mages started before that, but it is true that he didn't set out to exterminate them altogether until after Ilsa died."

"Do you think Ilsa's death somehow caused or inspired the Führer to kill them all?" Katja asked.

"I have no doubt Ilsa was Heinrich's balancing force. If she had remained in his life, I sincerely believe he would have made different choices for Ingleheim. In university, everyone could see how smitten he was with her. She was a stunning beauty as women from Luidfort are known to be." Ignatius adjusted the tie of his tweed vest and coat as he rode.

"Ample in beauty, but dull of wit. That is what they say of women from Luidfort Range." Katja smirked.

"I'll challenge any man that says that about Ilsa." Ignatius wagged a finger in the air. "In a battle of wits, she would have Volker, Bachman, and Heinrich scratching their heads at every turn. She was very opinionated, and the only person that I've ever seen win an argument against the likes of them. I think that's why Heinrich was so drawn to her. Intellectually they were the perfect pair."

In an attempt to talk about something other than Untevar's poverty and farming slaves, Katja had stumbled onto a subject even more dismal. To hear of her mother as someone so lively and with her own opinions and dreams, only for Katja to realize she would never know her, became too much to take in.

As soon as she started to tear up, Ignatius said in a lowered voice, "I'm sorry Katja. I know how hard it must be to speak of your mother."

Her heart froze inside her chest. "My—what?"

"It's all right. I've always suspected, but only after you asked about her did I know for sure."

"When did you figure out that I was Heinrich's daughter?" Katja asked.

"The moment you walked into your first lecture of mine. You are the exact image of both Heinrich and Ilsa. I had no doubt of your relation."

"If you had no doubt, then how come you chose me as your top acolyte? With your rebel ties, keeping the Führer's daughter so close was very risky."

Ignatius looked straight into his student's eye. "I chose you, Katja, because you are most deserving of the title. I put my responsibilities as a scholar and an educator far beyond my duty to the rebellion. You may resemble them, but you are not your parents. You make your own choices and it is by your choices that I pass judgment."

Katja felt her heart about to burst inside her chest. "Thank you, Professor. You have no idea what it means to hear you say that. I've always feared that someday I will be asked to account for the atrocities committed by my father for no other reason than being his daughter. It's nice to know that his legacy does not cloud your judgment of me."

"You never need worry about such things when I'm around." Ignatius's voice was quiet enough so the riders ahead couldn't catch a word. "Know that I never have and never will breathe a word of your parentage to anyone, especially to the Remnants."

"Oh, I never thought you would, Professor."

"Even so, you can trust me."

"I do, and you can trust me as well."

By the next day, the research team arrived at the Hot Lakes. Here one could find crystal golems in abundance. Miles away from civilization existed glistening crystal formations and smooth stone that formed into hills. Some of the larger hills formed into geysers, where steam from the ground water erupted into the sky and fed into beautiful warm lakes of dark teal blues and brilliant greens. Some of these lakes reached such staggering temperatures that the skin would sizzle off anyone who dared set foot in them.

Steam leaked from nearly every crack and crevasse in the smooth rust-colored stone, and hardly a plant or tree could grow. The team was fascinated by the many different crystal clusters that they spotted on their journey. They sang the Ode to some of them in hopes they were dormant golems; a surprising amount of them were, but none were giant. The team would have to go out much farther to find giant crystal golems and even farther than that to find the Alpha.

Their eye map indicated that they would find the Alpha at the Crystal Lake of Rainmier. It was a vast hot spring and at the center stood a crystal geyser so large that when it erupted, the warm mists of water would rain down on the terrain several miles from the lake. Katja could hardly wait to see it.

The Steinkamp knew the Hot Lakes fairly well and led them to a small valley between two hills. Because of the flatter landscape, the sun's light stayed visible longer, so they had more than enough daylight to set up their camp.

Katja finally removed her large-brimmed sunhat and facial net. They were far enough from the volcano that falling ash wouldn't be as much of a nuisance. Ignatius and Klemens shook off their hats and brushed the ash from their beards. Klemens had taken to growing a small beard and mustache during his mourning period. She preferred the beard—it made him appear more distinguished.

That night, she fell asleep quickly only to be awakened by Klemens's whispering voice and the jostling of the walls of her tent.

"Katja, Katja, wake up, hurry!"

Untying her tent flap just enough to stick her head through, she saw him wearing his vest and pants and holding a lantern. "What is it, Klem? It's the middle of the night," she croaked, rubbing the sleep from her eyes.

"Get dressed, quickly. You have to see this."

"It can wait until morning, surely," Katja protested.

"It can't. I saw a group of crystal golems fighting each other."

"But that's impossible. Golems have never been known to attack one another absent Mage command."

"I don't know what to tell you, Kat, but I saw it. If you hurry, you can see for yourself," Klemens urged.

With a groan, Katja turned on her lantern and found the blue ruffled blouse and brown cotton hiking skirt she had been wearing earlier that day. She tied on her boots and exited her tent fully dressed. On her way to the horses nearby, she tied her messy hair back in a ponytail to keep it off her face. She turned back toward her tent. "Wait, I have to grab my new journal."

Klemens took her arm and pulled her back toward the horses. "There's no time. The golems could have moved on already."

"Where is the professor?" asked Katja, mounting her horse that she noticed already had its saddle on.

Klemens waved a dismissive hand. "You know how long it takes to wake him. Let the old man sleep. We can report to him in the morning."

The two galloped off in a northwestern direction, circling the wide hill behind their campsite. Katja couldn't get rid of a sick feeling in her gut.

"Klemens, shouldn't we at least tell the Steinkamp where we're going?"

"Don't worry. I took care of it."

"Are you sure you saw golems fighting? It is highly unusual, and what's more unusual, is how you managed to see them in the middle of the night."

"I couldn't sleep so I took a walk, and they were on this road. I think they went down this way," Klemens said as they pressed onward.

They rode for a long time, and Katja continued to wonder if Klemens had seen golems at all. It didn't make sense—not only for golems to fight each other, but for him to be the one to venture off into the night alone. He had been acting strangely aloof for the entire trip and now he was determined to lead her far from the camp where there was a good chance they could get lost.

"I don't like this. I'm heading back."

"Just a little further. Please, Katja, once you see it, it will change everything."

To see golems in combat in the wild would be a significant discovery in golem behavior, but something still gnawed at her. She halted her mare. "I'm going back."

Klemens steered his buckskin toward her and grabbed Katja's reins to keep her from galloping away.

"What are you doing?" she asked shrilly.

"Don't go back to the camp. Trust me." Klemens's voice deepened.

"You brought me here under false pretenses without the protection of the Steinkamp, and I'm supposed to trust you? Tell me what is going on!"

Katja never dreamed that Klemens would harm her, but it had been two months since she'd broken his heart, and they had hardly talked in that time. Her heart raced.

"The Steinkamp is guarding the professor until the Karl come," explained Klemens.

"The Karl? No, Klem, we have to go back and warn him!" Katja tried to kick her horse into action, but Klemens kept his grip on her reins and pulled it back.

"We can't go back," Klemens snapped. "The Steinkamp knows about the professor and the Kings' Remnants."

"What? No, it's not what you think!"

"The Steinkamp spotted the Karl up the road before I woke you. They will arrive at the camp any minute to arrest him. I'm sorry you had to find out this way, but at least the Steinkamp warned me so that I could get you to safety."

"I'm not the one in danger here, our professor is. He is our friend, and we can't abandon him!"

Katja didn't understand how the Regime found out about him and why the Steinkamp, who was supposed to be working for the same rebel group, would sell him out.

"They are going to arrest you too!" Klemens said heatedly, careful not to let his voice carry. "They think you're his accomplice. But he knows it's not your fault. The Steinkamp said it has something to do with this Sigurd, the one you fell for. He's not who he seems."

Katja's heart sank. Klemens had been duped, and for reasons she couldn't begin to string together.

"None of that is true. You have to believe me. We are being set up."

"Ignatius must pay for his crimes, but you don't have to. The Steinkamp has been gracious enough to give you this chance to clear your name. I can use whatever leverage my father has left me to convince the Führer to exonerate you. He and my father were close friends."

"You don't know what you're talking about. Just let me go!"Katja kicked her horse again, but Klemens pulled back once more.

"I know everything, Katja, so stop lying to me! I read your journal, alright? I know all about the secret research you and Sigurd had been doing. I know you want to stop the Golem of Death from being awakened, but you don't know what you're getting yourself into—"

A wave of fury rushed through Katja. "How could you? My innermost thoughts! When did you read it?"

"I found it in the Crags after that quake."Klemens hung his head. "My leg was stuck under rocks, and your journal had somehow fallen right within my reach. I opened to a page where you referenced your secret excursions into Frost Woods with the Steinkamp, meaning you knew him before the Crags. I closed it immediately and planned to give it back to you, but then I noticed how the two of you were arguing at that farmhouse, and it made me crazy. I thought you were going to be my wife. I—"

"You had no right!"

"I know. I'm sorry. Once you told me that you loved him—I couldn't help myself. I read it all in an attempt to understand why you would fall for someone like him and not me. I discovered far more incriminating things, and I wish more than anything I had never seen that book."

"I wish you never had either," Katja hissed. "Now, where is it? I want it back."

"It's at the university in my safety deposit box."

"You idiot. If they arrest Ignatius they are sure to check all of our safety deposit boxes. You are a part of this too, Klem."

Klemens broke eye contact. "Not exactly. A month ago, I confronted the Steinkamp to see if he had any information on my father's death and why the rebels would target him. He told me that our professor has been leaking information to them about the Golem of Death. I felt so betrayed . . . the information he leaked is the reason why the rebellion abducted my father. I never told him about your journal, though. The Steinkamp was in the process of investigating so he asked me to keep quiet until he could mount more evidence." He ran his hand over his hair, revealing beads of sweat on his forehead. "A week ago today, he discovered that this Sigurd had ties to the Remnants, which implicates both you and Ignatius. I was able to convince the Steinkamp that you knew not what you were doing, and he agreed to let you escape arrest for the time being. Because *I* agreed to cooperate, I have been absolved from any actions against the Regime that I have unknowingly committed. They will not search my safety deposit box."

Katja screeched, "Klemens, how could you? You sold out your own professor so that you could be absolved?"

"Hey!" Klemens barked, clutching Katja's reins again. "I am not going to pay for the crimes Ignatius committed and neither should you!"

"Don't you see?" Katja shot back. "I am just as guilty as he is. I made my choice to team up with the professor and with Sigurd. I am not some nitwit who didn't know what she was getting herself into. I will accept the consequences of my actions, and I will face my arrest."

Katja knew that her father would likely vouch for her freedom as long as her journal remained in Klemens's safety deposit box. She might even be able to convince her father to show mercy toward his old friend. All she had to do was make it back to camp.

Instead of trying to kick her horse forward, Katja pulled hard on the reins and backed the horse up. Her bay reared, jolting Klemens so suddenly, he fell from his saddle. Before galloping off, Katja stopped her horse for a moment to check if he was all right. She hated him for selling out the professor to the Regime and reading her journal, but she didn't want to leave him alone and injured either.

"Kat, don't do this!" Klemens yelled. He pushed himself off the ground and onto his unsteady feet. His ankle had healed enough to walk, but it still bothered him, and he needed to be careful not to overuse it.

"I don't have a choice," Katja declared.

"You will be executed along with Ignatius! I won't let you die for that traitor!" Klemens cried as he staggered toward his horse.

"You've been deceived. The Steinkamp who is arranging all of this works for the Remnants too."

Klemens was so taken aback that he couldn't find the strength to lift himself back into the saddle. "The Steinkamp back at the camp . . . h-he's a rebel?"

"He is a Steinkamp long defected. Sigurd arranged for him to be here before he set off for war," Katja explained.

"That doesn't make sense." Klemens's brow furrowed. "If he and Ignatius are working for the same rebel group, why did he arrange for him to get arrested and label Sigurd as the defector?"

Katja's heart broke at the supposition she wished she'd had moments earlier. "I think the Regime captured Sigurd, and now the Kings' Remnants want to scapegoat him as the Rogue Steinkamp. The Regime would demand a reason for how the Remnants got word of the Golem of Death. The professor is no longer sharing information with the rebels, and the Steinkamp in our midst knows that. Ignatius's arrest would serve to get rid of someone no longer of use to the Remnants while satisfying the Regime that they've won for the time being."

Then she thought of something else that didn't quite fit. ". . . But the Remnants don't seem to want *me* to fall into Regime hands. That's why they wanted you to take me away."

"So?"

"Why should I matter to them? I'm the one who convinced Ignatius to start keeping secrets from them. Why didn't they sell out both of us? Unless—"

Her eyes widened in terror as she looked to Klemens. He only returned her glance with one of confusion.

"They know—they know who my father is," Katja whispered in shock.

How the Remnants discovered her true identity, she had no idea. Her parentage was the one thing she never wrote in her journal. Nobody knew she was the daughter of Herrscher Heinrich, not his closest allies, not even Sigurd. Ignatius only guessed at it, and he would never tell a soul, she trusted that.

"Get on that horse, Klem," Katja urged. "We need to leave at once. I don't think this is about the professor."

"You're right about that, fraulein," a gruff voice echoed from the darkness.

Two Steinkamp soldiers approached like manifesting shadows in the night. One pointed his crossbow straight at Klemens's face. He jumped at the sight and put up his hands.

"You're a sharp one," the Steinkamp with the crossbow said to Katja. His voice didn't sound like that of the rebel who had been guarding them for the past two months. She assumed these were the other two Steinkamp defectors Ignatius had mentioned.

"The apple doesn't fall too far from the tree, does it, Princess Kriemhilde II of Deschner," said the second Steinkamp, bowing facetiously to Katja.

"Princess?" Klemens sputtered in shock, still trembling before the crossbow.

"What do you want?" Katja murmured.

The Steinkamp with the crossbow replied, "Please step down from the horse, and do it now, or your friend here gets a bolt through the eyeball."

18

BROKEN THINGS

Katja's body shook as she got down from her horse. Putting her hands up, she slowly walked over and stood beside Klemens.

"Alright . . . I'll go with you. You don't have to hurt him."

"Kat, no!" Klemens protested.

"Shut your mouth," the Steinkamp barked and cracked Klemens across his temple with the crossbow, sending him to the ground.

"We have no need for him," said the other Steinkamp. The crossbow-toting comrade took aim for Klemens once again. Without a second thought, Katja stepped between the crossbow and her research partner.

"Move aside!" the Steinkamp commanded.

"Don't be a fool," Katja said with the firmest tone she could muster despite her quavering voice. "Do you know who this man is?"

"Our orders are to take the Führer's daughter—no one else."

"The man you just struck is the firstborn son of the late Kanzler Volker."

"This is no son of Volker," scoffed the other Steinkamp.

"The smart thing to do here is to take us both. My father and Volker were very close. Trust me when I say that the Führer will want Volker's son alive just as much as he wants me alive," Katja said.

"I suppose it wouldn't hurt to take them both to the Kaiser," the Steinkamp said to his comrade.

"The Kaiser?"

"That's right, fraulein." The second Steinkamp bound her wrists. The bindings became one with Katja's skin, fusing her hands together. The flesh felt like it would tear at the slightest movement.

His comrade did the same with Klemens. "The leader of the Kings' Remnants is looking forward to meeting you."

The Steinkamp led Katja and Klemens down the road, leaving their mounts behind. They came to a large prison coach pulled by two black horses. Once they locked the prisoners inside, they set off for somewhere unknown. It was dark, and Katja could hardly see Klemens's pale face right in front of her. The coach was so tall that even on the tips of her toes, she couldn't reach through the thin window slots at the top.

"Please," she begged the Steinkamp driver. "Just tell me what happened to our professor. Was he arrested?" Neither man responded. Katja pressed, "Why betray one of your own?"

"Woman, if you don't shut your mouth, Volker's son dies!"

"Please just do as they say, Katja," Klemens groaned.

Her eyes adjusted enough to find him sitting in the far right corner of the coach. His body was slumped over in fatigue as he nursed the welt on his temple with his handkerchief.

Katja, too, slumped against the wall and slid down in defeat. "I guess there's no use. The professor is as good as dead."

"You should stop worrying about him and start worrying about us," Klemens whined. "It's only a matter of time before they kill us too."

"They aren't going to kill us. They need us as leverage."

"For what? You should know that the Führer has a strict policy to not negotiate with rebels. As soon as these guys figure that out, it's off with our heads."

"Will you stop?" Katja moaned, her head starting to pound. "We don't know exactly why they want us, so until we do, will you at least pretend to be anything other than a coward for once in your life?"

Immediately, she regretted saying those words, but it was too late. Even in the pitch black of the coach, she could sense Klemens's expression darkening.

"Oh, so it has finally come to this. Your true feelings reveal themselves. 'Klemens is such a yellow-belly. He's no son of Volker. Now there's a hard man, intimidating and lethal, a great military leader he was. But not young Klemens, oh no—" He let out a demented chortle. "'He won't join the military, he wants to be a *scholar*.'" Putting his finger in the air, he spoke with an authoritative tone. "'Son, if you're going to spend your life with your nose in books, then you'd better use those books to win a war or two.

Then and only then can you call yourself a *real man*.'"

"I-I didn't mean it. I—"

"Yes, you did." Klemens now brought his attentions squarely on her. "And you're not wrong. I am a coward. You're the brave one. The way you stood between me and that crossbow . . . had I not recently emptied my bladder, I would have certainly wet my breeches staring down a Steinkamp like that. I suppose you have a lot of experience in that area."

"Klemens, not now." Katja sighed. She was not in any mood to talk about Sigurd. For all she knew, he was suffering in a volcanic cell, awaiting his execution at the Mouth of Verishten. As a man believed to be of low birth and a defector at that, Sigurd would never be granted a trial. She felt her heart tearing at the thought.

"I may not be able to kill someone with my bare hands or stare death in the face, but that doesn't make me any less of a man, you know," Klemens continued vehemently. "There is more might in one corner of my mind than there is in an entire force of Steinkamp soldiers. All they do is blindly follow orders. It is men like me who make those orders!"

"Your manhood was never in question. I've always admired your intellect, and so much more."

Klemens only scoffed. "Don't patronize me."

Katja's blood boiled over. "Do you want me to tell you that you're obviously the better choice? Fine, if that's what you want to hear. You are the better choice, Klem, but I didn't fall for you. I fell for a killer, and not only that, a defector who would rather murder his own kapitän than be with me."

"Is it really surprising that a Steinkamp would choose murder and mayhem over you?" Klemens slumped further into the coach wall.

Katja deflated. "No . . . I mean, *yes.* Why wouldn't he just stay?" She looked to Klemens diagonal to her, unsure of what kind of answer she expected from him.

"There is no point in making sense of what goes on in a Steinkamp's head." Klemens looked down at his bound wrists. "They're broken men."

"I know that. So what does that tell you about me, hmm? What kind of woman collects broken things? Maybe one who is broken herself." Katja admitted.

Tears flooded her eyes and threatened to pour down her face, but she kept them back with all her might. The last time she cried in front of Klemens it didn't turn out so well between them.

"You're not broken, Kat. Far from it," Klemens said softly as he shuffled along the wall of the moving coach to be closer to her.

"If only that were true, I'd marry you in a heartbeat. I truly would." Katja sniffed. "But you cannot begin to understand the nightmares from my past that have shaped me. There is darkness in me just as there is darkness in him, and for the first time in my life . . . it started to feel okay."

They grew silent as the coach trundled along the Hot Lakes countryside. Just when Katja thought that was the end of their tirade, Klemens suddenly spoke. "I can have darkness in me too. You don't know."

"Please." Katja snorted.

"My father was Kanzler Volker, the darkest man that ever lived. He ate Steinkamp soldiers for breakfast every morning."

"Oh, right, I'd almost forgotten." Katja couldn't help but giggle.

Whether he was serious or not, she got a kick out of his attempt at appearing austere. However, having Volker as a father could not have been easy, and she appreciated Klemens trying to make her feel better.

"But don't you forget my father is the Mighty Führer, the man responsible for killing hundreds of families, and now he wants to awaken an Alpha Golem whose sole purpose is to burn the life force out of anyone caught in its view. So, I win." She poked Klemens in the chest with both forefingers.

"I still can't believe it. You don't look like a Kriemhilde at all."

"Thank Verishten for that." She rested her head against the vibrating coach wall. "But you look like a Klemens through and through. What is your real name?"

"Klemens," he said with a shrug.

"Your real name is Klemens?" Katja cackled. "Why don't you use an alias?"

"There were somewhere between twenty and twenty-five Klemenses born around the same time I was, most of them highborn. Since nobody believed I was a son of Volker anyway, I didn't bother with an alias."

"Oh, you may be a braver man than I thought," Katja teased.

Klemens nodded, scratching his sideburns. "Yes, I am nothing if not a risk-taker. Does that intrigue you?"

Katja found herself giggling again. "Yes, it does, but you know what really intrigues me? You know exactly who you are, and you make no apologies for it."

"I do? I don't?" Klemens grinned, redness overtaking his pale cheeks.

"Don't ever change, Herr Klemens of Breisenburg. I know there is a woman out there who is perfect for you, and when you find her, you will make her the luckiest woman alive."

Klemens sighed through a reflective grin. "Is her name Princess Kriemhilde II?"

Katja presented her wrists to him. "Do I look like the luckiest woman alive?"

He shook his head, chuckling. "No . . . no, you don't."

"And please, just stick with Katja."

"Alright." Klemens clasped his bound hands around hers. "I promise from now on to respect your decision in not choosing me as your husband, which by the way, is a foolish decision."

"I know," Katja replied with a roll of her eyes. "I know."

"I am a grown man. I can get over it. But in the meantime, I will be here for you . . . as a friend."

"Thank you," said Katja, struggling to keep her tears back again. "Because you may be the last friend I will ever make."

"I won't be," Klemens replied thoughtfully, "because we will both get out of this . . . somehow."

Katja nodded, letting her head rest on Klemens's shoulder as he rested his head on hers. By the coach's rumbling, they eventually fell asleep.

Katja wasn't sure what woke her up, whether it was a rough bump in the road, the deafening hustle and bustle outside the coach, or the putrid smell of trash and urine. Sweat coated her from head to toe. The afternoon sun had been beating down on the black coach all morning, and the temperature inside it was stifling. Katja lay on her back underneath Klemens's arms with her head resting on his chest. Somehow, he was still asleep, and his hand was dangerously close to cupping her left breast.

Carefully peeling her sticky body from under his arms, she groggily got to her feet and attempted to look outside. From the chatter and odor alone, she knew where they were.

"Klemens, wake up. I think we're back in the City of Untevar." She shook him awake.

A few minutes later the coach came to a halt, and soon thereafter the back door swung open. The brightness from the outside world stung their eyes as the two Steinkamp ducked into the carriage to collect their hostages. They led them to a pristine courtyard gated off from the rest of the city. Up a long stone path was a sparkling castle nestled into a cliff face at the mountain's base. It was the crystal mansion of the Kanzler of Untevar.

Now Katja was more confused than frightened. She began to wonder if sometime during their slumber, Regime Steinkamp had overtaken the prison coach and were now taking them to safety in the hands of her father's other dearest friend. Hope began to creep into her heart the closer they came to the glistening structure.

"Why are you taking us to the kanzler?" she asked the Steinkamp.

"Quiet. Don't make me regret not knocking you out before coming here," he said in the same gruff voice as before.

Her heart sank, and she looked to Klemens, his eyes filled with fear. The two of them were no safer here than they were in the coach.

The Steinkamp took the hostages into the castle through a set of doors, thirty feet high. The sunlight reflected off of the decorative crystal, obscuring some of its more intricate details, but it took Katja's breath away nonetheless. Castles of this size were remnants of the Age of Man. Many golems were utilized in the construction of the great cities where they built grand castles into the mountains themselves.

They waited in a wide hallway lined with chandeliers made from crystals of various colors. Reflective glass formed the walls, creating the illusion of an open atrium bustling with activity when in fact it was an enclosed hallway. The luminous architecture made the scholars gape in awe until a large man with an unkempt ginger beard, dressed in a silk lounging robe strode into the hall.

"It's early, comrades, what do you have for me?" said the man in a hearty voice.

"Herr Kanzler, we present to you Kriemhilde II, daughter of Herrscher Heinrich," said the Steinkamp holding onto Katja's bindings.

"While I live and shit! So it is!" the kanzler boomed.

The Steinkamp released her bindings as Kanzler Bachman approached and took her by the shoulders to get a good look at her.

Katja got a look at Bachman in turn. From how Ignatius had described his intellect, she expected him to look more like an older version of Klemens. Instead, before her was a gigantic barrel of a man with graying red hair sticking out from all sides. He had a large bulbous nose and twinkling hazel eyes.

Bachman turned to Klemens, who the Steinkamp also released from his bindings. "And who is this lad?"

"This one claims to be Herr Klemens, the son of the late Kanzler Volker," said the second Steinkamp.

"How unexpected." The kanzler smacked his own impressive girth. As Klemens massaged his reddened wrists, Bachman clasped his own sausage-sized fingers around one of Klemens's hands and shook it eagerly. "It is an honor to meet you, lad. I am still reeling from the loss of your father. He was a formidable man."

"Thank you, Herr Kanzler," Klemens replied in confusion.

"It is a great pleasure to have you both in my home. Welcome," Bachman exclaimed. "Begitta, take my esteemed guests to their separate accommodations, and see them to fresh water, clothing, and what not."

A stout woman in a simple servant's gown suddenly appeared from behind his large frame. "Yes, my lord, it is plain to see what our guests are in need of."

"Spare me the lip, woman, and see to it." Bachman waved her off.

Begitta rolled her eyes and motioned for Katja and Klemens to follow her.

"May I ask why we were brought here by members of the Kings' Remnants?" Klemens asked before following Begitta.

"Isn't it obvious?" Katja said. "Kanzler Bachman is the Kaiser."

"Yes, what she said," Bachman chuckled, shuffling them out of the hallway. "Now off with you two, rest and freshen up. I will call on you to join me for dinner, and there I will be happy to answer any and all questions you may have."

Katja wanted answers now, but she also hadn't had use of a lavatory in what seemed like forever, so she submitted to following the servant.

Begitta led them up a glossy stairwell with dormant man-sized crystal golems holding up the massive banister. Golems of every imaginable shape and color decorated the halls, and it irked Katja to see them. Not even her father, with access to all the world's golems, had ever used them as pieces of furniture.

They reached Klemens's room first. There was no chance for either of them to speak to one another before Begitta demanded that Katja continue to follow. Her room seemed to be located on the other side of the castle from Klemens's, judging from how long it took to reach it. Inside her quarters she was met by a handmaid who helped her out of her sweaty blouse and skirt and into a polished marble tub with warm water already prepared for her. The handmaid scrubbed her clean, dried her off, and fitted her with exquisite silk robes. She then left Katja to rest in one of the softest beds she had ever lain in.

The canopy posts were held up by polished crystal golems. She stared into the dormant eye of the nearest one. In it, she saw the familiar markings that made up the Untevar Mountain Range. It gave her an idea of how she would leave this place when the time was right, but first she needed to uncover Bachman's intentions.

An hour before dinner, the handmaid returned to assist her with her evening wear. Katja chose a forest green, embroidered corset with bunched shoulders and satin gloves, cut through to leave her fingers exposed. The skirt was laced with green and black satins and fine beadwork. The gown flowed to the ground gracefully hugging around her legs ever so slightly. She liked dresses with modest crinolines to keep her movements unhampered. She curled and pinned her hair up with a fascinator to the right side of her head while allowing a few ringlets to drop freely to her shoulder on the left. Katja could hardly remember the last time she'd worn such an elegant ensemble. It made her actually start to miss the designer gowns she had hanging in her closet back home, many of which she hadn't had the chance to wear. *I'm sure Brunhilde found some use for them,* she thought bitterly.

"Fraulein?" Begitta said from the doorway, breaking her out of her reverie. "The kanzler is expecting you now."

The graying servant escorted her to the dining room. A string quartet played in the far corner. As soon as she approached the table, the two men rose from their seats in respect for the lady in their presence. Katja hardly recognized Klemens, clean-shaven again, save his sideburns. He wore a handsome embroidered vest with a ruffled cravat and form-fitting dark brown trousers.

"Katja, you look ravishing," Klemens stated as he took her hand and bowed, rubbing his thumb across her bare knuckles. She curtsied and turned to Bachman.

"Welcome, fraulein," he said, rubbing his thumb across her knuckles as well.

The kanzler looked much more refined than he had that morning. He wore a dark red embroidered suit, large enough to fit over his husky frame. His wild beard and hair were now trimmed and brushed, but still, a few ginger wires stuck out where they didn't belong.

Once everyone sat down at the large marble table at their respective ends, the servants paraded in fine crystal dishes bearing every type of meat, fruit, and bread they could want. Despite the mouthwatering smells coming from the food, the anxiety fluttering about Katja's stomach kept her from eating.

When the servants poured the red wine, she took advantage of it. She sipped the tart beverage while admiring the artwork around the room. She almost took some of it down her windpipe when she caught sight of two giant crystal golems standing as iridescent pillars on either side of the dining room entryway.

Crystal golems were unique in that they were taller than the others, but possessed a thinner build with long gangly legs and arms. They appeared headless, with their diamond-shaped eyes embedded deep in their chests. As strange as they looked, they were beautiful in their fragility, but that fragility also made them deadly.

"Impressive, aren't they?" said Bachman upon noticing her staring. "A Golem Expert like you must appreciate my artwork more than most."

Katja looked away from the golems and put down her wine glass. "To me, they are not artwork, Herr Kanzler. They are sentient beings, deserving a better existence than that of decorations in a lavish estate."

"Not so sentient at the moment, though," replied Bachman with a smirk.

Katja swallowed hard as she tried to hide her disgust.

"How did you get them to lie dormant in the open like that?" asked Klemens.

"They've all been here since I moved in," answered Bachman. "The King of Untevar, or some other Golem Mage of this house, would have commanded them into position and then into dormancy. As I am not a Mage myself, I cannot move them, so they will stay that way."

Katja took another sip of wine to hide a smirk. She put her glass down again and said, "Until my father decides to animate them from the comfort of his study."

"And what would give our Führer a reason to do that?" asked Bachman.

"One reason would be finding out that you, his closest friend and ally, is leading the rebellion against him."

"Leading a rebellion, mind you, that got his other closest friend and ally killed," Klemens added.

"And again, you have my deepest sympathies, herr. Believe me, Volker's death was never our intention. Once we learned of the Golem of Death, I knew Volker would be one of the few men who had knowledge of where it was held. All we wanted was to extract that information and send him on his way."

"Then tell me how he ended up dead," Klemens demanded, clutching his cutlery in a white-knuckled grip.

"How do you think?" posed the kanzler with his mouth full. "The Regime sent a Steinkamp to kill him before he revealed that information, if but a second too late. Volker revealed the secret location of the Alpha and he ended up dying for nothing. So, in that sense, the rebellion didn't kill your father at all. Her father did." Bachman pointed his fork at Katja. He then washed down his chicken with wine and proceeded to wipe the grease from his beard. The look of him repulsed her so she looked to Klemens instead. The two made eye contact briefly, but he cast his eyes angrily to the floor.

"You expect us to believe that my father would order the death of one of his dearest friends?" Katja challenged.

"Well, you don't order a lone comrade to rescue one of the Regime's most important offiziers if your intention is to do just that," Bachman said before biting into his bread.

"If you will all excuse me, I must retire," Klemens muttered, throwing down his napkin and rising to his feet.

All of the sudden, the guards in the dining room perked up at Klemens's movement. Bachman put out his palm without getting up from his seat.

"That won't be necessary, herr. Might I mention that although I wish to treat you as an honored guest in my house, you are in fact a prisoner? So, I cannot allow you to leave my sight just yet. Please sit down." He motioned to Klemens's chair.

Klemens flashed Katja a look of alarm and did what he was told.

"Apologies. I hope you understand." The kanzler continued eating.

"So we are hostages after all." Katja placed her fork down. "Then what is it that you want?"

"Can you not guess?" Bachman pointed to each of them at the dining table. "I want what I, your father, and your father, set out to accomplish long ago. I want a free and prosperous Ingleheim under one fair and balanced ruler."

"And I imagine that ruler would naturally be you?" Katja took another generous sip of her wine.

"Can you think of anyone better?" Bachman said heartily after downing the rest of his beverage. The servants quickly moved to refill his glass.

"You may want to take a walk through your mountain range once in a while," said Katja. "The Führer awarded you one of the wealthiest ranges, and your economic policies have brought it to ruin. I realize my father is far from a perfect leader but I'd rather die than see this nation ruled by the likes of you."

Bachman only chuckled at her outburst. Klemens glared at her.

"I understand your concern, fraulein. I am well aware of how Untevar suffers. But it is a temporary state, I assure you. To build a secret force against the most powerful Golem Mage in history is no simple task. Sacrifices must be made. Rebel soldiers are not created in times of plenty; they are born from the gutters. The more gutters you have, the more rebels you will make. It's simple economics."

Katja blinked several times, dumbfounded. "You enacted policies that you knew would strip wealth from your citizens to create an environment for rebellion?"

"Exactly," Bachman said between chews. "Well, the Führer is doing that mostly on his own. I am just using my mountain range to speed up the process a bit. Twenty-some odd years ago, I told Heinrich that to build a better Ingleheim, we needed trade with outside nations, and he agreed. Then a nasty plague broke out in Del'Cabria, and our borders had to close before they'd ever opened. Long after the plague had run its course, there was nothing that could convince Heinrich to reopen the borders for any reason. He didn't trust outsiders. In fact, even trade among the ranges angered him. He said that *'unrestrained trade between the regions will cause too much disparity in wealth, and will bring them right back into conflict.'*" Bachman puffed out his chest in an offensive impression of Katja's father. "I told him trade restrictions would impoverish all of Ingleheim in the long run. He no longer agreed. So, I used the range he awarded me to show him exactly the kind of Ingleheim he was destined to get."

"You let thousands of your people starve just to prove a point to my father?"

Bachman sighed thoughtfully. "I thought you would understand." He paused to take another bite of his chicken. "Your mother would have."

"I am not my mother."

"Evidently not." Bachman swallowed and finally put down his utensils then folded his hands together and looked intently at Katja. "But Verishten burn me alive if you don't look just like her. Heinrich gave you those amber eyes and those sharp Deschner cheekbones but you have Ilsa's hair and her full lips. That figure, waiflike yet curvaceous in a way that could cause the Third Eruption in any man's loins. . . ."

Katja wished the floor would swallow her up. The way the kanzler's gaze poured over her made her ill. She went for her wine again.

"Herr Kanzler, I ask that you show more respect for the lady at your table," Klemens said, coming to her aid. She was glad for it, even though it would do little good in protecting her from the kanzler in his own home.

"Accept my apologies, Kriemhilde. I didn't intend to cause you discomfort. Memories of your mother when we were young have me getting carried away."

"You loved her too." Katja swallowed and put her glass back down.

"Ilsa always had my full attention," responded Bachman with a smile. "She and I would stay up for hours debating feverishly into the night about various political and economic policies during the Age of Kings."

"But they say it was Heinrich who was her intellectual match," Katja inputted.

"Bah!" Bachman dismissed the notion with a wave of his large hand. "Heinrich won her over with his claim to Deschner's throne, not his mind. Ilsa did not want any part of the sanctimonious nitwits of Luidfort's high society, and who better to cement her position outside of that than the Prince of Deschner?"

"It all makes sense now," Klemens cut in. "You believed she should have chosen you for your intellect, but instead she chose Heinrich for his title. This entire rebellion is just a pissing contest between you and the man who got the woman you wanted."

"You misunderstand, herr. My love for Heinrich was beyond that of any mere woman, even one as exquisite as Ilsa. I was content to let him have it all. However, after they died, nothing was ever the same. It's as if Heinrich wanted someone to come along and end it all for him. As his last friend, it's only fitting that I be the one to do it."

Katja put out her hand. "Wait, you said *they* died—you mean my mother and Volker?"

"No, your mother and Gunnar."

Katja raised a questioning eyebrow.

"Gunnar, he was . . . may Verishten rip off my balls, your father never told you!" Bachman banged his hand down on the table in disbelief.

"Never told me what?"

"Heinrich didn't just lose a wife in the birthing bed, but a son as well—your twin brother," said Bachman.

Katja felt like she had been struck over the head. That explained why she had never grown to bear the Eye of Verishten, even though, she was the oldest and only child of a Golem Mage. She had never actually been an only child. The Eye was supposed to appear on her brother. No wonder Heinrich couldn't look Katja in the eye, for she reminded him of the loss of both his wife and his heir. A tear suddenly fell down her cheek.

"I'm sorry that you had to hear this from me, Kriemhilde. I thought your father would have told you about your brother," said Bachman.

Katja shook her head and dabbed her eyes with a napkin. "No . . . H-he didn't."

"More wine." Bachman motioned for a servant to come and refill her glass. She barely registered that it was empty. *How much have I had?*

Bachman offered to change the subject, and everyone at the table agreed.

"I've got a new topic." Klemens cleared his throat. "How are we to serve as your hostages, oh gracious host?"

"Ah, that's why I invited you to dinner, as it so happens," Bachman replied. "It's very simple, really. Kriemhilde will provide assurances from the Führer not to send his war golems and retake the Fortress of Mortlach."

"Has the fortress been taken already?" Katja asked.

"Not yet, but my most prized rebel fighters are marching toward it as we speak. My General Rudiger has acquired a secret weapon, an archer they are calling Gershlon Reborn. With his help and that of a very powerful little sorceress, we will fell the war golems currently guarding the fortress."

"You do realize that our research has not found any way of awakening the Golem of Death?" Katja reminded.

"It isn't what the Golem of Death can *do* that matters to us. It's what it *represents*. If the people believe it can be awakened, even someday, whoever holds it holds all the cards. I've read Ignatius's reports that state awakening it is impossible and that your research is a lost cause—"

"So he is now useless to you. That's why you let him get arrested," said Katja.

"Someone must take the fall if the Regime is to believe that it has won. Shortly they will receive word that the Führer's daughter is in rebellion hands, and they will be forced to stand down until further instruction."

"My father will never negotiate with you. We are not very close as it is."

"I think you are wrong about that." Bachman pointed at her. "What the Führer says and what he does tend to differ. You are the last thing he has left in this world. Trust me, he will do anything to keep you safe."

"If the Führer does agree to stand down, what then?" asked Klemens.

"I reveal myself as the Kaiser to my people. I tell them, as I have been indirectly telling them for years, that all of their ills can be cured—that it is time to take back what's theirs from a Führer who has mistreated them. They will rally behind me and my General Rudiger, and we will advance upon Deschner and seize Heinrich's seat!" Bachman sat back and slapped his enormous belly.

"You think it will be that easy?" Klemens scoffed.

"Verishten, no!" Bachman waved his hand down. "But I am sure your military insights can be of use, Herr Klemens."

"Why would I do anything to aid the rebellion? I am no traitor!" Klemens spat. His anger now made his words more brazen. Sweat formed under Katja's fascinator.

"Because under the current law, your father's kanzlership will go to someone of the Führer's choosing—someone who is not likely you or your brother Brenner. I intend to bring Ingleheim to a new Age of Kings. I can make you the heir to Breisenburg, a viceroy under my rule. You will be able to pass down all the wealth and honor that seat brings for generations to come."

"You can't tempt me with wealth and power. My father's inheritance will suit me just fine. I do not wish for his position." Klemens finished wiping his mouth with a napkin and tossed it carelessly down on the table.

"Or you can die." Bachman narrowed his gaze at Klemens. "I don't require two hostages, and I can always find another military man to fill your shoes. Your choice."

Katja's breath seized. Klemens had less leverage than she did. He had to tread lightly.

"Verishten curse you, Bachman!" Klemens violently knocked his dishes from the table, which hit the floor with an echoing clatter. He was on his feet, red and breathing hard. It was admirable to see that he wasn't going to sit down and take the kanzler's threats, but now was not the time for flexing muscle. Katja met his eyes and shook her head slowly in warning. Bachman was as still as a statue, watching him. Guards and servants stood on high alert.

Finally, Bachman ordered, "See our young guest to his quarters. He needs more time to formulate a proper answer."

His men approached Klemens, who swiftly turned and stormed out with the guards following close behind. The servants stepped out as well, leaving Katja alone in the dining room with Bachman. Her heart pounded in her throat.

Katja gave Bachman a pleading look, and he responded, "Not to worry, I don't plan on killing him yet. He is a smart lad and will come around."

After a sigh of relief, she asked, "What is going to happen to me once you get what you want?"

"Well, that all depends on what the people demand of their new leader and how much they hated the previous one. My guess is that they will call for the heads of the Führer, his pretty young wife, and his daughter. I will have to oblige them. I hope you understand," Bachman said with regret in his voice. Katja closed her eyes and took a deep breath as Bachman poured himself some wine. "Of course, I'd sooner just wed you."

He rose from his chair and walked over to where Katja sat. Planting his husky frame on the table next to her, Bachman took hold of her chin, turning her head to look at him. "I consider myself a traditionalist. I'm hoping the people think similarly. If we return to an Age of Kings, you will be the sole heiress to the throne of Deschner. My claim to that throne would be better supported if we were bonded in marriage. So, we'll just have to wait and see."

Bachman let go of her face, drank his entire glass of wine in one gulp, and set it down on the table beside Katja's. She heard a rumbling belch from under his breath upon swallowing, and it made her want to retch. *I would rather be executed before the people of Ingleheim than marry this repulsive man.*

"May I retire to my quarters, Herr Kanzler?" she asked, wanting to get as far away from him as possible.

"Yes, you may." Bachman moved aside so she could stand. "If there is anything you need to make your stay here more comfortable, don't hesitate to let me or Begitta know."

"That is very kind of you. The accommodations are satisfactory, though I would greatly appreciate some paper and pencils to be provided to me."

"I didn't provide such things because they could be used to pass messages along that may undermine our plans. I hope you understand," Bachman said while walking her out of the dining room.

"You can have every page counted and every picture inspected for all I care. I need to draw something to occupy my time and stave off thoughts of self-harm. I sense some dreary days ahead of me. I hope *you* understand."

"Begitta has already removed anything from your room that could be used to . . . take yourself out of the equation. However, I'd hate to cause you any more misery than necessary under the circumstances. Let me see what I can arrange."

"Thank you, Herr Kanzler."

By the following morning, Katja woke to a sketchpad and some charcoal pencils on her nightstand. The relief upon seeing them was almost overwhelming.

Now to plan our escape.

19
A WRETCH IN THE SLUMS

While holed up in the lavish estate of Kanzler Bachman, Katja kept herself occupied by drawing. To cast minimal suspicion, she drew various items from around her bedroom, the most important being a detailed rendition of a crystal golem eye. Begitta looked at her drawings during her daily rounds. Once, she had asked what the drawing of the golem eye was, and Katja simply told her the truth. Her attention to detail had impressed the woman, but there was nothing that tipped her off to Katja's plans.

On the fourth day, early in the morning, Begitta delivered an invitation from the kanzler. It read:

> *Kriemhilde II of Deschner. Please do me the honor of accompanying me to an early dinner tonight. I have pressing news to share with you and Herr Klemens.*

Katja put the letter aside and shook her head. They were prisoners and yet Bachman still felt the need to send written invitations for dinner when he could just send someone to retrieve her. *I suppose he wasn't kidding when he said he was a traditionalist,* she thought.

Her spine tingled at the thought of what Bachman's 'pressing' news might be. Whatever it was, it wouldn't be good. They had to make their escape tonight.

As much as Katja wished she could wear the comfortable blouse and skirt she came with, it would appear odd if she wore such casual attire to a high-status dinner. If today was the day of her escape, she might as well leave with the nicest dress she could find that wasn't too cumbersome. She put on a vintage gown of soft magenta. The fabric and beads were dyed darker on the bodice but faded gradually down the length of the layered skirts. She recognized the work of the famous dressmaker, Frau Ottilie of Deschner, with the low-cut bodice that exposed the shoulders but left the arms adequately covered. The old-fashioned belled sleeves of magenta and white lace also served well in hiding the rolled-up picture of the golem eye.

She was just pinning a jeweled hair net around her elaborate updo when Begitta came to collect her. "Come, fraulein, best not to keep the kanzler waiting."

In the dining room, the men greeted her once again. She hadn't seen Klemens since the last dinner, and it wasn't until now that she was certain he was still alive. He appeared to be nursing a few more facial bruises, courtesy of the guards that had escorted him to his room the night of their arrival, Katja guessed.

When he gave the formal hand greeting, Katja said, "I'm glad to see you well, Klem." She rose to kiss him on the cheek, using the opportunity to whisper in his ear. "Follow my lead."

She then greeted the kanzler and took her seat as before. String musicians played once again, but the cello remained unplayed for the time being. Perfect, she thought with relief.

The meal was served and was as impressive as the last. Despite her nervousness, Katja dove in and ate as much as she could. She didn't know how long it would be until her next meal. Looking to her, Klemens ate heartily as well.

After swallowing his grouse quite audibly, Bachman ended their idle chit chat to speak of why they were all there. "Last night, my men took the Fortress of Mortlach. Currently rebel forces hold it, and the Führer is—well, as you can imagine, rather incensed."

"Does he know that you have us hostage?" Katja asked.

"He knows the Kings' Remnants have you hostage, yes." Bachman grinned proudly. "And so far, there is no sign of him commanding legions of war golems to retake the fortress. It would appear everything is going according to plan."

"I'm curious," Katja began. "How did the Kings' Remnants find out who I was?"

"Heinrich was never foolish enough to reveal your alias when you went off to university," stated Bachman. "I had to find that out from my trusted general."

"Rudiger?" Katja's eyes widened. *Who could Rudiger have been in contact with that knew my identity other than Ignatius?* She wondered to herself.

"Yes, he is Steinkamp-trained and excellent at uncovering sensitive information. He was the one who arranged to have Gershlon Reborn help us take the fortress."

"And you never asked him how he found out about me?"

"Oh, I did. He said his contact at the university told him. I assumed he meant Herr Ignatius." Bachman continued eating.

Nobody at the university would have her identity on file. All students were personally vetted with Kanzler Gustaf of Nordenhein and the Führer. That meant Rudiger's contact was either Gustaf himself or the professor. She felt sick to her stomach and couldn't finish her meal. Could the professor have unwittingly expressed his suspicion of her parentage to Rudiger at some point, or was Kanzler Gustaf a secret rebel too?

Katja decided she'd learned as much as she was going to. It was time for her to make her move.

As soon as the violinists finished their song, she said, "You know, I used to play the cello rather well. If it's all right with you, dear Kanzler, I could play a little for you tonight."

Bachman's eyes twinkled with delight. "The cello was your mother's favorite. I can't refuse you. Go on, then!"

Bachman shooed the other musicians away and motioned for her to sit at the stool. Klemens gave her a nervous glance as she took her seat and set the cello in front of her. Swallowing the lump in her throat, she began playing a random song from memory to work up the necessary courage.

After a few minutes of stalling, she finally forced herself to start playing the *Ode to Golems*, but only the notes. At the table, Klemens glistened with sweat, but Bachman didn't notice, too enraptured by Katja's playing. It brought her some relief that he didn't appear to recognize the song. As she neared the last bar, she looked to Klemens again, who gave her an encouraging nod. She began the song over, but this time with the words.

As Katja sang she did everything she could not to look at the crystal golems at the entryway, focusing instead on everyone else's tranquil expressions.

"*. . . Golem, hear me, I am you,*" Katja sang the last bar.

The chandeliers above the dining table started to rattle, and the dinnerware on the table began to vibrate. Everyone except Katja and Klemens looked around nervously. All of a sudden, the entire dining room shuddered, and the golems guarding the entrance stepped out from the wall. Large pieces of the marble pillars surrounding the golems broke off with a deafening crack. Paintings shook from the walls and glass vases shattered upon the floor.

The servants screamed and the guards rushed to defend them from the two crystal giants coming to life. A guard moved toward Katja, but she swung the heavy cello low and knocked him off his feet. She pushed past the stunned kanzler and hopped onto the dining table where she took Klemens's hand to join her.

When they got close to one of the golems, a bright yellow light shone from its iridescent torso. They both covered their eyes as the light flashed so bright the guards, servants, and Bachman screamed in pain. Klemens and Katja opened their eyes, relieved to have avoided the initial blinding flash. She grabbed his shoulder and forced him to duck beside her. The golem's long spindly arm swung over their heads and came crashing down on the guards to the right side of the table, then again upon the guards to the left.

"What's happening? Find the hostages!" the addled kanzler roared.

Everyone blindly stumbled about with their hands in front of them. The other golem sped across the chamber and bashed more guards against the wall while defenseless servants ducked under the table or crawled out the side doors.

Katja shoved her hand up her sleeve and pulled out the parchment. She presented the picture of the eye to the golem closest to them. Its yellow light flashed faintly then dimmed before burning brightly within its chest. It turned its back to the researchers and leaned forward, placing its weight upon its arms while flashing another light beam at the approaching guards flooding in from the atrium.

"Get on!" Katja grabbed Klemens by the arm.

Klemens cursed as the two made a running leap off the dining room table and onto the golem's polished back. There were enough crystal clusters sprouting from its spine and shoulders for them to hold onto. The golem rose to a standing position and quickly dealt with the blinded guards blocking its path with a swift kick, sending them hurtling back into the atrium.

Bones crunched and men screamed as the golem plowed past the guards.

It had not been Katja's intention for anyone to get hurt, but she hadn't the time to work out the kinks in her plan. She was not in control of the golem, but she did expect it to take them far from Bachman's estate, toward its Alpha at the Crystal Lake of Rainmier.

As soon as the gangly behemoths entered the atrium, every man-sized golem acting as railings up the winding five-story staircase instantly came to life. Cracking stone and shattering crystal sounded from above as they broke free from the banisters. Shards of crystal rained down from the stairway with dozens of golems to follow. Some of their legs broke apart on impact with the ground, but many remained intact enough for their limbs to form piercingly sharp edges.

They impaled the guards left standing upon their sword-like appendages, blood staining the iridescent crystal. Katja gaped in horror at all the destruction, and she prayed the giant golems would soon leave and take all the smaller ones with them.

"The Führer must be doing this! How did he find out I had his daughter?" Bachman bellowed as he entered the atrium. His sight had finally returned as well as that of the other guards from the dining room. "Don't let them get away!"

The golem carrying the researchers continued toward the main castle doors, picking up pace as it prepared to break through. Katja and Klemens held on tight, positioning themselves fully behind the golem's back to avoid injury. The golem barreled through the tall crystal doors with a deafening crash. Chunks of the golem's body broke off, some of its shards cutting the exposed skin of Katja's shoulders and back.

It continued through the front courtyard of the castle with guards giving chase. Several sentries came to intercept. They could do nothing to stop the crystal juggernauts.

Another flash of light filled the courtyard, blinding more men. The surviving guards from the atrium had learned their lesson, dropping their visors down and remaining relatively unaffected. They threw a flurry of spears at the golem, piercing its long spindly legs, but could do nothing to stop its forward momentum. It barreled through the line of guards and then the gates, continuing down the path toward the City of Untevar.

Just when Katja began to believe their escape assured, two chains shot out across the golem's path. The rebel Steinkamp soldiers appeared on each side of the road leading to the city, their chain-linked splitting blades embedded in the trees that lined the path. They had already detached the ends of the chains from their dispensers and tied them around the tree trunks so they wouldn't give way. The golem did not slow down or otherwise move to avoid the obstruction.

"Stop!" Katja screamed at the golem.

Not heeding her pleas, the golem tripped. The chains bit into its spindly legs while grinding away the bark of the trees. It fell forward and Katja and Klemens screamed, ducking and rolling as they met the ground.

Following closely behind, the other golem halted before reaching the chain. One of the Steinkamp quickly stepped behind it and ran around its legs with a long strand of earth bindings. The bindings turned to crystal, fusing its legs into one. As it tried to lunge forward, the golem fell onto its hands and knees beside its companion.

Meanwhile, the other Steinkamp used his circular wind blade to chip away at the first golem's fragile legs. It didn't take long before one of the legs shattered from repeated strikes and the golem collapsed further. The Steinkamp ran in front of it with his crossbow loaded and primed. On its hands and knees, the golem flashed its light beam. Klemens and Katja closed their eyes just in time, but when they opened them, to their dismay, they found the Steinkamp unfazed.

The crossbow bolt hit the golem square in the eye, and its light extinguished. The other Steinkamp tried to stab the second giant's eye with his sword, but before he got too close, the golem managed to break apart the crystal bindings around its legs and rise to its feet. It knocked the Steinkamp several feet away with a swing of its angular arm.

By this time, Katja and Klemens had recovered from their tumble and ran toward the standing golem. She reached into her sleeve only to find nothing. Her heart sank. *The golem eye picture fell out!*

Grabbing each other at the same time, Katja and Klemens dove to the side and closed their eyes, avoiding the blinding light and the long crystal arm about to bash them into the ground. The crack of the arm shattering on impact reverberated through the air. They tried to crawl away as the glass giant stomped toward them. Right then, a Steinkamp's wind blade ricocheted between each leg until both shattered at the knees. The man climbed upon the helpless golem's torso and jammed his sword into its eye.

The researchers were now at the mercy of the one Steinkamp left standing.

"You're coming back with me, fraulein," he said gruffly.

The researchers rose to their feet and backed toward the edge of the road.

"Stay back. As you have seen, I am a Golem Mage just like my father, and I will—"

"You'll what? There are no golems around for you to play with now." He took out his earth bindings and pulled them taut. A short distance away, the other Steinkamp returned to his feet. While holding his side, he began limped toward them. *I just need to stall them long enough for—*

The horde of smaller golems raced around and leaped over the fallen giants on the road. Katja and Klemens dove into the bushes as the string of crystal bodies crashed into the two Steinkamp. Scrambling back up to their feet, the researchers ran for the city without looking back.

They could see the bustling thoroughfare in the distance, but it proved to be much farther away than it appeared. Eventually the Steinkamp would get away from the man-sized golems and catch up with them.

"We need to get off the main road," she said breathlessly.

They found a man-made ravine on the left side of the street where water flowed down into the lower levels of the city.

"Kat," Klemens wheezed, "I can't—"

"This way!"

She grabbed him by the arm and dragged him off the road. Without hesitation, they hopped into the ravine and onto a sidewalk beside the small stream. Klemens cried out as he landed hard upon the stone. "Agh! My ankle!"

"You're all right," she muttered as they hurried along. Soon the downward sloping sidewalk turned to steps, which they took in stride.

The two of them eventually had to catch their breaths. The bustling activity of the city was within earshot. They were almost there, but Klemens's ankle had started to swell.

"I think I strained it from that tumble off the golem's back." He winced while hopping up and down on one foot.

"Well, stopping is not an option."

They were about to set off again when they heard voices and heavy footsteps on the roadway above.

"You, take the lower level. They may have come down the ravine," said a man. He didn't sound like either of the Steinkamp, so he must have been one of Bachman's guards. In response to the guard's order, more footsteps rushed back westward.

"They're going to come down here. We have to keep moving." Katja pulled on Klemens's sleeve.

"Not with my ankle. I'll slow you down, and they'll capture us for sure."

"They'll capture us anyway if we wait here." Katja heard the heavy boots coming closer. They would soon be at the steps.

"You are going to run, and I am going to provide a distraction."

"Don't be stupid, you'll die if you return to the kanzler." Katja's voice broke.

"You've risked your life to save mine more than once. Let me do this for you."

"I won't let you die for me, Klemens." She clutched his sleeve tighter.

"I'll be fine," he said. "I'll take Bachman's offer and do whatever he asks in order to stay alive. I promise."

"If you die, I'll kill you!"

Klemens quickly took hold of Katja's face. "I'm sorry for everything that's happened. I love you, Kat, I've always loved you. Promise me you'll make it out of here—"

"Klem, don't—" Katja shook her head repeatedly back and forth, tears welling up in her eyes.

He let her go as the footsteps came closer. "As soon as they start chasing me, you run like mad, okay?"

She nodded and finally released his shirt. After a second or two of hesitation, Klemens ran around the corner and out of sight.

With a deep breath, Katja bolted in the opposite direction and ran as fast as she could toward the thoroughfare. Guards shouted and Klemens cried out. Tears flooded out of Katja's eyes, but she pressed on without looking back. She ran until she found another hiding spot under a small archway supporting the sidewalks of the upper level of town.

Upon catching her breath and seeing nobody following her, she continued along the lower street level next to the waterway, keeping close to the wall. Passersby gave her strange looks as she went. *I need to find something to cover myself,* she thought.

She eventually found a cloak left behind on a bench. It was heavily stained with ash and dirt, but she didn't have the luxury of being choosy. It was a man's cloak and large enough to cover most of her gown. She ventured into the upper levels of the city and blended in with the droves of citizenry going this way and that. She was still in a poor area—like most areas—so she had to be inconspicuous.

It took a while for Katja to find her bearings and figure out the direction of Deschner's north road. On her way to what she hoped was the right road, a short, heavyset man bumped her. While she attempted to recover from almost being knocked down, someone else came up behind her and pulled off her cloak. She gasped and spun around in anticipation of seeing Bachman's Steinkamp, but it was somebody else.

"That's a pretty dress you have on there," leered a tall man wearing a worn-out top hat and shoulder cape over long, filthy, dark hair. He stroked his greasy unwashed stubble as he casually approached and presented Katja with her cloak. Katja reached for it, but the man quickly moved it away from her. He chuckled huskily, revealing yellow, cracked teeth as he grinned. Katja's heart raced.

"Why's a girl like you got to cover up?"

"Keep it." She turned to rush away, instead she came face to face with the short stocky man who had first bumped her. He had a paunchy face with a bushy mustache and wore similar attire to his taller counterpart.

"You got schlepts, don't you, pretty fraulein?" the pudgy man asked.

She tore off the hair net that had tiny gemstones sewn into it. "Here, take this, now leave me be." She tried to run, but the other man stepped in front of her.

"Anything for me?"

"I don't have any schlepts with me."

"That's a shame. Bet that dress is worth a mighty sum, though." His eyes moved up and down the length of her.

The sun caused a shimmer, drawing her attention to a dagger in his right hand. Without a second thought, she darted in the only direction afforded to her, which happened to be a dark, underused alleyway. *Stupid, stupid idiot, this is exactly where they want you to go!* Glancing back, she found the two men following close behind, snickering all the while. Running frantically through the alley, she searched for an exit.

"Why are you running away? We just want to chat," the muggers taunted.

Katja pushed over a large bin of refuse, spilling it into the alley. Finally, she found her way to a crowded thoroughfare where she could attempt to lose her pursuers. Every face appeared more downtrodden and sickly than the last, and she realized she was no safer in this busy street than she was in the alley.

Glancing behind her again, Katja saw the robbers pushing their way through the crowd to get to her. They were more determined than she'd hoped they'd be. Masses of people congregated around her as she tried to push through them. Some of them reached for her, begging for schlepts and food.

"Please, frau, my babies are hungry, please." A haggard, middle-aged woman pulled on Katja's bell sleeve.

"I'm sorry, I can't help you," Katja cried.

She pulled so hard to get away from the woman the lace of her sleeve ripped. A flurry of outstretched hands came at her, and she suddenly couldn't find a way through the droves of vagabonds. They pulled on the fabric of Katja's gown, and one unknown woman among them even slapped her across the face.

"Highborn whore!" the woman screeched.

"*Schlepts—*"

"*Help us!*"

"*Bitch!*"

Katja heard her own screams among the slurs. There was just a blur of angry faces, and she could no longer tell one from the other. They grabbed at her, tugging her in one direction and then another.

"Let go of me!" Katja shrieked.

There were no city guards or Karlmen in sight to restore order. It was pure chaos in the streets, just as Kanzler Bachman had intended.

They will kill me, Katja thought. *I will die here like a wretch in the slums.*

That terrifying thought was further cemented into her mind at the sight of the tall robber in the top hat approaching. His knife was fully visible, ready to slice her open in the middle of the street. So many people around her, and not a single one would intervene. *They will watch me get gutted in the streets, and they will glorify it. And why shouldn't they? I am just a highborn whore to them.*

"No! Get away!" Katja struggled violently against various hands that shoved her down to her knees. The man in the top hat came even closer, flashing his rotting yellow grin.

Then a sharp *zing* followed by a cracking sound.

A bloody crossbow bolt poked out through the robber's larynx. Dark blood poured down his chest, and he collapsed face first onto the cobblestones. Everyone around him recoiled, but those holding Katja didn't let go. She struggled again only to find the man and woman holding onto her each collapse into a pool of blood. She hardly had a chance to contemplate this grisly turn of events when a black-clad arm seized her from behind and roughly dragged her off. Another Steinkamp soldier appeared in front of her and sliced away a vagabond that tried to grab her gown. The rest of the crowd dispersed in a blink of an eye.

The first Steinkamp carried her off so quickly she couldn't track where he was taking her. Katja's heart beat violently in her throat, and her arms and legs shook. Klemens's sacrifice had been in vain, and Bachman would likely kill him once she was secure in his grasp again. *I almost made it.*

The Steinkamp tied Katja's wrists so tight the skin broke and bled as the bindings molded to it. This time, they would not be gentle with her. They started walking her back through the city toward Bachman's castle. The gruff one led her by the bindings, and the other, with a limping gait, walked closely behind. A third Steinkamp sidled up to her left.

"Comrade, why are you back so soon?" Limping Steinkamp said to the one who'd just appeared.

Gruff Steinkamp asked, "I thought you were supposed to report to Rudiger after the old man's arrest?"

The third Steinkamp shook his head.

A sudden rage swept through Katja, and she lashed out at the third Steinkamp before he could answer. "How could you betray us? We trusted you!"

Gruff Steinkamp ordered Katja to shut up, but she ignored him. "At least tell me that Ignatius still lives," she demanded. The third man remained silent, enraging Katja even more. "Answer me, you bastard! You protected us for two months. Does that not mean anything to you?"

"That's it," said Gruff.

The team ducked into an alley and Gruff roughly pushed her down onto her knees. She cried out in pain as the bindings tore at her bleeding wrists. Limpy stayed back to prevent anyone else from coming into the alley.

"I'm definitely knocking you out this time." Gruff took his cudgel in hand.

With no means of protecting her head, all Katja could do was close her eyes, cringing in anticipation of a sound blow. She heard a crack, but it was not the cracking of her skull. Her eyes snapped open to find the silent Steinkamp having just struck the other one's head with the cudgel that should have hit her. Gruff's mask flew off, revealing the startled face of a middle-aged man that turned bloody as the silent Steinkamp bashed him against a wall and drove a dagger through his eye.

In a fluid motion, the silent soldier yanked his knife out of the man's face, spun around, and threw it at the other one coming up behind him. Limpy deflected it with a swing of his retractable blade. Grabbing the sword from Gruff's body as it collapsed, the silent one extended it, as well as his own.

Both soldiers slashed and blocked with their blades. The silent Steinkamp used one blade to block his opponent's flurry of attacks and drove the other upward through his lower abdomen. As Limpy doubled over, the silent Steinkamp drove the secondary blade through the top of his shoulder. He yanked the two blades free, and sliced Limpy apart, blood spraying against the building wall.

Katja clasped her hands over her mouth to keep from vomiting. She wanted to run, but her exhaustion kept her on her knees. The Steinkamp left standing flicked the blood from his two blades, retracted them, and placed them both at his back.

He then turned to Katja. She couldn't see his face or hear his voice, but she felt his steel gaze through his mask, and it penetrated her to the bone. It was in the way he stood, the way he breathed, the way he moved with such intent. Katja was immediately drawn into his dark presence. From that feeling alone she knew, beyond a doubt, the identity of the man looking at her from behind the black mesh. She was chagrined for not seeing it before.

"S-Sigurd."

20
REGARD FOR HUMAN LIFE

Sigurd couldn't believe his luck. There was Katja, standing before him, bound and stunned, but unharmed. *If I had been one second later...*

In her presence again, he was unprepared for how elated he would be, even under such dire circumstances. Not able to wait a moment longer, Sigurd pulled off his mask and hood. "Katja."

Relief flowed visibly through her body as she held her bound wrists out to him.

"Are you all right?" He strode over and unmolded the bindings from her raw flesh. "I'll take you to my horse, I have some bandages in my saddle bag."

Katja's hands shook. Their eyes met, and where Sigurd expected to see relief or gratitude, he saw only a fierce amber blaze, followed by a bracing slap across the face.

"You should have been here!"

"I'm here now."

Another slap came across Sigurd's other cheek.

"If you had never left they would never have taken us. You should have been here!" Katja moved to slap Sigurd a third time, but he stopped her. "Let go of me!" She pounded against his armored chest with her free hand.

Grabbing hold of both her wrists to keep her from hitting him, Sigurd pulled her into his arms. He felt her resistance, but he didn't let her go. He held her there, taking in her scent, sweet even when disguised in sweat and ash. It made him regret leaving her dorm room two months ago, even more than he already did. "I found you," he breathed. Katja exhaled heavily, her body finally relaxing against his. He released her, cupped her face in his hands, and leaned in to kiss her.

She responded with a hard shove. "Don't think you can just pick up where you left off!"

Sigurd stepped back. "Katja, I—"

"What are even doing here?"

"I was on my way to the Untevar Karl precinct to determine which road you'd be taken down on your way to Deschner. Then an angry mob drew my attention, and Verishten be good, who do I find but you right in the thick of it. I found a vantage point to shoot down your most immediate threat, but before I could retrieve you—"

"Wait." Katja shook her head in bewilderment. "You knew about my arrest?"

Sigurd pulled out the warrant from his back pocket and handed it to her.

"Where did you get this?" Katja asked.

"Your father gave it to me."

"My father—?"

"Wolfram."

"For Verishten's sake, Sigurd," Katja groaned. "Kapitän Wolfram is not my father!"

"That's not what he says. I already know he has a daughter named Kriemia, and he told me she's you right before I could kill him. He said you were under arrest for treason, so I came all this way to stop that from happening." He gestured to the dead men on the ground. "Then I find you being carried off by rebel Steinkamp. Obviously, you're someone important, so if Wolfram's not your father, who is?"

Katja continued to study the warrant, ignoring his heated inquiry. "This warrant is in the name of my alias and somehow from that Wolfram determined my true identity?"

"Clearly he knows your father. He named his daughter the same name, after all."

"Wolfram knows my father, but he does not know me. Nobody knows my university alias, not even my father's closest allies." Katja hugged herself, tucking the paper in the crook of her elbow.

"How can that be?"

"Because my father . . ." Katja's gaze drifted away from Sigurd. ". . . is the Führer."

Sigurd turned away from her and dragged his hands down his face. He had only briefly feared the possibility Katja could be related to the Führer, but never did he think it could be true.

Memories of Katja flashed through his mind—her disregard for expressing dangerous opinions, her apparent lack of fear of the Regime, her sense of entitlement that annoyed him from the beginning—it was all coming together. He felt sick to his stomach. All this time, everything he felt for Katja, everything he had done for her, was all for the daughter of the worst mass murderer in Ingleheim's history.

"So you're telling me that I could have let you get arrested, and you would have been just fine?" he said quietly, his jaw clenching.

"Yes," Katja began, "but the rebellion found me first. Apparently Rudiger discovered my true identity as well. How do you think that happened?"

"I don't know." Sigurd threw up his arms.

The sound of rapid footsteps echoed down the street near the alleyway. Not wanting to wait around to find out to whom the footsteps belonged, Sigurd grabbed Katja's hand while stuffing the warrant into his pocket. The pair avoided being seen as they found Sigurd's black steed waiting in another alley. He pulled her onto the horse behind him, and they rode through the least used streets and eventually exited the city without pursuit.

A mile or two outside of the city limits, Katja abruptly said, "Turn around. We have to go back."

"Why?" Sigurd halted the horse but didn't turn around.

"I need you to help me free Klemens from the Kings' Remnants." Katja filled Sigurd in on everything that happened to her in the past few days.

Sigurd shook his head. "We can't risk it. It's too late for him."

Katja shuddered behind him. "How can you say that? If it were me still imprisoned there, you would take the risk to get me out—wouldn't you?"

"Well, yes. But, that's different."

"How is that different?"

"Since you escaped, Bachman's security will be on high alert. It would be hard enough for me to infiltrate a kanzler's castle on my own in the best of times, but now it will be next to impossible."

"You are a Steinkamp!" Katja wailed as she jumped down from the horse in protest. "Nothing should be impossible. You already killed his Steinkamp. The golems slaughtered or injured a few dozen guards. His castle's in disrepair. There is no better time to infiltrate it."

Sigurd pointed to his own chest. "My priority right now is getting you out of rebel territory."

"You have the means to help him, but you choose not to. And to think I named Klemens the coward."

"Katja, get back on the horse!" He seethed. However, she was right in that rescuing Klemens was within his means, but doing so would put her in further danger and also give Wolfram a greater chance of either escaping or starving to death. He couldn't waste a single day in getting back to him.

"I don't know why I'm surprised," Katja continued. "I keep forgetting that you have no regard for human life."

Sigurd jumped down from the saddle and stormed toward her.

She backed away, so he stopped short. "I have a regard for yours. Can't that be enough?"

"If it weren't for Klemens sacrificing his freedom for mine, I would have been captured long before you found me on those streets. If you have such a regard for my life, then have a regard for his . . . please." Her bottom lip quivered.

"I cannot save him and keep you safe at the same time."

"Fine. If you won't help me, I am left with no choice but to go to the Karl and turn myself in. They will take me back to Deschner where my father will free me, and I can warn him of Bachman's betrayal."

Katja turned away and started walking back toward the city. Sigurd rushed over to her and grabbed her arm. "You're not going anywhere."

"That is not your choice to make. Unhand me!" she screeched.

"The Karl in Untevar are likely working for Bachman. They will sooner take you back to him than the Führer."

"Then I will return to Deschner on my own."

Katja tried to walk past him, but he held her fast. "Take a second to think, woman! If I were the Kaiser, I'd pretend to still hold you hostage, while I sent every man in my employ to intercept you on any of the roads to Deschner. Even if you manage to get past them, Klemens will be killed as soon as Bachman receives word you are safe."

"Not if I convince my father to negotiate."

"The Führer may risk his regime for his daughter, but he will do no such thing for your research partner."

"He is the son of Kanzler Volker. He and my father were very close—"

"Trust me, Katja. The Führer didn't care to rescue Volker from the Remnants before. Why would he do so for his son?"

"What do you know about what my father did or didn't do for Volker?"

"Because I carried out his order to kill him!" Sigurd shouted over her.

"What?" Katja recoiled from Sigurd in disgust. "It was you?"

It made his gut wrench and his heart sink simultaneously for Katja to look at him in such a way.

"For Verishten's sake." Katja clutched her head with both hands and pulled at her hair. "Who *haven't* you killed?"

"I've killed a lot of people."

"I know that. But . . . Klemens's father?"

"I didn't know he was Klemens's father, and it was not my duty to care. My orders were clear. Volker was a security risk that the Führer was not going to tolerate. He had to die," said Sigurd.

"He was not some assignment, Sigurd—he was a man! You killed Volker, and now you condemn his son to the same fate."

"I don't owe you an explanation. You already know exactly why I am the way I am. It's time for you to recognize that I am not the one you should be afraid of. The man you call father has more blood on his hands than any Steinkamp can ever imagine. He is the reason I was created. It is because of *him* that the rebellion is after you, and it is he who has condemned Herr Klemens to death." Sigurd shook his head and huffed. "For your entire life, you lived under the roof of the Regime's most bloodthirsty killer, but it is me, a single foot-soldier, that disgusts you?"

"Not you, Sigurd. I am disgusted by everything else!" Katja wailed. "The lies, the cruelty. I hate that this regime has to create men like you to do its awful bidding and that you never had a choice. For six years, I've tried to be anyone other than the Führer's daughter, but you were right. We cannot hide from who we truly are."

"And who are you?"

"Right now? I'm just a woman who doesn't want to lose another person she cares about."

"I'm sorry, Katja, but Klemens is a weak bargaining tool. It's you Bachman wants. If he gets his hands on you, Klemens is dead. If you return home, Klemens is dead."

Katja's legs gave way beneath her. She doubled over with her hands holding her stomach as if she were going to throw up. "There is no hope for him, is there? I won't accept it. I can't. Ignatius, Klemens, I can't lose them both. Oh, Klem . . ." Broken sobs kept her from continuing.

An uncomfortable thought came to Sigurd as he listened to her sorrowful murmurs. It hadn't even occurred to him that during his absence, Katja and Klemens may have become more than research partners, more than friends. Such a thought suddenly made him ill. This feeling alone proved that even after finding out Katja was the daughter of the man who had orchestrated the nightmare that shattered his world, it was only through her that he could ever hope to put it back together again. He would do anything to spare her heartache even if that meant he would have to let her go for good.

Sigurd crouched down and took her gently by the shoulders, helping her sit upright. "Do you love Herr Klemens? Is he the man you want?"

"I do love him," Katja sniffed. "But he does not possess my heart. You took that with you when you left."

Sigurd didn't know how to respond other than to stand back up. "Leaving your room that night was harder for me than . . ." He swallowed, almost unable to get the words out. "The time I spent in your service was the greatest month of my entire life."

"But you left anyway," Katja dismissed. "So it couldn't have meant *that* much."

Sigurd wanted to object, but when he opened his mouth, nothing came out. What could he say to convince her of how much she meant to him? How could he tell her that her light shone so bright, to look into it was too painful?

"We must press on," was the only reply Sigurd could give. He mounted his steed and offered a hand to Katja, who still kneeled on the ground. She looked up at him with tears pooling in her eyes.

"Where is there to go?"

"I'm taking you home, Katja. It is where you will be safest, and where you can do what you can to stop the coming war."

"But Klem—"

"If Herr Klemens is still alive, I promise to do all in my power to keep him that way. Now let's go."

21
BRAIN, THROAT, HEART, AND SPINE

I must be mad, Sigurd thought as he and Katja galloped through Untevar's wilderness. It would take more than a day to reach the City of Deschner if they rode through the night and another three to return to Kapitän Wolfram. He would have to add another few days to save Klemens. There was no way around it. He had made a promise to Katja, and he would follow it through, even if it meant that Wolfram would get away. *If Verishten is just, he will starve sitting in his own excrement before he finds a way to escape,* he hoped.

Late into the afternoon they came upon a part of the River Sleban that marked the border of Untevar into Deschner Mountain Range. Sigurd left Katja to rest and water the horse while he went ahead on foot to scout the crossing. As he feared, the bridge was heavily trafficked with Untevar soldiers. Though he had done his best to reach the bridge swiftly, even a Steinkamp was no match for the most talented messengers. Word had reached the kanzler's men at the crossing, and now getting to Deschner would be that much harder.

Sigurd returned to Katja with the distressing news. "We can't cross the bridge." Katja cursed, and he continued, looking out over the river, "We can still cross on our own and travel further north into Deschner before turning back south toward the city. It will add several more hours to our journey, but it's better than getting caught."

"So when you say '*cross on our own,*' you mean . . ."

"We're going in." Sigurd nodded then went to look for an adequate crossing point. Not giving Katja a chance to argue, he added, "Before we cross, though, it would be a good idea for you to leave the gown behind. It will weigh you down."

"Take my dress off?" she huffed. "I will do no such thing."

"We don't have time for this. The dress goes, or you don't."

She groaned. "Fine. Turn around, then."

He did so, taking the opportunity to refill his canteen in the river. After a few moments, he heard Katja huffing and puffing behind him with such exasperation, he turned to see her fumbling with the overabundance of ties connecting her bodice to her corset.

"I had a handmaid to help me get this thing on before." She grunted then sheepishly motioned Sigurd over with her head. "Will you?"

As soon as Katja turned her back to him, he noticed the hairline cuts all over her shoulders. He grazed his fingers lightly over them.

"The ribbons and connectors are on the bodice, Sigurd," Katja reminded.

He pulled on a few ribbons, but none would budge. He didn't have the patience to figure out which ribbon tied where. Growling under his breath, he took his knife, slashed the crisscrossing ties down the middle and tore apart Katja's bodice to reveal the cream-colored corset beneath.

She spun around. "What did you do? This is a vintage Frau Ottilie!"

"Spare me the history of the gown and strip."

Katja grumbled as he turned back around.

Since they wouldn't be able to take it across the raging river with them, Sigurd sent his horse away, hoping it would throw off any pursuers. He then aimed his splitting blade dispenser at the largest and closest tree on the other side of the river and pulled the lever. The blade shot out and burrowed cleanly into the tree's trunk. The chain was taut and just long enough to clear the body of water. A moment later Katja came up behind him and apprehensively wrapped her arms around his torso.

"Are you ready?" he asked.

"No, but I wasn't ready to jump into that snow-filled valley with you either, and that turned out all right."

With a nod, he marched into the River Sleban with Katja clinging to him. She squealed when the cold rapids flowed through her underclothes and shivered against his back. Even through his insulated uniform, he could sense the water's coolness. The rapids picked up as the two reached the middle of the river, and soon both of them were off their feet. Katja's grip tightened around his chest as the water rushed over their heads. Sigurd had to push up his mask. The water filled it faster than it drained out.

Within a few minutes, the pair was safe across the Sleban. Sigurd grabbed the base of the splitting blade and braced his foot against the tree trunk, tugging and jostling the blade until it broke free from the wood. It was blunted but would still work until he could replace it. After closing the blades back together, Sigurd took a seat on a fallen log to work on winding the chain back into his dispenser via the reel.

While doing so, he caught sight of Katja near the riverbank wringing out the lace of her underskirt. He expected her to be in an even fouler mood than before they crossed, but as she unpinned her drenched hair and whipped it over to one side, her face was alight with a refreshed glow and a smile he thought he'd never see again.

"I see, in order to make you happy, one must strip you of your finery and drag you through the Sleban," Sigurd quipped.

"After everything that happened back in Untevar, I have to admit, I kind of needed that cold, refreshing swim," she exhaled heartily then gathered her hair into a large braid off one shoulder. She had gone into that river an anxious, emotional mess and emerged a relaxed, vibrant woman. *Verishten strike me down, she is beautiful,* he thought.

It didn't take long for Katja to notice his unmasked eyes lingering upon her half-dressed anatomy. "What are you looking at, Steinkamp?" she said in a playful tone.

"I'm looking at you, fraulein." His gaze remained fixed on her as he continued to wind his chain.

"Well, look away." She blushed. Katja turned around and placed her hands over the appropriate places on her body to maintain a modesty long gone by that point. Such futile action only excited Sigurd more.

"That will be difficult, but I will try." And that was the truth. Katja's shape was elegant and irresistibly voluptuous. He imagined her legs wrapped around his waist while he held her against one of the trees and plunged inside her.

Katja cast him a bashful grin and continued to braid her hair, not bothering to move from his line of sight. Sigurd felt like his skin was set aflame underneath his damp uniform. It took everything he had to focus on his task. *Does she feel the same way?* he wondered before his reason quickly took over. *It doesn't matter. There is no time for this!*

After reinserting the splitting blade into its slot, Sigurd slapped his mask back on. "We need to keep moving." He motioned for Katja to follow him northward into the wilderness, trying his best to keep his thoughts on the task at hand and not his hands all about her body. The priority was getting to the nearest village before sundown so Katja could find clothing and he could dry out his uniform.

It was well past dusk when they came upon a quaint little farmhouse in a large clearing. Sigurd went ahead and performed reconnaissance on the property to see an older couple tending to their last chores of the day. They also had livestock consisting of hens, a few cows, and some hogs. Sigurd and Katja needed horses, but the couple had only one mule. It would not do, but they could at least scavenge some food and clothing.

Sigurd returned, crouching in the tall grasses to go over his plan with Katja. "I'll gain access to the house through that side window. Stay where I can see you and when I appear at the window again, signal to me if anyone comes around this side of the house."

"Are you planning on robbing this poor couple?" Katja was aghast. "Haven't you ever heard of asking nicely?"

"I'm not planning on leaving them destitute. I only wish to avoid complications. This couple has likely never seen a Steinkamp soldier before. If I approach them, they would probably run or attempt to defend themselves against what they perceive as a threat."

"That's because you *are* a threat. Maybe just sit this one out."

"What are you planning to do in your damp underthings?"

"Not every problem requires a soldier to solve it. Now take off that uniform."

"My entire uniform, or just—"

"All of it."

"I don't think so." Sigurd shook his head. He wondered if Katja was trying to get back at him for making her take off her fancy dress.

"Take it off. That's an order!"

"*You* don't get to give *me* orders," Sigurd argued, though he wasn't sure to what end.

"I don't see your kapitän anywhere, do you?" Katja looked around as if trying to search for someone. "Therefore, I am taking command. Now strip, comrade."

I should know by now that this woman will get her way no matter what, Sigurd thought as he begrudgingly unstrapped his armored vest.

"Now wait here until I return with further instruction."

"Yes, Frau Kapitän." Sigurd gave her a sarcastic salute.

A proud smirk appeared on Katja's face before she ran off toward the farmhouse. As soon as she approached the old man putting away his tools, Sigurd began to feel the fool.

"Herr! Dear herr, please help us!" she cried frantically. "Bandits came upon my husband and me. They stole everything, even our clothing and threw us in the Sleban!"

The old man immediately called for his wife, and the two of them ushered Katja inside. Sigurd waited in the grass, near nude, feeling cold and ridiculous. Moments later Katja returned wearing a peasant's dress and holding a smock and some trousers for Sigurd.

After putting on the clothes, he left his uniform hidden in the grass and went to introduce himself to the old couple whose names were Otis and Ingrid. They invited him and Katja into their quaint home for tea followed by bread and cheese. The couple set up a spot for them near the hearth to warm themselves. Sigurd couldn't remember the last time he had experienced hospitality—surely not since that family that found him bloody and broken as a child.

"Tell us," Otis began as he offered them both the plate of cheese, "what brings a young couple like yourselves to the Sleban?"

Katja looked at Sigurd briefly before providing a warm reply. "We had to leave our farm in Untevar Range. It has become increasingly difficult to make our living there and we were hoping for better fortune in the City of Deschner."

"How unfortunate that you lost everything to those awful bandits," said Ingrid as she poured everyone their tea.

"Not to worry. I have family in Deschner. Once we get there, we should be all right," Katja continued with her lie.

"Bandits are becoming a real problem, one that the Regime is not quick to rectify these days. Incidents like yours are not uncommon." Otis bit into his cheese.

"Be thankful that you two have come away unharmed," his wife added.

"Yes, were it not for my husband, I fear the bandits would have taken so much more." Katja placed her hand over Sigurd's, and a jolt shot through his spine followed by a warm sensation.

"And what of children?" Ingrid asked as she sipped her tea.

Sigurd could hardly listen to Katja's reply on account of her rubbing his arm affectionately, playing the loving wife while laying out tales of their ordinary peasant life. His heart raced at her touch, and his focus directed firmly upon her. He thought about what it would be like to have Katja as a wife on a small plot of land away from the horrors that currently plagued Ingleheim society. He thought of home in Kensloche and how much he missed running with the herding dogs and breathing in the clean air. He wanted to go back there—to forget about everything, to be something other than a killer. *Men like you don't get to have that.*

"If you'll excuse me for a moment . . ." he muttered, rising from his seat.

"If you're looking for the loo it's on the north side of the property." Otis pointed in that direction with his thumb.

"Th-thanks."

Sigurd went outside to collect his uniform and hung it in the barn to keep the ash from staining it. The night was still, and he could feel the exhaustion of the day weighing on him. He had hardly slept a wink since Breisenburg.

When he returned to the house, Katja was missing. Noticing Sigurd's confusion, Otis said, "She retired for the night, in the extra bed in the loft."

While Otis led him to the ladder that would take him up to join her, he said, "I was just telling your wife that the loft used to be where our son Benedikt slept."

"Where is he now?" Sigurd asked, although he wasn't sure if he should.

Otis's brown eyes darkened as he looked away. Ingrid came up beside her husband and replied, "He ran off to Untevar and joined the rebellion as many young men do in these parts."

"For me and Ingrid not to be branded traitors, we had to disown him. When he returns, we will have to send him away or turn him in. If he ever returns, that is. . . ." Otis put his arm around his wife in comfort.

"I hope that by the time the two of you have children, we will be living in a world where you never have to make such a choice," Ingrid said softly.

"Well . . . my wife and I have not gotten that far yet. Thank you for your kindness, frau. I hope that your son is safe wherever he is." Sigurd gave them a thoughtful smile. He knew many people suffered grievous losses at the hand of the Regime, although he had never given those people any thought until now, so wrapped up in his own loss and pursuit of vengeance. He started to see how selfish that endeavor might be.

He thanked the couple again and said goodnight before climbing the rungs to the loft. There, he found Katja fast asleep in the single bed, never looking more peaceful than she did right then. *At least she doesn't scowl in her sleep,* he thought.

The floor suited Sigurd just fine. He took a pillow that Katja wasn't using and laid himself down on the rug beside the bed. Within a few minutes, Sigurd tossed and turned. The roof was old and rotting in places, making the loft drafty. His uniform usually provided him with all the warmth and comfort required for nights like this, but in the peasant's rags, he felt cold and exposed.

That's it. Move over, Katja, Sigurd thought, no longer willing to tolerate the cold, hard floor.

"Katja. Kat!" he whispered while nudging her.

"Sig. . ." she replied groggily. "Are we leaving?"

"No, no. It's cold in here, and I thought—never mind. Go back to sleep." He once again took his place on the floor.

"What are you doing?"

"Going to sleep."

Katja motioned for Sigurd to get up. "Just get in the bed. You're supposed to be my husband, not my dog."

"As you say, Dear." He smiled with relief and climbed into the tiny bed beside Katja. She turned around and was out cold before he could settle in. With the warmth of her body against his, he felt a comfort never before experienced absent his uniform.

The sound of Katja's breathing and the smell of her hair soon cajoled him off to sleep.

Katja woke up the next morning warm and refreshed. Sigurd slept at her back with his arms around her and his face nuzzled between her shoulder and her neck. With a sigh she settled into his arms, content to never get out of bed again—until Ingrid called from below.

"I hate to wake you two, but breakfast is ready. Otis has cooked us some ham and eggs!"

Sigurd opened his eyes immediately and sat up in bed, excited as a dog about to receive table scraps. Katja's mouth watered even though she had enjoyed a presumably much more extravagant ham a few days prior with Bachman.

After eating heartily, Sigurd and Katja prepared to head out.

"We cannot express how grateful we are for the kindness you've shown us," Katja said at the door. "I wish there was something we can do to repay you."

"Nonsense," Otis said. "It was our pleasure. Perhaps someday when you are back on your feet you would consider paying us another visit."

"We would love that," said Katja as she shook both their hands.

Otis handed Sigurd a sack full of foodstuffs. "Take this. There should be enough food to get you to the City of Deschner and some schlepts for accommodations."

"We can't accept—" Sigurd began.

"Don't you start, young man." Ingrid wagged her finger. "Neither of you are in a state to refuse us." Turning to Katja, she added, "And don't worry about returning the dress, my dear. It no longer fits me the way it used to, so it's all yours."

"Thank you, thank you both," Katja gushed again.

When Otis and Ingrid went back inside the house, Sigurd took her by the hand and snuck into the barn at the edge of the property to collect his uniform. He started to undress so he could put it back on.

"Would it not be better to travel as peasants for a while? The rebels and the Regime are likely looking for a highborn woman with a Steinkamp soldier, not two commoners," Katja suggested.

After some contemplation, Sigurd replied, "Okay, but I will not be as formidable without my uniform."

"In civilian attire, you may not look as frightening, but you will still know how to kill a man, I presume."

"That goes without saying." Sigurd cinched his brow in concern. "Do you think I look frightening in my uniform?"

"I've gotten used to it, but speaking from experience, there is something innately terrifying about the sight of a dark and faceless figure right before you're sure he is going to kill you," Katja murmured.

Sigurd took slow steps toward her, silencing her with his hard steel gaze. It made her uncomfortable to look directly at him, so used to seeing nothing in front of her for so long.

"I'm sorry if I've ever scared you like that," he said, his voice low and husky. "But you never have to fear me."

"I don't, and if I ever made you think that I was afraid of you, I never meant to. The truth is you make me feel safer than anyone ever has."

"In all honesty, if you weren't a little bit afraid of me, that would worry me more. Even without the mask, I am still a Steinkamp, but know that above all, I will never do anything to harm you."

Katja nodded. "I know that."

"And I will do everything in my power to keep you safe. Unfortunately, there may be times when I won't be around, and I need to be sure you can handle yourself."

"You know I can. I handled that frost golem after it turned you into a human icicle, remember?"

"I don't doubt your ability to handle golems, but people are entirely different beasts. It would be wise for you to learn some self-defense to prevent a scenario like the mob in Untevar from happening again. This barn should give us the privacy and safety to practice."

Katja nodded in fervent agreement.

"Alright then. Now, I'm your attacker, and there is nowhere to run. Where are you going to strike me first?" Sigurd challenged.

"The groin!" Katja proclaimed.

Sigurd shook his head. "Such a significant weak spot will likely be defended quite rigorously, and if your attacker is female, then . . ."

"Oh." Katja flushed.

"Go for the throat and eyes—every time. You don't need to be strong, only quick. The element of surprise is paramount for you to escape any attacker. Let me show you."

Sigurd demonstrated where she should strike him and had her practice on him over and over until she got the hang of it. After a while, she started to enjoy herself. She didn't hold back when it came to doling out damage to Sigurd, and he took it all without complaint.

For attacks from behind, he taught her a few Steinkamp maneuvers that used the attacker's own weight and momentum against them. She was shocked that even with her smaller size, she was still able to toss Sigurd overhead and into the haystacks successfully after only a few practice runs.

"You are picking this up rather quickly," Sigurd panted while brushing bits of hay off his shoulders. "Everything you've learned here can be used against any foe. However, a Steinkamp has defenses against all of them and more. When one attacks, the key is to go on the defensive, never the offensive. You cannot hope to best him. He will always go for the quickest kill. Brain, throat, heart, and spine." Sigurd touched Katja in all four of those places to demonstrate. "They will attack one of these areas first, whichever is the most opportune at the moment."

Katja's spine tingled as Sigurd ran his finger along it. His touch aroused her despite the morbid subject matter. "If a Steinkamp means to kill me, what can I do to stop that from happening?" she asked.

"By staying alive just long enough for me to reach you," Sigurd replied. He went ahead and showed Katja the most effective ways to dodge a Steinkamp kill shot from each of the four areas. All it took were subtle body movements at the exact right moments to avoid instant death. That didn't always mean avoiding the wound entirely, but wounds could heal.

Sigurd grabbed her from behind and jabbed the end of his cudgel into the base of her skull. "If a Steinkamp has you in this position it means he intends to kill you in the quickest and least painful way possible. He will stick his skewer knife through this spot and into your brain to shut down your heart and lungs in one motion."

Katja's heart picked up pace. "What do I do in that case?"

Sigurd gripped her head still with his one arm and kept his cudgel on her skull with the other. "He will hold you in such a way so that you cannot move your head. Your first instinct might be to bend forward, or to the left where you perceive there to be a way out."

On his instruction, Katja struggled to the left and then forward, but Sigurd's grip didn't relent.

"Move your head as hard as you can to the right, toward the arm holding you."

Katja tried, but she could barely budge. "I can't move."

"You only have to move enough so the knife misses your brainstem. Keep trying. Put all your weight into it," Sigurd urged.

They kept at it and Katja soon found that it was much easier to move toward his arm and away from the gripping hand. "If my neck gets sliced open, I'll still die."

"Perhaps, but not right away. The faster you are, and the harder you push toward the arm holding you, the less chance the wound will be fatal. Every second you stay alive leaves one more second for help to reach you."

Sigurd then showed her ice powder and taught her that it could treat wounds. It was unable to freeze living skin, but could cool it enough to help slow the flow of blood and stave off infection.

"Thank you for doing this, Sigurd. It means a lot." Katja fiddled with the end of her braid.

"Anything for my new kapitän." Sigurd saluted.

"Oh, I'm no kapitän," Katja said, swaying from side to side. "I'm just a simple peasant girl."

"Evidently." Sigurd's eyes widened as they ventured up and down her body.

Without warning, he reached out to grab her. Katja snatched Sigurd's arm and twirled into him, using the leverage from her hips to flip him into the hay. She cheered in the delight of her new skill, but her victory was short-lived. He lunged forward, flung her over his shoulder and down into the haystack right next to him. Katja retaliated by stuffing a handful of straw down his shirt. He yelped and clambered after her while she kicked down one hay bale then another to keep him from reaching her, only to end up pinned beneath him at the top of the stack.

"Were you not listening? Never go on the offensive," Sigurd said with the widest grin she had ever seen on him. It was such a stark contrast from the unmalleable facial expressions he typically donned. It made her breathless to finally see him smile.

"Is this what you call defending the defenseless?" she asked.

"It's what I call punishing the wicked."

"You think me wicked, do you?" Katja dared, bringing her face as close to his as possible while still pinned down by the elbows. "Then do your duty, Steinkamp."

Sigurd pressed his lips to Katja's, devouring her in his passion. She moaned as he moved his lips down the length of her neck and chest. Her entire body loosened. Her heart and mind were free and waiting for Sigurd to do whatever wanton thing he desired.

His warm fingers migrated up her leg, underneath her gown. A jolt of self-awareness went through her upon realizing she no longer wore anything in the way of undergarments, yet she made no move to stop Sigurd's advance up her dress. As soon as he discovered there was nothing there but the moisture between her thighs, he stayed his hand and looked to her. Their eyes met. Sigurd's were alight with desire while Katja dared him to continue with a bite of her bottom lip.

Without taking his gaze from her, Sigurd's forefingers slid effortlessly inside her, making her breath catch in her chest. Despite her body tightening in response, she subtly moved against Sigurd's hand, inviting him inward. Her arousal threatened to capsize as his thumb stroked her in a way that made her entire body flush, and she threw her head back. He brought his lips to her exposed neck, gently biting and tickling her skin while his fingers dexterously caressed her below, and the wetness from her pleasure dripped down her thighs. Katja's whole body sang with desire as the Steinkamp had her completely at his mercy. His lips made her weak, and his fingers left her aching for more. All she could do was moan breathlessly.

Katja felt like she was under a spell until an older woman's voice rang out, "It came from the barn."

"Don't worry, Dear, I'm going to investigate," replied Otis, who sounded dangerously close.

Sigurd's fingers immediately withdrew from Katja, halting her rapture and jolting her back to reality. Cursing under their breaths, the two hastily gathered themselves and rolled off the hay bales. Sigurd picked up his bag with the food, uniform, and weapons, and both he and Katja snuck out of the back door they had used to gain entry.

Once they ran an acceptable distance away from the property, she and Sigurd burst out laughing. As sexually frustrated as she was, she was grateful to have had that brief moment of escape from her dreadful state of affairs. Ignatius was still under arrest, Klemens was still a hostage, possibly dead, and Katja was going to return to the house she had tried so hard to leave behind six years before. She feared becoming that sad and lonely girl again. But this time, things would be different. She had the self-defense tools that Sigurd taught her and the knowledge of how to influence golems without a Mage. Those two devices would protect her from whatever she would soon face. But the thought of being apart from Sigurd after everything they had been through left her with an incessant ache in her chest.

It had taken the better half of a day before they arrived at the next village. There, they hoped to find a means of transportation. Before they could enter the village proper, Sigurd took Katja off into the bush.

She thought he was going to continue what he'd started in the barn earlier but became disheartened when he said, "Stay here and keep out of sight. There is something odd down the road, and I need to investigate before we continue."

He hastily changed into his uniform and disappeared down the road. A few minutes later, he returned with dire news.

"A large contingent has taken the village ahead," he said. "They bear the triplet peaks crest on their flags. Some of them have it engraved in their armor, armor that dates back more than twenty years."

"What does that mean?" Katja asked, puzzled.

"The three peaks represent the Glacier Peaks of Nordenhein, worn as a coat of arms in the Age of Kings. Nordenhein has amassed a rebellion of its own, and they appear to be marching for the City of Deschner."

22

I RELEASE YOU

While Katja hid in the forest off the main road, Sigurd went back to the village to spy on the Nordenhein rebel army some more. He returned half an hour later.

"The rebels of Nordenhein had received word from the Kaiser that you were taken prisoner. Kanzler Gustaf was assassinated soon after."

"I suppose that means he's not part of the Kings' Remnants," Katja surmised. That also meant he was likely not the one that revealed Katja's alias to Rudiger. That left only Ignatius, but she still couldn't believe he would sell her out. There had to be somebody else who knew.

Sigurd continued, "The Nordenhein Karl precinct has been in disarray since the death of Vaughn. With rumors of his death being by the hand of the Rogue Steinkamp, it didn't take much to convince the rebel factions in the range to take up arms."

"But you killed Vaughn because he was partial in the death of your family, wasn't he?"

Sigurd shook his head. "Rudiger tricked me into eliminating Nordenhein's primary source of Regime corruption. He was furious that I hadn't concealed the fact that a Steinkamp perpetrated the killing, I think because I made it seem like the Regime was cleaning up its own mess. It sounds like he was able to feed the Rogue Steinkamp rumor instead, and now the common people see the Kings' Remnants as heroes. All Nordenhein needed after that was a sign the rebels might succeed. The Kaiser has since provided them with such a sign by taking you hostage."

"What does Bachman think he can do for them now that I've escaped?" Katja crossed her arms.

"What I told you he was going to do—pretend that he still has you and mobilize his army anyway. The rebel faction in Nordenhein will be marching south to join forces with the Untevar faction from the east. Together they plan to invade Deschner from the north while another Untevar contingent invades Deschner from the south. Most of the Führer's golem stock is being used to hold back the Herrani invasion—"

"And to stand by at the Fortress or Mortlach that the Remnants now hold," added Katja.

"With their greatest Military Strategist dead and the Steinkamp Kapitän missing, the Regime appears ill-equipped to stave off a rebel advance from two sides." Sigurd kept his eyes on the road to ensure no one was in earshot.

"If the Regime discovers that I am out of rebel grasp, that would turn the tide against the Kings' Remnants. My father could then siphon away his golems from the fortress to beat back the siege."

"All it would take is having you back in his safe keeping," concluded Sigurd.

"We're going to need to get back to Deschner, and quick."

"Let's find some horses and keep to the back roads around the village," suggested Sigurd. "If we ride through the night, you will be back in your father's care before the rebel soldiers are sighted near the city. However, there is still a chance that Bachman's southern contingent will lay siege to it before we get there."

Katja frowned. She wondered if Klemens was helping Bachman with his military strategy. *Do whatever you need to do to stay alive, Klem, and I will do what I can to convince my father to rescue you.*

She waited while Sigurd went ahead and stole two chestnut mares from a soldier encampment, under the cover of a twilight canister. The two of them rode hastily down a lesser used road heading southwest. As the hours passed, her heart began to feel heavy. The horse moved beneath her, but her mind stood still. She wasn't sure if returning home was such a good idea anymore. It was apparent the messengers used by the rebellion were faster than they were. The moment she set foot in the City of Deschner, she feared word would get out, and Klemens would die before she had a chance to talk to her father. However, she had more than just Klemens's life to worry about.

The pair finally rested at a creek near a junction. Once the horses had drunk their fill, Sigurd nudged his mare down the road toward the City of Deschner only to find Katja no longer following. He stopped and turned toward her. "What's the matter?"

"I can't go home." Katja swallowed a lump in her throat.

"I know you're scared to go back there, but it's where you'll be safest," Sigurd said.

"I might be safe there, but nobody else will be. The moment I step foot in my father's castle, he will engage all his golems from across Ingleheim against the siege. It will be a bloodbath."

"Then what do you propose?"

"If I return to Bachman, I will be put to death when his coup is complete, but if I return home, thousands of people will be laid to slaughter—innocent people like Benedikt, the impoverished masses, slave farmers, people who want to fight for a better life. Who am I to rob them of that, in the interest of my own safety?"

"Katja, we've been through this. I am not handing you back to Bachman," Sigurd said firmly.

"There might be another way." Katja gathered her reins in preparation to set off again. "We can go to Luidfort Range. It is naturally fortified and far enough away from rebel activity and Regime military oversight. My uncle Friedhelm is the kanzler there."

"You trust him?"

Katja nodded. "Out of all the kanzlers, Friedhelm is the most pragmatic. He will listen to reason and keep my presence at his estate secret from my father and Bachman. From there, we can send my father a message stating that my captors are treating me fairly and to insist on doing whatever he can to get Klemens back to Breisenburg safely. It might be his, and Ingleheim's, best chance."

"Two things are wrong with that plan," Sigurd began. "One, we will need to cross through Breisenburg to get to Luidfort. Two, the town there is teeming with military men because of the naja horde laying siege to the Barrier of Kriegle."

"Right, I forgot about the Herrani."

"Also, if the Remnants succeed in overthrowing the Regime, your uncle is their next target. The Luidfort natural springs are the primary water source for both Breisenburg and Deschner. Bachman will want to secure that area immediately after he takes power. When that happens, you will be trapped in a closed valley with little chance to escape."

Katja's heart sank. He was right. Bachman wouldn't be so foolish as to ignore Luidfort's water resources. He already controlled most of Ingleheim's food supply.

"Kensloche is our best bet," said Sigurd. "It's far from the rebels and the Regime. There will be messengers there who can deliver word to your father with a much lower risk of interception. In either scenario, however, Bachman stands a good chance of winning this war. Is that really what you want?" Sigurd maneuvered his horse closer to Katja's.

"It's not about winning or losing," she said. "It's about life and death. Ingleheim is nothing without its people. Sooner or later those people will get what they want, whether it's under Bachman or somebody else. Maybe Bachman is no better than my father, or maybe he is the only one who can bring Ingleheim the prosperity it deserves. Regardless, my father must answer for his crimes, and if he must pay with his life, I have to accept that."

Katja wondered if Bachman was right, that Heinrich was sowing the seeds of his self-destruction. She frowned at the realization that she would never get the chance to know her father as someone other than the Führer—never as the righteous, young idealist who captured her mother's heart. It was too late for that now. It was more important than ever for Ingleheim to avoid falling into another Age of Golems.

"We go to Kensloche, send a message to the Führer, and then what? You disappear?" asked Sigurd.

Disappear. The word sounded almost poetic. "Maybe."

"Are you sure? My parents tried to disappear, and the Regime still found them."

"Yes, but they had that bloodhound Wolfram hunting for them, and you killed him . . . right?"

"No, I didn't," Sigurd said as if that fact was obvious. "I left him tied up at the old farmhouse in Kensloche. He should be running dangerously low on rations by now, but probably still alive."

"You didn't kill him before coming to find me? Why?"

"Because he said he was your father. I didn't want to believe him, but he showed me that warrant and I couldn't go through with it."

"So you left him there in hopes that you could return in time to finish him off," Katja finished uncomfortably. "Is that why you were so resistant to go back for Klemens—because you knew you wouldn't get your revenge?"

Sigurd brought his horse even closer to Katja so that their stirrups touched. Taking off his mask, he looked straight at her. "It's true. I would rather kill Wolfram than save your friend, but that was before I saw the pain his death would bring you. If you still want me to rescue Klemens, then I will try. If you want me to take you home, I will. And, if you want to disappear just issue the command, and I will make it so."

"And Wolfram?"

"He will either starve to death or escape. He may never be punished for his deeds, and maybe he isn't meant to be. I know now that I am not Verishten's vessel for retribution. He no longer speaks to me. Maybe that means I'm unworthy, or that it was all in my head to begin with. I don't know. What I do know is that the world needs you and the work you do. It is more important for you to live than it is for Wolfram to die."

"Sigurd, I'm sorry for what Wolfram did to you," Katja said in a near whisper. ". . . For what my father did to you."

Sigurd had finally come to the conclusion that she'd hoped he would come to months before. Katja thought she would be relieved to hear him admit revenge was the wrong path, but it only made her feel guilty, like she was robbing him of something.

"You need not be," Sigurd replied. His gray eyes were steadfast, yet his features soft. "If my purpose is not to exact vengeance, then it should be to serve you. My life is yours, Katja. My blood, my spirit, and my heart, I pledge it all, not to the Mighty Führer, not to Ingleheim . . . but to you."

Hearing her Steinkamp soldier professing his undying love in the only way he knew how, didn't bring Katja comfort like she thought it should. Instead, it made her heart bleed more, but she wasn't sure why. All she knew was that she didn't want to go home, and she wasn't ready to be separated from Sigurd again.

When she didn't reply, he continued, "Give me the order and it will be done."

"I want to disappear," Katja said. Sigurd nodded, and she added, "And I want you to disappear with me."

He put his mask back on. "As you command, fraulein."

Riding day and night, they arrived in the Town of Kensloche by the second morning. Katja had managed to get in an hour of sleep here and there as Sigurd held her on his horse, leading hers behind them. He didn't appear even to want such a luxury, but she could tell that the lack of sleep was wearing on him.

Upon entering the town, Sigurd decided he didn't want to risk showing his brand to a haven clerk in case he or she alerted someone else to his presence there. He had changed into his civilian clothing, which did better to hide him than his metal mesh mask would have. Using the schlepts Otis and Ingrid had given them, they checked into an inn for the night.

Inside, they overheard conversations between patrons about Cragsmen raids in the western outskirts of town. When the people had sought assistance from Chancellor Waldemar in hunting down the raiders and bringing them to justice, they found the kanzler had vanished. The word was that Herr Waldemar, having sensed unrest amongst his citizenry, did not wish to go the way of his neighboring kanzler to the north. He made sure not to be around when the mobs came.

"Hmm, Cragsmen are not usually brave enough to terrorize locals so close to major townships," Sigurd whispered to Katja. "I don't think this sudden influx of Cragsmen activity is coincidental."

"It could be someone is incentivizing them to terrorize Kensloche. Whoever swoops in to save them will have the allegiance of the citizens. It might be the Kings' Remnants trying to pit Kensloche against their kanzler, like in Nordenhein."

"Made all the easier now they no longer have one," Sigurd added.

They decided not to think too much on it for the time being. Katja and Sigurd didn't plan on sticking around long. They would continue their journey to the Village of Leichstag, a higher altitude settlement nestled in a tight valley, isolated and self-sufficient. Leichstag would be the perfect place to hide from both the rebellion and the Regime.

Up in their room, Katja lit a fire in the hearth and both she and Sigurd dug into the last of the biscuits Ingrid had baked for them. They had just enough schlepts left over to buy more food in the town market the next morning. Sigurd went to lay his uniform out in case he had to jump into it quickly. From the black suit, Katja noticed a piece of paper drop to the floor. It was the warrant. She looked at it and noticed that the ink had smeared from their trek across the Sleban, but Katja's and Ignatius's names were still visible.

"Sigurd, why did Wolfram even have this warrant to begin with?" Katja asked as she sat down at the table. "My arrest is hardly a Steinkamp matter, is it?"

"In this case, it is," Sigurd answered. "Since a comrade was assigned to your protection, it makes sense a warrant would be run by the kapitän to garner information and cooperation."

"You mean the comrade working for the Kings' Remnants?"

Still laying out his uniform, Sigurd replied. "Yes, but Wolfram never knew that. His chosen replacement was intercepted. As far as I am aware, the interloper had been reporting under the other's brand to keep up appearances. I'm assuming Rudiger had the original Steinkamp killed."

"Something doesn't feel right about the whole thing," Katja muttered. "How did Wolfram find out that I was the Führer's daughter when you spoke to him?"

"Your father must have told him about you and your alias at some point. Probably as a way to better protect you from the rebellion," Sigurd surmised.

"That's just it. My father would sooner send a winged golem or my stepmother to retrieve me discreetly than to allow his Steinkamp Kapitän to arrest me like some dangerous criminal. It just doesn't make sense. The Führer can't possibly know about this warrant. It had to have been staged by the rebellion to get to me while throwing Ignatius to the wolves at the same time. Bachman did indicate that he'd wanted him to take the fall."

Sigurd sat down at the table across from Katja. "Then the real question is not how Wolfram found out about your alias, but how the rebellion discovered your true identity."

"Bachman said Rudiger found me through a contact at the university. I thought it could be Kanzler Gustaf, but we both know he was not rebel friendly, which leaves Ignatius." Katja sighed. "I just don't believe he would sell me out."

"Though, he did tell Rudiger a lot of things," said Sigurd with a furrowed brow.

"What did Rudiger say to you about Ignatius, anything suspicious at all?" Katja said while unbraiding her hair.

"Just that he was their mole and the one who told them about the Alpha project."

"Now, you see, I find *that* strange. Why would Rudiger trust a Steinkamp, who is not one of his own, with that kind of information? Why would he have been in contact with you in the first place?" Katja smoothed out her kinked hair with her hands.

Sigurd told her how Rudiger saw him hesitate to kill Volker in order to discover the location of the Alpha. "He tried to recruit me. I said no—"

"And he still told you about Ignatius's role with the Kings' Remnants?"

Katja interrupted.

"No, he never offered that information upfront. I got it out of him. I was suspicious of how he knew so much about my mission in Nordenhein. As it turned out, Ignatius alerted Rudiger to a Steinkamp security detail. He used his deductive reasoning to determine that it was me."

Sigurd's answer jolted Katja to her feet. "Ignatius never knew about any Steinkamp detail. He found out when I confronted him on his rebel ties. That was the day *after* you told me he was the mole."

Sigurd stood up with such vehemence his chair violently toppled over. "Rudiger lied about that too. Verishten burn him!" His jaw and fists clenched.

Katja gasped at the sudden outburst. There was definitely more going on between Sigurd and Rudiger that he was not telling her. *He will tell me when it is time for me to know,* she reassured herself, *but right now we need to get to the bottom of this.*

"If he lied about how he became aware of your assignment in Nordenhein, he probably lied to Bachman about how he became aware of me," Katja suggested.

"He's been lying to everyone about everything. Rudiger has an informer out there he doesn't want anyone to know about, not even his Kaiser. . . ."

"Someone who knows all about your assignments and my true identity."

Sigurd held Katja's gaze for a moment. "Kapitän Wolfram."

"Wolfram's secretly working for the Kings' Remnants."

"That would explain why Rudiger was so adamant on me not killing him until it was time. I wonder if Rudiger told him who I was before I got to him. Wolfram didn't seem all that surprised when I revealed myself on the Crags."

"If that were so, why did he take you under his direct command?" Katja asked. "He would have known you wanted retribution."

"To keep an eye on me, I suppose, to let Rudiger use me for his own purposes . . . to get me out of the way so he could stage your abduction." Sigurd scratched at his chin.

"I wish I knew how Wolfram found out about me. My father didn't even tell his closest allies of my alias, yet the Steinkamp Kapitän knew?" Katja shrugged.

"Take it from me. Wolfram has a way of uncovering things. He named his daughter a variation of your name. Maybe he's always known. Maybe he and your father are closer than you think."

Katja started pacing. "No, my father deferred most of his dealings with the Steinkamp Kapitän to Volker. Wolfram's daughter having the same name is likely coincidental, and he just capitalized on an opportunity to keep you from killing him. There has to be some other connection."

"That makes sense." Sigurd leaned back against the wall, crossing his arms. "A Steinkamp Kapitän is one of the few Regime offiziers who can approve of an arrest warrant issued by a Karl Kommissar. Rudiger needed the daughter of the Führer, so he sold out Ignatius to Wolfram to see it done. Having your name on that warrant was convenient for both of them, since I'm guessing at that point Wolfram had already received my letter convoking him to the cache where I was to ambush him. He was sure to keep a copy of it as insurance. He was willing to bet that I would see it as my duty to keep you protected."

"And with the threat of arrest hanging over our heads, it was easy to trick Klemens into taking me to the abduction site."

"Wolfram is the reason the rebellion knows who you are," Sigurd finished.

Katja mulled over all the people who knew her alias and who also had a connection to Wolfram, and only one name came to mind—a name that made the blood run cold in her veins.

"Melikheil!" Katja said in a quavering voice. "He worked very closely with my father and spent considerable time with Wolfram as well." *Could he be the connection?* A sickening dread formed a lump in her gut. Melikheil may not have had a reason to tell Wolfram about her alias, but if Wolfram wanted to know, what would stop Melikheil from telling him the truth? She wouldn't put it past the Mage to plan a coup of his own with all the power he and Brunhilde wielded between them. "It has to be him. He's behind all of this."

Her legs wobbled, forcing her to sit down on the bed. With a look of concern, Sigurd went to sit beside her.

"How would Melikheil know about your alias?" he asked. "Didn't your father keep you away from everyone?"

"Not everyone," Katja murmured as she hugged her knees to her chest and stared at the flames crackling in the hearth. "I was right in the open for Meister Melikheil." She didn't want to say anything more, but she forced herself to continue. Sigurd needed to know about her darkness, just as she had to know about his. "When it came to that wizard, my father was conveniently unobservant. I blamed his new young wife for distracting him, but it was much more sinister than that." Katja's eyes left the fireplace and fixated on her scarred fingertips.

Sigurd's voice was quiet but resolute. "What did he do to you?"

"It began innocently enough," Katja continued. "He would keep me company when I had nobody else to talk to. I found him interesting, and he seemed to find me equally so. It didn't take long before he became my first and only friend. I don't know exactly when he started using his magic on me. It was all so gradual . . ." She paused.

Sigurd placed a hand on her knee. "You don't have to keep going if you don't want to."

"No, I should. It's about time I tell somebody who will believe me." She clenched and unclenched her fists, trying not to focus on her hands anymore. "That sorcerer became my entire world. He'd summon me at various hours, and I did anything and everything he told me to do. Pleasing him was all that mattered.

"When he was away, I was rendered an empty shell whose only purpose was to wait for his return. I stopped reading, drawing, playing music—all the things I enjoyed were meaningless to me when Melikheil was gone. I would wait, like a dormant golem yearning for my Mage to return and breathe purpose into me again. It was like being asleep, but with a pathetic creature inside my head that lived out my wakeful days for me, doing things I'd never thought I'd ever do. And enjoying every minute of it. All the while, the real me faded away, but none of that mattered because my love for Melikheil was more important to me than my own existence."

"What you felt for him was not real. He forced it upon you," Sigurd muttered, his hands whitening with tension.

Katja nodded and wiped her eyes to keep tears from falling. "And discovering that fact nearly killed me."

(Seven years ago)

Kriemhilde, with her mind ever in a fog, watched a beautiful woman writhe sensually upon a man in Melikheil's bed. Loose curls of blonde hair fell from her bun and bounced over her bare breasts, her cries of pleasure echoing from the high vaulted ceilings.

It took her a moment to recognize the woman engaging in the throes of passion as her stepmother. Before she could question why Brunhilde was in the room at all, the man beneath her sat up and roughly pulled her head back by the hair to gain access to her neck.

Melikheil...

Kriemhilde stood before the two lovers, stunned. Her mind wouldn't allow her to make the connection between her beloved Melikheil and her father's wife.

"Meister?" she peeped.

Melikheil snapped his head around to look at her, but he made no attempt to move Brunhilde off. "I did not summon you, Kriemhilde," he chastised. "Be gone!"

Brunhilde gave a wicked grin and bit her lip mischievously. "Oh, there's no need to send her away just yet."

Kriemhilde was compelled to turn around and leave. *Everything is going to be okay. . . .*

"Stop," Melikheil called. She halted right where she was. "Sit down and wait."

Shaking, she sat down in a plush armchair near the hearth, facing the bed.

"Watch closely, now. Maybe you'll learn something," Brunhilde cooed as she took a fist full of Melikheil's shining black tresses and kissed him full on the mouth, smiling intently at Kriemhilde with her eyes.

From that point on Kriemhilde sat and watched her stepmother continue to ride upon Melikheil the way she herself had done countless times. She watched the woman lick, suck, and bite everywhere Kriemhilde wanted to, and she watched him do to Brunhilde the same things he had done to her. She never felt more at odds; watching her stepmother receive the pleasures she'd thought were for her alone made an unyielding vice clamp down on her heart. But on the other hand, having any chance to bask in the magnificence of her beloved Melikheil made her ache in longing between her thighs. She dared not look away.

The lovers stopped momentarily to look at Kriemhilde watching them. "Little Dove?"

"Yes, Meister?" Kriemhilde sat up straight and obedient. The wizard looked back to the woman astride him, his hand still roaming through her blonde waves. "If you're going to be here, you may as well pleasure yourself until we are done." He cast a sensual eye Kriemhilde's way, and immediately her right hand glided down her body without a single thought.

Melikheil nodded in approval before Brunhilde pulled his attentions back to her. As the pair continued in their lovemaking, Kriemhilde soon felt as if Melikheil's fingers were pleasuring her rather than her own. When he finished, she did also. Her entire body sang with an eruptive energy, but confusion swam about her mind as her self-awareness slowly returned.

"Why is she here, Meister?" she asked breathlessly.

"You're breaking the poor girl's heart," Brunhilde mocked. She rose from the bed and wrapped a feather-trimmed robe around her voluptuous form.

Melikheil ignored Brunhilde's callous words and beckoned Kriemhilde to the bed with him. "Undress for me," he ordered. *While Stepmother is watching?* She hesitated, but since it was what her meister wanted, she did as he bid.

"Do you wish me to pleasure you too, Meister?"

Melikheil chuckled and shook his head, "No, Dove. I'm quite spent. However, your stepmother is an insatiable one. How about you pleasure her?"

"Mel, what do you think you're doing?" Brunhilde scoffed.

Kriemhilde was even more confused. Melikheil had requested she pleasure other women for his enjoyment before, but they had been nothing more than handmaids. Surely he didn't really expect her to pleasure her own stepmother? She looked to Brunhilde, then back to Melikheil, hesitant to obey him.

The Mage took her face in his hands and peered deeply into her eyes. "You do love me, don't you, Kriemhilde?"

"More than anything in this life," she sputtered, her lips quivering.

"Then you will do this for me?"

She nodded repeatedly. "Yes."

Once Melikheil let go of her face, Kriemhilde crawled across the bed to where Brunhilde stood at the end of it. Rising to her knees, she reached for her stepmother and tried to lay a kiss upon her lips.

Before she could touch the woman's mouth, Brunhilde turned away and held up her hand. "Alright, that's enough. You've proven that she is completely under your control."

"Come on, Brunhilde. She is young, but I've instilled in her more than enough . . . experience." Melikheil grinned.

"I don't doubt that, but if it's all the same to you, I think I'll pass. Maybe it's about time you release her. It's not healthy for such a young mind to remain under thrall for so long." Brunhilde brushed an unruly strand of hair from Kriemhilde's forehead and tucked it behind her ear.

"Release me?" Kriemhilde whipped her head around to Melikheil.

"Her mind is strong for her age, which is why I chose her." Sitting up beside her, Melikheil ran his hand through her hair endearingly.

"But you're going to leave for Del'Cabria soon, so I suggest you get it over with."

"Get what over with?" Kriemhilde asked. The way the two Mages spoke of her as if she were not in the room made her stomach lurch.

Melikheil let out a heavy sigh. He took her by the shoulders again and turned her to face him. She stared longingly into his darkly powerful eyes that always made the blood flow hot in her veins. She remained perfectly still while he moved his hand across her line of sight, shielding his glorious face from her vision for one split second.

"Kriemhilde, I release you."

It came over her in an instant. A crushing dread, a monstrous emptiness, unlike anything she'd experienced when Melikheil would leave her before. This was different; this was a violation in its purest form. A handsome man stared back at her, but not in the way she expected to see him. He was wrong, distorted. This man was a perversion.

Kriemhilde jerked out of his grasp and frantically crawled backward on the bed. She would have fallen had Brunhilde not caught her from behind and dragged her over to the armchair.

Melikheil picked up his robe and put it around her naked body.

"Don't touch me!" Kriemhilde kicked her leg out. Melikheil shifted out of the way, and she hit nothing but air.

"This will be painful, but it will pass," Melikheil tried to reassure her.

Her heart felt like it was missing. There was an empty cavity in her chest, rapidly filling with an insipid horror. "No, get away! Stop!" she shrieked.

She shot out of the chair, burst from the room and ran down the echoing hallways of Deschner castle, ignoring the calls from the two Mages coming after her. Kriemhilde reached her room and locked the door. Weakly leaning against the hard oak, she felt the pounding of Brunhilde and Melikheil trying to come in.

It was all too much to bear. It was as if her entire being were stuck in a vacuum, and everything that made her who she was had been sucked into a void that thoroughly eluded her. All she felt inside was something foul, something putrid. She needed to get it out . . . somehow.

Wind railed against the stained-glass windows a few feet from her bed.

Those windows open from the inside. . . . She ran to the casements and opened them. Gusts of wind blew ash onto the bedspread behind her. She calmly stepped onto the windowsill, ignoring the repeated bangs against her bedroom door. Standing against the wind, she breathed deep as the ash tickled her face. With her eyes closed tight, Kriemhilde took one step. The air took her into its cold embrace.

Then, the wind suddenly picked up with so much force that her freefall stopped midair and she was catapulted upward. She landed on her bed and her window slammed shut all on its own. Melikheil had broken down her door and used wind magic to bring her back to safety.

How dare he? He has no right!

He grabbed Kriemhilde and shook her. "What are you doing?"

She went limp and heavy in his arms, and he eventually dropped her back onto the bed.

"Let me die," she begged him in whimpers.

"Well, now you've gone and done it." Brunhilde sighed as she appeared next to Melikheil. "I told you she has been under your thrall for too long. Now we have a blubbering suicidal mess on our hands."

"I can see that!" Melikheil snapped through gritted teeth.

"You were only supposed to thrall her long enough to see if she possessed the Eye of Verishten, but you just couldn't resist corrupting yet another virgin to add to your spiritual power."

"You know nothing!" Melikheil grabbed hold of Brunhilde's face and roughly shoved her away. She quickly regained her elegant composure while Kriemhilde curled up into the fetal position, willing the world to end. "I overestimated your intellect, Little Dove," Melikheil muttered into Kriemhilde's ear as she shook on the ash-covered blankets. "I didn't anticipate your mind breaking this easily."

"Don't blame the girl," Brunhilde interjected. "You underestimate your own power. This poor wretch has no friends and no real contact with the outside world to keep her grounded, and you had to go and turn her into your obedient little plaything."

"She is far more than that," said Melikheil as he reached down to touch Kriemhilde's head. She now lacked the energy to recoil at his touch, and his hand felt like it was sucking the life force right out of her. *Please, please go away. It's wrong, I'm wrong . . . Distorted . . .*

"While you're going off to war, what am I supposed to do with her like this?" Brunhilde stood with her hands on her hips.

"I only just released her. She is no longer under my thrall unless I choose to return her to it. She will be herself again in a month or so."

Myself? Who is that? Nothing in her life mattered the same way Melikheil had, and now he was gone. He stood right in front of her and yet he had disappeared completely.

"Focus on being a good little wife to the Führer, and I will focus on destroying that desert Mage," Melikheil said, taking Brunhilde around the waist.

"Then nobody alive will have the power to match ours," Brunhilde finished.

"Nobody alive, my beautiful Apprentice. I ask that you do one thing for me while I'm gone. Keep your stepdaughter away from windows and sharp objects, will you?"

Brunhilde groaned. "What do you want with this pathetic thing anyway?"

"She has something of mine, and I may need it returned to me if anything were to happen," he said quietly.

"Nothing is going to happen," Brunhilde retorted. "You are going to destroy Nas'Gavarr and return to me as the most powerful Mage in the known world."

"Even the most powerful Mage must have contingency plans."

Brunhilde sighed and rolled her eyes. "Fine, I'll see no harm befalls her. . . . You have my word."

"I was so desperate for the pain to stop. I begged Brunhilde to use her magic and make me forget," Katja continued, still hugging her knees to her chest. "Melikheil made her promise not to meddle with my mind for any reason, but she found other ways to torment me without using magic. She made my life so harrowed that I threatened to tell my father everything. She actually *dared* me to do it. So, I called her bluff . . . and my father didn't believe a word. It was as if he hadn't even heard what I said. I never felt so alone."

"Your stepmother must have bewitched him," Sigurd said as he reached out to stop her hands from shaking. "It is the only reason I can see why he'd ignore something so heinous."

Katja shrugged. "It didn't matter. From that day forward I focused all of my energies on leaving that place. When I turned eighteen, I convinced my father to allow me to attend University. Brunhilde didn't stand in my way. She was welcome to the life she and Melikheil stole from me. I made a new one. Melikheil did come to visit me once before he officially left for war, to tell me to await his *heroic return*." She let out a dark laugh through the tension. "It was his way of reminding me that I was still and always would be under his thumb. Now he's gone, but I still feel him with me. I'm so afraid he will make good on his promise."

"He's gone, I assure you."

"What if he's not? I don't think you realize how powerful he was. Has his death been confirmed?" Katja asked, her voice becoming frantic.

"As it happens," Sigurd said, squeezing Katja's hand within his, "I recently met a Del'Cabrian archer who witnessed him being ripped apart by Nas'Gavarr. Unless the archer is lying, which he'd have no reason to, there is no way that Mage survived."

"Are you sure?"

Sigurd went on to tell her about sunfire and how it was useless against Melikheil, but in the end it was flesh magic that did him in, just as Brunhilde had indicated. "Meister Melikheil is dead, Katja. I promise he will never touch you again."

She felt relief for the first time in so long, but knowing Melikheil was actually dead brought her a different worry. "I don't understand how I can still feel him with me even in death. It's like he's tainted my body and soul. I'm . . . soiled."

Sigurd took her by the shoulder and pulled her close to him. "That Mage damaged you, no one can argue against that, but you found yourself again. You fought your way out, and you never let go of what truly mattered to you. I only wish I can say the same for myself."

"What if a part of him still lives inside of me? Would you want me knowing his evil has infected me?" Katja stood up with the urge to pace again. *She has something of mine . . .*

"Nothing will change the way I feel about you, Katja," Sigurd replied, not letting go of her hand so she wouldn't stray too far from the bed. "No matter what darkness you may have inside you, it is there you'll find me, not him. I am your Steinkamp, now and forever."

The intensity of Sigurd's gaze caused her skin to flush. She could think of nothing more than sinking into his arms and succumbing to him.

"At this moment"—she loosened the ties on her bodice—"I don't want a Steinkamp."

When the bodice was loose enough, she slipped one shoulder out from the sleeve, then the other, and coaxed the remainder of her dress down until it was on the floor by her feet. Sigurd breathed heavy, and his pupils dilated at the sight of her fully exposed body. She grazed her hands over his soft, close-cropped hair. He let out a husky moan but didn't move to return her affections just yet.

"You're under no obligation to . . ."he murmured.

Katja didn't let Sigurd finish. Kneeling on the bed astride him, she pressed her lips to his, her kiss slow and deliberate.

"This is not my obligation,"she said between kisses. "This is my choice."

She continued to run her hands over his head and along the rigid contours of his face. For a while Sigurd remained stationary, simply content to let Katja caress him everywhere, places his armor had never allowed her hands to go before. She grazed her fingers under his shirt, feeling the firm musculature of his abdomen, the hair on his chest, and the hard strength in his shoulders.

Finally, a more feral instinct took over Sigurd. He swiftly flung off his shirt and put his arms around Katja, pulling her bare body hot against his. Sigurd kissed her ravenously as he fell backward on the bed, bringing her on top of him. His unbending manhood pressed hard against her inner thigh, causing her to become infinitely more eager. She reached down to liberate it from the soft wool of his pants only to have him stop her.

"All in good time, fraulein." Sigurd smoothly spun her around and laid her on her back. He proceeded to hold her down by the arms, giving her a devilish thrill. "There is something I've been meaning to do ever since we left that barn."His voice housed the quiet intensity that she had always been so drawn to.

He tenderly grazed his thumb over Katja's bottom lip like he had done the first time she felt his touch many months before on the Crags. That alone was enough to set her skin ablaze. Speechless, she was unable to ask Sigurd what he had in mind, but she didn't need to. She simply nodded in ardent agreement.

Katja's body repeatedly tensed and relaxed as Sigurd slowly caressed her in places she had only fantasized him touching. His lips traveled down the length of her neck and shoulders while he massaged her breasts. When his lips came to meet them, Sigurd swirled his tongue around her nipples and bit them softly, making her gasp in delight at the sensation. She closed her eyes and focused all her attentions on his hands, lips, and tongue.

Hands that had dealt so much death now made Katja feel more alive than she could ever remember. She let him venture further down her body, his short stubble tickling her. Sigurd never changed his course. He nudged her legs gently apart and teased her inner thighs with his lips. She moaned softly, urging him to keep going, the anticipation becoming unbearable. Her pleasure-filled moans became breaths of surprise when Sigurd's tongue finally arrived at her nether regions. Katja gripped the soft wool comforter beneath her as Sigurd spread her legs wider. Her arousal flowed from her body, drawn out by Sigurd's lips and tongue, bringing Katja ever closer to a sweet state of rapture.

This is not magic. This is real, she thought, gripping the blankets tighter as she cried for Sigurd to never stop. A molten pleasure threatened to erupt from inside, but then his lips continued back up the length of her body. She sighed with disenchantment, her body aching for more, but Sigurd had other things in mind. Now face to face again, he kissed her, their tongues entwined. She tasted herself on his lips. During the kiss, Sigurd removed his trousers and entered her. Her breath grew short as she wrapped her legs around his waist and squeezed him tight, coaxing him deeper inside.

Katja ran her hands firmly up Sigurd's back, exploring every muscle with her fingertips while receiving every inch of him, slow and deep. Soon enough the promise of ecstasy threatened to capsize her once again. She locked Sigurd between her legs so that he couldn't stop. For the first time, she was making love with a man of her choosing. He was her protector, her confidant . . . her Steinkamp.

As Katja's bliss mounted, Sigurd's passion grew insurmountable. His thrusts became harder and faster, filling her to capacity as he firmly held her down. He grabbed a fistful of her hair and pulled her head back, exposing her neck to him, where he proceeded to sensually nibble. Katja dug her nails into Sigurd's back as her own arched. She felt herself teetering on the edge, then waves of pleasure violently crashed through her body and mind, each one stronger than the one before it. She cried out Sigurd's name, inducing him to thrust more vigorously until he was spent.

Sigurd exhaled sharply, bearing his full weight upon her. She held his head in the nook of her neck and felt his heavy breath hot against her skin between his lingering kisses. His entire body deflated as if a wild force had just been released and he could finally rest.

After lying quiet and still for a while, Sigurd eventually pulled out of her and settled into her arms. She kissed him softly on the forehead while caressing his head and face. He moaned quietly, already half asleep.

Katja's heart suddenly felt heavy, and she realized she was still afraid. She worried that they were doing the wrong thing by disappearing and leaving Ingleheim to its fate. However, she chose to focus on the present moment, with Sigurd beside her, and dream of a future with him, far away from the pasts that haunted them.

It seemed possible now.

23

HARMONIOUS CHAOS

Sigurd opened his eyes the next morning to the vision of Katja sleeping peacefully next to him, only partially covered with a thin linen sheet. He had been trapped within the confines of his black armored shell for far too long. The softness of Katja's skin, the sound of her breathing, and the sweet scent of her hair ignited something instinctual deep inside of him. It wasn't anything he had ever felt before when either executing the perfect kill or taking the pleasure of the odd wench between missions. This was peace in its purest form, coexisting with the radiating inferno that now roared through his body. Sigurd could only describe his state as harmonious chaos.

He couldn't stop himself from gently caressing Katja as she slept. He touched her in every place he could reach. She moaned softly while still trying to sleep. Eventually her eyes opened to meet Sigurd's. She smiled, kissed him good morning, and proceeded to cuddle in closer.

As he held her, Sigurd imagined every morning starting this way, just the two of them together at a cottage in Leichstag where no one would ever find them. He pictured working a small farm together, like Otis and Ingrid. How hard could it be? Somehow, Sigurd's father went from earl to shepherd in just over a year, so surely, he could manage the same.

Suddenly, the image of his parents dying in front of him darkened his fantasy. Kapitän Wolfram was possibly still alive, and Rudiger was likely working with him. *I'm about to let those bastards get away with murdering my entire family,* Sigurd thought as he ran his hand through Katja's hair. Could he really disappear with her while Wolfram and Rudiger were out there plotting? Would they ever be safe with those men alive? His gut wrenched.

"I don't think we should go to Leichstag—at least not yet,"he muttered to Katja. "We need to know what Rudiger and Wolfram are planning first."

"That's what I was just thinking."Katja propped herself up. Voluminous brown locks fell haphazardly over one shoulder where Sigurd's hands continued to roam as she talked. "I don't understand why Rudiger would keep his dealings with the kapitän a secret from the Kaiser."

"Wolfram is an opportunist and obsessive contingency thinker. If the Kings' Remnants succeed, he will be rewarded for helping them, but if they lose, he won't be implicated by the current regime."

"How does Rudiger expect to control a man like that?"

Sigurd took a deep breath. "Rudiger was one of the comrades involved in my family's death. Wolfram later set him up as a traitor where he then escaped and joined the Remnants."

While he relayed the details of the story, Sigurd wondered about the boy who was killed in his place. Rudiger had told him that Vaughn killed the boy, but the Steinkamp present that day had veritably perished in the chasm. Why would Rudiger not just tell Sigurd the truth, that Wolfram killed the boy? He already had enough reason to go after Vaughn at the time so why pin the boy's death on him as well?

Katja gulped. "How did you keep yourself from killing him?"

"He promised me Wolfram. We were supposed to be on the same side. I was a fool to trust him as little as I did—never again," Sigurd said darkly. He flung the blankets off and sat up in the bed.

"What are you going to do?"Katja sat up as well.

"You know what I have to do." Sigurd grabbed for his undergarments. "Return to Wolfram and hope that he's still alive so I can uncover the truth."

Katja took him by the shoulder and turned him to face her. "And then . . . ?"

"I'm going to kill him . . . and Rudiger too."

"Oh."Katja cast her eyes down.

He cupped her face with both hands and made her look at him. "Please understand. This isn't about revenge anymore. This is—"

"It's okay, Sigurd. I trust you to do what must be done."

Katja's words were not those he expected. He thought she'd react the same way she did the last time he revealed his murderous intentions. He let go of her for a moment, unable to respond.

"If anyone deserves revenge, it's you. I was selfish to try to keep you from it before, but I was so afraid of losing you. I know now that one way or another, you have to see this through if the beast inside you can ever be put to rest," Katja said, placing her palm against his chest.

"No, Katja, it is you who puts that beast to rest." Sigurd held her hand flush to his skin. "Being with you is the only time I'm not thinking about death. For you, I can be something more."

"I don't want you to be anything more than the man you are. But I can't tell you who that man is. Only you can."

"I have lived and breathed vengeance for so long . . ." he began in a low voice. "When it's over . . . what if I'm nothing without it?"

"I think you'll find when that day comes, you'll know exactly who you are," Katja said, wrapping her arms around his shoulders from behind.

"Are you sure that's a man you truly want to know?" His arousal came roaring in at the feeling of her soft breasts pressing against his back.

"Yes," she whispered in his ear, "because I already know him. I'm just waiting for you to catch up."

Sigurd reached around and pulled her onto his lap. "Then I have a lot of catching up to do, don't I?"

Katja and Sigurd joined lips. Sigurd reached down and felt Katja's eagerness between her thighs, and it was not long until he slid back inside her tight, wet warmth. He rolled over onto his back, bringing her on top of him, kissing her all the while. Pushing down on his chest, she sat up, casting her wavy locks to the side.

The way she looked riding him, her wicked eyes of amber piercing him, and her hair disheveled in just the way he liked, made his more feral urges come forth. He held her tight as he plunged himself so deep she screamed his name, loud enough to wake the other patrons of the inn. He sat up to meet her, fisting one hand in her tangled hair and squeezing her breasts with the other. Sigurd kissed her ravenously, praying never to forget the taste of her lips for as long as he lived.

Once he felt the tremor of Katja's climax, Sigurd could no longer hold back. A molten pleasure erupted from him as if flowing from the volcano itself. He brought her down on top of him, exhaling heartily as his euphoria gradually died.

"That was quite the send-off," he said, still out of breath. He kissed her several more times before finally rising from the bed and getting into his uniform.

"I will find a message station in town and send an urgent letter to my father. Then I will go the market and buy some supplies for our trip." Katja ran her hands through her tousled hair.

"If all goes well, I will return before sundown so we can make headway during the night. However, if I don't return in twenty-four hours, you will have to find a way to Leichstag without me."

Before Sigurd put his mask and hood on, Katja leaped out of bed and threw herself into his arms. They kissed one more time. He wished he didn't have to leave. *We will never be safe if either Wolfram or Rudiger are still out there*, he reminded himself.

"Come back within twenty-four hours, Steinkamp. That's an order," Katja demanded with a hint of playfulness.

He ran his thumb across her luscious bottom lip. "Whether I'm successful in finding Wolfram or not, I will return before nightfall."

Once Sigurd let Katja go, he opened the door but found he was unable to walk through it. He looked back at her leaning against the doorframe, but hidden from outside view, beautiful in all her natural splendor. He would keep this vision of her with him until he returned.

"My name is Siegfried," he blurted.

Katja raised an eyebrow in confusion.

"That's the name I was born with. I just thought you should know."

"Oh?" Katja's eyes glowed with reverence.

Nobody had ever looked at Sigurd like that in his entire life, and for it to be Katja made him want to drop to his knees.

Not knowing what else to say, he said, ". . . So that the next time you scream my name in bed, it will be the right one."

Katja's captivated expression turned into a sardonic smirk to hide a blushing grin. "You'd best be on your way, comrade," she said as she playfully pushed him out the door.

He chuckled and put on his mask.

"Be careful," Katja said in a soft yet serious tone.

"I will."

He waited there for a moment, wondering if he should say more or kiss her one last time. *This isn't a goodbye.* He stepped away from the door as it closed behind him.

Sigurd took the north road that bypassed the Crags to sheep country. The trip only took half a day, even though he rode one of the stolen mares instead of the combat bred steed he was accustomed to. He couldn't risk borrowing one from a haven. Gone were the days Sigurd could depend on the conveniences of the Steinkamp outposts, but he had planned for this eventuality already. On the way to rescue Katja, he had buried some extra gear near an old farm property a few miles off the main road that he'd retrieved from a Kensloche haven. From the stash, he refilled his quiver and grabbed a twilight canister.

When Sigurd finally reached the crumbling farmhouse, he cursed Verishten to find it empty. *The bastard escaped!* He inspected the spot beside the wood stove where he had left Wolfram a week before. It stank of urine and feces. Some rations had been eaten, but at least half remained. Wolfram had been trapped there for three, maybe four days. Sigurd placed the time of his escape around when he found Katja in Untevar. He would never have made it back in time in any eventuality.

Then something strange came to his attention. The earth bindings that had held Wolfram to the wall were gone. If Wolfram had cut them or broken out somehow, he would expect to find pieces lying about, but there was no trace of them at all. That could only mean that they had been unmolded and taken away. Only another Steinkamp, or the rebel witch, could have done such a thing.

"Did you lose something, comrade?" asked a male voice from the doorway.

It was Rudiger, wearing his large hat over his loose auburn hair.

"Where's Wolfram?" Sigurd asked, crossbow primed and aimed for Rudiger's throat.

Rudiger placed his hands up. "He's returned to his duties, searching for you and the Führer's daughter."

"You freed him." Sigurd slowly stepped toward him.

"I told you it's not the time for him yet. I promised you we'd get him, and we will. You just have to start trusting me."

"Spare me your bullshit," Sigurd snapped. "I know the two of you are in collusion. What I don't know is to what purpose."

"Hmm, ever astute, that's what I've always liked about you." Rudiger pointed at him. "You disappoint me, though. First, you manipulated Jenn and my archer to help you abduct Wolfram. Then you had Jenn relay your threatening message to me, and if that didn't bother me enough, I received word of two of my closest comrades found slaughtered in the streets of Untevar in broad daylight. I assume you had a hand in that."

"You disappoint me too, Rudiger. You told me there would be no secrets between us. Were you ever going to tell me of your plan to abduct Katja and make Ignatius your scapegoat?"

"You never fully agreed to join my cause, so I was not about to tell you everything. Kriemhilde in the possession of the rebellion served to stay Heinrich's hand long enough for the Remnants to hold the fortress. Thank you, by the way, for finding us the archer who helped us take it in the first place. At least you came through on something." He smirked.

"Why hold it? The researchers have found no way to awaken Alphas."

"This was never about the Golem of Death. However, until you agree to follow my command, I won't divulge anything more."

"How do I follow a man who consorts with his and my worst enemy?" Sigurd demanded.

"Your worst enemy," Rudiger corrected. "Papa Wolf is not mine and never was."

"He set you up as a defector and turned you into the lowest form of Steinkamp."

Rudiger let out a husky chuckle. "On the contrary. My comrades and I are the only true Steinkamp still alive today—well, some of us are still alive." His grin quickly faded after the last words he spoke, and he continued more seriously, "I still have hope for you, though. Everything I've done in the last ten years has been for the Steinkamp and Ingleheim. I will see our pledge restored to honor, and I want you to help me do it."

The lies pouring from Rudiger's mouth made Sigurd's stomach churn. "How can the Steinkamp be restored to honor following a man who has none?"

"I never claimed to have any," Rudiger replied. "I sacrificed my honor long ago so those who come after me might stand tall. We've all done duplicitous things while wearing that uniform. I sincerely hope *you* don't intend to tell me what honor is. At least the sins I've committed have been in pursuit of a brighter future for the Steinkamp instead of foolish vendettas."

Why hasn't he once mentioned what the Kings' Remnants have to do with this? Sigurd wondered. He gathered the rebellion and Wolfram were both tools that Rudiger used to get what he wanted. Discovering who killed the orphan boy would determine which man, Wolfram or Rudiger, had power over the other. Wolfram killing the boy would mean Rudiger had something on him to use for his purposes. Rudiger being behind the killing could potentially put Wolfram in the position of control, and that was where Sigurd knew Wolfram always preferred to be.

"Tell me, then, Rudiger, now that we are being honest with each other," said Sigurd. "The other Steinkamp that was here with you twenty years ago—since we both know he died in the Crags, who did kill that orphan boy?"

Rudiger licked his lips while contemplating his answer. "Wolfram let that slip, did he? You must have rustled him pretty good."

"Did Wolfram go through all the trouble to adopt a five-year-old and mangle his body to make it unrecognizable, or was it you?" Sigurd pressed.

"Does it matter?" Rudiger replied stiffly.

"Yes, it matters."

Rudiger responded by pulling two long knives from his coat sleeves. Sigurd shot a bolt, but Rudiger dove out of the way just in time. He managed to dodge Sigurd's other two bolts as well. He cursed as he attempted to reload, but his opponent leaped forward and kicked the crossbow from his grasp. Sigurd tried to kick Rudiger's legs out from under him, but he jumped backward. The extra distance between them bought time for Sigurd to extend his two swords.

While the two men stood off, Sigurd's mind raced. *This is the Steinkamp who stuck his skewer knife into the back of my mother's skull.* He kept that memory in the forefront of his mind to fuel the hatred he needed to best him.

They rushed at each other, prepared to deliver their own blitz attacks. Every sword blow Sigurd dealt, Rudiger's knives blocked with ease. Along with his Steinkamp training, Rudiger's years with the Kings' Remnants gave him a type of hybrid fighting style that kept Sigurd guessing. He swung for Rudiger's neck but Rudiger grabbed his arm and shoved it hard into the wood stove, breaking off what was left of the smokestack while causing Sigurd to drop his sword. Before he could attack with the other, Rudiger grabbed the back of his head and shoved it down onto the stovetop, bent his last sword wielding arm back and disarmed him. Rudiger grappled Sigurd from behind and dragged him back from the stove.

"If you want honesty, I'll give you honesty," Rudiger hissed in his ear. "I killed that boy, and you are alive because of it!"

Grunting with exertion, Sigurd pushed off the ground with his legs. Even with his opponent's weight bearing down on him, he was able to bash Rudiger against the wall where Sigurd proceeded to elbow him in the ribs and the face then flip him overhead.

"So that's it." Sigurd kicked Rudiger on the ground. "Wolfram had no reason to brand you a traitor because you blowing the whistle on him would also implicate yourself. You never truly defected, did you? You're still Wolfram's dog!"

Before Sigurd's next kick could land, Rudiger grabbed hold of his foot and kicked him with his heavy metal-plated leg from the floor. Sigurd went flying head-first into the rotting table and chairs.

"I am nobody's pet!" Rudiger roared.

Sigurd climbed out from the splintered wood then Rudiger charged and bodychecked him into the wall. It crumbled as Sigurd crashed through it. A shuddering pain took the wind out of him, and plaster dust billowed through the mesh of his mask, making him choke.

He found himself on his back looking up at the ceiling of his childhood bedroom, much of it having rotted away where now, rays of sunlight beamed through the rafters. The *Ode to Golems* rang through his head— remembering his mother singing it to him in that very spot. *This is not my room anymore.*

Sigurd struggled to crawl out from under the broken wood and stone as Rudiger continued speaking from the other room. "I help Wolfram bring down the Kings' Remnants, the Regime rewards us both as heroes, and I advance the way Wolfram did. I will soon have command of the entire Steinkamp force, and it is through them that I will restore order."

Upon getting up on two wobbling legs, Sigurd staggered out of his room. "When you say restoring order, how is it that all I hear is the promise of mass death and destruction?"

"Because we are Steinkamp!" Rudiger exclaimed with an air of grandiosity. "Death and destruction are what we were created for. The world may not want to admit it, but it needs men like us. Ingleheim will not know peace until the refuse has been burnt away, and we are the only ones that can see it done."

"If burning refuse is what we must do, then we best start with you."

Sigurd charged Rudiger with a new onslaught of attacks. He struck him in the chest and the face, causing him to stagger back, blood and sweat spraying into the air. Rudiger blocked his subsequent strikes, so Sigurd moved to punching him in the midsection, so forcefully, clouds of gray plaster dust billowed out from Sigurd's fists. Rudiger doubled over, and

Sigurd took him by the collar and tossed him head-first into the other wall. The plaster made a satisfying crack.

Rudiger, now disoriented, gave Sigurd the opportunity to take out his earth bindings. He wrapped the bindings around Rudiger's neck and pulled until he was completely cut off from air. "You tricked me into inflicting undue suffering onto Vaughn, so it is only fair that you suffer in kind!"

At those words, Sigurd molded the leather to Rudiger's flesh. All he had to do afterward was step away.

Rudiger scraped his fingertips against the bindings suffocating him. He could not cut them off without slicing his own neck. Sigurd backed toward the door while watching the Rogue Steinkamp helplessly choke to death. Rudiger lunged for Sigurd, but he stepped aside, easily shoving Rudiger over. Rudiger needed his gloves to free himself, and that got Sigurd wondering. *Why does he not use the gloves he used to free Wolfram?*

Sigurd had to end this. He picked up the crossbow from the ground, preparing to finish the man off. As soon as he reloaded it, a small gray canister dropped into the house through the open roof. Darkness enveloped the space. *There is still one other Steinkamp defector alive*, Sigurd realized. He heard the quiet thump of a nimble man landing on the floor. Sigurd let a bolt fly toward the sound but heard the dull thwack of it hitting the wall.

Rudiger's choking became to gasps for air. Sigurd released another bolt to where he heard Rudiger's deep breathing, but it was deflected by what sounded like steel. In an instant, Sigurd's crossbow was knocked from his hands and soon he was fending off attacks from an invisible, fully armored Steinkamp.

He didn't know where his blades had fallen, so he only had his cudgel to block the Steinkamp's flurry of strikes. Turning toward the doorway, Sigurd attempted to get outside of the dark void and wait for his opponents to emerge to fight them in the daylight, but he was grabbed from behind and forced down onto his back.

Sigurd jumped back onto his feet and blocked a series of blows coming at him from all sides. Both men wailed on him with their own attacks. Continual strikes across the side of his head eventually broke off Sigurd's mask. Now his focus was less on finding his opponents in the dark and more on protecting his exposed face, but his defenses did little to block what felt like Rudiger's metal-plated knee coming up hard on his nose. He was violently shoved onto his back where he turned to his hands and knees. Sigurd spat out the blood flooding into his mouth from his nostrils, his ears ringing from the repeated blows to the head.

Rays of sunlight seeped back into the house, bringing the blood-splattered floorboards into view. He barely had a moment to decide his next move before Rudiger's heavy foot found him in the midsection, sending him rolling into a set of old wooden cupboards. The other Steinkamp grabbed Sigurd's leg and pulled him across the floor. Sigurd kicked him away and got back up only to be put down again by a powerful blow to the back of the shoulder by Rudiger. The other Steinkamp got behind him and grabbed hold of both his arms while bearing his full weight down on him with his knee. Rudiger quickly removed Sigurd's gloves while the other Steinkamp tied his wrists and ankles with earth bindings.

Rudiger loomed over him, his features cold, having lost his signature smugness. He roughly pulled off Sigurd's hood as the Steinkamp behind him pressed the point of his skewer knife to the back of Sigurd's skull.

"We didn't come here to kill you, as much as my comrade here would like to. We came here in hopes that you'd see things our way. Alas, revenge is stubborn. It prevents you from seeing past your own mask." Rudiger placed Sigurd's gloves into his inside coat pocket.

Sigurd spat out more blood. "It looks like you murdered that orphan in vain."

"If you won't join me, I have no choice but to see you into our kapitän's custody. You will see the inside of Verishten's Mouth by week's end."

"Verishten will choke on me, and I will return for you, Rudiger!" Sigurd seethed. The earth bindings tore at his bare flesh as he struggled, but he didn't care.

"There is no point. Wolfram and I spotted you and Kriemhilde in town last night. I came back here knowing you'd return. Wolfram surveilled the inn and waited for you to leave. He's taking the girl back home, and this rebellion will be quelled, permanently."

Sigurd felt like a splitting blade had slashed through his chest. He and Katja had been so careful—he had made absolutely sure there was no one spying on them. "You're lying!" he roared, wanting to rip Rudiger's throat out with his teeth.

The Steinkamp held Sigurd back so Rudiger, with his throat intact, was able to say, "No, Siegfried. Not this time."

24

THE VOLCANIC CELLS

Jenn drifted in and out of consciousness. It was quiet now, though she could still hear the sounds of battle in the distance. The quaking caused by marching war golems had died off.

She was partially stuck in a dream where she was a rat hiding from a giant serpent. The serpent slithered dangerously close to her furrow, its hiss piercing her tiny ears. Rat Jenn couldn't stop shaking. Any second now she would feel the serpent's jaws snap shut around her. These dreams were related to her spirit magic abilities, but she didn't know why she was always a rat or why she felt so powerless in them.

It was the spiritual rapport Jenn had with her mother Egret, that finally brought her out of the dream and into reality.

The Barrier has been breached! The Overlord will be upon us—we need your help, Jenn, please!

Egret's voice radiated through her mind. She could feel her mother's fear, her desperation. Again, she saw the images from the woman's consciousness. She was in a convent belonging to the Storm Sisters of Luidfort, the safe house Rudiger had found for her. They now used it as a refuge from the coming Herrani scourge.

Egret had called out to Jenn hours before the Regime attacked the Fortress of Mortlach. She had begged her to send more rebel soldiers to Luidfort. All she had been able to send was word to those soldiers already in the Town of Luidfort, to get her to safety. That message never made it out of the fortress. After she had reported Sigurd's abduction of Wolfram,

Rudiger took off, leaving her in charge. She had a responsibility to the men and women who helped take the fortress and couldn't abandon them. Shortly after Rudiger left, the line of war golems standing by moved to attack. Jenn had done all she could to protect the fortress, but it was no use. Dozens upon dozens of war golems came upon them all at once and the next thing Jenn knew, she was trapped under the rubble of it all.

I'm on my way, Ma, she projected to her mother.

Upon quickly taking stock of her situation, she found she was buried under mounds of stone and metal. She had no mortal injuries, but had she not used her earth magic to create a tiny alcove to hide in when the debris came down, it would have surely crushed her. Only a few faint beams of light shone through the cracks between the boulders. *Please let me have enough earth essence left to get out of here,* she prayed.

She concentrated hard on the vibrating aura embedded in the heavy stone. Placing her hands upon the rocks to help her focus, she broke the large rocks apart into smaller and smaller chunks until she was able to dig free. Climbing onto unsteady legs, Jenn staggered away from the debris that used to be Mortlach's southwestern tower.

All she could see through the falling ash and flame were bloody limbs and mangled corpses half buried under the stone. Pools of blood and entrails left in the wake of the golems' iron feet were entrenched deep into the dirt. Jenn had seen her fair share of gore in her life while working for the smugglers and fighting with the Remnants, but in less than an hour since the attack, the bloodshed proved to be too much for her. *Are there no other survivors?* she wondered.

It was the middle of the afternoon, and yet the thick smoke clouds combined with the usual ashfall made the sky look as dark as night. Screams, crashes, and clangs echoed through the air. The ground vibrated as golems walked about. *The north side is still under attack!*

"I've got to get out of here," Jenn muttered to herself as she turned south.

She was all sapped of essences and there was nothing she could do for her men now, but she could still save her mother. The persistent serpent dreams she'd been having lately must have been a sign Nas'Gavarr was close. *He has to be the giant serpent from my nightmares.*

Jenn soon came across two fallen war golems, one of them having had collapsed partially atop the other. As she walked around them, a scraping sound came from inside one of the golems. A man, smeared head to toe in ash and blood, struggled to climb out from between them. Jenn would never have recognized him if it weren't for his matted locks, caked with ash-laden mud.

"Jeth?" Jenn ran over to the golems and climbed up one of the arms.

"Take my advice," he grunted. "If you try to take down a golem from the ground, get out of the way *before* it falls on top of you."

"You're in oddly good spirits considering the circumstances." Jenn pulled the Fae'ren free with a good heave. "Anything broken?"

Jeth moved his arms back and forth and bent his legs. "Still got my limbs, and I can still use a bow. That's good enough for me."

The Fae'ren didn't look entirely unscathed. He was peppered in bruises, and Jenn wasn't sure if the blood he had on him was his own or someone else's, but she decided to take his word for it. She probably didn't look much better herself.

"We have to get out of here," she warned as they made their way back down the golem's arm.

Jeth looked to the slaughter continuing in the north and donned a deep frown. "So that's it? We're just going to go?"

From the moment they had taken the fortress, Jeth had been raring to claim his bounty, but Rudiger had promised him his Magitech when he returned. Jeth had said that he didn't trust Rudiger to make good on his deal and threatened to leave numerous times. Now it seemed like he didn't want to.

"If we stay, we die," she urged. "I'm low on aura, but I have an emergency sapphire stashed away in Deschner. That is also where we can find the rest of your Magitech. You can finally go home."

"I don't know where home is going to be yet," Jeth muttered.

"If I get you the Magitech, will you take me to the Town of Luidfort on the way out?"

Jeth finally turned back to her, his bloodshot eyes laced with exhaustion. "Is that where your home is?"

"That's where my mother is, and I *need* to get her out of there," Jenn said. "The Herrani have accomplished the impossible. They've breached the Barrier of Kriegle."

"How?" Jeth eyes went wide.

"All military efforts were focused on keeping the naja from climbing over it, but it was just a diversion while Nas'Gavarr's Earth Mages tunneled in from below."

"And how do you know what is happening in Luidfort all of the sudden?"

Jenn was too tired to explain the concept of spiritual rapports to the Fae'ren. "Magic."

"Oh, through a spiritual rapport or something like that?"

"Uh. . . yes, actually." Jenn cocked her head. *This certainly knows more than he lets on,* she thought.

"How does that work anyway?"

"I don't have time for this," she groaned, turning away from Jeth and heading southward.

"Come on, try it out on me now. Read my mind." Jeth seemed to have forgotten about the plight of the rebel soldiers.

With a heavy sigh, Jenn relented. "Spirit Mages can't just read anyone's mind at the drop of a hat. The object's mind has to be clear and receptive. It also takes time to do what we call *priming,* before it will let anyone in."

"But you did it," Jeth pressed. "The other rebels talk about how you got into that kanzler's head and made him tell you where the Golem of Death was."

"It took me two days of priming before I cracked Volker and that wasn't even to form a spiritual rapport, only to affect his perceptions enough to make him think I was the Führer, and I could only keep it up for a few seconds at a time."

"Oh, well . . . everyone is talking about how talented you are. I figured you'd be the next Melikheil." Jeth casually spat on the ground.

Jenn laughed a little. "I've been manipulating essences since I was twelve, so as an Essence Mage, I get by just fine. As a Spirit Mage, though—I only realized I had that ability at fifteen. My mother once knew a Spirit Mage who told her a few things, but most of what I know I had to figure out for myself. She allowed me to practice on her over the years, which is why I formed such a strong rapport with her. She's the reason I know the Herrani have breached the Barrier."

"Sweet Deity," Jeth said. "Then they'll be upon the Town of Luidfort in a little over a day. You'll be leaving this war zone for one far worse."

Before Jenn could respond, a war golem spotted them and made its way toward them, fast.

"I don't know." Jenn gulped. "Do I want to die under a golem's foot or between a naja's jaws?"

Jeth already had an arrow nocked and aimed upwards. Jenn's heart pounded as she helplessly watched the giant iron monstrosity get closer.

Beads of ashen sweat ran visibly down Jeth's forehead, the tension in his shoulders apparent. Never before had she seen an archer hold a bow so steady. He was a statue, his concentration unfaltering, even amidst the quaking of the ground with each of the golem's steps. It was almost upon them.

"Shoot!" she urged.

"Just wait," Jeth hushed. With a slow and calm exhalation, he released his arrow. Jenn had seen him hit several golems when they first took the fortress and each time she doubted the arrow would hit its mark, and each time she had been wrong.

The arrow zinged through the slits in the metal grating and straight into the glowing red eye behind it. The light went out instantly, and the golem collapsed to its knees. As it started falling forward, Jeth grabbed Jenn and dove to the side. The golem didn't even come close to crushing them, but apparently Jeth didn't want to take his chances this time around.

Lying on his back, Jeth looked to Jenn beside him on the ground. "Naja jaws it is, then?"

She nodded, and Jeth helped her to her feet. "How do you keep doing that?"

"Keep doing what?"

"Not missing."

"Magic." Jeth winked.

Rolling her eyes. "Whatever you say, Fairy Boy."

Sigurd was falling . . . falling deep into the blackness of the chasm. Its walls closed in around him as he fell farther into the infinite black. His fingers scraped along the rough stone. His skin tore as he struggled to find a handhold, anything to stop his descent. He screamed, his voice as a lost child's.

The chasm was alight in a burning red and then an unbearable, smoldering heat followed. Sigurd's skin sizzled and peeled. His lungs melted inside of his chest. Flames rose to meet him as he continued to fall deeper into the infernal abyss. The Golem of Stone would not save him this time.

He was alone now. Alone and burning alive.

And then that low rumbling voice sounded again, only this time, its message was much grimmer.

"The covenant is broken! The Age of Man has ended! You are lost!"

Sigurd regained consciousness on a wet floor in a darkened cell. He quickly realized that the floor's dampness was from the sweat dripping off his own half-naked body. The temperature in the cell was beyond stifling. It was enough to make Sigurd feel as if his very flesh were slowly burning away.

I'm in the volcanic cells!

He had heard all about the cells at the base of the Volcano of Verishten. Vents in the floor and ceiling allowed the volcanic heat to radiate through the cell block, making each so agonizingly hot that it wasn't uncommon for prisoners to die of dehydration before their sentence could be carried out.

Apart from the scalding air and the burning floor, Sigurd was further tortured by a violent thirst. The sweat entering his mouth was all the liquid afforded to him and every drop of it tasted like a life-giving spring. Sigurd began to look forward to his trip to the top of the volcano. At least then he would feel a breeze upon his blistering skin before his fiery death.

Sigurd clenched his drenched fists, causing the inside of his forearm to sting. The pain reminded him of the ritualistic and violent manner in which he had been processed before being thrown into his cell. The deed had been done by a group of comrades, including Rudiger, who had all stripped him down, exposing him as just an ordinary man of skin and bone. They had shaved off his wrist branding with a knife before taking turns beating him with their cudgels. Even some citizens had been invited to witness the humiliation. A Steinkamp traitor did not deserve to die with the dignity his mask and uniform afforded him.

The Age of Man has ended. You are lost. . . .

That sentiment ran through Sigurd's head over and over as he lay upon the burning floor. The more he thought about it, the more he trembled with rage. He was not ready to give up yet; he didn't care what some god said to him in a fevered dream. Sigurd rose to his feet and went for the cast iron door of his cell, looking for any flaw that could help him open it. Grabbing a bolt, he twisted it as hard as he could, the hot iron sizzling into the flesh of his palm. He grunted in pain.

Forced to let go, Sigurd inspected the peeling skin of his hand. *It's just one burn. You've suffered much worse than this at the age of twelve.* Sigurd ground his teeth, pushing through the searing pain as he continued to twist, but it didn't budge. He tried another bolt and it seemed to burn worse than the last. His angered shrieks ringing off the metallic walls of the tiny cell almost distracted him from the pain. Eventually, he cut his hand on the bolt and let go. He roared in frustration and slammed his whole body against the door before collapsing to his knees before it.

There is no use, he realized. Sigurd wiped the rivers of sweat from his brow and tried to catch his wind that would never come. The air was too hot and thick. He was going to die by Verishten's Mouth if he didn't die in this cell first.

Never before had he feared for his own death—that was until he fell for Katja. She probably worried about him, when it was she who faced the real danger. Even if Heinrich beat back Bachman's men and ended the rebellion, he would never see Rudiger coming. Rudiger was going to use his Steinkamp to overthrow his regime and Katja was going to be caught in the middle. If she did not submit, Rudiger would likely kill her, and there was nothing Sigurd could do to stop it. He could only trust that she would figure it out and run before it was too late.

Sigurd crawled away from the hot iron door just before it opened. A new air wafted into the cell, giving him a slight respite from the all-encompassing heat for just a moment. Several guards entered, dressed head to toe in leather armor and faceplates. Since Sigurd was too weak from heat exhaustion to put up a fight, they had no trouble shackling his hands and feet and lifting him off the ground by his arms.

Dragging him out of his volcanic cell, one of the guards said, "It is time, defector. May the Mighty Verishten save your soul."

25

VERISHTEN'S TEARS

Three days after her capture, Katja arrived at the Fortress of Mortlach in East Breisenburg. The southwest tower had partially collapsed, and golems worked to clear the rubble while men worked to rebuild.

"When was the fortress retaken?" she asked Wolfram as they arrived at the north gates.

"As soon as we spotted you in Kensloche with that defector, your father was notified, and he commanded his war golems accordingly."

Katja nodded. It had only been a few days before that the fortress was in rebellion hands. "When can I see my father?"

"He will send for you shortly, I'm sure."

Wolfram ordered one of his personal comrades to take her straight to her chambers in the northeast tower. There, she washed and changed out of her peasant garb and into something more appropriate for the Führer's daughter. A guard came to retrieve her a few hours later and took her to the central war room where her father waited with his offiziers.

Katja stood outside the large double doors taking deep breaths. She knew her father would be furious with her and likely ask a lot of difficult questions about her research and her involvement with Sigurd and the Remnants. However, she couldn't let herself worry about that. She needed to think of how she was going to convince her father to now spare Sigurd's life, along with Klemens's and Ignatius's.

The guard ushered Katja into the large, circular room under a breathtaking red, green, and yellow stained glass dome, depicting war golems and their

Mages. Her footsteps echoed loudly off the granite tiles. Five people sitting around a marble roundtable rose as she entered. The two people Katja noticed first were Frau Brunhilde and Herrscher Heinrich. Heinrich had aged considerably since she'd been gone. He had lost nearly all his hair, save a few white wisps behind his ears. Despite that, he still possessed the prominent jaw line passed on by Deschner kings and the daunting amber gaze that she'd inherited.

Kapitän Wolfram was at her father's right. There was also a taller man with long auburn hair, tied back, wearing the attire of a Steinkamp Kommandeur whom she didn't recognize. He nodded to her and sat back down, revealing a man of slighter build behind him whom she hadn't noticed until now. Her heart skipped a beat at the sight of him.

"Klemens!" Without a second thought, she rushed to embrace him, overwhelmed with relief. He looked paler than ever but alive.

"Thank Verishten you're all right, Kat," Klemens whispered as he returned her hug. "But I expected you to be here before me."

"I will explain everything later. I feared Bachman had killed you."

"Sit down, Kriemhilde, so that we may begin," Heinrich said in a stern voice.

Katja nodded and took a seat in the empty chair between the Steinkamp Kommandeur and Brunhilde. "What is it that you would like to discuss, Father?"

Heinrich's powerful voice echoed throughout the room. "First, you need to be updated on what has happened since you left for university." With a throat clearing, he continued, "We uncovered the identity of the rebel leader, who calls himself the Kaiser, months ago. To draw out his army, we needed to make him think he had a chance of winning."

"And how did you do that?" Katja narrowed her gaze at her father.

"Ten years ago, Wolfram enlisted his most trusted kommandeur to infiltrate the Kings' Remnants with the intention of revealing their leader and bringing them down. When Meister Melikheil left, I made sure I was not seen controlling golems that were too far from me. That way, Ignatius's theory about me needing the Spirit Mage's intervention looked plausible."

Katja glared at the man sitting next to her. *So, this is the deceptive Rudiger in the flesh,* she thought. Her skin crawled.

Brunhilde continued on her husband's behalf, "When we found the Golem of Death under this fortress, it provided a unique opportunity to get the Kings' Remnants to reveal themselves once and for all."

"So you knew all along that awakening it was impossible—that our research was pointless. Then why . . . ?"

"To draw the rebels out and test the loyalties of those most trusted in my regime," Heinrich said. "Herr Ignatius didn't waste a single moment informing Rudiger of our plans to awaken it. The rebels were chomping at the bit to get at it, so Rudiger and Wolfram arranged for Herr Volker's abduction with the expectation that he'd reveal the location to them."

"You could have had your infiltrator tell the rebels where it was located outright. Why make my father a casualty?" Klemens cast a vicious eye to Rudiger at his left.

"The information had to be gleaned by rebellion efforts," Wolfram cut in. "It would be suspicious if someone like Rudiger had that information without good reason. Volker was not supposed to die. The comrade Sigurd, who volunteered for the rescue mission, killed him despite my strict orders to keep him alive. I was careful to arrange it so Sigurd would reach Volker after he had revealed the information, but I underestimated his skill and his capacity for insubordination. It was an oversight that we have thusly rectified, my Führer."

Katja immediately noticed Klemens's tension as he looked from Wolfram to Katja, and then to Rudiger, in search of answers. *Wolfram is lying, which means that he did intend for the kanzler to die and he doesn't want Father or Klemens to know that,* Katja thought. "These are lies," she argued. "Sigurd was under order to kill the kanzler, and he claims that order originated with you, Father."

"I was there, fraulein," Rudiger insisted. "I saw Sigurd wait for the information to be revealed before shooting Herr Volker through the heart. I immediately reported his suspicious behavior to my kapitän before he returned to headquarters. He ordered me to confront Sigurd at his haven as a member of the Kings' Remnants. Sigurd admitted that he was working on his own directive and was, in fact, plotting to assassinate our noble kapitän."

"First thing we had to do was get him away from Fraulein Kriemhilde as carefully as possible," said Wolfram. "Rebel Steinkamp must be handled with care. If we had confronted him too quickly, it could have put her in danger, so I reassigned him to the front lines to keep tabs on him."

"I decided to put him to use in taking care of that crook of a kommissar, and in tracking down Gershlon Reborn," added Rudiger.

"Gershlon Reborn?" Klemens looked around the table in curiosity.

"Also known as the Desert War Traitor, someone of great interest to us," replied Heinrich. "Not only because he was witness to Meister Melikheil's demise, but because he was one of the few outsiders who could win Herran the war, as his namesake did for Del'Cabria a hundred years ago."

Wolfram put a finger up to interject. "We used him to give the Remnants a plausible means to take the fortress while allowing the Regime to off him as a potential threat when we took the fortress back."

"Once Sigurd delivered the archer to us," said Rudiger, "I promised him a chance to kill his kapitän. We were then going to set a trap for him and arrest him for treason. Had I known how difficult he would make things, I would have acted sooner to detain him. Despite that, our ruse was successful in the end, and that traitorous Steinkamp is right where he belongs."

Katja's gut wrenched. "And . . . where is that?"

"That is none of your concern, Kriemhilde," Heinrich stated firmly.

"Listen, Father—I don't know what these men told you already, but everything Sigurd has done was in the interest of protecting me. He saved my life and freed me from my rebel captors. He does not deserve to die for that."

Heinrich nodded solemnly before speaking. "I understand your confusion. It pains me to have put you through all of this, but your abduction was all part of a plan to embolden the Kings' Remnants to march against me. We allowed them to hold the fortress for a time so that we could see how far their influence stretched. It put them in a prime position to be eliminated, and now I know who my true enemies are. Kapitän Wolfram arranged for your subsequent rescue. They came upon Bachman's estate and found only Klemens. We later learned that you had escaped. It was a good thing Wolfram's hunch led him to Sigurd who he knew would return with you to Kensloche."

"This is madness, Father!" Katja exclaimed, standing and pointing at Rudiger. "Has it not dawned on you that this man whom you've had infiltrating the Kings' Remnants has been actively making them stronger than they otherwise would have been? Thanks to him, a marginal group of dissenters has been turned into a force of almost half of the population. How do you expect Ingleheim to survive this?"

"Sit down, foolish girl!" Heinrich snapped.

Her face flushed with rage. She wanted to yell, *I am twenty-four years old and six months shy of a doctorate. I am not some foolish girl.* Instead she kept quiet and sat down. A foolish girl would continue berating the Führer in front of his wife and colleagues. It was best she gather herself and speak more calmly if she had any hope of getting through to him.

"When undercover," Rudiger began, "it is important to gain your enemy's trust above all else. To reveal Herr Bachman as the Kaiser, I had to do things that benefited the rebellion for a time. I assure you, fraulein, it was worth the risk to finally bring them to their knees."

"Kommandeur Rudiger is right," the Führer said. "What appeared as a marginal group of dissenters had the potential to become a widespread revolt. Revolts must be quelled and with great force. If half the population is unwilling to bend to their ruler, that half is worthless to him. Ingleheim will be strengthened by the loss and you, Kriemhilde, will be safer for it."

"How will slaughtering half of your people make me any safer?"

"That is part of what we will talk about here today. As all of you may know, I have no heir bearing the Eye of Verishten. Most of the people do not realize this now, but when I am gone, they will soon learn no Golem Mage is around to lead them. This means that the ruling seat is ripe for the taking, and I fear, daughter, you will never be able to hold onto it unless we defeat our enemies now and reward our most loyal offiziers accordingly."

The Führer looked to his wife, and she continued on his behalf, "That is why our mighty Führer has awarded Herr Wolfram with a position second only to himself, the Kanzlership of Breisenburg, stewardship of this fortress and what lies beneath, and command of Ingleheim's military might. Klemens has agreed to wed his daughter Kriemia and remain in his father's house as Lieutenant Military Strategist under Herr Wolfram's command."

Katja looked to him with a start. Klemens didn't make eye contact with her. He didn't appear too impressed by the arrangement, but she figured it was best for him. With his father dead and his brother fighting the Herrani, Klemens had to think of his house and its continued usefulness to the Regime. She couldn't fault him for that.

Brunhilde went on, "And the position of Kapitän of the Steinkamp force has been awarded to Herr Rudiger for his years of unyielding loyalty in the midst of rebels." She held Katja's gaze for a lingering moment before finishing, "In addition, he has graciously agreed to a marriage pact with you, Kriemhilde. Your father and I insist on you two being wed as soon as possible."

Katja felt like she'd been thrown off a cliff. She looked to Rudiger beside her and was met by his raised eyebrow. "You can't be serious!" she scoffed angrily, unable to fathom how her father could sanction such a thing.

"We know it's sudden." Brunhilde primped her hair below her fascinator. "Your father and Herr Volker had wished for you to wed Herr Klemens—"

"That explains why my transfer to Golem Studies was approved so quickly," Klemens muttered, turning to Katja.

"Yes, well, as it turns out, your marriage to Fraulein Kriemia will be much more beneficial for everyone," Brunhilde replied.

"And how do *I* benefit, exactly?" asked Katja.

Heinrich sighed. "Understand that the future of Ingleheim, and your life in it, hangs in the balance. When there are no Golem Mages to keep the people in line, we must rely on the Regime's next most powerful resource, which are the Steinkamp."

"Under no circumstances do I consent to marry this beast. He is a liar. Neither Rudiger nor Wolfram can be trusted. When did you become so blind, Father?"

"Tell me, Kriemhilde, what evidence do you present that proves these two men, who have unfailingly supported this regime since its inception, are planning to betray me?" Heinrich challenged.

Katja had nothing. She wanted to tell him all about Sigurd being the surviving son of Earl Sigmund and that Wolfram and Rudiger conspired to deceive their Führer with the body of an orphan boy. Even if she could prove somehow that they were liars, doing so would only hasten Sigurd's execution. She shook her head silently.

"Let's all try to be understanding." Wolfram adjusted his spectacles. "It is common for a young woman to become unusually attached to her protector. As I've disclosed to you already, Sigurd is a deeply disturbed individual and has been feeding Kriemhilde lies, making her feel as if she could trust no one but him. In this way, he has made her feel dependent on him for survival. Verishten only knows what he had in store for her had we not intercepted them."

Wolfram speaking of her as if she weren't at the table brought Katja's blood to a boil. *If only you knew what it felt like to have someone invade your mind, making you think and feel things you otherwise would not!* "Father, I swear to you, none of what the kapitän is saying is true."

"Herr Wolfram has witnessed you and Sigurd together in Kensloche. He reports that you were staying at an inn there," Heinrich said, brushing right by Katja's pleas. "So now I must ask the question a father wishes he never has to ask, and know that if you are not honest in your answer, you will deeply regret it." Looking straight into Katja's eyes, he asked, "Have you allowed Sigurd to defile you?"

She struggled to keep herself from shaking. Pushing her tongue against the inside of her cheek, Katja shook her head in disgust. "I don't see how that is relevant to this discussion."

"If there is a possibility that you carry a traitor's bastard whelp, it is very relevant. Now answer the question!" her father barked.

It hadn't yet occurred to Katja that she may very well be carrying Sigurd's child. She prayed that she wasn't, for it would surely be terminated. She closed her eyes, willing her tears to remain inside them. With a deep breath, she muttered, "Not to worry, he did not *defile* me." It was partially the truth, since what happened between them was not something she would define as being defiled.

Heinrich harrumphed. "I suppose we will find out in a few months if you are lying."

"Meister Melikheil, on the other hand," Katja cut in, "defiled me on a regular basis under your own roof, but I suppose that doesn't count since it did not result in a *bastard whelp*."

The awkward tension increased tenfold around the marble table. Brunhilde looked to Heinrich, his mouth agape in horror. The Führer then sharply snapped his jaw shut and turned a violent shade of red. "Enough!"

"Tell that to your wife," Katja went on while eying her stepmother to her left. "Of all the times Melikheil defiled her, I'd expect he would have given her a child. Then again, maybe she is barren."

Brunhilde gasped then spat, "How dare you, you little bitch!"

Just as Katja hoped, Brunhilde let her guard down, and she could witness her father's angered glare regress and transform back into one of terror. He looked to Brunhilde for a split second, his lip quivering ever so slightly.

As if sensing the sudden change in her husband, Brunhilde immediately turned to him and said as sweetly as she could manage, "Don't believe her, Darling, she is simply lashing out. I can certainly appreciate how humiliating it is to have your virtue questioned."

As quickly as it came, the pained look in Heinrich's eyes faded as he reached out to touch Brunhilde's arm affectionately. Katja had finally witnessed it for herself. Brunhilde was controlling her father like Melikheil had been controlling her. That meant that the real Heinrich was still in there somewhere.

"My apologies to both of you for my harsh reaction. Please forgive me." Katja hung her head.

"Of course, Dove," Brunhilde cooed with feigned sympathy. "You've been through quite a lot."

Ignoring her stepmother, Katja turned to her father and Wolfram. "If you must know what Sigurd and I were up to in Kensloche, I'll tell you."

"Go on then," Heinrich said.

"We were on our way to the Crags to awaken the Golem of Stone— again."

"The Alpha of Crag Golems?" Heinrich said, aghast. "You've awakened it before? Why have you not notified me?"

"The professor and I were keeping it between us, of course. We wanted to be the ones who decided what to do with any and all findings."

"How did you awaken it?" asked Brunhilde.

"I didn't." Katja responded to her stepmother, then turned to the other men at the table. "Sigurd did."

Both Wolfram and Rudiger looked around the table with furrowed brows.

Wolfram leaned forward to ask, "Sigurd awakened an Alpha?"

Katja nodded. "We didn't know how he did it at the time, but we believe he is the key to awakening the Golem of Death. That's why I needed him. Ignatius and I were close to figuring out how a Mage could control an Alpha. Sigurd and I went to Kensloche to continue with our experiment until we were interrupted."

"Impossible." Heinrich pulled irritably on the collar of his buttoned military jacket.

"Klemens was there." Katja turned to her research partner. "He can validate my claims."

Everyone looked to Klemens. He sputtered, "Uh . . . she's telling the truth. The Golem of Stone did awaken."

"And you saw Sigurd do it?" Heinrich asked.

Klemens met Katja's pleading gaze and then shook his head. "I became trapped after a rockslide. I didn't actually see the Steinkamp do anything."

Katja sighed inwardly, but she was glad enough that Klemens told the truth. She didn't expect him to go the extra mile and lie to help her save Sigurd.

"Kriemhilde is simply trying to save the defector's life, Herrscher. I witnessed him try to awaken the Golem of Stone when he took me to the Crags and nothing happened," Wolfram protested.

"You didn't mention that in your report, Kapitän." Heinrich's amber glare burned into Wolfram.

"I didn't think it relevant. Sigurd is delusional."

"I'll understand if you don't believe me," said Katja, "but I know with Ignatius's help, I can awaken the Golem of Death. I believe we can come up with a way for you to control it, Father. That is, if Ignatius is still alive—"

"He has faced tribunal and is two days away from his execution," stated Heinrich.

"Free Ignatius and allow us to do what you requested three and a half months ago. Your dissenters can then truly be a thing of the past. However, I cannot do it on my own. I will need the professor's existing knowledge, and I will need Sigurd. If you wish to see them both beheaded for their crimes afterward, I will not stand in your way. Just give me this one chance to do what is right for the Regime." She squeazed her knees over her dress with both hands.

Heinrich looked straight at his daughter. "If you can deliver on this, there will be no force in this world that can stand against the Regime. However, it can also be the thing that destroys it. Are you absolutely sure that I will be able to control the Alpha?"

"Not absolutely, but if Sigurd and Ignatius die then we will never know."

"I suppose we never will," said Wolfram, "since Sigurd's death sentence is already being carried out. Word will never reach the volcano in time."

Katja's heart jumped into her throat. "Please, Father, command the winged golem taking him there to turn back!" *It can't be too late....*

Heinrich closed his eyes as everyone, especially Brunhilde, looked onward intently. Not many had the privilege to see how the Führer commanded his golems with a mere thought from the comfort of his chair.

After several minutes of concentration, Heinrich opened his eyes and looked to Katja. "I cannot reach it."

"What do you mean you cannot reach it?"

"There are no winged golems currently flying up or down the volcano at this time. I can only assume it has already returned."

"You can't know that for certain. Maybe it hasn't left yet."

Wolfram attempted an apologetic look. "It is well into the afternoon, fraulein. Volcanic executions always occur mid-morning. The Steinkamp defector is dead."

Completely devoid of air, Katja deflated in her chair. It was all she could do not to break down into tortured sobs in front of everyone. "I see," she murmured.

"Do you think that awakening the Alpha is possible without him?" Brunhilde asked. "Otherwise, I don't see why we should pardon Herr Ignatius either."

Brunhilde's voice was nothing more than a muffled drone as Katja's heart shattered inside of her chest. *It's too late.* She couldn't find the wherewithal to respond to her stepmother or her father's repeated requests for her to answer the question. She wished she really could wake the Golem of Death. She would gladly volunteer to be the first person to step into its deadly gaze.

"Yes, it is possible," Klemens replied on Katja's behalf. "Between me, the professor, and Kat—I mean, Kriemhilde, I believe we can still awaken it."

"Then it is agreed." Heinrich folded his hands together in front of him. "We will transfer Herr Ignatius to the prison here for the duration of the project. He will remain under strict guard. Progress made by any of you will be reported directly to Frau Brunhilde and myself through chaperones.

"Now, Kriemhilde," the Führer continued. "Let us return to the matter of your marriage to Kapitän Rudiger."

Before Katja could protest, a guard burst into the war room. "Mighty Führer, the Barrier of Kriegle has been breached. Nas'Gavarr's forces are making headway to the Town of Luidfort!"

The Führer and his offiziers stood with a start. Katja was too numb to take in the information properly. Although she worried for her uncle Friedhelm, she could only think of locking herself in her chambers and never coming out.

Heinrich dismissed the women from the war room so he could converse with his offiziers. Katja couldn't leave the room fast enough. She stepped into the hall where she hoped to find her breath, but it eluded her. She was jolted by Rudiger, having left the war room for a moment to catch up to her, just outside the door.

"You mustn't mourn for that Steinkamp, fraulein," he said, keeping pace beside her. "You'd do best to forget about him altogether. Only with Verishten can a delusional mind like Sigurd's find peace."

"Leave me be," she said coldly. Rudiger grabbed her shoulder and turned her to face him. An uncontrollable rage flooded her mind at his touch. She smacked him as hard as she could across his bearded face. "I look forward to our wedding night, Rudiger. It will grant me the opportunity to cut your heart out in your sleep. Then you'd know what it's like!"

Rudiger clutched her arm so tight it sent shockwaves of pain up and down it. She gasped, having forgotten with whom she was dealing. *Never go on the offensive.*

Pulling her closer to him, Rudiger hissed, "Do you really think I'm interested in Sigurd's leavings, hmm? I don't need you to rule. Remember that!"

It became clear to Katja at that moment what Rudiger was planning. *What good is a Golem Expert to him when he controls the entire Steinkamp force? What will stop him from overthrowing the Regime as soon as the opportunity presents itself?* "Let go of me," she seethed.

"Kommandeur—or Kapitän, whichever it is—" came the timid voice of Klemens from the doorway. Rudiger released Katja in a flash and stepped in front of her so that Klemens wouldn't see how frazzled he had made her. "The Führer requires your presence. Now."

Rudiger stepped inside as Klemens lingered behind for a moment to make sure Katja was okay. She mouthed the words "thank you," and Klemens nodded before stepping back into the war room.

Katja sprinted down the hallway and didn't stop until she found her chambers and locked the doors behind her. She went to open her window, letting Breisenburg's ashy air into the room. In the distance, she saw the Volcano of Verishten in the highest peak of the Deschner Mountain Range. The afternoon sun was completely hidden behind the ash clouds billowing into the sky. The volcano was more active than usual. Bright orange lava, which some referred to as Verishten's Tears, spurted sporadically into the air. Verishten wept heavily today. He had received the body and soul of the greatest man Katja had ever known—the only man she'd ever truly loved. Seeing the lava slowly pour down the mountain worked to stall her own tears. There was no room for self-pity and no time for mourning. Verishten would cry for her this time.

Gazing upon the volcano, Katja felt something inside her change as if a formidable darkness was awakening. But this wasn't her usual darkness. This wasn't what Melikheil had left behind. This was something else. It was Sigurd's darkness.

When she first met him, Katja had been so afraid of the man behind the mask. She had been anything but comfortable with how effortlessly he killed, even when it was to protect her. All she could think about now was that night when Sigurd had brutally dispatched those Cragsmen, where she had made the decision to trust such a man. It was under the stars where she gave him her heart and soul before she had even seen his face. It was that night when she had realized there were times when killing was necessary, even if she didn't want it to be. Now she understood. She understood Sigurd's darkness just like he had understood hers. They had both been victims; they had both been tools for the use of those who abused their power.

Not anymore. Katja knew what she had to do. Ingleheim was falling apart, but she would make sure that it fell apart her way. *Rudiger, Wolfram, Brunhilde. . . they will all pay for what they did to you. They will be stopped, and you will be remembered.*

In Siegfried's name, Kriemhilde would have her revenge and his.

26

FIND ME, HERE I STAND

A winged golem crouched upon a ridge off the base of Verishten's Volcano like a bird about to take flight. It looked to the ash-filled sky with its violet triangular eye before springing into the air. When it reached its peak altitude, enormous, sparkling granite wings, smoothed by rain and wind erosion, extended from its back. It glided downward, directing the winds with the power of its eye to aid its massive body in flight, something that would otherwise be impossible for a giant object made of stone.

Sigurd was helplessly bound to the front of the golem as it swooped into its ascent toward the mouth of the volcano. Unlike the other exhilarating moments he had spent flying beneath such a being, this flight would see him to his doom. That realization made his heart rage inside of his chest. He wasn't ready to die—not like this.

Thoughts of Katja were all Sigurd had to keep his panic at bay. He imagined her standing by the door of the inn and how she looked at him right before he left. His whole being lurched knowing that he was not going to be there to protect her from the dangers threatening her.

Katja, I am sorry. I have failed you.

Far below, a lone figure ran along a ridge. Sigurd was unsure if the figure was male, female, or even human, for that matter. It halted its sprint and pointed at the golem carrying Sigurd. *Wait, that's not pointing, that's aiming,* he realized. That's a man with a bow and arrow!

The arrow released, and Sigurd's gaze followed its trajectory all the way up and into the violet glow of the winged golem's eye. Its light went out, and the winds keeping the heavy granite wings in flight went with it. The golem hung in midair for an excruciating moment before free falling headfirst toward the jutting rocks at the volcano's base. Sigurd closed his eyes as he fell faster.

No, comrade. If you can inflict death on your foes, you can face your own.

As Sigurd plummeted to the ground, he forced his eyes open. The rocks came at him fast, yet they didn't seem to reach him. The winged golem hit ground, and that ground gave way. The earth took Sigurd and the golem inside it like a pool of liquid and then shot them back out like a geyser. The golem came back down onto its back with Sigurd still molded to its front. The afternoon sun barely peeked out through thick ash, but it was still enough to irritate Sigurd's sore, wind-whipped eyes.

The blurry, silhouetted head of Jeth eventually appeared over him. "So that's what you look like."

"How did you . . . ?" Sigurd rasped, unable to find the breath to finish his sentence.

"Hold on. I'll get him," said a familiar female voice. Jenn also appeared above Sigurd. She laid her hands upon the bindings and they returned to leather. He then slid off the golem's chest and onto his bare feet.

When Jeth took out his canteen, Sigurd's throat burned with a violent thirst.

"Water!" he croaked, snatching the canteen from his hands. He had drunk half the contents before Jeth grabbed it back.

"Ease up, will you? I need that to last me to Luidfort Range."

"Here, take mine," Jenn offered. "I'm bursting with essences, so I can always squeeze more water from the air."

"Oh, right, in that case, take both of ours," said Jeth.

Without hesitating, Sigurd took Jenn's canteen and drank down the beautifully refreshing liquid, followed by Jeth's. He drank so much he choked, having forgotten to breathe. "Thank you," he gasped between coughs.

"Take it easy there." Jeth patted Sigurd on the back until his coughing fit was over.

Sigurd leaned against the dormant golem to catch his breath. He was still dizzy and weak, and his skin dry and peeling in spots. "How did you two come to find me?" he asked in bewilderment.

"Divine providence, mostly." Jeth chuckled. "Jenn and I just came from the City of Deschner. There is a rumor going around that the Rogue

Steinkamp was captured and sentenced to death by the volcano. As luck would have it, on our way to Luidfort, we saw your winged golem taking flight. Both of us were more than curious to see who this Rogue Steinkamp was."

Jenn cut in, "As the golem was falling, I could see that it wasn't Rudiger, so we knew it had to be you."

"You two were supposed to be holding the Fortress of Mortlach. If you're here, am I to assume it once again rests with the Regime?"

"That'd be correct." Jeth nodded.

Sigurd ambled over to a precipice to get a view of the City of Deschner below. It was difficult to see the state of it through the ash-fall. "How does Deschner fare?"

Jenn began, "It's total chaos there. Two armies lay siege at its gates while the commoners riot in the streets, targeting Karlmen, and criminals, or anyone else who has ever acted as an oppressor. I also heard from some of my fellow rebels there that the townspeople of Kensloche have banded together in service to the rebellion and are marching toward Deschner to join with Nordenhein and Untevar."

"And the Führer and his family?" Sigurd asked. *Katja, please be all right.*

"Not that I took great pains to check, but from what I heard, the highborn areas are still untouched by the violence—they have lava golems standing guard. Rumor has it the Führer and his family fled to Breisenburg. The Remnants fear he is going to wake the Golem of Death."

Sigurd let out a quiet sigh of relief. He knew that waking the Golem of Death wasn't a possibility, but he hoped at least the part about Katja being safe in Breisenburg was. "So why do you make way for Luidfort? You'll find no rebels there, only yourselves hopelessly trapped in a series of isolated, rain-filled valleys," he warned.

"I haven't told you the worst of it yet." Jenn's lips formed a thin line. "The Herrani and their naja have tunneled through the Barrier of Kriegle and are a day away from the Town where my mother is . . . hopelessly trapped, as you put it."

Sigurd cursed aloud, then muttered, "This is my fault."

"How do you figure?" Jeth scratched at his bearded chin.

"If I had followed through with my mission, I could have killed that Naja Handler."

"What difference would that have made?" Jenn shrugged.

"For starters, there would be substantially less naja to deal with," said

Sigurd, "given that one Handler can control entire contingents of them through their spirit magic."

"Then this is your chance to make things right." Jenn stepped up to him. "Come with me and help me put a stop to them."

"It won't be enough to save them all."

"I'm not talking about saving them all, just a few, or at least one—my mother. I could use someone to keep man and beast at bay while I get her to safety."

"I can't," Sigurd muttered, shaking his head solemnly. He owed Jenn for saving his life, and it was partly his fault why her mother was in danger now, but how could he rationalize saving a woman he didn't know while leaving the woman he loved in certain danger?

"What do you mean, you can't?" Jenn threw up her arms. "Is it so much to ask that a Steinkamp actually fulfills his pledge to defend the defenseless?"

"Maybe leave him be, Jenn," Jeth spoke up.

"Why are you defending him?"

"Because it's not his fault, it's mine." Jeth looked down at his own foot, tracing lines in the ash piles on the ground. "I'm the one that kept him from completing his mission. My job, while I was waiting to get into Ingleheim, was to protect one of the most prominent Handlers, and I did just that." He looked back up to meet eyes with Jenn. "If you need someone to help you save your mother, I am your man. It's the least I can do. I have my Magitech now, and both Anwarr and my child will be taken care of. It's not like I'm behind schedule or anything."

"Thanks," Jenn said, her features softening.

Jenn then turned back to Sigurd. "I hope you enjoy the rest of your miserable existence that *we* allowed you to have. A witch and a thief will go save lives while the Steinkamp soldier sits and mopes."

"I am not a Steinkamp soldier anymore." Sigurd stared at the unsightly wound where his brand used to be. He could no longer call himself a Steinkamp, but all he wanted was to sink back into the shadows, protected yet ever formidable.

"Of course, you're not," Jeth said. "You don't have the proper attire, for one thing." He moved aside and presented the path leading back to the main road. On that road was a black horse hooked to a black armored cart.

"Is that what I think it is?"

Jeth nodded with a grin, and Sigurd jogged down toward the cart, flung open the doors at the back of it, and took in the sights and smells of brand new weaponry and Magitech.

Inside, he found a uniform for his build along with all the necessary weapons and gear required for a standard mission. Once he fastened his mask in place, he breathed in deep, taking in the metallic aroma of a freshly made, never before worn mesh. It was strange, however. He had worn a mask only a few days ago, but wearing one again didn't feel as natural as it once had. Nevertheless, as different as Sigurd's uniform felt against his body, it still felt right. It was still him.

I am not lost.

Sigurd walked back up to where Jeth and Jenn stood, and gazed out toward Deschner once more. This time he saw a different view. Before, he had always seen a world draped in darkness, a landscape void of humanity. Now, through the darkness of his mask, Sigurd could finally see clearly. He was beginning to understand the pledge he took so long ago. A Steinkamp must see the world through darkened mesh so that he may seek that darkness out and take it into himself.

'From the darkness we are born, from the shadows we fight, in the name of justice we kill.'

Sigurd knew that protecting the people of Luidfort should be his priority. They were the ones who stood in defense of Ingleheim while everyone else partook in petty power games or slaughtered innocents for the sake of chaos. It was his duty to make sure their cries were answered. The only questions remaining were, how could he do it on his own, and was he already too late?

Suddenly, he caught movement in his periphery. He snapped his head around to find a man-sized lava golem meandering down a steep gravelly slope above the winding path. It stopped on an outcropping not too far from where everyone else stood. Jeth and Jenn didn't seem to notice the obsidian creature gazing down on them. It stood there completely still, its round eye shining bright red before fading out and glowing again. Realizing Sigurd wasn't of its kind, the lava golem turned around and started climbing the mountain slope.

That's it! That's how I'll save them!

"Well, faceless man?" Jenn waved a hand in front of Sigurd's mask. "Are you going to help us or not?"

He turned back to them and nodded. "I will."

Jenn blinked a few times. "Really?"

"But there is something I need you to help me do first."

The witch groaned as she put her face in her palm. "If you say to help you kill Wolfram again, I will bury you in a landslide with one thought."

"Not this time. My aim is in the preservation of life, not the taking of it." Sigurd looked up to the top of the volcano. *The key to saving Ingleheim is up there, not down in the chaos below,* he thought. Verishten didn't call to him as he did for the Siegfried in the tales, but *this* Siegfried required no invitation. The lava golem was enough of a sign for him. "The Age of Man is not yet over, and I am not yet lost," Sigurd muttered.

Jenn seemed to know what Sigurd was getting at by how he gazed up the volcano. "Are you thinking about going on a pilgrimage right now? Don't waste your time. Verishten is not going to save us."

"Not with that attitude, he won't," Sigurd quipped. "It will not take me long to get up there with your help, Jenn. You said you were bursting with essences. Tell me, will it be enough to dismantle that golem up there?"

The Fae'ren scratched his ash-caked locks in utter confusion. Jenn, although looking confused as well, gave Sigurd the nod. With that, all three of them caught up with the golem on the mountain trail.

Sigurd began to relay his plan. "I need to find a giant golem that will take me as close to the Mouth as possible, and I need a golem's eye do it."

"Why am I agreeing to this?" Jenn griped.

When she and Sigurd got close enough to the golem, she lunged for it, grabbing hold of its rough shoulder of basalt and halting its step. Almost instantly, the creature shuddered and quaked. It stumbled to the ground and attempted to crawl away, but Jenn didn't let go. Made powerless by her earth magic, the golem writhed on the ground, humanlike in its struggle for life. She bit her cheek with the effort of driving her earth essences through it. A loud *crack* echoed as one obsidian arm broke away, then another *crack* and a leg detached. Soon the entire torso crumbled. Jenn grabbed hold of the golem's head as it broke away from its body. She crumbled the obsidian holding the eye in place, thus freeing it.

She handed the eye to Sigurd just as the bright red glow extinguished, leaving behind a fist-sized stone with hairline cracks resembling tiny magma fissures under its glossy red surface. It was beautiful even without its light, but Sigurd still felt a pang of guilt for which he wasn't prepared. *I know you would never approve of me killing a golem like this, Katja, but I didn't have a choice.*

The golem eye was too bulky to fit in one of Sigurd's pockets comfortably, so he molded an earth binding to the back of it and hung it around his neck. "Thank you both. If my pilgrimage is not the death of me, I will repay you.

You have my word."

"You can repay us now by coming with us," Jenn said.

"You and Jeth should head to Luidfort and keep your mother safe. Hopefully I can join you with enough aid to save us all from the coming destruction."

"What exactly are you going to do up there?" Jeth asked, scratching his head again.

"Most likely die," Jenn answered on Sigurd's behalf. "I think the volcanic cell cooked his brain." She turned to Sigurd. "Even if you manage to survive the ash clouds and attract enough golems with that eye around your neck, you're not a Golem Mage. The Führer will command them against you if he catches on to this asinine plan."

"That's not quite the plan," Sigurd corrected. "I intend to finally live up to my name. I will climb to the top of the volcano where I will face the Golem of Fire just as Siegfried did. I know it sounds like madness, but it's what I must do. It is why Verishten has allowed me to live thus far."

"You mean we allowed you to live thus far," Jenn muttered, pointing to herself and Jeth.

"We should get a move on, Jenn," said Jeth. "This fella's off his arse."

"I take it you are not familiar with the tales of Siegfried and the First Eruption," said Sigurd.

"Oh, I'm familiar with it—I just don't buy it." Jeth shook his head, gesturing to the fiery peak. "Your eyes will burn out of their sockets just by looking into that thing if the ash clouds don't suffocate you first."

"He's made up his mind," Jenn said. "Let the Steinkamp give it a try. You never know. Maybe he will be the one to usher Ingleheim into a new age. Or cause the Third Eruption that will destroy us all."

Maybe Jenn was right to mock him, but Sigurd could feel it in his bones that he was on the right course. He finally understood why the Golem of Stone saved his life when he was five and what it tried to tell him twenty years after. *Verishten, you are not finished with me yet!* "I wish I can help you understand, but you're just going to have to trust me."

"Trust you?" Jenn scoffed, then crossed her arms. "And what do you know about trust?"

"Only one thing . . . that it must go both ways."

It had always been about trust. Sigurd had to trust Verishten. For that to happen, he had to be a man Verishten could trust in return. Sigurd had to prove to the god, once and for all, that he was truly the first Steinkamp, that he represented the title's true meaning. Then maybe, just maybe, what was left of Ingleheim could be salvaged.

Once Sigurd was alone, he began to sing the *Ode to Golems* over and over. During his trek, he awakened five human-sized lava golems which then followed him. He prayed that he'd find a giant one soon, but he feared that the Führer had already enlisted all of them for other tasks.

It would take as long as two days to reach the top of the volcano, but Sigurd could cut out one of those days by ascending the Molten Slopes. Attempting to climb those slopes would be certain death, even for a Steinkamp since it was where rivers of lava from the Mouth made their slow descent. However, a lava golem was already made of such material and would fare a far better chance.

After a few hours, Sigurd came upon a line of men and women ahead of him, making the same climb. Some of them were wearing facial nets or air filtering masks. *Of course I am to run into pilgrims,* he thought. He had always thought these people mad to attempt a climb such as this, and now he was among them.

Sigurd caught up to them quickly. They gasped in awe at the singing Steinkamp marching past them with his five golems in tow. One of the male pilgrims at the front of the group called out to him, "Comrade, why do they follow you?"

Turning around, Sigurd replied, "They believe I have somewhere to lead them—I suppose."

"That song," said a woman, wearing a thick netting fastened to her hat to shroud her face. "Are they responding to the song you sing?"

Sigurd's first instinct was to ignore the question and continue, but then he had a thought. *Many voices can carry much farther than one.* "Yes," he answered. "I invite you all to sing along, if you like. The words are easy enough to learn."

"To what end?" said a male pilgrim, accompanying the woman.

"To find a giant lava golem to take me up the Molten Slopes."

At those words, all the pilgrims started to chatter amongst themselves before shouting out more questions all at once. Sigurd put up his hands to silence them. "If you want answers, listen carefully and sing along."

Before long, all nine travelers belted the Ode to Golems at the top of their lungs. Eventually, they heard the sound of crashing rocks, followed by the earth shaking below their feet. When Sigurd and his pilgrimage came around the trail's bend, out from behind the ash-covered mountainside stood a colossal twenty-foot lava golem blocking the path. It was wider than any Sigurd had seen yet, its arms thicker than its legs and reached all the way to the ground to support its gargantuan frame upon bulbous red fists. The pilgrims gaped in awe of it.

"Stay back," Sigurd warned. Only he and the golems still behind him approached the giant. Its eye flashed with a fiery red light upon a rounded obsidian head atop massive red-hot shoulders. Sigurd held up the eye and just as with the frost and crag golems before, the lava golem dimmed its eye's light and knelt, allowing him to climb its extended arm.

"What's it doing?" said one of the pilgrims, standing a safe distance behind.

There were enough rough basalt surfaces amongst the golem's joints to offer Sigurd grip as he climbed to the top of the obsidian titan.

"He's going to ride it!" a woman gasped.

The pilgrims stood frozen as Sigurd, now on top of the giant golem, began his dangerously steep ascent up the mountainside. The most diehard among them ran after him.

"Hey, get it to kneel again! Let us up, please!" one of them called. The two men and the one woman stepped in front of the golem.

Sigurd remembered the last time someone tried to get in a giant golem's way. "Get down!"

From the golem's eye came a flash of red light. One man tackled the other just as the fiery beam scorched the rocks, melting the ground where they had been standing. The woman screamed and ducked behind some boulders while the men scrambled to their feet to avoid being burned by the molten rock beneath them.

Sigurd quickly descended from the golem and slid down the steep mountainside. He put himself between the pilgrims and the golem, holding out the eye again. "Do not hurt these people—they are Verishten's true followers!" he exclaimed, unsure why he expected the giant golem to care. Its eye dimmed again, and it made no further attacks. With Sigurd's assistance, all three pilgrims climbed on top of the golem as well. As they set off, he said, "I suppose if you're all going to risk your lives to get to the top, I can help you get as close as possible."

At dusk, the golem, with the smaller versions climbing closely behind, came upon the Molten Slopes. The younger of the two men grew pale at the sight of the steaming streams of lava rolling down the side of the mountain, the origins of which were lost in the thick ash clouds above. Fiery red rivers flowed slowly around the charred rock formations, melting them and releasing their gasses into the air.

"This is as far as I'm going," the young man said.

"Are you sure?"

"Yes. I've gone farther than I ever imagined, thanks to you." The man removed his filtering mask and handed it to Sigurd. "Take this. You'll need it when you get to those ash clouds."

"Surely he's not going that far—are you, comrade?" the older man asked.

"If anyone can make it to the top and live, it is a Steinkamp soldier," said the young man, giving Sigurd a firm pat on the shoulder.

Sigurd thanked him and helped him down from the golem's back. Then he and the two remaining pilgrims made the harrowing ascent up the Molten Slopes.

The lava golem navigated its way easily around the molten rock formations. There were some instances where it had no choice but to step through the blackened crust, revealing the infernal red beneath. The golem's thick ankles and fists kept the lava from melting its arms and legs, and its height kept the pilgrims safe from any backsplash.

The farther up the slopes they went, the thicker the ash-fall became, the more stifling it grew, and the more man-sized golems stayed behind due to their inability to cross the widening lava streams. Although his Steinkamp mask kept out much of the larger ash flakes, it did little to keep out the finer specks that could make him choke. He was thankful for the filtering mask in that respect. However, nothing could keep the sweltering heat from hitting his face. Despite the torridity behind his mask, Sigurd's uniform did much to keep his core temperature down. The same could not be said for his travel companions. Sweat soaked through their attire. Sigurd feared that they would not survive, but he couldn't send them back down the slopes on their own, or they would surely perish.

It wasn't until the golem found the regular mountain path, on the cusp of the ash clouds, that the pilgrims had a chance to descend. The lava golem went into dormancy in the blackened cliff side, leaving the three travelers on a path that would have taken them days to reach on their own.

Sigurd and the pilgrims made camp, just off the path, to rest after the harrowing journey. At first light the next morning—although almost impossible to discern through the ash clouds—everyone awoke more exhausted than before they went to sleep, courtesy of the unclean air and uncomfortable heat.

"What do we do now?" The woman took shallow breaths between every word. Her male companion wheezed as well, despite them both wearing filtering masks.

"I continue on foot. It's not too far to the top now, but the ash clouds will make it difficult to see," replied Sigurd. When he was twelve, he had been dropped several feet from where he stood now, in the thick of the ash with nothing more than his undergarments. He had barely made it down alive. Now he was going to venture into it of his free will, and he was not coming back until he completed his task.

His uniform would keep the heat from overwhelming him, and the mask would keep him from suffocating, but nothing would protect him from a misstep into a lava pit that no amount of ice powder could freeze. Sigurd decided to leave behind his crossbow and splitting blade dispenser, two bulky pieces of equipment he could do without at this point. He nestled them between two rocks where he hoped he could collect them on the way down.

"You may never return," said the man.

"I must go anyway. I thank you for your support. May Verishten see you both safely down." He gave the man and woman the golem eye he carried. "Show this to any golem you come in contact with, and hopefully, they can keep you safe during the long trek down. As for giant ones, they will want to take you back up, but showing this to them will keep them from attacking you." He turned and walked up the path, nearly disappearing into the ash clouds.

"Who are you?" the woman called after him. "What is your name?"

Sigurd wanted to tell them what he always told people when they asked him for his name. *I am nameless.* But was he supposed to be? Why should he be? The first Steinkamp had a name, and so did Sigurd. He removed his filtering mask so he could toss aside the metal mesh that he wore underneath. Sigurd would meet Verishten and the Golem of Fire with a name and a face.

"My name is Siegfried."

"We will speak your name and tell all of Ingleheim of what occurred up here, whether you make it or not," said the man.

Provided there is still an Ingleheim to return to, Sigurd wanted to say. Instead, he nodded, fastened his filtering mask, and turned up the winding path where he vanished into the ash clouds.

Sigurd accomplished the remainder of the climb entirely on his hands and feet. Much of his gloves had burnt away, and the treads of his boots melted upon the sizzling rocks. The ash rained down so thick Sigurd could hardly tell the difference between solid molten rock or fluffy piles of ash. He had never been this high up before, and perhaps no Ingleman ever had. The bones of the dead would be crushed under mountains of ash or melted in the lava streams before they could ever be found. Sigurd was the only thing, living or dead, on that mountain.

For hours, he climbed toward the summit of the volcano, the heat making him wish he was experiencing the comforts of the volcanic cells instead. The incalescence and lack of fresh air sapped his strength until he could hardly bear his own weight. He started to lose the ability to determine up from down through the blinding ash and gaseous vapors.

Just as his body begged him to give up, the clouds parted in the wake of an infernal light beyond his reach. Now Sigurd could take a full breath within his filtering mask. He pulled himself up onto a blackened ledge, his lungs burning at the effort. Finally, he peered down into the destructive molten splendor, bubbling within a giant crater below.

He couldn't quite explain the vigor that returned to him once he looked upon it. It was a sight more glorious to him than the clock tower that led him out of Frost Woods so many years ago. The volcanic energy below did more than enliven him. It showed him his fate. This was where he was supposed to be all along.

How many men have laid eyes on such infernal power as this? he wondered in awe. There was only one other man to have looked into Verishten's Mouth and Sigurd shared his name. The idea made him laugh with elation. Being in the presence of the open volcano, feeling the scorching heat envelop him, and his lungs being singed from breathing it in, Sigurd remembered why he had come. He didn't have much time.

"Mighty Verishten!" he bellowed into the expanse. "It is Siegfried! I have come seeking your aid!"

The only reply to Sigurd's call was the bubbling molten rock below. He continued as loudly as he could manage, "The Age of Man is not yet over. I can save them, but not without your help! Please!"

Again, there was no answer. Sigurd wondered if he had risked everything in coming all this way only to have Verishten shut him out as he had done in the Crags. Perhaps the God of the Ingles was right. It was too late for Sigurd, which meant it was too late for Katja, for Jenn and her mother—for all of them.

And then it came. A rumbling voice shook him to his core. A voice that housed the power of the volcano itself.

"Do you remember where you came from?"

When Sigurd had been asked that question before, he could only think of death. He thought he was created in the darkness of that chasm and later shaped by the Steinkamp Academy. But since knowing Katja and remembering his childhood, he found there was much more to his origins. He was loved by a woman who believed in him, by a mother who sang to him, by a sister who showed him the constellations, and by a brother who bravely stood against two Steinkamp soldiers so that he would have a chance to escape the slaughter. Sigurd was the son of an earl who gave up his station and everything he knew to keep his family safe. Even if most of those people were now dead, it didn't matter.

"Yes," Sigurd rasped. "I am the son of Earl Sigmund and Frau Anja of Kensloche. I am the brother of Rosalinde and Kristoff. I am from the blood of Golem Mages, but I do not bear your Eye."

"Do you know why you were saved?" came a thundering reply.

That question was much harder to answer. Sigurd no longer knew why he was saved. It wasn't revenge, that was for certain, but was it to save Ingleheim? For all Sigurd knew, Verishten wanted humanity to burn this time around. Sigurd may not be Verishten's tool to save them, but to see them destroyed ever swifter.

"I don't know," he answered.

"You do not know?" Verishten's voice quaked within the crater, causing lava to spurt and ash to cough up into the air.

"I trust in you, Mighty Verishten, to do what you think is best. You say the Age of Man has ended, and maybe it should be. You made a sacred covenant with my namesake thousands of years ago for his descendants to forge peace with golem-kind. It was agreed that golems were to serve man. In return, man was to care for them, to respect them, not dominate and control them. You placed your trust in mankind and mankind has betrayed that trust. I understand why you must punish us."

"Why do you come before me?"

"Because I know there are many who search for knowledge long since lost. They still fight for what is right. If given the chance, those people will bring Ingleheim back to honor. I come before you to beg you to spare them your wrath by granting me the power to save them."

"Who are you to demand such mercy?" The volcano quaked again, causing more rivers of molten rock to pour over either side of the platform he was perched on.

Sigurd removed his mask briefly to wipe the dripping sweat from his brow, desperately hoping to get through to the great infernal god before he collapsed from heat exhaustion.

He finally understood who he was and why he was there.

"I know I am undeserving of your mercy. I am a man filled with hate, anger, and regret. All I've ever known was how to inflict death!" Sigurd bowed his head and continued, "That is why I leave myself in your hands— my life force, my spirit, it is yours to do with what you will. All I ask is that you spare Ingleheim its fate, and usher in a new Age of Golems and Man, together as one."

"You've already pledged your life and spirit to another," Verishten boomed. *"Would you renounce that pledge and forge one anew?"*

The mere thought of renouncing his pledge to Katja made Sigurd's heart break. His primary duty had been to her from the moment he heard her play the *Ode to Golems* on her flute in the woods. Even back when he didn't like her, he owed everything to her.

Could Sigurd give up Katja to give himself over body and soul to Verishten instead? He didn't want to, but maybe he already had. Instead of racing to Deschner or Breisenburg to rescue her, he risked her life and his to confront the God of the Ingles. For a true Steinkamp, Ingleheim was supposed to come first, and Katja would have been the first one to remind him of that.

"Hear me, Mighty Verishten," Sigurd called, his strength rapidly waning. "I, Siegfried of Kensloche, renounce all prior claims to my being and entrust it all to you. Take me as your vessel, now and for all time!"

"You are lost, Siegfried!" bellowed the molten god.

It was not enough. Verishten required more than words. He needed an offering of essence, spirit, and flesh. It wasn't enough to exhibit humility; he had to prove his bravery.

Sigurd pushed himself to a shaky stance and staggered toward the ledge. He took one last look at the lava below and removed his mask, letting it fall to the blackened stone at his feet. The clarity he gained seeing the volcano's eternal light below gave him all the strength he required. *Trust must go both ways.*

With his eyes to the ashen sky and his arms outstretched, he called out with all he had left, "Golem of Fire! Find me, here I stand!"

Sigurd relaxed his body, letting it fall from the ledge into the swirling fire below.

27
VERISHTEN'S WRATH

The rains were heavy as Jeth and Jenn traveled into Luidfort Mountain Range. Jenn expected dreary weather in the southernmost mountains of Ingleheim during the spring and would have usually welcomed it, but on this day she found it to be a dreadful hindrance. The Magitech had been slowing them down, so they left it in a safe spot just outside the eastern pass. Without it, they could ride unencumbered through the night and arrive at the eastern pass in only a day.

Jeth rode the Steinkamp gelding and Jenn sat behind, both of them caked in the horse's muddy backsplash. Droves of villagers and townsfolk moved through the narrow pass to escape their settlements while Jenn and Jeth rode through them in the opposite direction.

The state of the Town of Luidfort looked no more promising. People scurried about trying to evacuate or find secure shelter. Regime soldiers barely held the line against the barrage of Herrani warriors clambering to get over the south walls. *Does this mean the southern villages are gone now?* Jenn wondered. She was shocked by the absence of the Führer's winged golems. Many were likely being used to keep back the naja at the Barrier of Kriegle, but surely not all of them. There was no time to figure out what was going on; she had to find the convent where her mother was put up.

Ma, I'm close, lead me to you, she projected to Egret.

In a few moments, she was answered with a mental map leading to a temple, to which the convent was attached, built into the rocky cliffside at the edge of town. Jenn pointed out the directions to Jeth, who kept expert control of the horse as he steered it through the panicking droves.

Once they reached the convent, Jeth stayed behind to look for a safe escape route while she rushed inside. The old stone building was narrow and filled to capacity with frightened citizenry.

Ma, I'm here, where are you? Jenn didn't need her mother to reply. She soon found her tending to some of the children in one of the bedchambers. "Ma!" She exhaled in relief.

Egret, wearing the blue and black robes and bonnet of a Storm Sister, took Jenn in a tight embrace. "Jenn, my darling girl, I told you to send soldiers, not to come yourself."

"Rebel soldiers aren't coming. It's just us now. We should leave here." She took her mother's arm.

"I can't, the children need me."

"You will all die if you stay. We have to get out before the passes clog up with the town's entire population."

"Get yourself out. Go live the rest of your life. I have taken the Holy Storm Vows, my place is here now." Egret crouched down to help a little girl tie on her bonnet.

"They accepted you knowing who you used to be?" Jenn asked, wide-eyed.

Egret finished with the little girl and rose to address her daughter. "I told them that I was going to take my vows of chastity at the Cathedral of Verishten in Deschner before—until your father came upon me. I told the sisters here the truth of what he did, and that circumstances beyond my control left me no alternative occupation. The sisters took pity on me. I can never partake in the water purification rituals. Those are reserved only for virginal women, but in times like these the temple can no longer afford to turn away any who wish to serve."

"Be that as it may, I can't leave you here. Temples are always sacked during invasions. These doors will not hold when the naja come."

"I will not abandon the children." Egret took a baby boy from one of the other sisters in the room to change his diaper.

"There must be somewhere safer we can take them."

Egret's dark brown eyes widened with a thought. "Kanzler Friedhelm has agreed to take in as many commoners as can fit in his fortified estate. I would have brought the children there sooner, but the crowds were insurmountable and I feared they would get hurt. Perhaps you can think of a spell to get us through to it, without endangering the children."

Jenn agreed to help her get the children out of the convent with the assistance of the other Storm Sisters charged with their care. Once everyone was ready to leave, they went outside to find themselves in a torrential downpour. The roadways were littered with horses and carts stuck in the mud. Jenn cursed aloud in front of the children.

Jeth came up to meet them, his horse caked in mud up to its knees. "I don't think it is wise to take a horse through all this muck."

Groaning, Jenn looked southward and realized that seas of mud were the least of their worries. The line of forces keeping the Herrani back were suddenly trampled over by an unstoppable horde.

The naja had arrived.

Monstrous reptilian beasts leaped over the walls and raged into the town square, the mud hardly slowing them down.

"Back inside!" screamed one of the sisters amongst the children's cries.

"No!" Jenn ordered. "They will find you in there. We stick to the plan. We can still make it to the kanzler's."

"I can find us a way through," said Jeth.

The group followed Jeth between market stands and through shops to avoid the deepest mud puddles in the streets. Jenn did her best to keep the group unnoticed by bending the light around them. It proved useful for avoiding detection from the Herrani warriors, but it did little to prevent the naja from catching their scent.

The group was only a block away from the gates of the kanzler's estate when a piercing screech cut through the air. Everyone looked around frantically. Three armored reptilians made headway toward them.

Verishten have mercy, they're fast! Jenn thought, adrenaline rushing through her. The children screamed as the sisters grabbed as many of them as they could carry and burst into a sprint.

"Keep running!" Jenn called to the women and children. "I'll hold them off!"

"How?" asked Jeth.

"Just get them to the kanzler's!" Jenn had no idea how she would hold off three hulking naja, but she had plenty of essences stored in her sapphire bracelet since the stop in Deschner. Focusing on the glistening water auras and vibrating earth auras on the ground, she collected the mud into large clumps and pushed out three spinning spheres of water and mud at each of the naja running toward her. She ended up burying only one of them, and the other two leaped at her.

She screamed and ducked. One of the naja flew overhead and ran toward the women and children. The third knocked her back so hard into the mud she was swimming in it. Jenn lifted her head and wiped the mud from her eyes. A Storm Sister carrying a toddler slipped and fell, and a naja was seconds away from pouncing. Jeth shot an arrow through its open maw just before it landed on them. He then turned to shoot another arrow at the naja still advancing on Jenn and although it hit its mark, the wound had little effect on the its thick, scaly skin. Jenn hurled more mud and water at the beast, burying it for the time being.

"Jeth, get them out of here, I'll be fine!" she shouted, mud dripping from her face and filling her mouth.

"Wait, I see the Handler!"

Surrounded by several naja and dressed in orange and red robes, a man walked through the muddy square. Jeth quickly helped the sister to her feet and sent her on her way before taking another arrow from his quiver. He scurried up a large fountain to get a better vantage point.

Jenn didn't get a chance to see if Jeth would be successful. Another naja made way for Egret and the others. Clambering to her feet, she ran full tilt for the reptile, hoping to lure it toward her and away from of the children. Using her water magic, she pushed more rain and mud at the naja, having almost caught up to the fleeing group. *I can't reach it!* The reptilian was too fast.

"No!" Jenn screamed. Everything happened so quickly, and she couldn't think of what other magical attacks she could muster in time.

All of a sudden, the naja in front of her, along with every other in town, screeched in unison and collapsed to the ground. Jeth cheered from the fountain. The Handler fell dead with an arrow to the head, and all of the naja were now outside of his control. The naja in front and behind Jenn writhed in the mud. *Maybe I can control it myself,* she thought.

Jeth came running back from the fountain. "Jeth, go with my mother and the others, I have to try something," Jenn ordered. She then approached one of the disoriented reptiles.

"Don't go near it!" Jeth put his hands out to stop her. "They are no longer under Handler control, but they're still bloodthirsty killing machines!"

Ignoring his warning, she knelt down and laid her hands on the naja's head, attempting to read the spiritual aura within it. It was easier than she had expected to slip into the creature's mind, but she couldn't make sense of what she found. Images of blood, viscera, and teeth intermingled with overwhelming fear and pain, the loneliness of loved ones lost, and a raw urge to maim and kill. It felt so human. It was too much, and she had to let go. *There is a human being in there. This is not a true naja!*

Right then, every naja came to at the same time. The one Jenn had touched leaped at her so fast and ferociously that she had no time to react. The reptilian juggernaut knocked her down and bared its enormous fangs. She felt like the frightened rat from her nightmares about to get taken into the jaws of the giant serpent.

All Jenn could do was grab it by the head and force herself inside of its mind once again. The rain, mud, and chaos of the outside world fell away, and she became surrounded by blackness. From the depths came multiple eyeless faces with fangs and claws all around her. The growls and shrieks chilled Jenn to the bone, but she didn't let go. She ventured further in, digging her way past the teeth and claws that threatened to bite her. *They can't hurt me here—it's only in the mind.* she reminded herself.

Finally, she found a dark, quiet room where a man lay in the center of the floor, a giant snake wrapped around his head. He was naked and subtly convulsing, making short gurgling breaths beneath the snake that smothered him. Jenn was in her rat form, but much larger than she had ever been before, almost the size of a mid-weight dog. She didn't hesitate in biting the snake and whipping her head back and forth viciously. The serpent hissed and bared its fangs, but Jenn only hissed back. She didn't stop biting the snake until it eventually uncoiled and slithered away.

As the man gasped for air, Jenn was whisked back into the cold, wet reality of Luidfort. The naja on top of her shrieked and recoiled. "What just happened? Where am I?" it croaked.

"You can speak," Jenn gasped as she breathlessly got to her feet.

The naja's golden reptilian eyes dilated, looking fearfully all around. "What did you do to me?"

"I-I tried to take control of your mind, but I did something else instead. I think I just undid whatever spiritual hold your master had on you."

The naja looked upon himself and made an agonized screech. "T-that desert sorcerer . . . he did this to me!" Looking to Jenn with a pleading look, he said, "Please. You can change me back!"

"I can't." Jenn shook her head apologetically. "Flesh magic was probably used to transmogrify you. I don't know anything about that type of magic. I'm sorry."

Jenn! Egret's spiritual projection made her skull feel like it was struck from the inside. Herrani warriors charged at the sisters in the distance. One grabbed Egret, but Jeth rolled up and sliced him through the midsection with his scimitar. Another warrior came up behind Jeth and kicked him down into the mud while his partner went for Egret again.

"Ma!" Jenn bolted to her mother's aid.

The freed naja rushed past her and sank its teeth into one of the Herrani attackers, allowing Jeth to lift himself up and continue his assault. Within a few more seconds, the naja tore through the other Herrani. The women and children continued to scream even after their attackers were dead.

Jenn caught up to the rest of the group and got between them and the naja. "It's all right, this one is on our side."

The women huddled close together, pulling the children away from the reptile.

Jenn stepped aside to show that the naja wished not to attack them. Egret carefully approached the reformed beast. "Thank, you. What do we call you?"

The naja scratched at his green and brown marbled snout and slowly replied, "I was called . . . Sebastian."

"Will you help us, Sebastian?" asked Jenn.

"I am in your debt, young sorceress. Ask whatever you will of me and I will carry it out," he said with fervor.

"Good. Then you can bring me those naja that are on their way over here. I wish to free their minds as well." She pointed to two, quickly advancing.

Sebastian blocked the first of the naja from getting to them while Jeth distracted the second with a few arrows. Jenn got behind that one and entered its mind. She destroyed the snake that strangled the man's spirit and then did the same for the second naja as Sebastian held it back. After a short conversation with the two of them much like the one she'd had with Sebastian, Jenn now had three naja in her debt.

The three reptile henchmen effectively protected the women and children until they arrived at the kanzler's gates. The crowds that had been desperately waiting to be let in were now being slaughtered by the Herrani and the naja. Most of the dead bodies strewn about were the soldiers charged to protect the gates, their blood turning the brown mud puddles a darkened red. Jenn's heart sank at the sight.

"It's not safe in there either," Jeth said. "If these gates are knocked down, everyone inside will be slaughtered. Our best bet is using our naja to clear a path back through the pass, toward Untevar."

"The pass will be treacherous from the rains, not to mention the enemies at our backs. We should find somewhere else to hide," suggested Egret.

"There is nowhere to hide!" one of the sisters cried.

"The only safety is in that estate," Jenn said with fortitude. "And to ensure it remains safe we all have to defend the gates with whoever else remains." Jenn turned to the naja. "You three form a protective barrier around the women and children. Jeth, you and I will cleave a pathway through the enemy."

While Jenn contemplated which type of essence she would make use of, a ferocious wind picked up, practically blowing her bone-thin body right over. Lightning cast the dark storm clouds alight, and thunder boomed so unusually loud that people stopped fighting to look up at the sky.

One of the Storm Sisters shrieked and pointed to the cliffs in the north. "It's Verishten's Wrath!" She dropped to her knees and the other sisters followed suit, bowing and shouting prayers to the storming peak.

Everyone stopped to gape in awe at the black clouds swirling around Luidfort Range's highest summit, as if the storms were originating from that one place.

The storm clouds parted from Verishten's Wrath and the peak came alive, breaking away from the rest of the mountaintop. Huge stone wings unfolded, revealing a massive creature with enormously thick legs made up of the cliff itself. Great ram-like horns jutted from each side of the colossus' head where an amethyst beam pierced through the thick storm clouds, casting its light upon the stunned crowd of Ingles, Herrani, and naja alike.

"Is that . . . ?" Jenn murmured as the rain fell harder. "It can't be—"

"It's the Golem of Storms!" Egret gasped.

The Alpha of the Winged Golems launched into the air from the mountaintop, spread its colossal wings and cast the entire town square in shadow.

"We should run," Sebastian suggested.

No longer caring to fight one another, people and beasts bolted off in different directions. Jenn and her group ran to an old storefront to take cover, praying it was sturdy enough to withstand the increasingly violent winds. The sky outside turned black as night, and the thunder cracked at such deafening volume that it drowned out the children's cries.

Jenn ducked into her mother's arms like a scared little girl, her wind magic talents lacking and powerless against gales of such godly magnitude.

All she and the rest of the townspeople taking cover in the storefront could do was watch numerous cyclones spiral down into the thoroughfare, tossing about Herrani warriors and naja while strangely leaving the local residents and Regime soldiers relatively untouched.

"Look, the peaks!" One of the older children pointed toward the storming mountain. "The golems are coming to save us!"

Several winged golems glided over the northern cliffs and swooped into the town. They picked up only the enemy forces and smashed them back into the ground in a gory display.

"Sweet Deity," Jeth murmured, staring out into the storming violence in equal parts terror and awe.

"Jenn!" Egret directed her attention back to the kanzler's estate. "The gates are cleared, and the soldiers have regrouped. Now is our chance."

"Back to the estate!" Jenn called. She turned to her two most recently freed naja helpers. "Both of you need to go with the women and children and make sure they get there safely. Continue to guard them until the threat is gone. Afterward, you two can return to whatever homes you were taken from and your debt to me will be paid in full."

The two naja nodded.

"How may I be of additional service?" asked Sebastian.

Before she could answer him, Egret asked, "Jenn. You're not coming with us?"

"No, we are going somewhere else." She looked to the sky with the majestic and dangerous Golem of Storms circling above. "That Steinkamp bastard might have done it after all. The Alphas are awakening, which means we need to get back to the City of Deschner."

"Why?" Jeth asked.

"This is your chance to get away from all this, Jeth. You've done more than enough for us Ingles." Jenn didn't wait for his answer. She hugged and kissed her mother goodbye and motioned for Sebastian to follow her.

"What do you think you're going to do at the City of Deschner?" Jeth jogged out into the rain after her.

"The rebellion isn't going to win itself."

"But—"

A giant winged golem, made of blue and gray marbled granite, suddenly landed just feet from where they stood.

"I'll be fine. I've got Sebastian here." She patted her new reptilian ally on the back. ". . . And maybe I can hitch a ride on one of these things."

Jenn pointed to the winged golem perched on its haunches and staring her down with its violet triangular eye.

"Well, if it's all the same to you, I'll catch a ride along with you and see how the rest of this plays out." Jeth grinned.

Jenn turned to the Fae'ren sauntering up to her, mud running down every inch of his body, his light brown mats so caked in wet ash that they were made black. He was a gruesome sight, but she found a jovial charm shining through those mischievous hazel eyes of his. She had grown used to having him around. "I suppose we can make room for you, Fairy Boy."

As they walked toward the landed winged golem, he said, "I've always wanted to fly on one of these things. But do you think it will let us near it? I mean, it is being controlled by the Führer, right?"

The winged golem just stood there as if awaiting their approach.

"If there is any truth to the Siegfried tales, then it's not. But if we want to find out for sure, we'll just have to climb on."

28

PATH OF THE
HEDONIST

In the war room, Kanzler Wolfram presented a scout who had just returned from Deschner. "Tell your mighty Führer exactly what you told me, Herr Lanzel."

Herrscher Heinrich, along with Kapitän Rudiger, stood in wait for Lanzel's report.

"The Kings' Remnants have abandoned their siege of the City of Deschner and are moving toward this fortress, my Führer."

"How far out are they?" Heinrich asked.

"By my estimates, the southern army is a little less than a day away, and the northern troops will arrive a day after that, maybe sooner," answered Lanzel.

Heinrich nodded and stepped to the massive arched window that presented the northern landscape of Breisenburg. "What makes Bachman think he stands a chance in taking this fortress back?"

Turning to the scout, Wolfram said, "Tell him what you saw in Deschner—the reason for the rebel's shift in target."

"I'm not exactly sure what I saw, but whatever it was, it was powerful. . . ." Lanzel gulped and looked to Wolfram and Heinrich nervously.

"Out with it," the Führer demanded.

Lanzel cleared his throat. "Well, there was this giant moving light that came from Untevar Range that has now settled in the City of Deschner. It shines with every color, and so brightly, no one can look directly at it without going blind. Some said the light is brighter than the sun as it is visible through the thick clouds of ash. It illuminates the city to such a degree that the fighting and rioting ceased, and citizens were forced to run for cover."

"That's quite the poetic description, herr," Heinrich commented. "But did you find out what this light was?"

"I talked to some of the monks around there, and they claim this . . . thing . . . is the Golem of Light from legend, Verishten's Warning. Remnants who still had their sight intact followed the Kaiser in abandoning the city. They think it is pointing them in a new glorious direction.

Rudiger with his hands behind his back, spoke up. "Most likely, though, Herr Bachman learned that you, Herrscher, were not in Deschner, and he now believes his glory lies here."

"We must act at once," Wolfram began. "I advise that we send our forces to meet the rebel advance and keep the fight as far from the fortress as possible." *I'll be damned if this fortress is retaken so soon after it was awarded to me,* he thought.

"It is no matter," Heinrich said. "The Golem of Death will awaken in due time. I say let them come."

"With all due respect, Herrscher," said Rudiger. "I don't believe your daughter speaks true of her ability to awaken the Alpha. It was clearly a ploy to defer the execution of her professor and the Steinkamp defector."

The Führer nodded thoughtfully but didn't give Rudiger his full attention. He instead turned back to Wolfram. "Send as many men as you require, Kanzler, but know that I want Bachman returned to me alive. I wish to have him be the first executed by the Golem of Death."

"As you command, my Führer." Wolfram dismissed the scout and then turned to Rudiger.

Rudiger stepped forward and gave Wolfram the salute.

"You've been away from Bachman's side for too long, and he will soon suspect you've abandoned him. Act as his general one last time, regain his trust if need be, and bring him to me alive."

"As you command, Herr Kanzler." Rudiger nodded and turned to leave.

Wolfram watched Rudiger as he left. *What is he planning?*

It had come as a surprise to Wolfram when Frau Brunhilde announced Kriemhilde's pending marriage to the new kapitän. Before all of this began, Rudiger and Wolfram had agreed that Wolfram would become Kanzler, and Rudiger Kapitän of the Steinkamp force. That was as far as the two men's ambitions would take them, or so Wolfram had believed. He only wished for dominion over Ingleheim's military industrial complex. With that behind him, he could push for expansion into Del'Cabria and provide lifelong security to his family, not otherwise possible for a bastard. He expected only to become Führer if Heinrich died within the next few years.

Rudiger's marriage pact will put him in the running to rule, and I may very well have to start taking orders from a man who used to be a common foot-soldier. Wolfram broke out into a cold sweat. *What is stopping him from assassinating both the Führer and me, and taking control of Ingleheim's entire military might at the first opportunity?*

Rudiger's mission to capture Bachman would hopefully distract him long enough for Wolfram to rethink his options. One of those options may involve getting rid of Rudiger altogether and regaining control of his Steinkamp. Verishten forbid the Steinkamp were ever ordered to come after their previous kapitän.

Kanzler Wolfram joined Heinrich at the window. The Fortress of Mortlach was positioned in just the right location to provide a view from the war room that stretched across two mountain ranges. Not too far in the distance was the Volcano of Verishten and the City of Deschner at its base. From there, a beacon of yellow light shone through the ashen sky.

"What sorcery could cause such a light to shine there for so long?" Wolfram inquired, adjusting his spectacles.

Heinrich shook his head. "Legends say that the Golem of Light has the power to reflect it in the magnitude that we see here."

"But it's impossible for it to have awakened," Wolfram protested.

"It wouldn't be the first Alpha awakened in these last few months." Heinrich raised an eyebrow.

"Do you really think your daughter has something to do with this?"

"She never awakened the Golem of Stone, Kanzler, Sigurd did . . . supposedly." Heinrich's unnerving amber glare made Wolfram even more uncomfortable than it usually did.

"I assure you, Herrscher," said Wolfram. "That Steinkamp joined Verishten in the volcano yesterday. I received confirmation early this morning."

The truth was, the winged golem used to take the Steinkamp to the Mouth had never returned, but it was not uncommon for the odd one to burn up during its dive into the Mouth. For the few executions carried out that way, losing a winged golem here and there wasn't a notable loss.

Heinrich shrugged and turned from the window. "On another note, do you have anything more to report regarding Luidfort?"

"I've sent three battalions to Kanzler Friedhelm's aid. The pass into Luidfort Range is overrun with refugees, so the soldiers have been delayed, and with the current winged golem shortage, we do not have enough to fly all the soldiers into it. I anticipate damage to the range will be rather extensive, but I assure you, the Herrani threat will be contained there. We will destroy them all when the refugees clear out. Our water stores can easily hold out in the meantime."

"Pray that they do." Heinrich cast his gaze back out the window. "We cannot ship glacier water from Nordenhein until the rebellion is quelled, and that won't be until after we demolish the coming scourge here."

"I agree, Herrscher." Wolfram bowed. "And we will do away with this rebellion very shortly. Then we can focus our full military efforts on the Herrani."

With nothing more to add, the Führer sighed heavily. "You are dismissed, Kanzler."

Wolfram nodded and left the war room with clenched fists. *The rebellion is not getting near this fortress if I have anything to say about it.*

The day after the roundtable meeting, Katja, Klemens, and Ignatius were put up in the study in the northeast tower. Stacks of Golem Mage texts and other magical tomes, brought from the Deschner libraries and archives, littered the table.

The research team had no real leads on awakening or controlling an Alpha. The plan instead was to eliminate their most immediate threats: Wolfram and Rudiger. Katja had explained to Klemens before Ignatius's arrival of what those men had done to Sigurd, and how they were likely planning a coup that would see Ingleheim to even greater ruin. She didn't divulge her own desires to see the two men destroyed in revenge of Sigurd, but it didn't matter. Wolfram and Rudiger needed to be stopped for all of their sakes, regardless of her ulterior motives.

With Wolfram as the new Kanzler of Breisenburg and Rudiger the new Kapitän of the Steinkamp, their only hope was for Katja to get through to her father and have him act accordingly. To do that, they would need to free him from the woman controlling him.

Since Ignatius was under constant surveillance, she had to bring him up to speed through codes of phrase, words pointed out in various texts while pretending to research Alphas. It was understood that 'controlling the Alpha' meant 'breaking Brunhilde's thrall over Heinrich,' and the words 'Golem Mage' actually meant 'Spirit Mage.'

The guards posted in the study had been ordered to report all goings on to both the Führer and his wife. Therefore, the researchers had discreetly removed pertinent pages from Spirit Mage diaries and inserted them between pages in the hefty Golem Mage tomes.

Everything they had read thus far referenced only two reliable methods of breaking a Mage's thrall over someone, at the Mage's will or at the Mage's demise. There were also references to people having escaped thrall through cleansing spells performed by other Spirit Mages. Katja sighed with hopelessness, as the only other Spirit Mage she knew of was dead, but then she remembered someone Sigurd had mentioned.

Calling to the guard standing a few feet from where Ignatius sat, she asked, "What became of the rebel witch? Is she being held prisoner here or was she killed?"

"Why do you need to know, fraulein?" the guard inquired stiffly.

"We might be able to make use of her abilities—to assist us in controlling the Alpha."

"Frau Brunhilde's abilities should suffice—"

Ignatius cut in, "No disrespect to Frau Brunhilde, but the rebel witch happens to be a competent Essence Mage as well. It is those abilities we wish to make use of."

Katja gave Ignatius an encouraging nod. She had not been aware of the rebel witch's other arcane talents. An Essence Mage could produce sunfire, something Brunhilde, unlike Melikheil, would have no defense against.

The guard replied, "The witch escaped and has not been seen since the retaking of this fortress."

Everyone sitting at the table slumped back into their chairs. *Dammit! Now how are we going to break Brunhilde's spell?*

Katja considered killing her, and shivered at her own darkening thoughts. Despite everything Brunhilde had done to her, she had never wished death upon her. However, knowing that Brunhilde controlled Heinrich the way Melikheil had once controlled her forced bile to rise into her throat.

Realistically, she could not anticipate the consequences of killing her stepmother. If there was a way to break Brunhilde's spell without resorting to murder, she would much rather take that approach.

As she probed deeper into the Mage diaries, she found notes of one

Mage's desperate search for immortality through spirit magic. She thought about moving on, but the team was growing desperate, and she couldn't shake the feeling that this excerpt would finally give them something they could use.

It read:

There are two paths to immortality. One brings great pain and suffering, the path of the masochist; the other brings great pleasure, the path of the hedonist.

To not take the road full of worldly pleasures would be madness. What I was never told was that no matter how often I indulge my most persistent desires, it will never truly make me whole in this life or the next. Each method promises everlasting life, but with both paths, my body will never be my own, and in the path I've chosen, not even my soul is completely mine. What kind of soul will I be left with once I've accomplished this, anyway? One that has been rotted by the spoils of pleasuring myself. Is that any better than one dilapidated by self-torture? There is one thing I am certain. I cannot stop my pursuit now. What's done is done. My spirit is now forever bonded with another and I don't dare break that bond. I will be forever tethered to my vessel. In time, I will find a way to dissolve his sentience to make way for mine alone and then—

The pages had been ripped out like many of the other diaries, likely by Regime Censors or perhaps Brunhilde or Melikheil themselves. It was just as well, for Katja had read more than enough to make her spine tingle. She snapped the book shut.

Is that what Melikheil had been doing to me the entire time? She wondered in horror. *Was he bonding his spirit to mine while satisfying his most debauched, carnal desires? The path of the hedonist. . . .* Sudden nausea hit her, and she began to shake.

'She has something of mine, and I may need it returned to me if anything were to happen.'

Katja rose from the table and went to the window for some air.

"Are you okay, Kat?" Klemens asked.

"I'm fine . . . just frustrated."

"If you require an Essence Mage, we can send for one," the guard offered. "Although a good one is hard to come by these days."

"We don't have time to wait around for a Mage." Ignatius stood up to stretch his legs. "We should take a more obvious action in controlling the Alpha." He pointed to his magic tome that referenced the death of a Mage as his obvious action.

Katja shook her head. "I don't think that's wise in this case, Professor." Picking up the diary again, she found the pertinent page and showed it to him. "Controlling an Alpha that way may end up harming the Führer."

Ignatius read the excerpt then scratched his whiskers. With a sigh, he put the book down, a deep frown lining his face. Katja now feared that if Brunhilde had bonded her spirit to her father's, it was possible for her to regain her sentience through him upon her death.

"We need an Essence Mage," she said, crossing her arms. "Preferably one that manipulates all six essences."

The guards squinted with confusion at the researchers' conversation. Katja hoped they weren't becoming suspicious.

"Maybe we don't need one. Come look!" Klemens motioned for the others to look at his text. He pointed to certain words as he spoke. "This excerpt discusses a way we can keep the Alpha *(Spirit Mage)* from killing *(controlling)* the Führer upon its awakening *(death)*. That should be good enough, right?"

Katja read over the paragraph that referenced Mages using sunfire against Spirit Mages. "This doesn't tell us anything new. We will still need a Mage to combine these two essences." She pointed to the words *fire* and *light* on the page, the two essences required to make sunfire.

"Which two essences?" the guard who stood closest to the door asked.

"Earth and life force, of course, what else?" Ignatius huffed. "Obviously, the only two essences that can keep the Golem of Death from killing our mighty Führer."

"R-right." The guard nodded sheepishly. Katja bit her lip to keep herself from laughing out loud at the Professor's bullshitting tactics.

Klemens continued, pointing out words as he went, "Yes, but I'm saying that we might not need those essences *(sunfire)* at all. I reckon it's not the magic behind it, but the physical substance that makes it is so effective against golems *(Spirit Mages)*."

Katja read where Klemens indicated specifically—*Sunfire is hot enough to burn the spirit within where a regular flame will not suffice, thus severely weakening the Spirit Mage. . . .*

"You might be onto something, Klem." She gave the top of his shoulder a good squeeze.

"Let me see." Ignatius came over and read the excerpt as well. He then pointed to the words he couldn't say. "Ah, this suggests that this *(flame)* is not enough, which is why it must be combined with this *(light)* to make it more potent."

"All we need is something stronger than this *(flame)*. We don't need a magical combination," Klemens said.

"Like what, then?" Ignatius asked.

Katja knew of one thing. It was not hotter than sunfire, but it was much hotter than flame. It could cause just enough damage to Brunhilde's spirit to free Katja's father and keep Brunhilde from possessing him later on. It could buy Katja enough time to get through to him. She flipped through the pages of a golem text on the table. "In order to keep the Golem of Death from killing my father upon its awakening, I know just what we can try. . . ."

Finding the word she was looking for, she pointed to it while ensuring the guards couldn't see. *Lava.*

Klemens grinned at Katja and nodded to Ignatius. The professor looked as excited as he did on their first excursion into frost woods. "Well, you know me, I'll try anything once."

"Guard," Katja called. "Please send word to the Führer that we would like to see the Golem of Death as soon as possible."

"Already?" the guard asked with wide eyes.

"We are not prepared to awaken it just yet. We only want to inspect it."

What she really wanted was to look for any dormant lava golems that were not being utilized by her father to unearth the Alpha. She already knew their fire beams were hot enough to melt rock.

The guard nodded and headed for the door. Klemens called after him, "And find me three topographical maps of Ingleheim, if you please?"

The guard stopped. "What do you need maps for, herr?"

"I am the Lieutenant Military Strategist here, and I have other important duties I must attend," Klemens replied imperiously. "Now, fetch me those maps!"

"Apologies, herr, right away." The guard bowed and left the room and one other guard stayed behind.

"Are you going to map out military strategies while working on this project?" Ignatius asked.

"The maps may come in handy with this project as well," Klemens replied to Ignatius while giving Katja a wink.

Ever the clever Klemens, Katja thought with a grin. All of her golem eye drawings were still in her journal locked away at the university. Finding the opportunity to sketch a lava golem eye without being noticed would be difficult. Cutting one out from the map of Deschner and Breisenburg would be just as good once Katja had a chance to outline the two ranges and bring out the golem eye within.

"Have I ever mentioned how proud I am of you two?" Ignatius placed a loving hand on each of his students' shoulders.

"Yes, but not nearly often enough." Katja touched his hand and smiled up at him.

"Then, I'll say it again. I'm glad to have chosen you both as my acolytes, and I'm not just saying that because you saved me from my execution."

"Don't thank us for that yet, Professor," Klemens said, "because if this experiment goes awry, they'll put us all up on the chopping block."

Klemens was not wrong, but they could not let that deter them. For better or worse, Frau Brunhilde was going to burn.

By the next day, the chaperone guards escorted the research team down to the tunnels underneath the fortress. Fortunately, the Führer was tied up in meetings, and nobody knew where Brunhilde was. The guards had already been given Brunhilde's key to gain entry to the tunnels. The researchers could search for dormant lava golems more or less on their own.

Beyond the enormous steel doors sealing off the tunnels from the rest of the castle was a massive cavernous opening where stone walls gave way to a porous, nearly white, igneous rock. Hundreds of stalactites and stalagmites were cast in light and shadow by several hanging braziers. Flashing red molten beams erupted from lava golems' eyes, burning away rock formations throughout the area. Two large tunnels, one to the left and the other to the right, branched off from the rest of the cavern.

"Where do those tunnels lead?" Katja asked one of the guards.

"They connect to another open cavern like this one on the other side of the Alpha."

"And where is the Alpha exactly?" Ignatius inquired as he spun in a circle, looking all around him.

Katja expected there to be a gargantuan, man-shaped pillar of stone right in the middle of the cavern, but there was only iron scaffolding built against the far wall. She ventured a little further into the large stone vault. To her left, she found a rigid gray pillar embedded in metamorphic rock. Her gaze followed the pillar up, fifty feet above her head, to find it wasn't a pillar at all, but the beginning of a protruding arch connected to a strange centerpiece, surrounded by stalactites.

Katja gaped at the sight of the round, iridescent fixture on the ceiling. It was the size of a clock tower, roughly fourteen feet in diameter, facing the ground. She couldn't see it all because of the scaffolding, but there could be no mistake. Above her was the lethal eye of the Golem of Death. The gray arch to her right was one of its giant legs, attached to its stalactite-covered head. The other three were partially embedded in the stone that the lava golems worked to melt away.

The Golem of Death was not at all what Katja had expected, though there were no smaller versions of it to give her a clue as to its appearance. It was the only one of its kind, unique in its terrifying magnificence. It was all she could do not to go straight up to the Alpha and study it, to satisfy her scholarly curiosities. *That's one part of me that will never die,* she thought. She had to concentrate first on the team's plan to awaken golems absent the watchful eyes of their chaperones.

Professor Ignatius went to play his part to get rid of the first one. "Dear me," he said, looking back toward the door. "It appears I have left my notes in the study. I'm sorry everyone, I need to retrieve them."

The guards groaned. Being an enemy of the Regime, they couldn't allow Ignatius to venture back to the study on his own.

"Come on, then," said one of the guards, who took Ignatius by the arm and escorted him out of the cavern, leaving the second guard behind. One chaperone would be easier for Katja and Klemens to deal with, but they had to think quickly before Ignatius and the other guard returned.

"Klemens," Katja began, "go through that tunnel to the other side of the cavern. See how many lava golems are excavating, and tell me if you find any still in dormancy. If so, we will have to notify my father so he can command them to life. We will need all the golems we can, working around the clock, to uncover this thing."

Klemens nodded and continued along the stone walkway toward the left tunnel.

"Herr, stay within sight until my partner returns," ordered the guard.

Turning to the guard, Klemens snapped, "I'm not a traitor who requires close watch. If you don't mind, I'll explore the other cavern while you make sure the Führer's daughter doesn't fall from that scaffold."

"The scaff . . . ?" The guard turned around, baffled to find Katja already making her way up the ladder so she might get closer to the Alpha's eye.

"Oh, do be careful, fraulein!"

While Klemens was in the other cavern, Katja would take this time to draw a picture of the Golem of Death's eye. She was curious as to what design it would have, since it didn't hail from any one mountain range, as far as she knew.

She walked across the wooden planks at the top of the scaffold while taking out a small notebook and pencil. Stopping under the dusty glass eye, she saw no scratches or etchings of any kind—just a dark gray ash inside. It was akin to looking into an endless ashen sky. If the Alpha were to awaken at that moment, there was no picture she could show it in order to appease it, and that was probably the point. It was Verishten's eye of final judgment that no soul could escape. Shivers ran down her spine.

On her way back down the ladder, a series of echoing booms sounded upon the metallic doors. The guard told Katja to stay put as he went to open it. *Surely they can't be back from the far northeast tower already,* she thought uneasily. While the guard's back was turned, she decided to head into the tunnels to find Klemens. *This might be our only chance to discuss our plan of action absent the guards.*

She didn't get far when she heard a sudden gasp followed by a body collapsing from behind her. Looking back to the door, she found it partially open and the guard motionless on the ground. Nobody else was in sight. She looked around to no avail.

"Professor?" she called out in a wavering voice. With no reply, Katja's heart picked up pace. She quickly turned and continued down the tunnel. As she walked, Katja heard heavy footsteps behind her, urging her to walk faster.

"Kriemhilde . . ." a deep voice echoed through the tunnel, halting her step abruptly as if she had hit an invisible wall.

The voice twisted her insides in an agonizing manner, and she had to hold onto her chest with one hand and her stomach with the other. Her entire soul threatened to pour out of every orifice as the footsteps came closer, finally stopping a few feet from her back.

"No . . . i-it can't be," Katja trembled. She could feel deep in her gut, a sickening certainty, born of a vacant dread she hadn't felt in years.

Meister Melikheil.

29
UNBLINKING

"Kriemhilde."

He was so close.

"You can't be here. You're not him," Katja whispered, shaking her head. She stood frozen. *If I turn around, I will see those dark eyes, and my soul will fall back into oblivion.*

"You know it's me, Little Dove. You feel me because a part of my spirit is bound to yours. We are connected despite my releasing you so many years ago," said Melikheil.

He was so close she could smell the outside's ash-fall on his coat. Her heart heaved inside her chest. It was as if Melikheil were pulling it toward him with a ghostly hand.

"I have just returned from the desert. Frau Brunhilde told me I'd find you down here. I put the guard to sleep so we could be alone—"

"You're dead," Katja interrupted. "This isn't real."

"Face me and see how real I am."

She thought about running, but if Melikheil was truly behind her, she couldn't allow him to find Klemens. *Please, Klem, stay away until I can figure something out.* She gradually turned around, struggling to steady her breath.

There he stood, the Mage that had held Katja's heart and soul prisoner for two whole years before shattering them both into a thousand pieces. He wore his black tailcoat over a satin vest and a white ruffled collar. His long dark hair was tied back in a low ponytail under a modest top hat. The only thing missing from the darkly handsome picture of Melikheil was his raven-adorned walking stick.

As soon as she saw him, she felt the urge to jump into his arms like she'd always done when he returned from a long absence. Her gut twisted. *I will not let him take me over.* She had to get far away from here.

"Why did you come back?" she asked quietly as she edged along the tunnel wall to get to the other side of him.

"Isn't it obvious? I've come back for you." Melikheil reached out to touch Katja's face, but she jerked out of his reach and continued backward toward the tunnel's opening. "Where are you going?" he asked with concern in his voice.

"Stay away from me!" Katja hissed. She couldn't allow her voice to carry too far, lest her echo travel into Klemens's ears and he come to her aid. There was no telling what Melikheil would do to him.

The dark Mage swayed toward Katja with his palms up, to signify he meant no harm, but she knew he did not need to lift a finger to cause her such. "There is no need to fear me. I do not intend to put you under my thrall again. You will come to love me on your own as it should have been in the beginning."

"You're demented," Katja said through gritted teeth. "To think I'd willingly give myself to a beast like you—I'd rather be gutted."

"But you have given yourself to a beast already. That Steinkamp, I know all about him. I can sense his degenerate essence on you still. But he is gone from this world, and it can once again be the two of us."

How does he know Sigurd's dead? Katja wondered. Did he learn it from Brunhilde before coming or did being tethered to her spirit allow him to share in her experiences from afar? The nausea she felt at that moment overwhelmed her. *I have to get away.*

Once back in the open cavern, she turned to run, but Melikheil swiftly moved to block her. He grabbed her firmly around her bicep. Melikheil's other hand brushed aside her hair and took a tender hold of her head.

"You should be with me, Kriemhilde."

"No." Katja tried to pull away, but Melikheil managed to cage her between him and the scaffolding. He tried to lay a kiss upon her forehead, but she shook her head away. "I can't—I won't go with you!"

She accidentally met his eyes, and they instantly reminded her of how wonderful it had felt to lose herself in them.

"Meister." She touched his face, and then abruptly recoiled. Despite Melikheil promising not to thrall her, she could still feel him subtly pulling her in with the power of his spirit. *Sigurd is the one you loved. He was real,* she forced herself to remember.

"I left a piece of myself with you, and I won't be separated from it another day. You belong to me, Kriemhilde, and deep down you know it to be true."

Katja closed her eyes and forced thoughts of him from her mind. She took deep, controlled breaths and fought as hard as she could to think of what was real. She thought of her research, her dream to see Ingleheim enter a new Age of Man, and her love for Sigurd. Depictions of his strong face and unyielding gray eyes replaced the face of Melikheil in her mind. Sigurd's quietly intense voice kept her grounded. *'No matter what darkness you may have inside you, it is there you'll find me, not him.'*

Melikheil's voice broke through Katja's introspection as he gripped her arm tighter and pulled her away. "Come with me, and I will bestow pleasures upon you that you have never imagined. I will give you everything—"

Katja's body weakened as he led her from the scaffolding. With all her mental might, she fought to keep her mind clear and firmly planted herself in place. *You are not taking me anywhere,* she seethed inwardly.

"Melikheil, wait." She opened her eyes.

"What is it, Dove?"

"This will be painful. . . ."

Katja struck him in the throat with speed akin to a snake's. Melikheil staggered back, clutching at his neck and choking.

". . . But it will pass," she said coldly. She followed up with a low sweeping kick to Melikheil's ankles, knocking his feet out from under him, and he fell to the ground.

Katja's perceptions suddenly shifted. The person choking and gasping upon the ground was not Melikheil. It was a blonde woman wearing a teal gown and coat with puffed sleeves.

"Brunhilde!" Katja gasped in shock. "How were you able—? You promised Melikheil that you'd never use magic on me!"

Brunhilde continued to hack and choke. She staggered to her feet while rubbing her red throat and taking labored breaths. "That was when he was still alive," she croaked. "Now the greatest sorcerer of our time is dead and for some idiotic reason, he felt the need to bind part of his spirit to yours as well as mine. You are still vulnerable to him. I used what I have of his spirit, within me, to make you see him."

"Why would you do that to me?" Katja recoiled. "You're sick!"

"It would have been very pleasurable for you, had you just submitted to one final bout with your old flame. However, the small fraction of Melikheil's spirit inside me only allows me to wield an equally small fraction of its power—power needed to thrall you. My intention was only to unbind Melikheil's spirit from yours and take it into mine," Brunhilde replied, still rubbing her throat.

"And what could you possibly want with that lecherous soul?"

"In my Meister's absence, my spirit has grown powerful enough to feed his. In time my body will be a worthy host. Then he and I will rule this world as one like we were supposed to." Her hazel eyes looked as if they were about to tear up at her words.

Katja's stomach churned at her stepmother's actions, but her fear of her waned. "You're pathetic, to wish to share a body with as wretched a soul as his. Although, perhaps you both will be happier as two debauched minds trapped together for eternity."

"Don't presume to be better than me," Brunhilde lashed. "Melikheil and I shared almost everything. I know about every sordid act you performed for him, and I felt how hungry you were for more. Even now, with the short time I spent in your mind, I can see all the wicked things you've done and wanted to do to that filthy Steinkamp. You are just as depraved as any of us, and the sooner you admit that, the better off you'll be."

"It is not me you should concern yourself with." Katja crossed her arms. "You should be worrying about giving my father an heir. A rebel army and the Herrani are coming to sever the Golem Mage line forever. Without the Führer's body that you use to control golems, you are nothing."

Brunhilde looked away, shaking her head and scoffing as lava golems continued their excavation, paying the two women no mind. "Oh, Verishten forbid I deny the mighty Führer an heir. I am not a mountain for future Golem Mages to be mined from. If Verishten wants more, he can make more, but he will never do it through my womb. My power transcends man and golem. I've grown beyond such degrading and primitive purpose. Once I've joined with Melikheil, all mankind will tremble at our feet. Verishten himself will not oppose us."

Katja shook her head. "You two truly belong together."

"If that is how you feel, then give me his soul, and you will be forever free of him, and me," Brunhilde offered.

"And allow you to pleasure me as Melikheil?" Katja turned up her lip in disgust. "The only pleasure you can give me right now is jumping into that golem's fire beam."

Brunhilde waved her arm dismissively. "Don't be so dramatic, Dove. It won't take long. All you have to do is close your eyes and relax. I promise I'll release you immediately after."

Katja fought the urge to spit in her stepmother's face, but she took a deep breath instead. She had an idea. "Fine, I consent, but only if you release my father first." She locked eyes firmly with Brunhilde's.

"Release your father?" The Mage cackled at the notion. "Oh no, I'm afraid I can't do that. We are bound together, our spirits so assimilated, we are practically of one mind. If I release him now, the poor man won't be able to walk, let alone command a single golem against the coming charge. I cannot return your father to you, and why would you want me to? He never loved you. He was never good to you, not like *Sigurd* was."

Brunhilde took slow steps toward Katja, who found herself backing into the scaffolding again.

"Your Steinkamp is seared into your mind and heart. Allow me to bring him out. You can say goodbye, make love one last time. Your mind will never be able to fathom that it is me. You will be completely lost in the man you love. How can one last moment with him not outweigh any desire to see your father's feeble mind freed?"

"Maybe," Katja muttered as Brunhilde ventured even closer. Remembering Sigurd's lips upon her and how the sound of his voice in her ear left her breathless, but she was not about to soil Sigurd's memory by taking the sorceress' offer.

"Allow me to do you this one kindness and help me put Melikheil's spirit where it belongs."

Brunhilde quickened her approach, reaching her silken-gloved hands out. Before the woman could lay a finger on her, Katja smacked her hard across the face with the back of her hand, the sound echoing off the cavern walls.

"His soul belongs to me now."

"You cannot keep it from me!" Brunhilde shrieked while holding her cheek, now red to match her throat.

"You insist on keeping my father, so I will keep your Meister," said Katja. "Besides, I'm starting to get used to him."

Brunhilde hissed, "There are two ways a Mage can unbind a spirit, and I offered you the painless way. When I'm finished with you, there will be nothing left of that so-called brilliant mind of yours!"

With a determined screech, she lunged at Katja and tried to grab her head. Using Brunhilde's forward momentum, Katja moved to the side and shoved her to the ground. She grabbed her stepmother by the hair, tearing off her lace fascinator and pulling her blonde curls loose from their bun.

"Guard, wake up and stop her!" Brunhilde screeched.

The guard lying on the ground by the door snapped to sudden consciousness. Without a moment of hesitation, he bolted to Brunhilde's aid. He took Katja by the arm and yanked her off his mistress. Brunhilde then returned to her feet and composed herself.

Katja struggled against the guard's grip as Brunhilde said, "You were always so sullen and cynical for such a pretty girl. I still cannot understand why Melikheil chose you when he already had me. I wish he had let you fall out of that window. What a fool he was!"

"Then why resurrect him?" Katja yelled, no longer caring about her voice echoing through the caverns. "Are you incapable of ruling this world with your power alone?"

"You cannot begin to understand what it feels like to watch such extraordinary spiritual power fade away untapped. He is my Meister, and it is my duty to see him returned to former glory."

"I do understand. I know how it feels to have the one you love torn from this world. Only most of us don't get to bring that person back."

"Melikheil is not yet gone," Brunhilde corrected. "He still lives in the two of us. His spirit roams between our living realm and the spiritual one until I bring him back, but only if you give me the piece of him you carry."

Brunhilde attempted to lay hands on Katja's head once again while she was still restrained, but Katja jammed her elbow into the guard's ribcage, taking the wind from him long enough for her to flip him overhead. She dove to attack Brunhilde, but before she could reach her, the guard grabbed Katja's leg and pulled her onto the hard ground with him.

"Hold her down!" The sorceress commanded.

The guard put his full weight on Katja's chest, forcing all the air from her lungs. She struggled violently, gasping for air as Brunhilde kneeled at her head. As soon as she laid her hands on Katja's temples, the cavern darkened to pitch black. Katja heard the ravenous growls of a canine. A silver wolf sprang out of the darkness and sank its teeth into her chest.

She shrieked in pain as the wolf jerked its head from side to side, its fangs tearing into her mercilessly. Blood splashed as the wolf worked its way through her flesh. It then took what appeared to be an enormous black raven into its jaws and began to pull it from her chest. The raven was soaked in blood, embedded in her sternum, unable to come loose. The wolf pulled harder, and Katja cried out in agony. She desperately wanted the wolf to just rip the bird out, but it was part of her body, and the pain was too great.

With one more gargled shriek, the world returned to Katja once again. Her head pounded as she looked around dazedly. Brunhilde was on the ground amongst broken chunks of rock, holding her bleeding temple and moaning in pain. Katja looked up just in time to see the guard punch Klemens in the face, and in an instant he was on the ground as well.

Where did Klemens come from? What's happening? Katja held onto her head, trying to steady herself as she wobbled to her feet. She jolted back into full awareness by the cavern shuddering, sending her back down to the ground. A giant lava golem burst from the left tunnel, crashing through stalactites and stalagmites. Relief flooded over her. *Klem, you did it!*

"Subdue him!" Brunhilde screamed at the guard as she tried to get back up.

Klemens was still on the ground recovering from the last punch when the guard bent over, took him around the neck, and strangled him. Katja clambered to her shaking feet to come to Klemens's aid, but she found it wouldn't be necessary. A bright red fire beam burst from the golem's eye and hit the guard on his side. The guard's uniform burst into flames, but the burning hole through his ribcage ensured he was dead before he hit the ground.

Katja took out the map piece from her sleeve and held it up for the lava golem until its red eye flashed and dimmed. Despite her disorientation, she ran for Brunhilde, who was completely stunned, grabbed her by the hair, and dragged her over to the golem.

Presenting Brunhilde to the it, Katja yelled, "This woman is a threat to you all. Take her too!" *She won't have time to call on Father to stop the golem before its fire beam claims her,* Katja hoped.

To her alarm, the golem moved its gaze from Brunhilde on her knees, to Katja holding her there.

"Fools!" Brunhilde sneered. "Heinrich and I are of one mind and soul. He does not have to be in the room for me to use his power."

"You won't kill me, not while I still have your precious Meister inside of me." Katja reaffirmed her grip of Brunhilde's hair.

"I suppose I can't, but this handsome fellow . . ." The golem slowly turned from Katja to Klemens. "I would hate to kill young Kriemia's betrothed, but he does have a brother who would do just as well."

"Klem, watch out!" Katja screamed.

Klemens cursed aloud before running to take cover behind a cluster of stalagmites against the cavern wall to his right. The golem's beam hit the ground where he had been standing, rendering it bright red and molten.

Katja let Brunhilde go and ran after the golem that now stomped toward Klemens. The golem shot its beam again, and a few of the stalagmites around Klemens melted into puddles of lava. He yelped and crawled further into the cluster. Brunhilde's sickeningly sweet laughter echoed off the cavern walls.

Snatching the guard's spear, Katja ran in front of the golem with the intention of distracting it. *What am I going to do, throw it into its eye fifteen feet up?*

The entire cavern shook again as another giant lava golem crashed through the right-side tunnel. Instead of attacking Klemens, the second golem rammed itself into the first. Screaming, Katja dove out of the way. She crawled over to join Klemens, and the two of them ran for the tunnel where the second golem had emerged.

"You woke two of them?" she asked Klemens breathlessly. "How did you get it to come around the other way?"

"I thought I only awakened the one."

The golems bashed together. One fell backward onto the scaffolding, taking down the entire iron structure and making a deafening clank as it crashed to the stone floor. The same golem shoved the other into the cavern wall so hard that several stalactites shook loose and shattered over its obsidian body. A string of braziers broke from the ceiling, pouring fiery hot oil onto the remnants of the scaffolding and igniting the wooden planks.

Brunhilde stood amongst the chaos, looking intently at the fighting golems, her fists clenched. It didn't take long before her determined expression turned to one of horror. "I can't control it. Impossible!"

As the second golem's fist prepared to strike the other, Brunhilde, lost in shock, didn't get out of the way in time, and it knocked her down hard. Klemens and Katja continued to watch the two giants burn molten holes into each other's obsidian bodies as well as anything else around them. If Brunhilde wasn't controlling the golem and Klemens wasn't influencing it, did that mean the Führer's mind was somehow free?

There was no time to contemplate how or who controlled the golem. The cavern began to quake again, this time, so severe the stalactites shook from the ceiling. Katja's blood froze in her veins. The last time she had experienced an earthquake of this magnitude, the entire Crags transformed into the Golem of Stone. More stalactites crashed down around them as Klemens grabbed Katja's hand and made a run for it.

"Wait!" Katja looked back to her stepmother still on the ground.

"Just leave her!"

"I have to free my father." She pulled out of Klemens's grasp and made way to the disoriented sorceress. Dodging the falling rocks, Katja picked her by her frilled collar and shook her. "Let him go, Brunhilde!"

Once she realized it was the Golem of Death that stirred, Brunhilde's bloodshot eyes widened in terror. The rock around the Alpha's giant limbs crumbled as it struggled to break free from its stone prison. The other lava golems continued to excavate mindlessly while the two, still in combat, crashed through the left tunnel and out of sight.

"We must leave here at once! It awakens!" Brunhilde cried.

"Release him!" bellowed Katja.

Breathing frantically, Brunhilde closed her eyes and said as clearly and as calmly as she could, "Heinrich, I release you. There. It's done. You've won, Little Dove."

If she can release him without requiring him to be in the room, then she can put him back under her thrall just as easily, she realized. *There is only one way I can be certain he remains free.* She eyed the melting scaffold behind Brunhilde, rapidly forming into a pool of lava.

"I am no dove."

With all the strength she could muster, Katja pushed Brunhilde into the lava. She stood there, breathlessly watching her stepmother writhe about, her clothing aflame, her vibrant curls singeing away. The sorceress' skin blackened and peeled. Her agonizing screams blasted through Katja's mind as Brunhilde managed to roll away from the molten pool. She desperately tried to smother the flames engulfing her gown.

It is done.

Then came an ear-shattering crack behind her. One of the Alpha's legs broke free from the wall. The massive glass eye above illuminated the cavern in a ghostly glow.

"Katja, come on!" Klemens bellowed.

The tremors within the cavern intensified, and Katja rushed toward Klemens. The two of them sprinted to the door, leaving Brunhilde and her agonizing pleas behind.

Klemens opened the door while she took one last look back. With the fire put out, but her body badly burned, Brunhilde crawled along the ground toward the door. An ethereal spotlight from above shone down upon her and held her in place. Her weakened whimpers returned to shrill screams while she floated into the air, reaching desperately for Katja or anyone to pull her outside the Golem of Death's terminal light. Katja gaped in horror as Brunhilde hung helplessly before the great colorless eye of Verishten's Judgment.

Brunhilde convulsed. The light filled her until it streamed out of her eyes, nose, and mouth, leaving emptiness behind. Her agonizing shrieks faded as her body shriveled, rapidly decomposing, burnt skin flaking until it fell away as ashes.

Klemens pulled on Katja's arm. "We need to go!"

They closed and locked the doors behind them. The quaking continued as they ran up the stairs, trying not to falter from the ground's movement. They didn't stop running until they ascended three more floors and the shaking lessened to a faint vibration. It seemed that the Alpha had settled for the time being.

As they emerged in the southeast tower, Katja's heavy heart weighed her down. There was no satisfaction to be had in what she'd done to Brunhilde. Ingleheim was better off without her, yet Katja didn't feel any better for it. She only felt a revolting dread. The fact that Sigurd had to kill nearly every day since the age of thirteen only proved to her how strong he truly was. Her heart lurched within her chest, missing him all the more.

When Katja and Klemens left the southeast tower and ran into the upper battlements outside, they were met with heavy rainfall. Soldiers ran about and barked orders from one man to the other.

"What's happening?" Katja wheezed, her chest still heaving from the stairs.

"I think the fortress is under attack!" Klemens replied.

The bailey bustled with soldiers rushing to their posts or getting weapons from one place to another.

"My father is likely in the war room," said Katja.

The war room was in the Keep on the fortress' north side. In the interest of avoiding the bailey, they took the most convenient way around the battlements. When they reached the northernmost battlements, Klemens stopped to find out what was going on. He found a pair of mounted binoculars to give him a better view beyond the fortress walls.

"Verishten save us." Klemens gulped. "It looks like all of Ingleheim is out there."

"Does it look like they'll get through?"

"Not really. I've never seen this many war golems in one place before, and they are not holding back."

"Let me see." Katja stepped in front of Klemens and looked through the binoculars herself.

Lines upon lines of war golems advanced toward the rebel armies of Untevar and Nordenhein. Each stomp laid several men to slaughter at the bottom of their iron feet. Arrows and spears deflected off them like rain off stone. They were unstoppable. This was exactly what Katja was afraid of, if and when she returned to her father's side.

"I don't understand," Klemens said. "Frau Brunhilde is dead, and yet the golems are still carrying out her commands."

"Brunhilde used my father's spirit to command the golems, so the commands technically came from him. Once a golem is given its order, it will continue to carry it out without the Mage needing to be conscious of it. We need to get my father to make them stand down."

"How will he do that without his Spirit Mage to amplify his power?"

"As long as they are in his sight, he will have access to them."

Katja was about to walk away from the binoculars when a red light further northeast caught her attention. Turning the glass eyes toward it, she couldn't believe what she saw. There, in the distance, toward the Volcano of Verishten, was a colossal flame-covered figure rapidly making way southward. Its body shone molten red from beneath charred black rock. The size of it was comparable to the Golem of Stone, perhaps even larger.

Its terrifying fire and brimstone majesty gave Katja a beautiful calm. The mighty Verishten was awakening the Alphas to make things right again, but what she didn't know was whether that involved saving the Ingles or destroying them. Either way, it was out of their hands.

"It's the Golem of Fire!"

Klemens was aghast. "Are you sure?"

Before she could give Klemens the binoculars, she noticed movement on the Alpha's shoulder. "And there's somebody on top of it!"

The Golem of Fire was still too far away to make out the mysterious person. She could only discern that it was a human dressed head to toe in black.

Her legs wobbled. She stopped peering through the binoculars and steadied herself against the bastion. *It can't be him, can it? He should be dead, but he managed to awaken an Alpha before. Could he have awakened the Golem of Fire too?* Katja didn't want to let her mind go there. If she held onto any hope that Sigurd was alive then found it not to be the case, her heart would shatter all over again.

Klemens looked through the binoculars, and his jaw dropped. He turned to her, his brown hair wet and plastered to his head, his spectacles dotted with raindrops. "You were telling the truth. He can awaken Alphas."

Tears instantly poured from Katja's eyes and got lost in the rain running down her face. "I was bluffing. Sigurd had a connection to the Golem of Stone, but I swear I didn't know how. . . . Is it really him?"

Klemens nodded. "You should go to him. I'll find your father."

Incredibly touched, dumbfounded, and exhausted all at once, Katja shook her head. "Not yet. I stand the best chance of getting through to him after what Brunhilde did to him. We go together."

With a nod, Klemens turned to lead Katja down the steps from the battlements and toward the Keep. She looked back to the volcano one more time. *Thank you, Merciful Verishten, for bringing Sigurd back to me.*

Suddenly, there was a loud crack followed by breaking glass, distinctive amongst the pelting rain and booming thunder. Klemens grunted, falling back against Katja. A blood-covered arrowhead stuck out the back of Klemens's head. Katja clutched his arm, but she couldn't keep him from falling.

"Klem!" she shrieked.

A crossbow bolt was embedded deep into his right eye socket, his spectacle lens shattered through. His other blue eye—dark and unblinking.

30
PRIMAL INSTINCTS

Katja fell to her knees before Klemens's motionless body, shaking as she touched him with a quivering hand.

"No, Klem . . . please . . . no, no, no, no." She shook him as if somehow he would come to and brush off the crossbow bolt embedded in his skull.

The rain came down harder, washing away the blood pooling under Klemens's head and drenching Katja in her grief. She didn't care that the one who used the crossbow now walked toward her. She doubled over and wept. *This wasn't supposed to happen to you, brave, brilliant Klem.*

"It's time to come with me, fraulein."

Katja lifted her rain-soaked head. Standing before her, wearing the long black and silver-buttoned coat of the Steinkamp Kapitän was Rudiger, accompanied by ten of his faceless foot-soldiers. She couldn't imagine hating the man more than she already did.

"You didn't have to kill him!" she cried.

"He was in the way."

"He was no threat to you!"

"You're probably right, but even a Steinkamp can't be too careful these days. I can't have Volker's successor given a place in my regime. Men like Herr Klemens and Herrscher Heinrich cannot be allowed to live in the new Age of Order."

"Say what you will of my father," Katja said through gritted teeth, "but it is men like Klemens who make this regime worth preserving at all. And men like you are the reason the Alphas will destroy it!"

Rudiger smirked then grabbed her roughly. She didn't fight him. Her grief weighed her down. The rain sapped her energy, and she knew better than to try and escape one Steinkamp, let alone ten.

"No, fraulein," growled Rudiger. "It's time for *men like me* to restore order to this nation, and you will join your father in solidifying that."

"Listen to me!" Katja protested. "The Golem of Death has awakened, and it will kill us all. My father is the only one who can command his war golems to fall back and help get everyone out of here."

"Don't make me execute you right here and now." Rudiger shoved her into the arms of one of his comrades. "I prefer to do it where I will have an audience. The people will demand to see the vestiges of the old regime that oppressed them be destroyed before they will recognize a new one."

"There will be no new regime!" Katja screamed.

"Take this mad woman to the Keep," Rudiger ordered his comrades.

"Let me go! Sigurd!" Katja struggled against her captors, hoping that Sigurd would hear her somehow.

"Not to worry, fraulein, you'll see your Steinkamp again very soon," Rudiger taunted as he motioned for his comrades to follow him down the steps.

"Dammit!" Jenn cursed into the howling winds from atop the winged golem. "It's taking us to the Fortress of Mortlach!"

As the golem flew down beneath the dark storm clouds, the ashen wasteland of Breisenburg became visible, along with the fortress in the distance.

"So this thing is being controlled by the Führer after all," said Jeth, holding onto the back of the golem with Jenn and Sebastian. The rains had washed away much of the mud caked into his locks. "He's taking us back here to be executed. Whose bright idea was it to get onto the back of a winged golem during an open rebellion again?"

Jenn glared at him. Before she could reply, Sebastian cut in, "If I recall, you volunteered to come along for the ride, my Fae'ren friend."

"I'm a risk taker, I'll admit that," said Jeth. "Doesn't make this idea any less stupid."

"Everyone just shut up and let me think!" Jenn barked.

The golem continued its descent toward the Fortress of Mortlach.

Rows upon rows of war golems plowed through the lines of rebel soldiers. It glided over the armies on the ground and over the fortress' outer walls toward the northwestern tower. Then, it suddenly changed course, veering sharply to the left and making a steep drop toward the bailey.

"Looks like it's taking us to the Keep," said Sebastian with a raspy, nervous chuckle.

"Wait a minute, is that Rudiger?" Jeth pointed to a tall auburn-haired man in a black uniform leading a line of Steinkamp and their female captive onto the bailey. The faceless soldiers took their prisoner southward, around the west side of the Keep, to get to the main entrance on its south wall.

"What is he doing?" Jenn wondered aloud.

"I don't know, but I no longer trust him." Jeth glared down at men below.

"You *never* trusted him."

"Oh, right." Jeth nodded. "Well, now we have our chance to find out what he's really been up to all this time."

The golem landed abruptly in the bailey, trapping the marching Steinkamp between the Keep's western wall and the western battlements. Other Regime soldiers about the bailey didn't pay too much mind to the winged granite creature, likely having seen many of its kind before. Rudiger, not as quick to dismiss the obstruction, motioned for his comrades to halt.

The golem went dormant, allowing its three riders to descend from its back. Jenn didn't care that she had been brought here to be executed—she was not going to go quietly with her questions left unanswered.

"Rudiger!" she called as she stepped out into his path. "Why are you wearing that uniform?"

Both Jeth and Sebastian remained hidden behind the dormant golem.

"Jenn?" Rudiger squinted in confusion as if she were the last person he expected to see. "I'm glad you're alive. I have the daughter of the Führer, and in the Keep there is the Führer in the flesh. Soon we will be victorious."

Seeing him dressed in the uniform of the Steinkamp Kapitän made Jenn sick to her stomach. *He doesn't care about the Remnants, he never did. He's double crossed us!* She clenched her drenched fists, her fingernails cutting into her palms.

"Are you going to step aside?" Rudiger made a sweeping gesture with his arm.

"I don't think so." Jenn shook her head and took a step forward. Jeth came out from behind the golem and stood beside her.

"Ah, so the Del'Cabrian is here too." Rudiger turned to Jeth. "I don't have time to give you your Magitech right now. I have a regime leader to kill."

"Don't worry about it," Jeth said. "I already took it off your hands."

"Well, good . . . so go home."

"I can't. I made a promise to a Steinkamp to help him kill his kapitän. I suppose that kapitän is you now?" Jeth tilted his head in question while pointing at Rudiger.

"Jenn!" Rudiger barked. "Either fall in line, or my comrades will have to take you both out. I suggest you do the former because in that Keep is your mother's salvation."

"If I'm to assume you mean to take the ruling seat for yourself, then you never gave a *shit* about my mother's salvation!" Jenn yelled back.

"Under Steinkamp rule, all smuggling rings will be put down permanently. I promised you that. Choose your side wisely, Jenn."

She felt torn. All she had ever wanted was to help the rebellion that had gotten her and her mother away from those smugglers, but now . . . *Jeth was right. I should never have put so much trust in Rudiger.* Jenn looked to the sky and saw billowing storm clouds forming as they did in Luidfort. An enormous winged shadow flew overhead, hidden behind the clouds it created.

"The Golem of Storms," she whispered.

"What?" Rudiger looked up as well.

"The Alphas are awakening," screamed the Führer's daughter, still within a Steinkamp's grasp. "The Golem of Storms is above, and the Golem of Fire is on its way. Please help me get everyone out of h—" Her desperate pleas were cut short by the soldier's smothering grip.

Jenn knew what side Verishten was on, judging by how he had directed his wrath on the Herrani and favored the lives of those who tried to defend the defenseless. It brought to mind Sigurd's words. *My aim is in the preservation of life, not the taking of it.* That would be her aim as well.

"You're too late, Rudiger," she said. "My mother is safe now, no thanks to you."

"I'm glad to hear it, so why are you even here?"

"I'm here to repay my debts."

"Kill them," Rudiger ordered his comrades, and they immediately aimed their crossbows at her and Jeth.

Jenn had absorbed plenty of wind essence from the storm during the flight, so it was easy enough to pull away the air in the Steinkamp's immediate vicinity. They clutched for their throats, choking inside their masks. The two Steinkamp holding the Führer's daughter weakened their grip, and she was able to wriggle free.

To save his comrades, Rudiger threw two knives at Jenn, but she quickly wrapped a whirlwind around herself to deflect the blades. She then pushed out the winds and knocked all those standing in front of her to the ground. This gave Jeth the chance to attack the Steinkamp while they were down. With his scimitars, he delivered death blows to the two men closest to him and killed another who tried to retrieve the Führer's daughter with a well-placed arrow to the jugular.

"Sebastian! Now!" Jenn called, not willing to wait for any Steinkamp to recover.

The reformed naja sprang into the fray, startling everyone on the bailey. He barreled through the Steinkamp as they began to regroup, slashed through their protective face plates and dug out their throats with his claws. Other Regime soldiers, alerted by the naja's presence, flooded into the bailey to assist. Numerous crossbow bolts and spears punctured deep into Sebastian's scales. Bright orange blood leaked from the wounds, but he was unfazed as he continued to rampage through the soldiers.

Rudiger left his comrades to fight Jeth and Sebastian themselves while he snatched up the Führer's daughter. He weaved expertly through the battle with the woman over his shoulder, knocking Jenn down with his elbow to get by her.

"Hey!" she growled. "I'm not finished with you!"

As Rudiger ran for the Keep's entrance, Jenn focused on the aura of the stone he ran upon. She stretched the earth essence out so the stone became malleable, as she had done to prevent Sigurd from smashing into the volcano's base. The rock liquefied under Rudiger's feet, and he sank. Jenn let go of the earth essence, and the stone reverted to its normal state, sealing him in the floor to his waist.

On her way to confront him, Sebastian flung a Steinkamp in front of her by accident. The masked man jumped to his feet and turned to her. She use a whirlwind again to block the Steinkamp's sword blow, which nicked her arm through her coat sleeve.

"Shit!" Jenn cried, holding her bleeding arm.

Before she could think of her next move, Jeth broke away from the brawl and shot an arrow into the Steinkamp's neck. With a grateful nod to the archer, Jenn went to aid her friends in battle before confronting

Rudiger. *It's not like he's going anywhere.*

Once Katja realized Rudiger was stuck in the ground, she struggled violently to get out of his grasp.

All the other soldiers were too distracted by the Del'Cabrian archer and the naja to pay mind to either their kapitän or his captive. Unfortunately for Katja, even waist-deep in stone, Rudiger's grip would not wane. From over his shoulder, she reached the ground behind him and pulled herself along it, kicking furiously. Rudiger reached one arm back, roughly took her by her blouse, and yanked her right back into his inescapable hold.

"No!" she wailed.

She no longer cared what he was capable of doing to her. She knew that if he wanted her dead, she already would be. It would mean little to execute Herrscher Heinrich's daughter while stuck in the ground with nobody watching.

Katja's primal instincts took over. Kicking and flailing, she scratched down Rudiger's face, drawing blood into her fingernails; she even bit into him. Everything became a blur. Rudiger's grip weakened, and she fell onto her back. He still had both hands around her waist, but she kept kicking wildly. For a moment, she thought she would get free. Then Rudiger returned with a force so powerful, Katja's determined rage quickly transformed into sheer terror. He lunged forward, his long arms reaching for her. The kapitän grabbed her by the hair and yanked her head back hard. Her cries cut off once he clamped his fingers around her neck. She gasped for air as he dragged her back to him.

Before she could retaliate any further, his fist cracked hard across her face. A numbing pain reverberated through her head and neck as bright flickers of light danced across her line of sight. She tasted blood as it flooded into her mouth from her nostrils and she went limp, rocking her head from side to side and doing all she could to stay awake after such a brutal strike. Rudiger raised his fist in preparation for another hit. If this one didn't kill her, it would knock her out for certain.

Then, the point of a guard's spear pressed against Rudiger's jugular, staying his hand.

"Let her go, Rudiger," demanded the tiny witch holding the spear.

"You should know better than to threaten a Steinkamp, Jenn."

"I have a naja, and you are rapidly running out of Steinkamp."

Rudiger took a deep breath, glancing around the bailey at the naja tearing through his comrades. He slowly loosened his grip around Katja's neck. She dragged herself out of his reach as quickly as her exhausted body would allow and wiped the blood from her mouth. She tried her best to remain alert and ignore the aching of her face and the ringing in her ears.

"How in Verishten's name did you get a naja under your control? You've been holding out on me, haven't you?" Rudiger smirked.

Jenn smirked right back, whacking him over the head with the shaft of her spear before pointing it back at his face. "Tell your comrades to stand down or my naja will tear through every single one of them!" she hissed.

Rudiger didn't have a chance to respond. The ground quaked so violently, anyone left standing hit the ground. The bailey cracked apart and started to crumble with chunks of stone falling into the cavern below. An incline rapidly formed beneath Katja, and she began to slide down it.

"Help!" she shrieked.

The Del'Cabrian leaped to her aid and grabbed her hand, but his footing soon crumbled away and he began to slide alongside her. The entire bailey caved in. Soldiers and Steinkamp desperately scrambled for the edges where the floors were still intact.

Just as the ground completely fell away beneath them, a whirling gust of wind engulfed Katja and the Del'Cabrian, blowing them safely to an unbroken ledge at the bailey's eastern edge. Jenn appeared from the whirlwind as soon as it dissipated.

"What just . . . ?" Katja sputtered.

"Thanks for the wind save, Jenn." The out of breath Del'Cabrian gave her a firm pat on the arm.

Jenn winced as she held onto the bleeding gash on her left bicep.

"Sorry, you all right?" The Del'Cabrian asked with concern.

"I'll live." She turned to Katja. "What about you, fraulein?"

Despite the throbbing of her face and the taste of blood in her mouth, she nodded. "Yes, thank you, Jenn and . . ." she turned to the matted haired man, who finished for her.

"The name's Jeth."

"Well, that's shit," muttered Jenn.

"Hey, I happen to like my name—in its shortened form anyway."

"Not you! Him!" She pointed to the western edge across from them. Rudiger had broken free during the collapse and climbed to safety up the western battlements using his earth bindings.

"Don't worry, he won't live much longer," Katja said darkly, not taking her eyes from the murderous kapitän.

Jeth and Jenn exchanged confused glances, but before they could say anything, the bailey erupted in quakes again. A bright white light beamed up from the pit below. Katja glanced down, and her whole body trembled at the sight. The Golem of Death's head had broken free and now had the ability to rotate in any direction. Instead of facing down into the caverns, it now faced upward. The soldiers who had fallen into the pit were caught within the light's mysterious hold.

"Sebastian!" Jenn yelled, reaching out for the naja helplessly floating. Katja held her back so she wouldn't get caught in the light as well. Jenn sent wind gusts toward the beam in an attempt to push the naja outside it, but strangely the wind was redirected around. To Katja's amazement, the naja spoke.

"Thank you, Jenn. If you find others like me, do for them what you've done for me. Free them—"

The naja, along with everyone else caught in the Golem of Death's sight, convulsed and exploded into light in the same manner as Brunhilde.

"I will!" Jenn yelled back at him, tears wetting her dark bloodshot eyes.

Katja's eyes flooded with tears as she covered her ears to block the shrill screams of the victims' life force burning within them. Each scream came to an end at the same time, and each corpse disintegrated into ashes, swirling in the wind. Then the light went out.

"Is-is that the Golem of Death?" Jeth's eyes were wide with horror.

"Yes, and we will be next if we wait here another minute," Katja affirmed.

"We'll get you out of here, fraulein," offered Jenn.

"No, we need to get inside the Keep. My father can help."

"How is the Führer going to help with this?" Jenn asked.

"Only he can release the golems currently under his control. You're the rebel witch everyone is talking about, aren't you?"

Jenn nodded.

"Then you have to come with me, please," Katja begged.

"Uh . . . Okay."

"And Jeth—a friend of mine, Herr Ignatius, is being held prisoner here. The dungeons are below the northeast tower just there." Katja pointed to the tower. She figured the guard would have taken Ignatius there when he discovered the rebel armies had the fortress surrounded.

"Say no more." Jeth's hazel eyes twinkled. "It'll be good practice for breaking myself out of prison someday."

Katja gave him a brief description of Ignatius before he climbed nimbly up the wall and into the eastern battlements that would take him to the tower.

The two women proceeded to edge carefully along the crumbling boundaries of the bailey toward the Keep's entrance.

"Are you sure we should be going in there with the bailey caved in and the Golem of Death just below?" Jenn asked nervously. "I've already been buried alive once this week. I'd like for it not to happen again."

"Then we'd better be quick about it."

31
DIVINE GIFTS
(Two days ago)

There was nothing but bright, molten red all around Sigurd. The ash suffocated him and the heat waves flowing from the volcano were sweltering. As he plummeted closer to the inferno, he felt a singeing burn on the skin around his left eye, more than anywhere else on his body. The pain made him want to scream, but he could only gasp for air as adrenaline flooded through him.

Blackened rock manifested out of the magma below, and a fiery hand rose to meet him. The hand caught him in midair, and he landed hard. The awakening creature was so large that Sigurd was but a schlept in its charred palm. He instantly lost his orientation. Massive black fingers, with lava glowing through the cracks in the stone, closed around him, cutting off any light.

It was too hot inside the clenched hand. Sigurd couldn't breathe. Whatever air he managed to take in made his lungs sting. *What good is it to be spared the death of the hot pit, only to be roasted to death within the Golem of Fire's infernal grip?* Sigurd had never been more terrified than he was at that moment, but he had to trust Verishten to keep him safe.

Ignoring the searing pain of his entire body, he lay back against the burning rock of the Alpha's palm and closed his eyes. Doing so hurt the scorched skin around his left eye, but he would have to ignore it for the time being.

After a few painful breaths, the giant hand disappeared from beneath him. When he opened his eyes, it was all blue sky above. The heat no longer bothered him. In fact, it cradled him. A hot, limitless strength coursed through his core, as though the lava had entered his veins.

With a powerful heave and a giant leap, Sigurd flew out of the volcano. The ash clouds parted before him, presenting all of Deschner Mountain Range to the west and Untevar Mountain Range to the east, dressed in a crimson magnificence. These mountains belonged to *him*. They were *his* home, and he now knew he would do anything to protect them.

When Sigurd tried moving his arms and legs he found that he could not. He didn't feel like himself. He was something else entirely. He then realized he was no longer in his body, no longer looking through his own eyes. He now saw Ingleheim through the solitary red eye of the Golem of Fire.

This was what the legends spoke of. It was the ancient Golem Mage power that was awarded to the hero Siegfried and the other five Steinkamp Warriors' sons. Power, not through domination but through the intermingling of spirits, and it now belonged to him. The spirit of man and golem joined as one, and Sigurd never wanted to be severed from it.

The Alpha put Sigurd's body onto one of its enormous scorched shoulders, far enough from the lava continuously leaking through every crack of its blackened form. Sigurd felt the sizzling rock through his gloves. The sensation brought his consciousness back into his own body, making him small again. Much of his uniform was burnt through, but the inner layer remained, along with his vest which was a little melted and charred, but still useable.

Breathing hard, Sigurd flickered back and forth between his perspective and that of the Alpha. "Mighty Verishten, this power—I can't control it," he rasped. All the pain and fear returned in a thunderous wave.

The Golem of Fire's booming voice radiated through Sigurd's being. *"Such power is not for you to control!"*

Immediately, he realized the foolishness of his words. It was the need to control it that led mankind to break the covenant in the first place. It was not about control. It was about letting go. He breathed deeply and closed his eyes, letting himself fall back into the Golem of Fire, but when he opened them, he was somewhere else altogether. Sigurd looked through new eyes—not the Golem of Fire's, nor his own.

The sun shone bright, unhindered by dark clouds of ash. There was a glistening body of water before him, lit with every imaginable hue of blue, green, and orange. Lines of giant crystal golems stood in wait for their

Alpha to awaken—Sigurd was among them. He was at the Crystal Lake of Rainmier.

Numerous geysers erupted violently under the great lake as the water bubbled and boiled. A deep rumbling came from beneath the gargantuan crystal geyser at the lake's center. An explosion of blistering steam burst into the sky, causing gallons of water to rain down onto the lakes below. The glistening geyser cracked apart, crystal shattering and flying through the air. A graceful and iridescent titan emerged from the wreckage, long limbs unfurling before taking its first steps in over two millennia. Waves of hot water crashed onto the rust-colored shore as the Alpha of Crystal Golems stepped out of the lake.

Yellow light emanating from the eye at the Alpha's midsection bathed Sigurd and all the surrounding golems in its bright, warm glow. Its crystal refracted the sun's rays into every color of the spectrum.

Katja should be here to witness this, Sigurd thought, realizing how unfair it was that she could not experience the beauty of this moment with him when she was the reason he was there at all. *Will I ever see her again?* he wondered, his heart heavy.

"Who awakens Verishten's Warning?" the Golem of Light asked. Its voice sounded pure and melodious.

At that moment, Sigurd found himself hundreds of feet above the lines of crystal golems. He was within the Alpha, and he could respond to it.

"Golem of Light, the people of Luidfort need your help," he said.

"They are for Verishten's Wrath to salvage," sang the Alpha.

"There must be something you can do for them."

Beyond his control, his mind pushed out of the Golem of Light. He found himself in the middle of a burgeoning storm, high above Verishten's Wrath and looking down upon its shuddering peak. He could feel the torrential power of the Golem of Storms awakening.

Sigurd looked through the eye of a winged golem in flight. Numerous other winged golems glided around with him. Focusing on one, Sigurd let himself go, his mind falling into it so easily that he felt compelled to do it again. Up in the crackling storm clouds, he cycled his consciousness in and out of various golems. Soon enough, he discovered he could subtly influence them all by sharing his thoughts with them just as he did with the Alphas.

The golems didn't respond to Sigurd through language like the Alphas did, but they spoke to him through emotion. he felt tethered to them like they were extensions of his being. They flew through the swirling storm clouds to save the people of Luidfort, not because Sigurd commanded them—he didn't have to. He nudged them into action through his heart. They understood his yearning for Luidfort's salvation and were impassioned to comply.

Once the Town of Luidfort came into view below, Sigurd suddenly felt the desperation of the populace trapped in its valleys. He could hear their screams, taste their suffering. All the pain and anguish of the people was so poignant it was as if he were experiencing it all first hand. Through the golems, Sigurd felt the fear of so many. *Golems have always had a spiritual connection with humans,* he realized. *It was humans that had lost the connection with them!*

He became weak and an overwhelming urge to weep came over him. *It's too much. I shouldn't have this kind of power. I am not the man for this. . . .*

He fell violently back into his own body, still standing on the Golem of Fire's shoulder at the volcano. Collapsing to his knees, he gritted his teeth, trying desperately not to fall apart.

"Now do you see? Now do you know why the golems have kept your kind away for so long? Humans are weak and deceitful. They squander the divine gifts given to them and take for themselves those that were not given!" the Golem of Fire boomed.

Tears streamed down Sigurd's ash-stained face, falling as black drops from his eyes. "I never knew . . ." he rasped. "What have we done?"

The Golem Mages in the Age of Man had so much more than the legends led anyone to believe. Verishten gave them the power of connection, not only with golems but with each other—to all humanity. Sigurd had that power now, and he could see why the Mages before him had severed the connection, opting instead for simple domination and control. How could the Kings of old have ever enacted war on each other if they were able to feel the fear and anguish of their foes? It was no wonder Verishten was angered by mankind. They forced golems into submission for their own selfish purposes rather than use their power to advance them both. They were not strong enough. How could Sigurd expect to be?

"Do not make us regret giving you this last chance for redemption. Give up now and an Age of Golems will return! Never again will man set foot in the Mountain Ranges of Ingleheim!"

"Man is . . . man is weak," Sigurd sputtered.

"And they will perish because of it!"

Another Age of Golems was Katja's worst nightmare, and although he didn't realize it until that moment, it was Sigurd's as well.

"No." With great effort, he rose to his feet. "I won't let that happen."

He wiped his ever-sweating brow and looked out over the Deschner Mountain Range below, beautiful even covered in ash. *This is where I came from. This is why I was saved.*

Once Sigurd accepted his newfound ability and all the costs associated with it, he found it easier to cycle his consciousness through the golems all over Ingleheim. At first, he could only see through the eyes of giant golems or the Alphas. Unlike the Alphas, giant golems were receptive to Sigurd's influences. They felt more like a part of him.

Sigurd spent a day or two at the volcano practicing cycling his mind throughout the lava golems around him. He learned he could feel even the smallest of them in his vicinity and influence them without needing to enter them. With the smaller golems, he felt how easy it would be to bend their will completely to his own, how open and vulnerable their spirits were to the mind of a Golem Mage like him.

In addition to learning how to use his new power, his mind pulled back and forth between the remaining awakening Alphas. The Golem of Ice in the Glacier Peaks, known as Verishten's Wisdom, and the Golem of Stone from the Crags, known as Verishten's Grace. Both rallied to assist him in saving Ingle lives.

When Sigurd let his consciousness fall into the Golem of Light, he found the Alpha seated in the main square in the City of Deschner before the great Cathedral of Verishten. The city was quiet. Not a single person could be seen or heard. They all huddled in their homes with the curtains drawn to keep out the Alpha's blinding light. Sigurd felt no souls outside the city gates either.

"What happened to the siege?" Sigurd asked.

"The rebellion has moved on. They make way toward Breisenburg Mountain Range," said the Golem of Light in its melodious voice.

"They are heading for the Fortress of Mortlach! We need to stop them." Sigurd would have felt his heart jump into his throat if he were anywhere near it. The last thing he wanted to do was bring the rebellion to Katja.

"The City of Deschner has been spared. Let those that march toward further destruction face Verishten's Judgment."

"We can't let that happen. None are worthy. They will all die!" Sigurd protested.

"Fear not," the Alpha responded. *"Verishten's Judgment may also be Verishten's Mercy."*

"I know what mercy can mean," Sigurd said with bitterness, "especially to an Alpha keen on ending any, and all, human life that crosses before its eye."

Not receiving a reply, Sigurd fell back into his body upon the shoulder of the Golem of Fire. Every lava golem not currently under the Führer's control amassed around their Alpha as if waiting for an order two thousand years overdue.

"Golem of Fire," said Sigurd. "We must go to the Fortress of—"

"We know why you wish to go there, but there is no need. The human rebellion will end at the resting place of Verishten's Judgment."

"I made you a promise to uphold the covenant, but you made a promise as well—to offer mankind a second chance, to help me save them, even if it is to save them from themselves. There are good people at that fortress."

Sigurd couldn't help but cycle in and out of the hundreds of lava golems surrounding them. Every single one was ready and willing to follow him and the Golem of Fire to the fortress. Golems and humans were still connected, and Verishten had agreed to allow that connection to continue.

"Very well, we will march," the Alpha agreed. *"But know that there are some who must face judgment and you shall not stand it its way."*

"What of mercy?"

"We will leave that up to you, Siegfried."

32

THE PLEDGE

As the Golem of Fire and its golem army made for the Breisenburg Mountain Range, Sigurd sweated profusely, even after having left the volcano. He'd never felt so anxious in his life. The rebellion had more than a day's head start. It was possible he would come upon the Fortress of Mortlach already decimated.

More than anything, he feared for Katja's safety. *I have to trust her to take care of herself.* He felt the Golem of Storms and its army of winged golems arriving at the fortress. *Keep her safe,* he urged them, *keep them all safe.*

He and the Golem of Fire eventually reached the fortress. A horde of rebel soldiers faced off against the legions of war golems. The Führer had a hold over them still, and Sigurd would not be able to influence them to his side.

He realized that to keep Heinrich from potentially taking control of his own army, Sigurd would have to dominate some of them temporarily, just like he had with the lava golem in the caverns below the fortress to keep Frau Brunhilde from taking it over. Sigurd cycled his consciousness through a dozen of the golems below him. *Carefully make your way through the rebel armies and take down those iron titans,* he commanded, bending their will with hardly any resistance.

Dominating every golem left in his sight, severed Sigurd's connection to them. This was one of those few moments when the domination of golems was necessary, and Verishten trusted him never to abuse that power.

The Golem of Fire made its approach toward the fortress after the first wave of lava golems cleared a path through the chaos. The rebels and Regime soldiers were so stunned by the arrival of the Alpha that many of them fled, but many more stayed to fight, praising the mighty Verishten for coming to their aid.

The eighty-foot Golem of Fire stepped over the war golems to reach the outer wall of the fortress. Laying its hands upon it, the Alpha sent its molten energy through the stone, melting it in mere moments. Sigurd and the Alpha walked into the outer ward of the fortress to meet the next line of Regime soldiers and war golems. The lava golems made entry afterward and went to task taking down the war golems as commanded.

The winged golems flew around the fortress, giving Sigurd the opportunity to jump into them and get a better picture of what was going on behind the walls of the inner ward. The Golem of Death had caused significant damage to the bailey, Katja and Jenn were alive and making their way toward the Keep, and Rudiger was on the western battlement, aiming a crossbow at them from afar.

"You're mine, Rudiger," Sigurd whispered to himself. He closed his eyes and fell into the winged golem nearest Rudiger to intercept his shot. The bolt ricocheted off the golem's granite body as it flew toward him.

"Shit!" he growled, and the golem took him by the waist with its giant stone hand.

Sigurd directed it to the southwest tower, under construction, where he intended to face Rudiger himself. The golem crashed through the scaffolding of the tower's second floor, still missing its entire south wall. There, it would stand guard over Rudiger until Sigurd and the Alpha could arrive.

Unfortunately, Rudiger's crossbow-toting arm was free, and he shot a bolt through the golem's eye, jarringly disconnecting Sigurd from it.

"Damn you!" he grunted once he was back in his body. In desperation, he closed his eyes in search for another winged golem nearby and summoned a smaller one coming in from the east. Opening his eyes, he jumped down from the Alpha's shoulder and landed cleanly on the golem's back as it flew by. He mentally guided the gliding creature over the inner wall and into the tower's exposed second floor. Sigurd stepped off the golem's back just as Rudiger found his bearings.

"You!" Rudiger gaped in shock. "How are you still alive?"

"I told you Verishten would choke on me."

Rudiger pointed to Sigurd's left eye. "Did he cough up that mark on your face as well? Your sister had the Eye in your family. You aren't supposed to have it!"

Sigurd touched the burn encircling his left eye, still sensitive to the touch. *So that's what happened*, he thought. "Verishten gave me the mark I bear. Who gave you yours?" He pointed out the scratches running down Rudiger's left cheek.

"Courtesy of your Golem Expert. I never imagined the daughter of the Führer to be so . . . plucky." Rudiger grinned. "It's a shame I have to kill her before I wed her."

Thoughts of Rudiger's hands on Katja in either capacity made Sigurd's fists clench so hard they cramped. "Your only shame was not killing me in that farmhouse a week ago," he said with a low and controlled voice.

"A week ago? I should have killed you twenty years ago," Rudiger spat. "That is a mistake I will not repeat today."

Rapid footsteps scuffled up the stairs from the floor below. Several Steinkamp soldiers appeared, each one swiftly and silently fanning out across the room. Rudiger gave Sigurd a smug grin and made a quick exit up the stairs to the floor above while even more Steinkamp flooded in. Sigurd cursed Rudiger's cowardice before he sprang into action alongside his winged companion.

The golem spread out its thin granite wings and whirled around the room, taking down two Steinkamp with each one. Sigurd extended his blade and entered the fray. All of his opponents were prepared to block any and all attacks from him, and he was further disadvantaged with his head and face unprotected. However, the golem fighting alongside him more than made up for that.

Sigurd found he could experience the battle partially through the golem's perspective and used his ability to tap into his opponents' emotions and intentions. He caught them off-guard and accessed the vulnerable areas in their armor. Arms were lost, tendons severed, and jaws stabbed clean through. Sigurd acquired a second sword from a fallen comrade and dispatched those remaining twice as fast.

He stood amongst his departed foes to catch his breath for a few seconds. *That's a lot of dead Steinkamp*, he thought. His victory was short-lived when he heard several more coming up the stairs. *Oh, come on!*

Sigurd sighed. "I can't deal with this right now. Hold them back for me?" he asked his golem. He raced up the stairs just in time to see a flash of Rudiger's feet dashing up to the fourth floor and beyond. "Where are you going?" Sigurd muttered.

He heard the droves of Steinkamp combating the golem downstairs.

Just let them pass and fly out of the tower to catch me when I come out above, Sigurd mentally suggested to the golem.

He took out his blast gel dispenser and sprayed a generous amount of gel along the floor starting near the top of the stairs and working his way backward. When he finished, he bolted for the opening in the tower wall and turned around to face the Steinkamp pouring into the room. Their crossbow bolts and splitting blades were aimed and ready to release, but Sigurd didn't give them a chance. He clenched his gloved fist just as he made his backward leap out of the tower. The gel detonated and the resulting explosion blew away the soldiers on the third floor while crushing those on the second floor with debris.

He only fell a foot or two before his winged companion came up underneath him, and he landed on its back. "Nice job," he said, patting the golem on the back as he laughed out loud with relief that he came away from that many Steinkamp unscathed.

The golem carried him up the rest of the cylindrical tower to find Rudiger having just reached the top. Sigurd slid off its back and landed on the top of the tower. Rudiger stepped onto the bastion and grabbed hold of a flag pole. Fastened to the pole, extended a rope and banner that connected the southwest tower and the central dome of the Keep. Sigurd guessed he intended to use it to get to the Keep without being noticed.

"I found you to be a lot of things, Rudiger, but a coward wasn't one of them," he commented.

Rudiger froze then stepped down from the bastion. Turning to face Sigurd, he said, "I won't hurt your beloved Katja if that's what you want, but the people demand the head of their Führer. If I am to lead this nation, I must be the one to give that to them."

"I can't let that happen."

"I mean to kill the monster that set all this death and destruction in motion," Rudiger exclaimed. "And you, of all men, want to save his life? It was his order that led to your family's death, don't you realize that?"

"Heinrich will face Verishten's justice, but you will not be the one to execute it." Sigurd shook his head slowly.

"I will return honor to the Steinkamp. I will bring Ingleheim into a glorious new age, one where all the wretched elements are purified. Only the Steinkamp can usher in such an age." Rudiger's eyes were wide and crazed.

Sigurd saw the desperation dripping off him like the rainwater running down his face. "That is not what a Steinkamp is," he said plainly.

"*You* dare speak to *me* of what a Steinkamp is?" Rudiger spat. "I stripped you of your uniform. I cut off your brand. You are a Steinkamp no more!"

"No, but I will be the first."

The two men circled ten paces from each other on the top of the tower.

"Have you forgotten?" bellowed Rudiger. "I gave you a chance to stand beside me, to put the malice of our pasts behind us, and yet you spit in my face and shit on the pledge!"

"You're right," Sigurd admitted. "I never lived by the pledge. I was too fixated on vengeance, something that has no place in the Steinkamp mantra."

"To fight means to kill, to kill is mercy," Rudiger recited.

"Today," Sigurd declared. "I will retake the pledge and let you be the first man to experience *my* mercy."

Sigurd extended his dual blades while Rudiger unsheathed a two-handed longsword.

The new Golem Mage and the new Steinkamp Kapitän clashed swords in tandem with the thunder and lightning. Sigurd knew not to underestimate Rudiger's skill and superb strength in battle, but he felt a radical calm—a newfound perception that was not solely his own. He utilized his winged golem circling the tower to get glimpses of the fight from different angles, and more importantly to tap into Rudiger's emotions. Underneath his feelings of superiority and all his pent-up rage, Sigurd felt his violent intentions at every moment. He felt Rudiger's aim to cut off his head, giving Sigurd the opportunity to duck at just the right time. He gained insight into Rudiger's plan to sweep his longsword across his midsection, and he parried back.

Comforted that his focus was sound, Sigurd began reciting, "I hereby pledge to uphold the Steinkamp mantra at all times." He ducked a couple of Rudiger's strikes.

"Fight me, dammit!" Rudiger growled with frustration, and Sigurd responded in kind with a series of frenzied dual blade strikes.

"I pledge to never waver and never retreat. To defend the defenseless—"

Sigurd knocked the sword out of Rudiger's hand, but the kapitän rolled away from Sigurd's follow up strikes.

"—And punish the wicked."

He made a jumping slice with both swords. Rudiger did not back away in time. The first blade slashed the belted coat open, and the second found skin beneath his shirt. With a loud grunt, Rudiger faltered, putting his hand to his sternum.

"To never cause undue suffering to my enemies."

"You should see me ended, then, lest you break the pledge right out of the gate," Rudiger rasped.

But I no longer consider you my enemy, Sigurd thought. Rudiger was the real Steinkamp traitor and always had been. Only the God of the Ingles, in the form of the Golem of Fire, advancing toward the tower where the two men fought, could keep his soul.

"And to leave no trace of myself behind—" Sigurd continued. Just after those words left his mouth, Rudiger kicked his legs out from under him.

"You have no right to say those words!" Rudiger kicked Sigurd before he could regain footing, stomped on his left arm, and separated him from one of his blades. He then took Sigurd around the back of the neck, wrenched his last blade out of his hands, and shoved him head first into some empty storage barrels filled with rainwater.

The barrels capsized, pouring their contents over Sigurd. Water and ash flowed into his eyes, disorienting him for a moment, but he didn't stop reciting. "From the darkness, I am born—"

He didn't see Rudiger's next kick coming. A bracing blow to the chest knocked him hard into the bastion.

"Shut your mouth!" Rudiger snarled, taking Sigurd by the buckle on his right shoulder and punching him repeatedly in the face.

Each bracing strike helped solidify Sigurd's resolve. He caught both of Rudiger's fists in hand and pushed back on him, bracing himself against the bastion with the heel of his boot. He then slowly rose to a proper footing.

"In the shadows, I fight!" Sigurd overcame his opponent's strength enough to force his arms outward, allowing him to step into his space. "In the name of justice, I kill!" He finished with a well-placed headbutt, sending Rudiger to the ground. He shook off the reverberating pain in his skull and kicked Rudiger in the sternum. "And in obscurity, I die."

"Though I am not faceless." Sigurd picked Rudiger up and returned his repeated punches before sending him to the ground. "Or nameless! I will devote my life, my blood, and my spirit—"

Rudiger sprang back to his feet and came at Sigurd with a flurry of punches, each one sloppier than the next. Sigurd dodged and blocked them all.

"—To Ingleheim and its people!"

Rudiger's metal-plated leg came hurtling for Sigurd's side, but knowing what to expect, Sigurd caught his ankle.

"As one heart—"With a burst of speed, he whipped out his skewer knife while simultaneously ducking below Rudiger's extended leg.

"One mind—" He sliced underneath Rudiger's thigh, successfully severing his tendons just above the knee.

Rudiger cried out in pain, falling onto his hands and knees, and cursing into the thunderous sky. Sigurd drove his boot down hard upon his leg, rendering it all the more useless. "And one force!"

The Golem of Fire now stood right next to the damaged tower, the top of which only came to its shoulder. The Alpha placed a fiery hand upon the south bastion, causing the stone to bubble and liquefy. The tower wept lava from its walls, the top floors dripped down into those below. It began to slant as blistering molten rock spread slowly across the rooftop.

Sigurd summoned his winged golem again as Rudiger molded his earth bindings to the stone to keep from sliding into the advancing lava.

"I suppose you think you're the hero. Siegfried Reborn,"Rudiger panted. "You may be worthy in the eyes of Verishten, but what about the eyes of the people? Do you think they will follow yet another Golem Mage?"

Being a Golem Mage didn't automatically mean Sigurd was a leader, but the more he let Rudiger's words sink in, the more he realized that Ingleheim was going to desperately need one very soon. Could he be that for them? Would he be any better than Heinrich or Bachman or all of the warmongering kings who had come before? All Sigurd knew was that he was the only man alive with the ability to know exactly what the people yearned for, but giving that to them would be an entirely different matter. Deciding not to dwell on the notion, he let himself slide forward down the slanting rooftop.

Rudiger cried out shrilly, "Wait! No!"

Sigurd completed his pledge with a roar. "I am Steinkamp!"

He kicked Rudiger in the chest and sent him reeling backward. Rudiger rolled helplessly toward the inferno. He clambered to stop his descent, clutching onto red-hot rock. He screamed as his gloves sizzled away, along with his boots and coat until his entire body lit ablaze. Grabbing hold of the earth bindings left molded to the roof, Sigurd stopped himself from sliding off along with him. The tilt of the tower allowed him to watch the

Steinkamp Kapitän's entire fiery descent into the lava pits bubbling at the base.

As soon as the winged golem flew in sight, Sigurd pushed off the nearly vertical rooftop and into the scorching air. The golem caught him upon its back and carried him away from the sinking tower.

33

SAVE THE BOY

Kanzler Wolfram had taken a sizable force to meet with the rebel soldiers advancing from the north. At an outpost a few miles from the fortress, he sat at an old wooden desk waiting to hear the latest report from his scout.

"Did Herr Bachman receive my message to have words with him?" he asked Lanzel, sitting across from him.

"Yes, he and a modest contingent are making way to the location you have indicated, Herr Kanzler," Lanzel replied with a curt bow.

"And what of his other contingents? Why have we not run into any of them yet?"

One of Wolfram's personal guards entered the room with the tea he had requested, served in a tin cup and poured from a kettle of the same material.

"I've spotted a few. They are spread out, taking various backroads, and some have gone off-road completely. They have been able to get around all our offensives. If we come up behind them now, we risk getting trapped between them and any additional contingents still heading south."

"We don't need to go after them," Wolfram said, blowing on his steaming tea and taking a sip. "Our Führer has every war golem surrounding that fortress by now. They will not get far. Tea?"

Wolfram offered Lanzel a second cup, which he graciously accepted. Motioning for the guard to pour Lanzel his tea, he continued, "Any sign of Kapitän Rudiger?" He drank more to aid in swallowing the anxious lump in his throat.

Rudiger was supposed to retrieve Bachman and bring him to Wolfram alive. Not trusting the man for a second, he had sent Lanzel and some other scouts further north. Lanzel had just returned, but there was still no word from his new Steinkamp Kapitän. *What if that arrogant prick is plotting something with the Kaiser instead? He could be the reason Bachman agreed to negotiate, but then why not send message informing me of that? Instead, I get confirmation from a scout!*

"Still nothing," Lanzel replied, taking a sip from his cup. "But the rebel armies farther north have been reporting some . . . strange things."

Wolfram felt a chill despite the hot beverage. "What kind of strange things?"

"Stories similar to the mysterious light in the City of Deschner," Lanzel said in a low voice. "The rebel armies from Kensloche have been caught in severe rockslides. They report that two cliffs have collided with one another. It was as if the cliffs were moving of their own volition, they say."

"Well, that's fortunate for us." Wolfram loosened a bit.

"Stranger still, reports of sudden ice storms in northern Deschner have completely frozen out the rebel reserves stationed in the villages there. All that are left to fight in the rebellion are Bachman's men from Untevar, and the one Nordenhein contingent that left before the storm hit."

Wolfram drank back the rest of his tea and set down the cup with a grin. "Well, Lanzel, my boy, it appears the tables are swiftly turning against the Remnants now, doesn't it?"

"Maybe." Lanzel gulped, placing his cup on the desk without finishing. "Although, I wouldn't celebrate yet. Rumor has it these fortunate occurrences were caused by Alpha Golems."

"Or maybe Verishten is truly on the side of the Regime." Wolfram rose from his chair, still chilled to the bone. *If all the Alphas are awakening, how long will it be before the Golem of Death does the same? And can Kriemhilde and her team really control it?* he wondered. Perhaps she wasn't bluffing after all.

Wolfram forced that particular worry from his mind for now. He had to take care of Bachman first. "Come, Herr Lanzel, let us go and set up the meeting point."

A few hours later, Wolfram waited alone in a tent a mile from the outpost with his men outside. As a sign of good faith, both Wolfram and Bachman agreed to leave their men a few yards away with orders not to enter while the two kanzlers conversed.

Rain pelted hard onto the tent's roof as a low rumble of thunder boomed from the south. The storm of the century was brewing, making Wolfram even more eager to get this meeting over with and return with Bachman in custody.

After a while, Bachman trundled into the tent. "Wolfram, you tricky bastard, it's been a whore's age since I've seen you last."

"Welcome, Herr Kanzler." Wolfram approached to shake Bachman's hand.

"I must say," the bear of a man continued, "the kanzlership lifestyle is already agreeing with you."

"As is the warlord lifestyle for you, Herr Bachman," he replied with a cordial nod.

"I know what you must be thinking." Bachman planted his large frame down on one of the chairs. "Why do I risk showing myself to you?"

"Don't tell me you have another hostage."

"No, no. I come here to offer you terms instead."

"Of your surrender?"

"May Verishten singe the hairs from my balls if I were to ever surrender," Bachman guffawed. Wolfram winced. *Such things can be made reality,* he thought as the so-called Kaiser continued. "If Heinrich graciously steps down and declares me his successor, I will agree to banish him and his family as opposed to executing them. If she is willing, I may be moved to allow Fraulein Kriemhilde to remain in Ingleheim as my wife. If Heinrich does not agree to these terms, then I will have all of their heads by the end of tonight."

"You'd be wiser to surrender. Your Kensloche armies are impossibly delayed, your reserves are frozen out, and the City of Deschner is kept from you by a mysterious light. Rebel casualties have grown so large that you are now desperate. Therefore, you come to me to offer these terms in hopes of intimidating the Mighty Führer to give up his seat when there is no danger in you ever taking it by force in the first place."

Bachman smirked, scratching at his graying ginger beard. "I've always admired your talent for reading people. That's why I agreed to see you rather than any other one of Heinrich's representatives. I happen to know that you, like me, are an opportunist and of great intelligence. You can see that even without this rebellion, Heinrich's rule is coming to a rapid close.

When he dies, and the golems no longer obey, who would you rather have lead this nation? His sorceress whore? One of Volker's whelps? They will never hold that seat, and your position in the Regime will never be secure. Help me become Ingleheim's Kaiser and I will not only ensure you maintain rule of Breisenburg and all its military might, but guarantee your progeny will inherit it for generations thereafter."

Wolfram crossed his leg over the other and smiled. "Your offer, although generous, is no different than what my Führer has already given me. Whether I hold the title of Viceroy or Kanzler, the power afforded to me is the same. My daughter gains a beneficial marriage to Volker's eldest son. That alone will grant me and my family favor in the Regime long after Herrscher Heinrich's demise. You have no heirs, Bachman, no one fit to see her taken care of in this new Age of Kings you speak of."

"I have no *legitimate* sons, this is true, but I have many young men loyal to me, one in particular that would suit your daughter's needs quite nicely. My General Rudiger, has been promised Untevar Range as well as control of the Steinkamp force."

Wolfram wanted to laugh out loud at Bachman's offer. *It would appear that Rudiger was not so quick to betray his Kaiser as ordered,* he thought. Clearing his throat, he said, "General Rudiger, you say? I must meet him at once. Did you happen to bring him with you?"

"I'm afraid my general is indisposed at the moment," Bachman said. "However, I can arrange a meeting between the two of you shortly."

"Tell me of his accomplishments."

Bachman rose to his feet with a groan and said, "Well, he planned the taking of the Fortress of Mortlach a few weeks ago, in which he was successful. I then charged him with tracking down Fraulein Kriemhilde after her escape, but you beat him to that. I haven't seen him since, but I have received messages from Kensloche periodically. He has successfully fueled the uprising there like he did in Nordenhein. He is leading the Kensloche rebel armies toward Deschner as we speak. He even managed to enlist some Cragsmen to our cause. I fear he has been held up by the rockslides, but sooner or later they will break through."

Wolfram studied Bachman's expressions as he talked and there was no indication that he was hiding anything else about Rudiger. Everything Bachman said tied into Rudiger's whereabouts up until Sigurd's and Kriemhilde's capture where he joined Wolfram at the fortress. *What is Rudiger planning? He hasn't reconnected with Bachman in the first place. He probably never left the fortress and instead waited for me to set out after him. I must return to the fortress now!*

"Thank you for coming, Herr Bachman," said Wolfram as he rose to lead the rotund man to the tent's exit. "I will give your offer heavy consideration."

"When can I expect an answer?"

"When I've had a chance to size up your general."

Once Bachman was out of sight, Wolfram gathered his personal guard made up of his most trusted infantrymen and a few Steinkamp. They mounted their steeds and set off into the heavy rainfall.

They arrived at the fortress' north walls in a couple of hours only to find it in a state of disorder. Wolfram couldn't believe his eyes. Golems were out of control, fighting one another as well as men on the ground. War golems were stuck in the mud or cut down by lava golems. Winged golems crashed into each other in the air. Man-sized golems of all types ran about, blocking attacks aimed at one group of soldiers against another.

Wolfram feared that he was too late. Herrscher Heinrich had to be dead for all the golems under his command to have fallen into chaos. The only man who would dare kill him was Rudiger.

Fortunately for Wolfram, his personal contingent would be sufficient for fighting his way back inside the fortress walls. The Steinkamp kept close to him as they rode through the swarms of rebel soldiers and around the combating giant golems. They used their crossbows to take out any rebel that dared come near the kanzler and his men.

"I am going to place some blast gel ahead," one of the comrades said as he rode off into the fray. A few moments later, a series of explosions blew a path through the rebel fighters and a couple of man-sized golems. Wolfram and the rest of his men steered their horses through the smoke and wreckage toward the north gates.

Once he gained entry through the gates, Wolfram was met with a sight that made the blood freeze in his veins. Darkness enveloped the grounds in the wake of a giant flying creature weaving in and out of the thundering storm clouds. To the west, an enormous golem glowing molten red melted the southwest tower with its giant hands.

This can't be happening—this place is mine! Wolfram's breath grew short as his head began to spin. He thought about turning back, but where would he go? Everything he worked for was here. This was his mountain range! This was his castle! All of it rightfully earned!

With his eyes to the Keep, he pressed onward. If Heinrich were still alive, he'd be in there; if he were dead, Rudiger would be there in his place. One way or another, Wolfram was not going to give up everything he had worked so hard for over the last twenty years.

Katja and Jenn went to look for the Führer in the war room. His personal guard was there, but Heinrich was not.

"Where is my father?" Katja asked the guards as she burst through the doors.

The two guards stepped out to block them. "You can't go any further, fraulein."

"There is no time. Let us through or everyone in this fortress is going to die."

The guard stood firm. "The Führer will not be disturbed. The fortress is under attack. I advise you to return to your tower and—"

"I can see that the fortress is under attack. What is worse is that the Golem of Death is awake, and I don't think it's interested in choosing sides. Now let us through!" Katja demanded.

One of the guards nodded toward Jenn. "Who is this? She looks like a Remnant."

"She's your Führer's last hope!" Katja said firmly.

The guards exchanged glances as she stood there in a cold sweat. To her relief, they stepped aside. One of the men led them to a small meeting chamber down a set of stairs just off the war room.

"Your father is unwell. A short time ago he collapsed and has been in an incoherent state ever since." He opened the door.

There, on a cot, lay the once mighty Führer, his cheeks pale and sunken and his hair even whiter than when Katja had seen him a few days before. A nurse tended to Heinrich, who periodically twitched and muttered nonsensical phrases. A few words stuck out, such as Ilsa's name, then Brunhilde's, and strangely, the words '*save the boy.*'" There was almost nothing left of Heinrich's mind, and it broke Katja's heart to see the damaged state Brunhilde left had him in.

"Father." She knelt at his bed and nudged him. "It's me, Kriemhilde. Please wake up."

Heinrich's eyes fluttered open in response to his daughter's voice, but he was far from lucid. He touched Katja's arm lightly and looked in her general direction. "S-save . . . the boy."

"What does that mean?" Tears rose to the surface. She looked to Jenn standing unobtrusively on the other side of the room. "Is there anything you can do?"

"Maybe," Jenn said hesitantly, "though I am not as experienced in spirit magic as the one who did this to him."

"She's dead now," Katja said. "You are all we have."

Jenn looked around uncomfortably at the Regime offiziers in the room. Katja could only imagine how difficult it was for her, considering her previous loyalties, but there were far more important matters at hand than Remnant or Regime ambitions. The nurse stepped aside and allowed Jenn to take a seat at Heinrich's bedside.

"Well . . . given his condition, his mind is vulnerable enough so I should be able to slip right in without any priming." Jenn closed her eyes, and the room fell silent. After a few moments, she took Katja's hand and said, "I'm in. I'm going to pull your spirit in with me, if that's okay."

Katja's breath caught in her throat. The thought of having her spirit pulled back into a Spirit Mage's world terrified her. "What for?"

"I might be able to transfer you into his mind with me. It will be easier if it is someone familiar to him that makes contact. Otherwise I will have to spend countless hours scouring his innermost thoughts for images of you to project onto myself."

Taking a deep breath, Katja nodded. "Okay, I'm ready."

She closed her eyes and waited for several minutes before she dared to open them again. Katja gasped. She was alone in a darkened corridor, similar to the castle halls of the Deschner estate. The old artwork of Frau Blomgren hung crooked, most pieces covered in thin, tattered sheets. Layers of dust blanketed the tables and chairs, looking as if no one had touched them for years. There were four identical hallways in each direction, all of them too dark to see to the end.

"Jenn?" Katja called. There was no answer, just the echoing of her own voice.

She ventured down the hallway in front of her and reached another corridor identical to the one she just left. Next, she went right and found a dust-filled study. Going through the door at the end of the room brought her back to the corridor where she'd started. When she turned to go back, the door was gone.

Katja breathed hard as she briskly walked down more and more hallways. "Jenn!" she shouted, her voice cracking. "Father?"

Lost in the maze of her father's mind, the loneliness Katja knew all too well began to resurface. Her heart ached as a hopeless terror set in. The walls seemed to close in on her the farther she went, and the air grew so dusty she could choke on it.

"Father, please! Where are you?" Katja cried down the infinite hallways. "Is anybody in here?"

"Sorry, I lost sight of your spirit for a while there," Jenn said from behind her. "This is the first time I've taken another person into someone's mind. I wasn't even sure I could do it."

When Katja turned around, she was startled by an enormous rat-like creature in the corridor with her.

"Don't be scared, we Spirit Mages have different forms here," said the rat with Jenn's voice.

"Why do you choose the form of a rat?" Katja asked as they continued down another hallway.

"I didn't choose this form—it chose me. Growing up impoverished makes one very familiar with rats. I'd go to sleep every night listening to their squeaking and scuffling around in the dark. I guess they had a profound effect on my spirit."

"That explains why my stepmother used a wolf to tear into me when she was trying to—she wasn't using a wolf—she *was* the wolf."

"Yes, I've dreamed about the she-wolf before," Jenn revealed. "She had great power, but I never knew who she was in real life."

Katja stopped where the hallways intersected and threw her arms up. "Why isn't my father here?"

Rat Jenn sniffed the air and replied, "It is up to us to find him. You knew him best, where do you think he might be?"

Katja looked down each dark hallway that led to nowhere. "I don't know. He could be anywhere, or nowhere. I really . . . don't know him at all," she said with a defeated sigh.

"I do. Go left," a faint male whisper replied, and she shivered.

They looked around the corridor. A small black raven sat perched on a dusty torch sconce high on the wall. She didn't know where it came from, but she knew exactly who it was.

"We should go left," Katja said and headed down the left hallway.

The raven kept appearing everywhere they turned, whispering

directions to them as they ventured through the dark and dusty castle.

"What is that raven doing here? I think I've dreamed of him before too," Jenn said as she scuttled down the hall behind Katja.

"It's a long and horrible story. . . ."

Just then, Katja turned a corner and nearly tripped over a soft obstruction. It was a wolf carcass, its fur stained with dark red blood, its tongue hanging out of the side of its mouth. Much of its body was burnt and hairless. The wolf lay before a pair of doors. *It once stood guard here—Father.* Katja pushed the doors open and marched through them.

Beyond, was a large bedchamber, illuminated by the light of the double full moons shining dimly through an ash-filled night sky. Katja's father stood at the foot of the bed, staring at the woman lying on it. His jaw was clenched and eyes wet with tears that threatened to fall down his face.

Katja walked closer to the bed to get a better look at the woman. She was beautiful and in grave pain. Her long brown hair was plastered to her head with sweat, her face pale, her eyes shut tight as she writhed in blood-soaked sheets.

"Mother?" Katja croaked. Ilsa didn't respond.

"She can't hear you. She's just a rendering from your father's memory." Jenn scuttled up next to Katja.

Nurses and midwives materialized in the room. They swarmed Ilsa's bed, dabbed her forehead with a cool cloth, gave her liquids, and encouraged her to push. Katja couldn't bear to look upon her mother, a woman whom she never had a chance to meet, in so much agony and so near death.

Stepping away from the bed, Katja let the nurses close around her mother. She approached Heinrich at the foot of the bed. Placing a hand on his shoulder, she said, "Father. Don't stay here any longer. You can't save her."

"Save the boy," Heinrich murmured.

"Why do you keep saying that?"

"That's what I told her." Heinrich motioned to the midwife. "I stood here, knowing I was about to lose everything. And all I could think of was losing a possible heir. '*Save the boy*,' I said."

"But it was a girl that lived." Katja sniffed back tears. She felt an unyielding weight on her chest upon hearing her father confirm what she'd always feared was true.

"Kriemhilde, I . . ." Heinrich stammered. "What I wouldn't give to have you all with me, you, your mother . . . and Gunnar."

"I'm sorry, Father," was all Katja could think to say.

Heinrich turned to his daughter and held her by the arms before him. "Never be sorry, Kriemhilde. You are not at fault. It wasn't what would happen to me if my son died, but what would happen to you if you had lived that worried me. How was I going to protect a daughter, my only child, and a woman, absent the Eye, from the horrific ills of a brutal and selfish nation?"

"So you moved to change it," Katja said in a broken voice. *It was all for me.* . . . That realization made her want to break down into tears, but she still quivered in anger. If everything Heinrich did was to protect her, why did he leave her alone? Why didn't he protect her from the ills inside of his own house?

He turned back to his wife, crying out in agony. "Ilsa always knew what to do. She always had a plan. Once she was gone, I—I became afraid. Everything I'd done to unify Ingleheim before your birth created many enemies. Without me or a brother to protect you, I feared Ingleheim would not be kind to you."

Heinrich turned to Katja again, his eyes still red, his teeth clenched. "You see, the Earl of Deschner, the King of Untevar, they all had their greedy sights on my throne—your throne. They all had sons to bear the Eye into the next generation. My line was done, and they knew it. With me as the last Golem Mage, I thought I could create a safer Ingleheim for all of us."

"Was a safer Ingleheim worth tearing apart so many lives, the poverty, and fear, the freedoms lost?" Tears ran down Katja's cheeks. She wondered if her tears were figments inside her father's mind or her own.

"I didn't care, at least not enough. I am weak, Kriemhilde, and more than that I am ashamed because even after all the terrible things I've done to ensure your safety, I didn't protect you from the sorcerers that made it all possible. What I allowed them to do . . ." Heinrich broke eye contact, turning his gaze instead to the full moons outside the window. "I knew what was happening, but whenever I thought about it, the urge to stop it was always cast from my mind. I . . ." Heinrich took a ragged breath. ". . . I allowed it to continue, and for that, I am truly sorry."

"It wasn't your fault," Katja said, pulling him to face her. "They were controlling you with magic. Trust me, I know what it's like. There was nothing you could have done."

"You don't understand." Heinrich's voice was so faint, she barely recognized it. "I sought Melikheil out in the first place. I begged him to make me a Golem Mage whose power rivaled those from the first generation. He told me how he was going to do it, and I willingly gave myself over to him. I never let myself think that he could abuse the power he held over me. A part of me wanted to be absolved from everything I went on to do."

Nausea crept into Katja's gut. She was beyond sick, beyond angry, but her compassion for her father's suffering at the hands of those monsters, and his remorse upon realizing his mistakes, kept that anger at bay. She swallowed the lump in her throat. "Well, they're gone now. They can't control us anymore, but they left an awful mess, and you are the only one that can clean it up." She began pulling him toward the door.

"I can't." Heinrich pulled out of her grasp. "I deserve to be in here."

"Maybe you do. You failed me. You failed Ingleheim. But now you have the chance to make things right."

"Nothing I do will ever make things right."

"The Golem of Death is awake. If you stay here, you will die. Your people will die!"

"I'm sorry," Heinrich muttered faintly, shaking his head.

"I didn't come all this way to leave you in this room forever, watching your wife suffer until the Golem of Death puts you out of your misery," Katja said with vehemence, but her voice softened as she deflated. "Please, Father, your people need you—I need you."

Heinrich gave Katja a pained look, the rigid blaze of his eyes all but dead. "I've been trapped here for so long . . ."

"All you have to do is walk out that door." She pointed to the door behind her.

"No!" Heinrich recoiled and turned back to Ilsa, who now lay cold and still in her blood-soaked sheets. "She's out there. She won't let me leave. . . ."

Turning angrily to the raven perched upon her mother's bed post, Katja demanded, "You and Brunhilde did this to him. Now help me get him out of here!"

The raven stared blankly at her with its glossy, ebony eyes and squawked. *How much of Melikheil is really in that little bird?* She wondered.

Before she could turn to Jenn for help, the room shuddered and violently collapsed in on itself.

"Father!" Katja screamed while ducking to the ground. She was suddenly back in the tiny bedchamber where her father lay on the cot, half-conscious.

"What happened?" Katja asked with alarm.

One of the guards went to investigate the crash and returned supporting his bleeding partner. "It's the war room. The entire stained-glass dome has been shattered by an enormous flying . . . thing."

"It's the Golem of Storms." Jenn bit her lip.

The other guard, bleeding from a gash in his right arm, collapsed into a chair with a grunt. "We must get the Führer out of here."

"Not yet. We just have to get him to leave that room. We almost had him," said Jenn.

"What are you talking about?" the first guard asked while assisting the other.

"I've got a plan to get us out of here," said Katja. "Jenn, get back in there, do whatever you can to get him out of that room. I'll be right back."

Jenn called after her, but Katja didn't have time to explain fully. She emerged in a war room completely exposed to the elements just as the Golem of Storms disappeared into the black clouds. Shards of broken glass crunched beneath her shoes as she walked to the middle of the platform and peered out. From her periphery, she saw the southwest tower collapse, bringing her attention straight to the Golem of Fire. It was there where she saw him flying upon the back of a winged golem.

"Sigurd, Sigurd!" Katja hollered through the howling winds and clapping thunder, waving her arms above her head.

It seemed impossible, but Sigurd turned toward her in only a moment. Crouching upon the shoulders of his flying golem, he glided toward the Keep. To see his face, even from far away, made her heart thud furiously in her chest, and she smiled despite the horror around them. *He can get the winged golems to fly everyone to safety,* she thought with relief.

Sigurd was only a few feet away from the Keep when his own relieved expression transformed into one of utter panic. From behind came the crunch of glass, then a man's arm grabbed her and put a knife to her throat.

"Sig—" Katja cried out just as he landed. The golem perched on a crumbling piece of wall and Sigurd walked carefully toward Katja and her captor. Several other Regime soldiers, as well as three Steinkamp, appeared around her.

With his palms out, Sigurd said in a firm voice, "You don't have to hurt her, Wolfram. I'm right here. We can settle this between the two of us."

"There is no settling anything!" Wolfram snapped, his grip on Katja tightening. "This fortress is mine. This mountain range belongs to me! Do you have any idea what it takes for a man of my birth to reach the heights that I have? I've dug through mounds of shit and ash to get here—"

"What of the Golem Mage families?" Sigurd asked. "Are they the shit and ash you speak of?"

"What I did to them was mercy!" Wolfram yelled, dragging Katja backward and farther away from Sigurd. "I gave your family a painless death. You should have had the same back then, and I will offer it to you now if you take one more step forward."

Wolfram's men pointed their weapons at him. Sigurd halted his step, his shoulders tense.

"I see you somehow came upon some Golem Mage abilities," continued Wolfram. "Pull back every golem, put the Alphas to rest, and leave this place. You can take your woman to the far reaches of the known world for all I care—just never return."

"Wolfram," Sigurd began slowly, "I can call back the golems, but the Alphas do not follow any directive but Verishten's."

"Lies!" Wolfram spat. "Kriemhilde swore before her father that you are the key to awakening them and that she was close to figuring out how they could be controlled. Now here you stand with all six of them doing your bidding."

"I made it up, you fool!" Katja exclaimed.

Sigurd locked eyes with Katja as if to tell her she should stop talking then looked back to Wolfram. "I realize this fortress is important to you, but if you stay here, you will die. Let Kriemhilde go, and you will survive. The Golem of Storms flies above this fortress. It will take you and your men to safety before the Golem of Death gets free."

Katja felt a surge of relief. The Golem of Storms alone could fit every person in the fortress upon its body and carry them away from certain destruction. *Shame that Wolfram's life will be spared, after everything he has done,* she thought bitterly.

"Don't bargain for my life, Sigurd. Save Jenn and my father first. She will bring his mind back so that he can release his stock of golems to you," she pleaded.

Wolfram pressed the cold knife against her skin. "Do I hear this correctly? You would let me go free? Forgive my disbelief after our last, not so amiable, confrontation where you tried to kill me and left me to starve in my own shit!"

"You have no choice, Wolfram," Sigurd snapped. "It's over!"

"For some of us, it is." Wolfram dragged Katja toward the southern edge of the platform overlooking the bailey. Below, the Golem of Death had three legs free.

"Wolfram, stop!" Sigurd took rushed steps forward and Wolfram's men moved to halt him.

At that moment, a violet light parted the black storm clouds to the north to make way for the Golem of Storms. Lightning cracked around the floating mountain, creating rumbling thunderclaps as it soared toward the Keep.

While Wolfram's men were distracted, Sigurd made his move. He pushed through the soldiers in his way, not caring to engage in direct battle. His determined gaze was fixated on Wolfram and Katja.

Too afraid to struggle, Katja was dragged farther and farther away from Sigurd. When Wolfram reached the edge, he stopped, wrapped his left arm around her head to hold it in place, and pressed the point of his knife to the back of her skull. Her adrenaline raced through her entire body, realizing she only had one chance at getting out of this alive.

"Take one step closer and her heart will cease to beat."

"If she dies, so do you!"

"Just call off the Alphas!" Wolfram roared.

Katja and Sigurd locked their eyes again, both of them knowing that calling off the Alphas was impossible. Sigurd shook his head.

Without warning, Katja jerked her body toward Wolfram's left arm as hard as she could. The cold tip of Wolfram's blade broke the skin and a sharp pain followed.

34

REMEMBER THE COVENANT

The tip of Wolfram's knife emerged bloody through the side of Katja's neck. Time slowed to a crawl as Sigurd scrambled to her aid, his heart having already leaped from his chest the moment Wolfram had come up behind her. Wolfram flung Katja to the side, making her spin on her heels before she fell backward. She reached out for him as she fell off the platform. *She's not dead—I can still save her!*

Wolfram stepped out of the way and pulled out his sword to attack. Sigurd paid him no mind as he ducked the swing of the blade and dove off the edge after Katja. Not giving a single thought as to how he would survive the fall, he sped vertically through the air, gaining on her descent, and wrapping his arms and legs around her.

Spinning around in midair so that he was beneath her, Sigurd pleaded with all his mental capacity, *Winged golems, we need you—any of you!*

Like back in the chasm and again at the volcano, Verishten was not about to let Sigurd fall to his death. The Golem of Storms directed a whirlwind straight downward with the power of its triangular eye. The winds swiftly wrapped around Sigurd and Katja, whipping them in circles until they arrived safely on the ground.

Without pause, he fished for a packet of ice powder from his back pocket and applied it to Katja's wound. He clenched his fist and activated the water magic in the powder, spreading a fine frost along the gash. The bleeding slowed but didn't stop. She had lost so much blood during the fall, she shivered in his arms, her lips becoming a startling blue.

"Sig . . ." Blood dripped from her mouth as she tried to speak.

"You're going to be fine. I have you," Sigurd muttered while applying firm pressure to her wound with shaking hands. *There is too much blood, why isn't the ice powder working?*

Color drained from Katja's cheeks, and her eyes struggled to stay open. She reached up and faintly traced the scorch mark around Sigurd's eye with her fingertips. "Y-you . . . reached the top of . . . ?"

"Yes, and I'll tell you all about it soon, just save your strength."

At that moment, Jeth and Ignatius came running from the east side of the bailey. Ignatius knelt down beside Katja and Sigurd. "Oh no, oh, Katja. How did this happen? Quick, Jeth, go fetch a field medic or anyone that can close this wound!"

"A medic in a fortress with too many wounded to count? I'll do my best." The Fae'ren archer bounded away.

Sigurd didn't let her go. "Forgive me, Katja. I swore to always be your Steinkamp, but I gave myself to Verishten. I never meant for you to—"

"It's okay." She gulped back more blood. "You protect Ingleheim now . . . only you can repair the covenant. I . . . trust you."

"I can't do it without you," choked Sigurd.

Katja weakly smiled as she put a hand out for Ignatius who frantically tied his handkerchief around her neck. "Professor, don't . . . let our research . . . end with me. The people must know . . . that they can influence golems too. . . ."

"Of course," Ignatius nodded with tears in his eyes. Blood already soaked right through his handkerchief.

"And Siegfried . . ."

It killed Sigurd to hear his real name spoken from her lips. "Don't say anything more," he pleaded, his eyes flooding with tears.

"Show them . . . that Golem Mages need not be . . . feared. . . ."

"We will show them, both of us together. You are not going to die." Sigurd's voice cracked as he said the last word.

"Sieg—"

Katja choked up more blood as Sigurd frantically looked around for Jeth and that medic. *What is taking so long?* He held Katja's head against him as Ignatius helped keep pressure on her wound, but it was no use. Her breath slowed to near nothing. Her eyelids grew heavy.

"No, Katja, hold on!" He tried to shake her awake, but her eyes wouldn't open, her body only grew colder. All the while, his blood boiled with panic and rage. "Fight it, Katja, dammit, hold on! Verishten, please—you can't take her—you can't!"

Ignatius, with his finger on Katja's pulse, looked at Sigurd and said with deep sadness in his voice, "Her heart beats no more."

Sigurd's anger threatened to capsize him, but he lacked the strength to express it. "You can't take her—anybody but her," he murmured as he held Katja's unmoving body so tightly he feared he'd break her bones, and he bellowed into the storm winds.

Through his rage, Sigurd's consciousness fell into the Golem of Storms above. It could feel his pain, and it hurt with him. He watched Verishten's Wrath send a maelstrom of wind upon the Keep, blowing every man still standing on the platform off it, including Wolfram. The frantic shrieks of all twelve men falling to their deaths brought Sigurd back to his body. The men rained down one by one, blood and bone splattering onto the wet stone. The Kanzler of Breisenburg landed with a bone-crunching thud just a few feet from where Sigurd held Katja. He could hardly glance over to him, lying in a puddle of flesh and blood.

It doesn't matter anymore. He has lost, and so have I.

Sigurd's mind fractured. He desperately cycled into one golem after another to escape the raw helplessness he felt while holding Katja's lifeless body in his arms. He fell into crystal golems in the Hot Lakes, crag golems in Kensloche, but no matter how far he let his mind stretch, he kept coming back to the fortress—right back to Katja.

"I'm sorry," he whispered as he laid her down. After brushing wet strands of hair from her face, Sigurd pressed his lips to her forehead, the coldness of her skin making his body tremble with rage and despair.

While Sigurd wept upon her, the bailey erupted into quakes. Cracks ripped through the stone, fanning out from the pit in the center. A gargantuan, igneous rock creature burst out of the rubble and crawled rapidly toward them like a four-legged spider, its iridescent gray eye encompassing the entirety of its spherical body from which stalactites still hung.

"Verishten have mercy," Ignatius sputtered. "It's—"

"Golem of Death!" Sigurd's scream rippled across the bailey. The Alpha responded to Sigurd's call and crawled over to him. Ignatius backed away as it caged Sigurd and Katja with its four legs, dimming the light of its eye.

"You dare call to me?" Its voice sounded ominous and feminine.

"Is it within your infinite power to give life as well as take it?" Sigurd asked the harrowing titan above him.

"*It is.*"

"Then I humbly ask you to give life to this woman." Sigurd let go of Katja's cold body and rose to his feet.

"*That is no humble request!*" the Golem of Death boomed.

"You are Verishten's Mercy, are you not? I beg you, show that mercy to her. There is no one else, alive or dead, more deserving of it."

The Golem of Death bent its massive stone legs and lowered its eye toward Katja's body. It shone its gray light upon her and dimmed it again. It then raised its head once more. "*She is unworthy. Her spirit is tainted by a corrosive evil. It shall not be allowed back into this world.*"

"I don't give a shit about the evil that lives inside her. It does not begin to touch her! Any mere human can see that, why can't you?" Sigurd seethed.

"*Only a life of immeasurable value can even the scales for one as unworthy as she.*"

Sigurd's blood boiled over. "If that is your decree . . . then I will offer mine. As the last Golem Mage and first Steinkamp in this Age of Order, as Verishten's vessel on this plane, I ask that you take my life and give it to her."

The Golem of Death brought its head low again, staring Sigurd down with its dead, ashen eye. "*Your life, I do not want. You pledged your heart and soul to Verishten. Would you renounce your god?*"

"This woman is the reason I fight for humanity at all. Given the chance, it would have been *her* at the top of the volcano to take the leap. It should be her that bears his Eye, not me. Only she can see Ingleheim returned to a state of which Verishten would be proud. For your divine judgment to find such a person unworthy brings into question whether he is a god worth revering. I would gladly renounce my pledge to Verishten to trade places with her," Sigurd declared with fortitude. Although he shook with fear, he knew no other course. He clenched his fists and stood tall and firm before the Alpha.

"*Very well, Siegfried. Your life for that of Kriemhilde's,*" the Golem of Death said. "*But if she does not uphold the covenant between golem and man, she will be the first to pay the price for breaking it.*"

"She will not disappoint you."

With outstretched arms, Sigurd looked up at the giant disk above his head. The Alpha's light shone down, making his skin prickle. He lifted off the ground, helplessly stuck. *I hope you forgive me someday for this, Katja.*

"Wait!" yelled a man from the Keep's entrance.

Suddenly the light went out, and Sigurd dropped to the ground. An old man hobbled toward the Golem of Death with the assistance of Jenn. Sigurd recognized his piercing amber eyes. Herrscher Heinrich stepped away from Jenn and continued with his walking stick to move himself forward.

"You are whom they call the Mighty Führer, who dares declare himself a god among men!" blared the Golem of Death.

"Yes, I am!" the Führer replied in fortitude despite his appeared frailty. "I broke the covenant. I brought the Mages' insipid evil into this land. I am the reason my daughter has been tainted by it. However, unlike me, she is stronger than it. I am unworthy of Verishten's Eye."

Heinrich walked up to Katja's body where Sigurd stood and ripped open his shirt, bearing his mark, singed onto his sternum.

"What are you doing?" Sigurd asked Heinrich.

"I may not know my daughter as well as you," he replied. "But I can bet your life means more to her than her own, and for you to throw it away for her sake—I reckon it will kill her all over again."

"But—"

Heinrich cut Sigurd off to yell up at the Alpha. "My life for my daughter's, Golem of Death!"

"I plan to claim your wretched life in any instance," boomed the Alpha. *"You do not provide adequate sacrifice."*

"Then we both stand as a sacrifice." Sigurd took his stance beside Heinrich. "Where his life does not suffice, take from me what you require."

"And from me," Ignatius took a step beside Heinrich as well.

"I'm probably going to regret this, but take a little from me too. Just let the woman live already," Jenn said in frustration. Everyone looked to the little witch in surprise. She responded, "It's no big deal. I can just reabsorb more life force from somewhere else . . . when I figure out how to manipulate life force, that is."

They all nodded in agreement and faced the Alpha above. The Alpha said nothing and simply shoved Jenn, Ignatius, and Sigurd outside of its light beam with its legs, leaving only Heinrich frozen within it.

The light lifted the Mighty Führer off the ground. Amongst his screams of anguish, the light poured out of his eyes, ears, nose, and mouth as his body convulsed. His skin glowed a blinding white before the light faded, leaving behind a withered corpse that burst into cinders.

"This is where we finally part, Little Dove," Melikheil's voice sounded from a howling abyss. "Wherever your spirit goes, so does this small piece of mine."

"Am I dying?" Katja wondered aloud.

"You're dead, and you will finally be free of me, just like you've always wanted—unless the Golem of Death drags you back. Spirit, essence, and flesh, it is all connected, and I am connected to you. Whatever you do, wherever you go, a part of me will be forever with you."

Katja felt her spirit pulling away from the abyss, pulling toward the bailey where Sigurd had held her. "You may be a part of me now, Melikheil, but you do not control me anymore. If you ever try, I know a powerful Spirit Mage who can push you back down," she said.

"The trick of immortality is not putting all your eggs in one basket. You and Brunhilde are not the only ones I've bound my spirit to. For now, I am content to remain here in wait."

Katja heard screaming from beyond the abyss, screaming that she recognized. "Then you'll be waiting a *long* time." She let go and allowed herself to be pulled into her body.

In the next instant, she gasped for air, choking on ash and coagulating blood. Sudden pain reverberated from her neck. She grabbed it. Although there was blood, there was no wound, and the pain soon subsided. Her body was cold and heavy, and she struggled to sit up.

Katja didn't have to struggle long. Sigurd was at her side brushing mounds of ash off her face and body. Then, there came a stinging pain on her chest. Without caring where she was or who would see, Katja undid the top buttons of her blouse and revealed the Eye of Verishten singed into her sternum.

Breathing so hard she could barely speak, she murmured, "The Eye— these ashes—Sigurd, what happened?"

He didn't have to say a word. Katja remembered the awful screams she had heard before getting back into her body. Everyone she knew stood around the bailey, but not her father; the only parts of him that remained were his cane lying beside her and his Eye of Verishten now burned onto her own chest. Tremors ran through her.

"F-Father!" she sobbed. "What—?"

Taking her into his arms, Sigurd said, "It's all right. It's finally over."

She felt his words of reassurance were for his benefit as much as hers.

Father, I never really knew you . . . but thank you.

The rains stopped, and Katja's tears did too. She looked up at Sigurd, his steel gray eyes wet and bloodshot, his skin stained nearly black with wet ash. Sweat glistened off the distinctive scorch mark over his left eye—his Eye of Verishten. Katja grabbed his face and kissed him full on the mouth. He tasted of salt and earth—of life—and she would never let him go.

The Golem of Death, stirred above them, abruptly interrupting their passionate reunion. Katja yelped, having not noticed it before now. Sigurd held her tight to his chest as they watched it return to its caves below the bailey.

"Remember the Covenant!" the Alpha boomed.

As she watched the Golem of Death disappear, Katja slowly began to understand that her father gave up his life so Sigurd didn't have to. It was the greatest gift he could have given her, and in the end, he was able to leave behind his Golem Mage legacy to his daughter when he wasn't able to with his son. She lifted her head to Sigurd and touched him tenderly over his scarred eye.

"I will do more than remember it. I will cherish it."

35

DIVINE BLEMISH

(Six months later)

When Siegfried and Katja had arrived at the City of Deschner with all the golems and survivors from the Fortress of Mortlach behind them, the Alpha of Crystal Golems put out its all-encompassing light and left the city to its people to rebuild. Afterward, Siegfried was declared Ingleheim's Kaiser by the people, and Bachman soon abandoned his loyal followers.

In the meantime, a small religious following headed by the two pilgrims that accompanied Siegfried up the volcano had already taken hold in the city. They helped rally support for him to lead the nation under one fair and just ruler. The Fortress of Mortlach had been left in the hands of the Golem of Storms and the Golem of Fire to destroy and subsequently use the molten rubble to seal away the Golem of Death, where it would remain lest mankind break the covenant again.

Now, six months after the destruction of the fortress, Siegfried stood before the unruly crowds in the City of Untevar where he prepared to carry out Herr Bachman's death sentence. It would be the first and most important execution Siegfried would perform as Kaiser.

Scores of sunken, dirt-stained faces lined the fences around the stage where the execution would take place. Despite Siegfried's efforts to send food and supplies to the poorest regions of Ingleheim, there was never enough. The shortage would continue until the grain fields of Untevar could yield to their full capacity again. Such things took time, and summer was almost at an end.

The anger people already felt at Bachman's abandonment was set further ablaze when his trial revealed that the man they had rallied behind to deliver them from their impoverished state was also the man behind the policies that put them there in the first place. Siegfried didn't have to feel their emotions through a golem to know their thirst for vengeance was unquenchable.

Two execution offiziers brought Bachman out in chains. The masses clambered to get over the fences, demanding that he be thrown to them so they may deliver their own brand of justice. Siegfried stepped in front of the prisoner, raised both hands in the air, and brought the screeching masses to a relative calm. Beads of anxious sweat formed on his brow. To have so many eyes upon him made him feel sickeningly exposed, but he quickly learned how to hide his fear. It was a whole new type of mask he had to wear, one that didn't offer the same comforts as the previous.

"As your Kaiser, I promise to always take the needs of the people into account. I understand your desires for violent retribution against this man, but this will not be a nation that causes undue suffering to its enemies. Anyone sentenced to die in this new regime will be given the mercy of a quick death. That is my final decree."

The crowd erupted with boos and hollers. Siegfried knew exactly what they wished he had decreed instead, but it was up to him to show them a better way.

One of the offiziers placed the heavy broadsword in his outstretched hand while another forced Bachman to kneel at the chopping block. Siegfried was about to perform another unprecedented act which he felt was lacking in regimes prior. He was going to carry out the sentences with his own hand. Ever since Siegfried retook the Steinkamp pledge, he was no longer comfortable having someone else do his killing for him.

"Herr Bachman of Untevar, I, Kaiser Siegfried, and the people of Ingleheim have sentenced you to die. You may issue your final statement."

Bachman spit on the ground. "You cannot hope to control my people, young Kaiser. They will eat you alive."

I don't need to control them, Siegfried thought. "Take solace that you have been spared from that very fate." He raised the sword above his head and brought the blade down hard and swift. Bachman's cleanly severed head fell into the basket beneath the chopping block.

The roars of the crowd were deafening. Some sounded satisfied by the execution while many others screamed obscenities. Siegfried had done more for the people of Untevar than anyone had in decades, and yet he was still far from winning them over.

He and his offiziers left the stage, and he ducked into the armored coach that would take him back to Deschner. Joining him in the coach was his Viceroy of Luidfort, Herr Friedhelm and the newly appointed General and Viceroy of Breisenburg, Herr Brenner.

"There will be mass riots because of this," Brenner said as he scanned the raging crowds outside.

"I've already ordered the city guards to double their patrols for the next few days," replied Siegfried.

"We should send some war golems to maintain order."

"No. It is important that the people of Untevar understand that I'm not going to be another Heinrich." In addition to picking up the pieces of a failed regime, Siegfried's priority was helping the people regain trust in their leaders, if such a thing were even possible.

"With all due respect, Herrscher, I think you are too lenient with them," said Brenner. "Those people are animals and need to be treated as such until they learn."

"They have been treated like animals for over twenty years. I believe they will learn not to act as such, as long as they are shown a better alternative," Siegfried countered.

"I respect your ruling, but I do not agree with it. Helping them is paramount, but in the meantime, they need a firmer hand until order is restored. It's for their own good."

"And your counsel is always appreciated, General." Siegfried tipped his head.

It became clearer every day to Siegfried that Brenner was nothing like his late older brother, Klemens. Where Klemens had devoted his life to studying war, Brenner had lived it. Despite his darker outlook however, Brenner proved himself to be an honorable leader in battle. He led several battalions against the Herrani scourge from the beginning and was integral in liberating Fae'ren Province after the Golem of Storms cast the Herrani from Ingleheim. Nas'Gavarr's forces retreated to the desert a month after Luidfort was reclaimed and the Barrier of Kriegle sealed.

What impressed him the most about Brenner was the fact that even though he was aware of Siegfried's involvement in Volker's death, he never outright blamed him, understanding that Siegfried had been following Wolfram's orders. His ability to separate his emotions from his duty made Brenner a much more trustworthy man than Siegfried would have been not too long ago.

Herr Friedhelm then spoke, "I say you should have given them what they wanted. If anyone in Ingleheim deserves their revenge, it's the people of Untevar."

"Trust me, I know better than most the thirst for violent reprisal, which is why I also know how pursuing it will corrode any humanity they may have left. This nation cannot begin to repair itself if we allow those within it to be lowered to the level of men like Bachman."

"For someone who didn't think he was fit to lead a nation when he started, you appear to be picking it up rather quickly." Friedhelm's eyes twinkled as he scratched his bushy brown mustache.

Siegfried chuckled. "It helps when you have an outspoken partner to guide you."

"That sounds like my niece," Friedhelm quipped. "So much like my sister. Ilsa was the only person who could tell Heinrich what to do."

"A wise friend once told me, no matter how clever, how ordinary, or how monstrous the man, there is always a woman behind him calling the shots," Siegfried said thoughtfully while glancing out the coach window.

"Really?" Brenner grinned. "Does this *wise friend* happen to be Fraulein Kriemhilde?"

The two men chuckled between themselves while Siegfried smiled and nodded. "Laugh all you like, Herr Brenner. Your time will come."

Brenner scoffed, making Friedhelm and Siegfried laugh all the more. He never did honor the marriage pact of his deceased brother. Kriemia and her mother had decided to join a convent in Deschner after they both refused Siegfried's offer to see them well cared for.

"What of your time, Herrscher?" asked Friedhelm. "When are you planning on taking my niece from Fraulein to Frau?"

Siegfried grimaced slightly, growing weary of constantly answering that question. "Your niece insists on earning a doctorate before subjecting herself to the confines of marriage."

"Just as well." Friedhelm chuckled. "Kriemhilde is not one easily confined. Enjoy your freedom now while you still can."

As Friedhelm and Brenner snickered away, Siegfried smiled to himself. The only time he ever felt free was when he was with Katja, and he couldn't wait for her to return from Nordenhein.

A week later in the Castle of Deschner, Siegfried strolled into a private meeting chamber to touch base with Jenn. She had been left in charge while Siegfried and his viceroys were in Untevar. Siegfried had also offered her the position as the Kaiser's official Mage, as well as Meister Melikheil's old castle with all the magical paraphernalia locked within. She had proven herself to be a very resourceful and influential young woman, and one of the few people Siegfried could trust in his new regime.

Although still a slip of a girl in body, Jenn had become much larger in spirit. She no longer wore the old uniform of the Kings' Remnants, but she wasn't the type of woman to wear a dress either. She now wore form-fitting trousers and an embroidered women's vest with a dark blue military-style coat, her short dark hair now grown out just past her ears.

"Have you given any more thought to my offer, Jenn?" Siegfried asked as he closed the doors to the meeting room.

"I have," she replied with her eyes wandering to the floor, "And . . . I respectfully decline."

Siegfried frowned. "I'm surprised to hear that. You and your mother would never want for anything ever again, and you can help a lot of people."

"Oh, I don't doubt that. But I'm not ready. I've never been properly trained in spirit magic and given that every Spirit Mage I've known of so far has been pure evil, I'd like to know how not to become so myself before delving into that level of power."

"You have nothing to fear in that regard. You're stronger than the others. I believe you can resist any pull toward evil." He sat down and put his feet up on his large granite-topped desk.

"I appreciate the confidence you have in me, Siegs," Jenn said, plopping herself down in one of the plush armchairs diagonal to him. "It's just that . . . this nation doesn't need nor want another Spirit Mage right now. The people trust you and part of that trust comes from knowing you won't make the same mistakes Heinrich did. I think it's for the best that I leave."

"Leave where?"

"Ingleheim." Jenn fiddled with the silver buttons on her coat sleeves.

"What is this really about?"

She sighed. "My mother is in a good place with the Storm Sisters, and I can't thank you enough for trying to make a place for me here with you, but there are other people out there that need my help more."

"People outside of Ingleheim?"

"People in the desert."

Siegfried nodded. "I see. This is about the Fae'ren, isn't it?"

"Jeth?" Jenn sputtered. "No, why would—? I mean, he said he and Anwarr were going to settle somewhere far away from the thieving life. I'm likely never going to see that fairy boy again, not where I'm going."

Siegfried chuckled at her flustered expression before returning to the subject at hand. "You'd better not be thinking of going against Nas'Gavarr. The Overlord leaves trails of dead Mages behind him." His brow furrowed.

"May Nas'Gavarr end me then if I ever become that stupid." Jenn laid back on the sofa and rested her head on her hands behind her. "The desert is where I can find other Mages, someone with whom I can learn. And it's there where I'll find more corrupted minds to free."

Siegfried nodded again as he stood back up. "Well, good luck to you then . . . and be careful. The more naja you free, the more likely you will capture Nas'Gavarr's attention."

"Don't worry. For the first little while, I'll be learning more about spirit magic, maybe become an Apprentice. Who knows?"

"That, I can appreciate," said Siegfried. "There is so much that I still need to learn about my own abilities."

"At least you have a Golem Expert and fellow Golem Mage to help you navigate through it."

Siegfried went to look out the large window that granted him a view of the Volcano of Verishten. Even now, he had trouble keeping his mind on the task at hand rather than flipping between every golem in existence. It took nearly all his concentration to recognize that he stood with Jenn and not in the Iron Mines or the Crags. Especially with Katja not being around, it was difficult for him to stay grounded.

Katja had inherited her father's abilities—limited only to domination. Just like one would expect, she wasn't apt to dominating golems and was content only to communicate with them using the depictions of golem eyes. For the time being, she was more interested in studying Siegfried's unique abilities to satisfy her scholarly urges.

"Speaking of which, Katja told me before she left that she'd be presenting her thesis at her graduation ceremony. How was it received?" Jenn wondered.

"I don't know. She hasn't presented it y—" Siegfried's mind slowly emerged from a cloud of blinding ash. A jolt of panic pierced through his chest. "Shit! What day is it?"

Jenn told him, and Siegfried's panic quickly turned to a sickening dread in the pit of his stomach. "Oh no!"

"It's her graduation ceremony today, and you forgot?" Jenn shot up off the sofa.

"I thought it was still a week away and that this week was last week—she's going to kill me!" Siegfried's voice noticeably went up in pitch.

"Okay, this is bad—really bad, but you might still have time if you travel by air—"

Siegfried didn't wait for Jenn to finish her suggestion. He had already nudged awake a winged golem lying dormant just outside. He was out the window and flying away from the castle with Jenn looking after him.

"Siegs!"

"Just hold down the castle until I return," Siegfried called back, then muttered more to himself, "If I return alive, that is."

He's still not here! What could be so damn important that he wouldn't show up? Katja fumed inwardly as she came to the end of her thesis presentation. She stood at the podium overlooking an engrossed group of scholars from all the fields of study that the University of Nordenhein had to offer. All of them eager for her thesis' conclusion. However, she found it hard to focus, plagued with worry for the reason behind Siegfried's absence.

Did something go wrong during Bachman's execution in Untevar? Surely I would have received word by now if it had.

Closing the worn leather-bound journal that she had recovered from Klemens's safety deposit box, she concluded her presentation. The university's covered rooftop terrace came alive with applause. The warm reception from her peers for all her hard work made her forget about disappointment for a moment, and she basked in the feeling of finally having accomplished what she set out to do from the start. *I'm done!*

Ignatius, standing in the front row just off to her right, smiled wide through his neatly trimmed and waxed whiskers. She returned the smile before turning back to the rest of audience.

"In closing, I would like to express my gratitude to all those who have made these discoveries possible. I'd like to thank my professor and mentor, Herr Ignatius of Nordenhein. He has recently earned the position of Viceroy of Nordenhein Range, so let us congratulate him on such a prestigious appointment."

Ignatius took a bow as everyone cheered.

"Herr Ignatius possesses a thirst for knowledge and a passion for sharing that knowledge that I will always admire and strive for. He never stopped believing in me and never gave up on me no matter how difficult I was to work with at times. For that, Herr Ignatius has my limitless gratitude."

After waiting for the audience to finish clapping, she continued, "Of course, I must thank the Steinkamp soldier who had been assigned to my security here at the university and went on to become my greatest love and your Kaiser. . . ."

Katja scanned the audience again to see if he had made it and found he still wasn't there, making her heart sink deeper. "He regrets not being here, but he deserves to be recognized today. Were it not for his unfaltering commitment to keeping me from harm during often dangerous expeditions and his assistance in finding the key to the resulting breakthroughs, I would not be here to present these findings to you. In fact, there would be no findings to present."

After more cheers, Katja went right into the most emotionally tumultuous part of her speech. "And finally, I'd like to thank a man whose integrity, brilliance, and commitment to golem-kind will never be forgotten. His passion for his scholarly pursuits set him apart from his peers. His intellect was unrivaled, and more than anything, it was his brave and kind heart that inspired me and continues to inspire me. . . ."

Katja took a moment to force back a tear. Ignatius had offered to say this part of the speech before she had come up to the podium, but she owed it to Klemens to do it herself.

"His sacrifice is the reason many of us can stand here today in celebration of the reaffirming of human and golem relations. He is the reason why Herr Ignatius and I still draw breath. Therefore, I dedicate this thesis to the memory of my research partner, my friend, and my hero, Herr Klemens of Breisenburg. He will be forever missed. Thank you all for coming."

Katja nodded, dried a tear mid-fall, and quickly stepped away from the podium. She shed a few more tears in Ignatius's embrace before coming down from the stage to shake hands with her many congratulators.

Once she went through the endless line of people, the celebration was at hand. From such an emotionally charged day, Katja decided to go outside the stained-glass enclosure and onto the large square balcony to get some fresh air. A bracing chill coated the breeze, making her shiver. She rubbed her arms with her hands, wishing she had retrieved her coat before going outside. *Summer in Nordenhein shouldn't be* this *cold*, she thought.

As she walked over to the balustrade to take in the view of the campus, an enormous golem covered with a sparkling layer of ice and snow emerged from the distant tree line, clouds of condensation billowing off it. There, upon its shoulder, stood a man wearing a long black coat with silver buttons over the finely threaded vest and pants ensemble of the high-born Ingleman. It was a manner of dress that satisfied both roles of Kaiser and Steinkamp Kapitän—until a replacement for kapitän could be found. Herrscher Siegfried rode upon the shoulder of the Golem of Ice, a spectacular titan Katja had not been given the chance to see until that moment.

Verishten's Wisdom stepped over the university walls with ease and made its way to the balcony where Katja stood in awe. It came right up close so that Siegfried could speak directly to her from its shoulder only a foot or two below the balustrade.

"The Golem of Ice! How did . . . ?" Katja trailed off, almost forgetting how angry she was with him.

"While flying here, I happened to come upon it on its way to its resting place. I convinced it to come here with me since it was on the way. Think of it as a graduation gift from your very adoring and oh so proud Steinkamp."

Katja leaned over the balustrade to bring her face closer to his "You forgot the *very late* Steinkamp. And I mean that in the *'you missed my entire presentation'* sense as well as the *'you are a dead man'* sense."

Siegfried winced. "Did I mention an extremely sorry Steinkamp?"

"Oh, you will be."

"How did it go?"

"Fantastic, especially the part about how my protector quite foolishly stepped into an ice beam and I had to drag him to a hot spring to thaw out. That little anecdote got quite a few laughs."

"Really? You told them that? Did you mention that I stepped in front of that ice beam to save your life?"

Putting her forefinger to her chin, Katja hummed and hawed before answering. "You know, I'm not sure I mentioned that. Maybe you should have been at my speech!" She turned and stormed off as Siegfried leaped over the balustrade to keep her from going back inside.

"I'm really sorry, Katja. I got mixed up with the days."

"And here I thought only a national emergency would keep you from forgetting something this important to me! I thought something bad had happened to you!"

"It's like I told you before. When you're not with me, it's difficult to remain in my own head. The golems—they tug me all over the place."

"Oh, so it's my fault for not being there to constantly remind you when the most important day of my life is. I understand how golems can be distracting, but enough with the excuses."

Siegfried put up his hands in defeat. "You're right. You're absolutely right." Reaching into his inside coat pocket, he said, "I was going to wait until after the celebration to give you this so we could be absent the eyes of every scholar in Nordenhein, but . . ."

Katja glanced behind her to find a bunch of people, including Ignatius, peering through the windows out to the balcony. When Katja turned to face Siegfried again, there was a bracelet in front of her made of shimmering red obsidian, unlike anything she had ever seen before.

"This was handcrafted by one of the people that I met on my pilgrimage," Siegfried began.

Katja let out a quiet gasp, not able to peel her eyes away from the bracelet. "Those people that started a religious movement in your name—they made that?"

"It was made from the lava golem eye that I used to ascend the Molten Slopes. I went to visit their temple a while back, and they presented it to me. I told them that I would only require a piece. It is the last eye that shall ever be ripped from a golem's body by a man. You should be the one to keep it, to remind you of how this world has changed for the better . . . because of you and the work that you do."

The bracelet was so beautiful and Siegfried's words so touching, Katja forgave him for his lateness ten times over, but she couldn't help giving him a hard time anyway. "Siegfried, it's beautiful . . . but, like you, also late in coming."

"Oh, so that's a *no*, then?" Siegfried backed away playfully. "Alright, well, I guess I'll just toss this bracelet made from what some say is a sacred relic over the balcony here and—"

Siegfried held the bracelet over the edge, making Katja's heart leap into her throat. She rushed over to him.

"Don't you dare." She carefully snatched it and admired the glimmering etchings that represented parts of Deschner Range. "I love it. Though, do be careful, Siegfried Reborn, that those followers of yours don't inflate your head to the size of Verishten's Volcano."

"With a woman like you to keep me humble, that won't be possible."

"I put a high value on humility in a man." Katja settled into Siegfried's arms. "Especially if that man is to be my Kaiser."

"Then what say you? Will you be my Kaiserin, Kriemhilde the II of Deschner?" He brushed a lock of hair behind her ear.

"On one condition." She smiled. "Don't call me Kriemhilde."

"Fine by me."

"Oh, and since you weren't here, I should inform you that it's Doctor Katja now."

"Ah, of course, forgive me—Doctor Katja," Siegfried said with the quiet intensity that always made her heart flutter.

With the bracelet in hand, she wrapped her arms around Siegfried's neck and kissed him passionately without a care to the cheering onlookers. During the kiss, she slipped the bracelet on.

Siegfried took hold of Katja's face and kissed her again, this time as her husband. She pulled away from him before he finished so she could marvel at the Alpha standing patiently just below the balustrade. With a squeal of delight, she waved to Ignatius and the other scholars and cast herself over the railing.

Everyone on the terrace gasped in fright while Siegfried cried out in alarm, "Dammit, Katja, don't do that, it's icy!"

She landed with a grunt upon the Alpha's snowy shoulder. Siegfried immediately dropped down beside her, and the icy colossus began to move.

"You worry too much." She cackled.

"How would it look if the Kaiser's new bride fell to her death?"

"Good point. One fall to the death was enough for me," she said, waving to the onlookers.

The scholars continued to wave from the balcony until they were out of sight. Siegfried put his arm around her shoulders as they turned to face north. "Now to sit back and enjoy the ride."

"I've always wanted to pay a proper visit to the Glacier Peaks, but we will arrive there ill-prepared for the cold. It's nearly autumn."

"Forget the Peaks. You mentioning the hot springs earlier made me realize that you, darling wife, have yet to indulge."

Katja met her husband's gaze with a cheeky grin. "That was because you were saying *'go away, don't look at me, I have to remain mysterious.'*"

Siegfried laughed and pointed to the mark around his eye. "Yes, well, since I've earned this divine blemish, everyone in Ingleheim has seen my face now."

Katja traced her fingers along the scar endearingly. It was rare for the Eye to appear in a place so visible, especially the face. She liked to believe Verishten put it there intentionally, out in the open where Siegfried could finally be seen for the man he truly was. To her, it was his divine blemish outside, as well as inside, that she was drawn to the most.

"You jump into a volcano and come out with ancient Golem Mage abilities and a scar envied by every man in Ingleheim. Remind me to feel sorry for you when we get to the hot springs."

Siegfried leaned in and kissed her tenderly on the neck. "Once we get to the hot springs, there will be no need to feel sorry for me."

Katja giggled and rested her head on her husband's shoulder. The newlyweds sat upon the Golem of Ice, experiencing each giant step as if it were their own while gazing out at the entirety of Nordenhein's glacier splendor laid out before them.

The End

INGLE TERMS GUIDE

FRAU   Formal address for a married woman
FRAULEIN   Formal address for a young, unmarried woman
FÜHRER   Leader
HERR   Formal address for a male of high standing
HERRSCHER   Formal address for a male sovereign
KAISER   Emperor/King
KAISERIN   Empress/Queen
KAPITÄN   Captain
KARL   Regime police force
KOMMANDEUR   Commander
KANZLER   Chancellor
KOMMISSAR   Commissioner
MEISTER   Master
OFFIZIER   Officer
SCHLEPTS   Currency of Ingleheim
STEINKAMP   Regime's elite fighting force used for specialized missions
requiring highly efficient execution

MAGIC TERMS GUIDE

MAGE   A person, also referred to as a witch/wizard/sorcerer, who can
manipulate one or all three components of existence: essence, spirit, and
flesh.
ESSENCE MAGE   A Mage who manipulates the six essences of
wind, light, water, earth, fire, and life force.
AURA   The energy that makes up each of the six essences (see
Essence Mage).
SPIRIT MAGE   A Mage who manipulates spirit, the energy that gives
all living creatures their sentience.
PRIMING   The process in which a Spirit Mage prepares a subject's
spirit for manipulation (see Spirit Mage).
FLESH MAGE   A Mage who manipulates the physical tissues of living
organisms.

MAGITECH   Items that a Mage has enchanted with magical properties for the use of people without magic abilities.

GOLEM MAGE   A person with a god-given ability, based on a combination of spirit and earth magic, to influence and/or control golems.

MOUNTAIN RANGE GUIDE

DESCHNER MOUNTAIN RANGE
Leader: Herrscher Heinrich; the Führer
Golem: Lava
Alpha: Golem of Fire; Verishten's Voice

NORDENHEIN MOUNTAIN RANGE
Leader: Kanzler Gustaf
Golem: Frost
Alpha: Golem of Ice; Verishten's Wisdom

KENSLOCHE MOUNTAIN RANGE
Leader: Kanzler Waldemar
Golem: Crag
Alpha: Golem of Stone; Verishten's Grace

UNTEVAR MOUNTAIN RANGE
Leader: Kanzler Bachman
Golem: Crystal
Alpha: Golem of Light; Verishten's Warning

LUIDFORT MOUNTAIN RANGE
Leader: Kanzler Friedhelm
Golem: Winged
Alpha: Golem of Storms; Verishten's Wrath

BREISENBURG MOUNTAIN RANGE
Leader: Kanzler Volker
Golem: War
Alpha: Golem of Death; Verishten's Judgment/Mercy

STEINKAMP WEAPONRY

MAGITECH EQUIPMENT

WIND BLADE   Round throwing blade enchanted by wind magic to allow the wielder to control its trajectory.

TWILIGHT CANISTER   Cylindrical item that breaks apart and creates a void to shroud all light essence within a fixed radius.

ICE POWDER   Granular substance that freezes anything not warm blooded. It is useful in putting out fires and making objects more brittle.

EARTH BINDINGS   Leather bindings that come in various lengths. They can take the form of whatever they touch (i.e. wood, rock, metal, skin). Used as handholds for climbing or for tying up captives. All Steinkamp rock climbing equipment share similar earth magic enchantment.

BLAST GEL   Clear, highly explosive gelatinous agent enchanted by fire magic, and is discharged from a small dispenser.

CUDGEL   Blunt force instrument that also acts as a light torch when the light magic is activated at its base.

STEINKAMP GLOVES   Made with grips to aid in climbing and weapon holding. They are connected to all the magic essences used in the Magitech equipment. Squeezing the glove in a fist will activate the essences within the various substances when they are ready for use.

STEINKAMP MASK   Made of a thin metal mesh, easy enough for the wearer to see out of, but the light essence coating creates the illusion of a dark void.

STEINKAMP UNIFORM   Is resistant to the essences of fire and water/ice, which helps maintain the wearer's body temperature in various climates.

NON-ENCHANTED WEAPONS

RETRACTABLE BLADE   A sword that can extend and lock in place when equipped, then retracts to easily store in its sheath at the wielder's back. They are not overly strong, but light and thin, used for quick kills only and not extended sword play.

CROSSBOW   A Steinkamp's crossbow allows for three bolts to automatically load and fire before having to reload. They are compact and light with a small crannequin so the wielder can cock it quickly and easily, but they have relatively shorter range. A Steinkamp's ability to approach unseen allows them to get close enough to a target to make up for this lack of range.

SKEWER KNIFE   Long, pointed knives used for close quarter executions. Their length is adequate to pierce a target's brain stem to shut down heart and respiratory functions when driven through the back of the skull.

SPLITTING BLADE   A chain linked blade released from a dispenser worn around the wielder's forearm. On impact, the blade splits into three prongs to further embed into the target. It is used mainly to kill a foe from afar while allowing the wielder to drag the foe toward them via a crankshaft mechanism. It may also be used as a grappling device.

CPSIA information can be obtained
at www.ICGtesting.com
Printed in the USA
LVHW09*2310050918
589318LV00004B/13/P